A surprise delivery...

SNOW
Bride

She's pregnant!
She's stranded with a gorgeous stranger!
And she's about to find out that love
happens when you least expect it...

Stella Bagwell began her writing career almost by accident. Although she always loved reading romances, she never thought to write one herself. She was a hairdresser, but developed a severe allergy to hairspray and was forced to resign. With time on her hands, she wanted to do something creative. She remembered a high-school English teacher telling her she could be a writer if she wanted. Armed with that notion and an old manual typewriter, she went to work. The result was her first book for Mills & Boon! Stella's plan for the future is to continue writing romance novels as long as there's an audience to enjoy her work.

Kay Stockham sold to Superromance in 2005. Within ten months of that first sale, she sold three more stories to the Superromance series, and attributes her success to perseverance and a true love of the romance genre. You can find Kay hanging out online in her cyber home at www. kaystockham.com where she hosts a monthly contest giveaway and blogs about what it's like to be a newly published author.

Laurie Paige grew up on a farm in Kentucky. Shortly before she started primary school, her family moved to town. Heartbroken at leaving, she recovered upon discovering the library. It was the most wonderful place – thousands of books. She read *The Little Engine That Could* at least once a week. She met her future husband in the Sweet Shop. (That really was the name of the place). After Laurie finished high school, they married and headed off to Florida and the US Space programme. There they worked, attended college, learned to surf, met the Original Seven astronauts, had a daughter, and adopted a dog and two cats. Laurie's e-mail address is LauriePaige@AOL.com. She loves to hear from readers and share thoughts, recipes, and ideas.

SNOWBOUND
Babies

STELLA BAGWELL
KAY STOCKHAM & LAURIE PAIGE

M&B™ and M&B™ with the Rose Device
are trademarks of the publisher.
Harlequin Mills & Boon Limited, Eton House,
18-24 Paradise Road, Richmond, Surrey TW9 1SR

SNOWBOUND BABIES © Harlequin Books S.A. 2009

New Year's Baby © Stella Bagwell 1993
Another Man's Baby © Dorma Kay Stockham 2008
An Unexpected Delivery © Olivia M Hall 1996

ISBN: 978 0 263 86902 6

025-0109

Printed and bound in Spain
by Litografia Rosés S.A., Barcelona

New Year's Baby
STELLA BAGWELL

To Mary-Theresa Hussey, Melissa Jeglinski
and Eliza Shallcross for all their hard
work on this project.

Also, a special thank-you goes to my editor,
Valerie Hayward,
for her wonderful guidance and support.

Chapter One

Kathleen Gallagher Hayes knotted the white towel between her breasts, then tilted her head toward the faint pinging noise at the bedroom window. Was that sleet?

Scurrying across the room on bare feet, she pulled back the heavy drapes. The warm moist air that had escaped the bathroom during her shower had misted the window. She wiped a hand over the glass, then peered into the dark night.

The window faced north and was partially shrouded by a huge gum tree. At the moment the bare branches had little effect in stopping the small bits of ice from viciously pelting the windowpane. She groaned aloud at the sight.

Oh, how could this happen tonight of all nights?

It was New Year's Eve! Her family and friends were gathering for her brother Nick's engagement party. She'd even bought a special bottle of champagne to add to the celebration.

Snatching up a red robe lying across the foot of the bed, Kathleen quickly slipped her arms into the sleeves and tied the belt at the waist. She hadn't noticed any precipitation before she'd gotten into the shower. Maybe the highway would still be clear enough for her to make it down the mountain safely.

At the front of the house, Kathleen stepped gingerly onto the small concrete porch. The latticework covering the north end had blocked out some of the sleet, but the steps and the sidewalk along the side of the house were coated with a clear glaze of ice. Kathleen could see it growing thicker by the minute.

Shivering, she carefully stepped into the house just in time to hear the phone ringing. She clutched the heavy robe against her as she hurried to answer it.

"Hello."

"Kathleen. Thank God you answered. We were afraid you'd already started over here in your car."

She instantly recognized her brother's voice. "Nick, I just got out of the shower. It's sleeting like crazy here. The ground is already covered!"

"I figured as much. It's snizzling here."

"Snizzling? Is that some weather term the army uses?"

He laughed. "No. It's a cross between snowing and freezing rain. I thought everyone knew that."

"I guess I'm just not as with it as you, dear brother," she answered dryly, then plunked herself down on the arm of a sofa. "So what am I going to do? I think the highway is probably already glazed over. Nick, I can't miss your and Allison's engagement party. If it hadn't been for me you might not even be engaged!"

Nick laughed. "Give me some credit, sis. After all, I am the man Allison fell in love with."

Kathleen smiled. Her brother sounded on top of the world and she couldn't be happier for him. "Yes, but don't forget that I gave her a little push in your direction. Now I can't even be there to celebrate with you." She groaned, then cursed. "Damn! Damn! I should never have come home today. I should have just stayed on the farm and worn some old rag to the party. At least I would have been there and not stranded up here!"

In the voice he used to train army recruits Nick barked at her, "Kathleen, don't even think of trying to make it over here to the farm tonight! You'll break your neck, or something worse."

Kathleen grimaced as disappointment flooded through her. "I have new tires on the car. Maybe if I just crept along at a snail's pace, I could make it."

"No! I forbid it and so does Dad. There's not a highway more hazardous than 71 when it's slick.

And my engagement party isn't worth you sliding off the mountainside.''

Kathleen knew he was right, but that didn't make her feel better. "I know. But I don't want to miss out on the merrymaking. I'm so thrilled that you and Allison are getting married. And Sam and Olivia have just gotten home from their honeymoon. It's New Year's Eve! I bought champagne! There's too much to celebrate for me to be stuck up here!''

"I know, honey. We want you to be here with us, too. But not at the expense of your safety.''

"That's easy for you to say. You're there. I'm the one stuck up here alone!''

Sounding just as upset as his sister, Nick said, "Well, Sam and I could try coming after you in his pickup. It's a four-wheel drive. We might make it up the mountain to you, but I wouldn't promise you we'd make it back down.''

He didn't sound very keen on the idea. And Kathleen knew it would be foolish to encourage her brothers to come after her. "No, it would be just as crazy for you two to try it as it would be for me. Allison and Olivia would kill me if something happened to either one of you. Besides, if it keeps this up very long the authorities will close the highway, anyway.''

"We're really sorry, sis. We're going to miss having you here. Maybe you can make it tomorrow for dinner,'' he added hopefully.

Kathleen could hear music in the background and her father playing some sort of tickling game with Benjamin. The boy's giggling and squealing was punctuated with her father's deep laughter. It was easy for Kathleen to picture her family and friends gathered together in the old farmhouse, roasting marshmallows in the fireplace, dancing in the parlor and toasting Nick's engagement and the New Year with all sorts of food and drink. Knowing she was going to miss it all sent her spirits plummeting.

"Yes. Well, kiss Allison for me. And tell Mother and Daddy I'll see them tomorrow. If the road's clear, that is. Otherwise, don't worry about me. I have plenty of groceries in the pantry," she told her brother.

"We'll call you later this evening to see how you're faring," he promised, then added with a laugh, "Remember, sis, *you* have the champagne. If nothing else, dress yourself up and enjoy it."

"Alone?"

Nick chuckled. "If you drink the whole bottle you won't know you're alone."

"You're horrible," she said with a laugh.

"Bye, sis. Talk to you in a little bit. And don't go outside for any reason. We don't want anything happening to you."

Kathleen promised she wouldn't leave the house, then slowly hung up the telephone. Well, what was she going to do now? she asked herself.

Impulsively, she reached for the remote control and switched on the television set. A local weatherman was on the screen, tracking the ice storm by radar. From his predictions, it was going to be a nasty one, and Kathleen knew she might not be stuck here for just tonight. It might be several days before she could drive off the mountain—a fate that wasn't all that unusual in the steep Boston Mountains.

With a defeated sigh, she rose from the couch and headed to her bedroom. Her hair was still wet from the shower she'd taken earlier. She decided she would dry it, put on a bit of makeup and the new outfit she'd bought to wear tonight. From the looks of things, she was going to have to spend the evening alone, so she might as well make the best of it.

Ross Douglas considered it a miracle when he got the pickup he was driving onto the shoulder of the highway without sliding into the ravine below. And since it was only about fifty yards away from the driveway leading to his house, he considered himself lucky, indeed. He could walk the rest of the way, and worry about getting his vehicle later.

After depositing the keys in his jeans pocket, he zipped the heavy coat he was wearing up to his neck and tugged the baseball cap lower on his forehead. It was going to be a long, frigid walk, and as he slid out of the truck into the icy sleet and wind, he wondered how he could have given up warm southern Texas for this.

The climb to his house was incredibly slick. Several times he lost his footing and was forced to cling to branches and dried weeds on the roadside to keep from sliding back down the steep, winding mountain. No cars passed him, either going up or coming down. Ross supposed nobody but him had been stupid enough to get caught in this weather. Coming from the warm climes of San Antonio, Ross had ignored the weather forecast this morning, thinking a little snow couldn't be that much of a problem. Next time he'd listen!

Once he made it to the more-level driveway, the going was much easier. Ross quickened his pace, eager to get inside the house to warmth and the supper he had yet to have. Since it had been early in the afternoon when he'd left for Fort Smith, he hadn't thought about turning on the porch light. Now he wished the meager gaslight fixture in the yard was nearer to the front entrance of the house. He couldn't see a damn thing and he knew the steps, and more than likely the porch, too, were coated with ice.

He was digging the keys from his pocket when he spotted something on the porch sitting next to the door. As he gingerly made his way across the concrete floor, he saw that it was a box of some sort.

He hadn't left a box on the porch. Had a neighbor been by? Left something for him? Hell, Ross, you don't even know your neighbors yet, he reminded himself.

Careful not to slip, he unlocked the door, flipped on the light, then carried the box into the house and set in on the kitchen counter. Obviously, someone had wanted to give him something, he thought, as he shrugged out of his coat and tossed it over a kitchen chair.

Rubbing his hands together in an effort to warm them, he turned a wary eye on the box. It was made of cardboard, and the top flaps were tucked and neatly closed. Ross was hesitant to pull them open. Maybe one of his new colleagues had left it as some sort of prank, and balloons or something crazy would burst out all over the room.

But that didn't make much sense. Who would be out in an ice storm, especially on a mountain road, just to pull a practical joke?

Deciding to put his curiosity to rest before he made himself supper, he tugged back the flaps and looked inside. Ross frowned quizzically at the navy blue woollen material bundled inside the box. It was heavy and looked like a coat of some sort. Who in the world would be giving him a coat? He'd moved to Arkansas only two weeks ago and into this house more recently than that. No one around here even knew him, except for those at the school in Fort Smith who'd hired him.

He reached to take the coat from the box, then

suddenly stopped as the folds of fabric pulled away to reveal what was underneath.

Dear God, it was a baby! A newborn baby! The sight was so shocking, so unexpected, that for long seconds Ross could only stare down at the tiny human with its scrunched-up face and thatch of fine dark hair.

Was it alive? The question galvanized him into frantic action. Jerking the coat aside, he lifted the child from its makeshift cradle.

The baby was wrapped in a towel that was stained from birth waste. To Ross's utter relief, the child let out a lusty squawl and squirmed in his arms.

For God's sake, how long had it been on his porch in below-freezing temperatures? Thirty minutes? An hour? It couldn't have been very long, he decided, because the box was dry and free of snow.

With the baby in his arms, he ran out to the living room, where the phone sat on a low end table. "Oh, hell!" he cursed, then slammed the receiver back on its hook before he even got it to his ear. The phone was useless. The phone company hadn't yet been out to hook up his line. It would be next week, they had told him. Next week would hardly help him now!

All right, calm down, Ross, he told himself. Don't panic! Think! What are you going to do? This baby obviously needs medical attention, or at least someone who knows how to care for a baby. You don't!

Fear plunged through him as he glanced down at

the baby's wrinkled face. He had to do something! The child could be suffering from hypothermia!

Warm it! Yes, wrap it up and get it warm!

Ross ran back through the house to the bedroom and snatched a flannel shirt and a thick sweatshirt from the dresser. When he pulled the soiled towel from the baby, he discovered it was a girl. In a hasty inspection, she looked to be perfectly formed and unblemished, as far as he could tell.

With the tiny girl bundled in the shirts and tucked in the crook of his arm, Ross frantically paced around the room. As his mind churned, trying to formulate some sort of plan, the baby let out a loud cry, making Ross instinctively cuddle the newborn closer to his chest in an effort to warm her with his own body heat.

Dear God, what kind of person could have left this child on his doorstep, where it could easily have died from exposure.

Never mind that, Ross, he quickly told himself. You have more pressing questions to deal with at the moment. Like how are you going to get this baby off the mountain to someone who can care for it properly?

Who was he kidding? Short of walking five or six miles in freezing rain, there was no way to get down the mountain. This wasn't a heavily populated area, but it wasn't isolated, either. Although state highway 71 was no more than a hundred yards from his house, it was so steep and winding that he doubted a standard car or truck could drive on it in this weather.

This newborn infant didn't need to be exposed to the cold again after what she'd already been put through. So what did that leave? Neighbors? Could he possibly make it up the mountain?

The question had Ross literally racing to the front of the house and the picture window in the living room. He knew there weren't any houses close to him on the way down the mountain, but maybe there was one on the way up.

Silently praying, he swiped a hand over the frosted glass and peered across the front lawn to the highway, then upward through the dense woods. Faint lights flickered through the bared limbs and tree trunks, making Ross sigh with relief. Lights had to mean someone was there. Someone who could help him.

He put the baby down long enough to throw on a coat, hood and gloves. Then he bundled the baby in a heavy quilt and left the house.

A mixture of snow and sleet was being driven by a vicious north wind. The ice stung Ross's face, almost blinding him while the slick glaze under his boots made it slow going as he headed in the direction of the truck.

The frantic desperation Ross felt made everything inside him want to run, but he forced himself to creep safely along the driveway. He knew if he fell and broke his leg, he and the baby might both wind up dying from exposure.

When he finally reached the truck, he discovered the door handle was frozen. Ross banged on it several times with his fist before the ice broke loose enough to allow the latch to open. He was shivering and out of breath by the time he got the baby and himself into the cold interior.

Just let the engine start, he prayed as he twisted the key. Let him make it up to that house and to help.

The truck fired to life. With a sigh of relief Ross turned the heater on full blast, then wrapped the seat belt around the bundled baby as best he could. If there was one thing Ross was certain of, it was that the next few moments were going to be a rough ride.

Ross somehow managed to get the truck off the shoulder and onto the highway, but as soon as he did, it began sliding sideways. The more he gunned the motor in an effort to straighten it out, the more the tires spun helplessly on the ice.

After several failed attempts to move up the hill, he eased his foot off the gas, which had an equally disastrous effect. The truck began sliding backward, and Ross instinctively jammed on the brakes. However, the snow and ice made them useless and the truck continued to slip faster and faster down the steep, curving road.

"Hold on, baby. Hold on," Ross whispered, feeling more helpless than he ever had in his life.

Seeing they were headed straight toward a deep ravine, Ross made a split-second decision to wrench the steering wheel and deliberately ram the truck into the ditch.

For long moments after the truck came to a jarring halt, Ross clung to the steering wheel and drew in long, shuddering breaths. He was shaking with fear, not just for himself, but also for the baby who lay strapped in the seat beside him. He could have killed them both!

There was nothing left for him to do now but walk, he realized once he'd gathered his wits. Somewhere in the back of his mind he remembered warnings about not leaving a vehicle in a blizzard, but Ross also knew he couldn't sit here in a freezing truck waiting for help that might never come. The baby couldn't survive in this. He wasn't even sure he could.

Bits of ice pelted Ross in the face and eyes as he struggled to carry the baby up the mountain toward the faint lights flickering through the heavy woods. He was sure his face was frozen, along with his hands and feet. He'd never been this cold in his life, and he was afraid to imagine what the cold was doing to the baby. She was securely bundled in the heavy quilt, but it was quickly becoming covered with snow. Soon the dampness would seep through to the inner folds and onto the baby.

He had to hurry! He couldn't let anything happen to the new little life he carried in his arms.

Kathleen attached the dangling rhinestones to her earlobes, then stood back in front of a floor-length cheval mirror. She was dressed in winter white wool slacks with a matching cashmere sweater. Rhinestones were splashed across the bodice and round the cuffs at her wrists, giving the outfit a party look. Her hair was finally dry and lying in loose curls around her face and shoulders. Beneath the coal dark tresses, the outlandish earrings swung and glittered against her neck.

Not bad for a night on the old homestead, she thought with an impish laugh. Then she turned away from the mirror to add the final touch—a pair of silver high heels.

There was no way she was going to feel sorry for herself tonight, she thought as she left the bedroom. It was New Year's Eve. Tomorrow would begin a fresh year. And more than anything Kathleen wanted this coming year to be different from the past one. She was determined to begin it with a sparkle and a smile. It was time that her life went on. Good or bad, Kathleen believed, she was finally ready to face the future again.

She was in the kitchen, arranging an array of

snacks on a lacquered tray, when a knock came at the front door. She couldn't imagine anyone being out on a night such as this. But perhaps Nick had decided to try to make it up here after all. He'd been known to do crazier things, she thought, as she hurried to answer the door.

Safety made her flip the porch light on, then look through the peephole. It wasn't Nick standing outside in the freezing cold. It was a man holding a bundle of some sort in his arms.

She opened the door as far as the safety latch would allow. "Can I help you?"

Ross's face felt so stiff he wasn't quite sure he could make his lips move enough to talk. "I'm Ross Douglas," he said after a moment. "I live just down the mountain from you."

Kathleen continued to study his face, or what little she could see of it under the hood of his olive drab army coat. Was he the person who'd recently purchased the old Mabry place? She'd passed it a couple of days ago and vaguely noticed someone moving in.

"Are you having some sort of trouble? Did you wreck your vehicle on the ice?" she asked.

Ross was becoming impatient. Good Lord, couldn't she see he was freezing? The baby was freezing! Why was she being so damn cautious? This wasn't Houston, or even New York City!

"No, ma'am. I need help. A phone. I have a baby here that—"

"A baby!" Kathleen gasped. Before he could say more, she hurriedly pulled the chain latch from the door. "Please come in," she urged, pushing aside the metal storm door to allow him to enter the house.

Ross stepped past her and into the blessedly warm room. It had taken him at least thirty minutes to make it to this house. As he'd slowly worked his way up the side of the wooded mountain, he'd not seen a solitary vehicle, and before this woman had answered the door, he'd begun to feel as if he and the baby were the only two humans left on earth.

Kathleen slammed the door shut against the icy wind, then turned anxiously to the man, who'd walked to the middle of the room, still holding onto the bundle in his arms. "Is something wrong with the baby?" she asked quickly. "Should I call an ambulance?"

His teeth chattered fiercely as he said, "Hell, lady, an ambulance couldn't make it up here!" He glanced down at the baby as he hurriedly peeled the quilt from it. "Besides, I don't know if the baby is all right or—she needs care! I think she's just been born!"

Stunned, Kathleen looked at him stupidly. Was the man out of his mind? Or had hypothermia settled in to make his thinking incoherent? She rushed over to them. "What do you mean, you don't know? Isn't it yours?" Kathleen's attention was caught by the thick head of hair and little cries. Her heart turned over as she looked at the baby, swaddled in a sweatshirt much too big for it.

Ross glanced up at Kathleen, but he was so distraught that the only thing that registered in his mind was a young face and long dark hair. "No, she's not mine. She's been abandoned—I don't know who she belongs to. Just call someone, damn it!"

The panic in his voice sent Kathleen racing to the phone. It wasn't until she'd picked up the receiver that it dawned on her she didn't know exactly what she was doing. "What—who do I call? We don't have emergency service here!"

Ross tossed the snow-covered quilt to the floor, then looked desperately around the room for something to use as a blanket.

"Call, uh, call the hospital. Surely someone there can tell us what we need to be doing for her!"

He spotted an afghan on the seat of a stuffed armchair. Snatching it up, he wrapped it around the baby and carried her over to a fireplace, where a fire burned low on the grate.

Kathleen's hands shook as she punched out the number of the nearest hospital, then she grabbed the pad and pencil she always kept near the phone.

"I need help!" she blurted when a female voice answered, then stopped suddenly as a wave of fresh fear rushed over her. "Yes, I'm still here," she said, trying to collect herself. "I, uh, we've had an emergency childbirth here and, uh—no, no, there's no mother.'' Oh Lord, she sounded insane! "I mean—there is, but the baby has been out in the cold and—'' She paused and took a deep breath. "Yes, calm down. Yes, you're right. If you could just give us instructions—what to do for her until we can bring her in to a medical facility. What? Yes, I'll wait.''

Kathleen slapped a hand over the receiver and looked at the man and baby. "They're switching me over to pediatrics. They wanted to know about the mother. Where is she?''

"How the hell should I know! This baby was on my front porch when I got home, and that's all I can tell you!''

Chapter Two

Ross was pacing back and forth in front of the fireplace by the time Kathleen got off the telephone.

"What do we do? What did they say?" He fired the questions at her as the baby began to cry.

Kathleen ripped the sheet of paper from the pad and hurried over to the stranger and the baby. "I've got it all here." She waved the paper at him. "There just happened to be a pediatrician making his rounds, so I talked with him. He said to take things one step at a time and everything would be fine."

"Fine? What does he know? He doesn't know this baby has been out in a blizzard!"

One of Kathleen's dark brows shot up. She didn't care for this man's attitude. Not one whit. "Yes, he does know. I told him."

"Then why is she crying?"

The baby's cries had grown louder with every passing second, and were now rising up over the adult voices. "I don't know. I've never had a baby!"

"Oh, my God," he yelled in disgust, "I find a woman and she's not a mother!"

If it hadn't been for the baby, Kathleen would have put him out of her house right then and there. "I don't even let people I know yell at me, mister, much less people I don't." Her eyes cut an angry path over his face. "Not every adult is a parent. Are you?"

Ross shook his head, ashamed that he'd let his emotions take over. "No, I'm not. And I'm sorry for yelling. But I've—been going a little bit crazy ever since I found her on the porch," he said, looking down at the crying baby in his arms.

Kathleen quickly reached for her. "We're going to take care of her," she said, trying her best to sound reassuring.

Ross released his hold on the baby, albeit reluctantly. In the past hour she'd come to feel like a natural part of him. As though in some strange way she'd become his child, not just a baby he'd found in a cardboard box.

"Oh—oh my," Kathleen gasped as she carried the child over to the long plush sofa. "You weren't kidding, were you? This really is a newborn infant," she said to him.

He followed her to the sofa, his face consumed

with worry. "I don't know for sure, but it looks like she was born only a few hours ago."

Kathleen had noticed earlier that he'd referred to the baby as a girl, but she didn't know whether he'd merely said it out of panic or confusion. "She? Then it is a girl?" Kathleen asked, darting a quick glance over at the dark stranger, who seemed to be suddenly filling up her living room.

He nodded, then pushed off the hood of his coat. Kathleen watched the garment fall away to reveal a head of thick, dark hair and a set of rough, craggy features.

"I'm Kathleen Gallagher Hayes," she told him. "What's your name again?"

Quickly he closed the small gap between them to extend his hand. "Ross Douglas."

She reached out and for a brief moment his fingers closed around hers. They felt like ice, instantly reminding her that this man had made a trek up the mountain in an ice storm. "You're freezing! How long did it take you to make it up here?"

He shrugged and unzipped his coat. "I'm not sure. It seemed like forever."

Kathleen jerked her head toward the fireplace. "If you want to build up the fire, it might help to warm both of you up." She looked back at the child and felt a stir of panic in spite of the pediatrician's warning for her to remain calm and collected while dealing with the baby. "First he said to make sure she was breathing without difficulty. Like a wheeze or cough.''

"And how do we know?"

"He said if she was able to cry freely, she was more than likely breathing freely."

"Well, she certainly seems to be doing that. So what next?" he wanted to know.

"We need to check her temperature. The doctor said she should feel warm, but not hot, and her skin should be a pinkish red, not ashen or blue. How does it look to you?"

Ross came back from tossing a couple of logs onto the low bed of coals in the fireplace. "Well, she doesn't look blue, but her face is pretty red."

Kathleen figured that was caused from her crying, but since she hadn't been a parent either, she could hardly say for sure. She ran her hands lightly over the baby's arms and legs. "She feels warm. I'll go find a thermometer."

She hurried out of the room, leaving Ross to watch over the baby. He tried quieting her with soothing words, but she ignored the sound of his voice and kept on crying.

Frantic to hush her, Ross picked her up and cradled her in the crook of his arm. Thankfully, the contact with his body seemed to pacify her somewhat, and slowly her cries turned to faint whimpers.

Ross let out a heavy sigh and raked his hand through the damp hair falling over his forehead. He

was a man who worked around children everyday,
but they were the teenage kind. They weighed more
than a few pounds, could digest anything that went
under the heading of food and could communicate in
their own strange ways. Teenagers were nothing like
this tiny life he held in his arms. This child had
thrown him for a loop!

Kathleen hurried back into the room with a thermometer in her hand. "I don't have the kind that you
use on babies, but the doctor said we could use the
armpit method in this circumstance."

Both Ross and Kathleen gave a sigh of relief when
they'd taken the baby's temperature and it registered
normal.

"Well, now that we know she's not suffering from
hypothermia, she needs to be cleaned and fed,"
Kathleen said, glancing at the hasty notes she'd
scratched during her conversation with the doctor.

"Do you know how to do that?" he asked.

Kathleen could hear the desperate edge in his
voice. She was feeling that same desperation, but she
knew it wouldn't do for either of them to give in to
it. For now she and this man would have to do the
best they could and hope it would be enough.

"I'm going to give it my best shot," she said with
far more confidence than she felt.

Ross looked at her with renewed hope. "You've
cared for children before? Baby-sat?"

A classroom of twenty-five students sometimes

felt as if she were baby-sitting, she thought. "Yes, but not for an infant like this."

"Me, neither," he muttered. "They were all a lot—" he measured off a space with his hands "—a lot bigger than her."

Kathleen looked back at him and felt a faint flutter in the region of her heart. Ross Douglas was dark, brawny and utterly male. He was a man who looked like he knew much more about making a baby than taking care of one.

The thought tinged her cheeks with color as she replied, "Well, I think I have some books that might help us."

Books. Ross groaned, but not so that Kathleen Hayes could hear him. She was already on the way out of the room. After those books, he supposed. Hellfire, he muttered to himself, she was a grown, mature woman. She should know about babies. Women were supposed to have that internal thing that automatically clicked on when they had a child.

But Kathleen Hayes hadn't had a child, he reminded himself. So he could hardly blame her for not knowing. But damn it, he'd never felt quite this helpless in his whole life. He knew he was being irrational and tried to calm down. It made no sense to take his anger and frustration out on this woman. He looked at the baby, then shook his head. "Hold on, little girl, and I'll try my best not to let anything happen to you."

In the study, Kathleen frantically scanned a row of books. Once she found the titles she was looking for, she jerked them from the shelves and hurried back to the living room.

Ross Douglas was still by the fire and the baby was still in his arms. He'd said he'd never had a baby, she mused. But he didn't hold the child with the usual awkwardness men had when dealing with infants.

The observation took her thoughts a step further, to whether the man had a wife. He looked to be somewhere in his late twenties, certainly an age where most men had already settled into the role of husband. But he didn't appear to have that attached look about him that married men usually did.

At the moment, whether Ross Douglas was attached or unattached was hardly important, she told herself as she joined him on the hearth. They had a baby to attend to.

"This book about childbirth and baby care should tell us a few things," she said, hurriedly flipping the pages. She'd purchased the book when she and Greg had planned on starting a family. Unfortunately, she'd never been given the chance to use it. She'd never conceived, and then Greg had been killed. "It's obvious she needs to be washed, and something needs to be done with her umbilical cord, otherwise it will heal in an ugly shape."

Ross grimaced. "Right now I'm not worried

whether she'll be able to wear a bikini when she's a teenager. I want her to eat!''

Kathleen gave him a sidelong glance that told him she didn't appreciate his lack of patience. ''So do I, Mr. Douglas. But we can't very well give her plain old cow's milk!''

''Why not?''

Kathleen groaned at his innocent question. ''Because it's too hard to digest. Babies don't drink that sort of milk until—well, way down the road from now. The doctor gave me a make-do formula that I can mix up until this storm is over and we can get to town.''

The baby began to cry in earnest again, and Ross gently rocked her in an effort to quieten her. ''Even if you know what to feed her, how are you going to give it to her? Do you have a baby bottle around here?''

Kathleen ignored his questions and kept reading. Ross wanted to curse a blue streak at her. He was a man of action and this waiting around while Kathleen Hayes educated herself about babies was driving him mad.

Finally she looked up at him and blinked, as though his question had just registered with her. ''What? A bottle? Oh, yes, I believe I do. One of my friends with a baby left a bottle here some time ago.'' She motioned for him to follow her out of the room.

"Come on. We'll take her to the kitchen and I'll start gathering things together."

Ross followed her through the house, his eyes flickering from her to the large rooms they passed through. The house was opulent compared to the one he'd just moved into. It was furnished with modern, expensive furniture, deep, thick carpeting, draperies that showcased rather than covered the windows. Oil paintings decorated the walls, while fragile art pieces and potted plants sat here and there in carefully chosen spots.

Still, the house couldn't hold a candle to Kathleen Gallagher Hayes, he realized. She was tall and long legged, her figure lushly curved in all the right places. Her nearly black hair hung to the middle of her back in a fall of silky curls, and as she walked ahead of him, the sweet scent of jasmine trailed after her.

Earlier, when he'd started up the mountain with the baby, he had prayed to find a woman in this house. Well, he'd found one all right, he thought. But was she the kind of woman he'd been praying for?

"Were you planning to go out tonight?" he asked. Surely she didn't sit around the house dressed as she was now.

"Yes. To my family's house. We're having an engagement party for my brother tonight. I was getting ready to go when the sleet started."

She glanced back over her shoulder at him and

smiled, dazzling Ross with the sudden transformation of her features. "And what about you? Were you planning to party, too?" she asked him.

He shook his head. "No. I'm still in the process of moving. I was going to unpack boxes." He looked at the baby girl in his arms. It was still hard for him to believe that all this was happening. "I guess I ended up unpacking the most important one, though, didn't I?"

"Thank God you did," Kathleen exclaimed. "I can't bear to think the baby was out in the cold. Do you have any idea how long she might have been there?"

She hurried into the kitchen and flipped on the overhead lights. Ross followed her to a work counter. "Not really. I drove into Fort Smith sometime before noon and didn't get back until the storm hit. She could have been left there anytime during the afternoon."

Kathleen shuddered at the thought. "Well, it will be up to the authorities to figure out who might have done this. But let's take care of her first before we bother calling the sheriff, or whomever. Do you agree?"

Ross nodded. "Yes, I agree. Besides, the authorities can't get up here to her, and we certainly can't take her down. Not tonight, at least. And even if we could, I don't think it would be good for her to go

back out into the cold. The weather out there isn't
fit for human or beast, much less a newborn infant.''

"You're right. We'll just do the best we can until
we can get her into the city."

His eyes on the baby, he said, "I guess we'll have
to be her mommy and daddy for right now."

Ross Douglas couldn't know how his words struck
her. He couldn't know how often Kathleen had
prayed to become a mother and how she had grieved
with everything inside of her when she'd realized she
couldn't bear children. Now, through some crazy
twist of fate, she had a baby needing her care.

She gave him and the baby a quick glance as she
tried to figure out the strange surge of emotions well-
ing up inside her. "Well," she said, her voice un-
expectedly husky, "if you're okay holding her, I'll
get what we need to clean her."

Kathleen had turned and taken a step away from
him when he practically shouted, "A bath? I thought
we were going to feed her!"

Frustrated, she turned back to him. "We are, Mr.
Douglas. If you'll just calm down and think about it,
you'll see that she needs to be bathed before she
eats."

Ross watched the rhinestones on her wrists sparkle
as she jammed her fists on either side of her waist.
This woman, he realized, looked the furthest thing
from a mother that he could think of. She looked like

a woman just ready and waiting to seduce the man she wanted.

"Oh, and how did you come to that deduction?" he asked. "Is that what the doctor said to do?"

She drew in a long, bracing breath. "He didn't say. He just instructed me on how to wash her and feed her. But I do have enough common sense to know that once she eats, she'll more than likely go to sleep. A bath would disturb her."

"Look, Ms. Hayes, like I told you a minute ago, I don't know how long she might have been on my porch. And I sure don't know how long it's been since she was born. It could have been hours and hours ago. The little thing could be starving to death!"

Kathleen's frustration with the man flew out the window as she watched his other arm come up to cradle the baby in a totally protective gesture. How could she not be touched by his obvious compassion?

She crossed the few steps between them and gently brushed her fingers across the baby's head. "Mr. Douglas," she began, trying her best to sound reassuring, "I am woman enough to know that a mother's milk isn't always present when a baby is born. Sometimes it's several hours before the—uh, well, before the baby actually receives milk."

Although her face was bent over the baby's, Ross could see a blush spreading across her cheek. Apparently she wasn't comfortable discussing such basic things as a woman's breasts with a man. But as far as that went, he wasn't, either. Not because it affronted him, but because it told him that even though he was twenty-nine years old, there were things about a woman's body that he didn't know. Especially when it came to childbirth. Well, Ross, you never professed to know everything, did you?

Kathleen kept waiting for him to say something. When he didn't, she lifted her eyes to his face and was instantly jolted with sensations. Gray was supposed to be a cool color, she thought, but Ross Douglas's eyes were anything but cool. She could almost feel their warmth sliding over her face, her hair, her throat and finally her lips.

"Mr. Douglas—" she began, only to stop when he shook his head.

"It's Ross, ma'am," he said. "I figure we might as well be on a first-name basis."

Suddenly she was quivering and she didn't know why. It wasn't because of his voice, or the hot look in his eyes. And it wasn't because he wanted her to call him Ross. It was something within her, something that she'd thought had died along with her husband. But this man's closeness, his scent, his rough maleness was sparking it back to life. And scaring Kathleen in the process.

"Okay, Ross," she said, taking a step away while trying to give him a casual smile. "So—so I'd better…get the things for the baby."

This time Kathleen didn't wait for him to agree. She quickly turned and left the room.

Her high heels made a tapping noise on the tile. Ross watched her leave, saw the rhythmic movement of her hips, the sway of her hair as she moved her head. She was an enticing sight, to say the least, he thought. He couldn't ever remember seeing a woman with such ivory white skin, dark green-brown eyes and hair the color of midnight. He'd stumbled onto an Irish rose in the middle of an ice storm. And he wasn't quite sure if he'd been cursed or blessed.

Chapter Three

Kathleen returned to the kitchen after a few minutes, carrying an armful of blankets and towels. After making a pad with them on the kitchen table, she hurriedly gathered warm water and mild soap.

While she scurried around the room, Ross paced from one end of it to the other. He'd never known having a baby could leave a man so helpless and overwhelmed. No matter that this baby had come to him under extreme circumstances, he felt just as responsible for her at this moment as he would if she'd truly been his.

"Okay, I think everything is ready. Put her on the blankets," Kathleen instructed him.

Ross placed the baby on the pad of blankets, only to have her immediately begin screaming with red-faced fury, her little arms waving rigidly at her sides.

"Is she warm enough? What's wrong with her?" he asked as he stared helplessly at the infant.

Kathleen scarcely registered his question as she pulled away the afghan and began to examine the baby. She believed Ross Douglas was right in saying she might be only hours old. The umbilical cord had been raggedly cut and left untied. Neither had the birthing fluids been thoroughly washed from her skin or hair. Kathleen wanted to burst into tears at the pathetic way in which this child had been welcomed to the world.

She didn't realize she'd made a sound, but she must have, because suddenly Ross Douglas was touching her shoulder.

"What's the matter? Are you crying, too?"

Swallowing the lump in her throat, she quickly shook her head. "I'm—I can't bear to see how this precious little thing has been treated. Tossed away like some old, unwanted rag." She reached up and wiped away the tears that had fallen onto her cheeks. "How could someone do this? Why did God allow it?"

Ross knew exactly what this woman was feeling. He'd felt the very same thing when he'd pulled the baby from the cardboard box. His hand tightened on her shoulder as he said, "Maybe God allowed it because he thought she deserved parents who would really love her."

Kathleen had to believe that, because she certainly

didn't want to believe in suffering of any kind. "Yes, you must be right. And we have her now. That's all that matters."

With fresh determination, she went to work washing the baby. And as the signs of waste began to disappear, so did Kathleen's tears. This baby was loved, she told herself fiercely. Because she loved it.

"She's still crying," Ross said, as Kathleen continued to wash and rinse the baby's thatch of dark hair. "Do you think something is wrong with her?"

From the moment Kathleen had laid the baby on the padded table, Ross had taken up a position at her left shoulder. All the time she'd been washing the baby, Kathleen had tried not to notice his nearness, but it was terribly hard to do when he was standing so close she could feel the heat from his body.

"Going by what the doctor said, she seems all right. And she sounds like she has a healthy set of lungs, so that's good."

"But it couldn't be good for her to cry like this," Ross said anxiously.

"From what I can remember my mother telling me, it's pretty normal. She said my brother Nick screamed for the first three months of his life with the colic, and he turned out so healthy it's practically disgusting."

He watched as she finished washing the child from head to toe, then dried every wrinkle with exceptional care. She seemed to handle the child with confidence for someone who'd never had a baby before.

"I don't suppose you have any diapers around here," he mused aloud. "What are we going to use?"

Kathleen gave him a brief smile. "You're going to make some while I mix up the formula."

He stared at her in amazement. "Me? I can't make a diaper. I barely know how to put one on a baby, much less make one!"

If the baby's cries hadn't been so disturbing, she probably would have laughed at the panicked look on his face. How could men bravely face an enemy in battle, but want to turn tail and run when confronted with caring for a newborn?

"Surely it can't be that hard," she assured him. "When I went after the blankets, I found a white sheet. You can cut it into large squares while I fix her a bottle."

Ross would do anything to finally get a bottle in the baby's mouth. He somehow felt that once he saw her eating, he'd know that she was really okay.

"So, show me what to do," he said, resigning himself to the task.

Kathleen got the sheet and scissors and cut a pattern for him. While he made the diapers, she pinned a thick hand towel onto the baby for the time being, then wrapped her loosely in a flannel sheet.

"She looks beautiful," Kathleen said, her voice

tender as she dabbed a little baby oil onto her fingertips and smoothed the dark baby hair.

"You know, the more I think about the whole thing, the more I wonder what kind of woman could give birth, then just leave the child with a stranger," Ross said with angry dismay.

Kathleen looked up at him, her expression suddenly thoughtful. "Maybe it wasn't a stranger. Maybe it was someone who knew you," she said.

He brushed her suggestion aside with a doubtful shake of his head. "I only moved here two weeks ago. The only people I know are the ones I'll be working with."

"Where is that?"

"Fort Smith. I'm a high school baseball coach and history teacher."

So Ross Douglas was a teacher, she thought curiously. He certainly fit the coach part, but it was hard to imagine this virile-looking man lecturing about history to a group of high school students.

"This is a strange time to be taking a teaching job," she remarked.

"Not really. It's in between semesters. But as far as knowing anyone that might leave me her..." His shoulders lifted and fell, telling her he was just as much at a loss as she was. "I don't know anyone here or back in Texas who would do such a thing."

"Then I guess your house was just a random choice," she said thoughtfully.

Ross looked back down at the baby. She seemed to be drifting off to sleep again. He was relieved that her crying had finally stopped. No matter what Kathleen Hayes had said about it being normal, he didn't want the baby to cry. It might mean that something *was* wrong with her.

"But why?" he wondered aloud. "Why pick my house?"

Kathleen shook her head sadly as she turned toward the cabinets behind them. "People do strange things for strange reasons. I suppose the mother must have been very desperate."

"What makes you think it was the mother? It could have been the father who put her on my porch."

Kathleen grimaced. "I doubt she has a father."

Ross reached out, and Kathleen watched his finger gently stroke the baby's delicate cheek. He had big hands, she thought, with tough palms and long fingers. His skin was startlingly dark against the baby's ruddy complexion, and would be even more so against her own white skin.

The unexpected image of Ross Douglas touching Kathleen's own bare skin had her mentally shaking herself. What was she doing thinking such...erotic things? she wondered desperately. This man was a total stranger! And right now she should be thinking solely of the child.

"She has to have a father. Otherwise she wouldn't have been born," Ross reasoned.

"Biologically speaking, yes. But something tells me that if this little girl had a real father, she wouldn't have been placed on your doorstep."

"You're probably right," he conceded with a rueful twist of his lips. "And I suppose we'll find out soon enough."

Kathleen turned back to the cabinets to search for the baby bottle. Behind her, Ross realized he was still wearing his coat. Shrugging out of the damp garment, he placed it over a chair.

"Thank God, I found it," Kathleen said a minute later as she pulled the plastic bottle from a bottom shelf and held it up for him to see. "I think we would be in far worse trouble without this."

Ross joined her at the cabinet. "Maybe we could have used a rubber glove like you see in all those old movies," he said dryly. "It always seems to work."

Kathleen smiled at his suggestion, thinking they might as well try to find what humor they could in the situation. At least that was better than dwelling on the tragedy that would have occurred if Ross Douglas hadn't found the baby in time. "Well, actually, I was thinking a moment ago of an old movie where circumstances force three cowboys into taking care of an orphaned newborn."

"*The Three Godfathers.* John Wayne," he said with a grin of instant recognition.

The lazy smile caused lines to crease in his lean cheeks and sparked his gray eyes with a devilish light. Kathleen felt her eyes drawn to his face, as though there wasn't a thing in the room to look at but him.

"You've seen it," she said.

"Yes. But let's not put axle grease on this baby of ours," he said with a low chuckle.

Kathleen was glad to see that this man was able to joke in spite of the circumstances they were in. And she was glad she could laugh along with him, because she wanted to show herself that finding this man attractive really wasn't anything to worry about.

"No. If she needs oiling, I think I can find something lighter than axle grease."

Resting his hip against the cabinet, Ross watched her punch a hole in a can of condensed milk. "Is that what the doctor said to give her?" he asked.

Kathleen pointed to the note lying on the countertop. "See for yourself."

His eyes scanned the piece of paper. "Thank God, we have something she can eat. Do you have plenty of that stuff on hand?" he asked pointing to the can.

"Plenty. I do a lot of cooking and baking and I like to be prepared," she said, finding she could not keep herself from looking at him and smiling. He returned her smile as he folded his arms across his chest.

The movement drew Kathleen's attention to the fact that he'd removed the army coat. He was wearing jeans and a dark blue crew-necked sweater with a white shirt beneath. He was built just as she'd imagined, with broad, thick shoulders and a lean, trim waist. She knew instinctively that he would be strong, as strong as her brothers, who were both as powerful as bulls.

"You don't trust me with this baby stuff, do you?" she asked more amused then resentful.

A sheepish expression crept over his face as he watched her pour a measured amount of water into the rich milk. "It's not that. I just…want the baby to be okay."

From the corner of her eye, Kathleen saw his gaze travel over to the table where the baby lay sleeping on the folded blankets. Something inside her stirred at the tender look on his face.

"So do I. And if it will make you feel any better, I'm not a complete dimwit. As a matter of fact, I'm a schoolteacher like you. Although I'm not teaching at the present."

Ross was surprised by her admission. He'd already decided she was a wealthy woman who didn't have to work at anything. Not even at looking beautiful.

"Why not? I mean, why aren't you teaching now?"

Kathleen's eyes remained on the milk she was mixing. "My husband was killed about a year ago. It took awhile for me to gather myself back together and…want to go back to work. By the time I did it was too late to find a junior high teaching position that was open. Maybe when the next school year starts something will be available."

He felt like a heel. But how could he have known that she'd had a husband, much less that he'd been killed?

"Sorry. That was nosy of me."

Tomorrow is the beginning of a new year, Kathleen reminded herself. She wasn't going to let thoughts of Greg drag her down anymore.

"Don't apologize. You didn't know about my late husband. Besides, friends ask me the same thing. Why aren't you teaching? Why don't you go back to teaching?"

"Does it bother you that they ask?"

Kathleen smiled wanly as she looked over at him. "Not anymore. I'm looking forward to returning to the classroom."

Ross didn't say anything as she went back to the task of making the formula. He only hoped she didn't teach high school. He couldn't imagine any boy over the age of fifteen being able to concentrate with her for a teacher.

"This ice storm," he said, "is it something that happens very often around here?"

"It doesn't happen frequently. But we usually get a dose of it every winter."

"Are you kidding?"

Kathleen merely smiled at his shocked expression. "No. It's not uncommon to get stranded here on the mountain because of snow, sleet or freezing rain. Especially in January."

"I'm from south of San Antonio. We don't have weather like this. In fact, while I was slipping and sliding up the mountainside, I was wondering why in he—heck I'd moved up here."

"Why did you?" She poured a portion of the prepared milk into the bottle and placed the remainder in the refrigerator.

Ross went back over to the baby. Even though she appeared to be healthy and normal, he had the uncontrollable urge to keep checking. "A longtime friend asked me to take on the job as a favor to him. And since I was looking for a school anyway, I decided to accept the position."

Kathleen made sure the lid and nipple were fastened tightly on the bottle before she hurried over to the microwave. "Is it his job you're taking over?"

"No. My friend is the principal. The coach I'll be replacing was in a bad car accident and broke his leg. He'll be in a cast well into summer."

She placed the bottle in the microwave, then switched it on. While waiting for the bottle to heat, she turned around to face him. "So this is just a temporary position,'' she asked, ''until he gets back on his feet?''

Ross shook his head. ''No. This was his last year. He's retiring. That's why I bought the house. I didn't want to start out renting.''

So he was planning to stay in the area, she thought. The news pleased her, though she couldn't say why. She doubted their paths as neighbors would cross once this thing with the baby and the storm were over. ''It must have been hard on you to move up here on such short notice.''

''Not really. I only have myself to move. And since I wasn't teaching last semester back in San Antonio, I didn't have to worry about giving notice and all that sort of thing.''

If he hadn't been teaching, what had he been doing? Kathleen wondered. But she kept the question to herself. She'd already shown too much interest in the man.

Behind her the microwave dinged. Kathleen removed the bottle and tested the milk on the inner part of her arm. ''Do you want to feed her?'' she asked, offering the bottle to Ross.

''No,'' he said a bit awkwardly. ''I think I'll wait and see if she can get the hang of it first.''

Beneath the veil of her lashes, Kathleen gave him a long, pointed look. ''If I wanted to be mean, I'd remind you of how you've continually yelled that she needed to be fed. But since I'm not that kind of person, I won't say a thing."

An hour and a half ago Ross hadn't met this woman. So why did he feel as if he was beginning to know her already? Why did he instinctively know that she was teasing him instead of mocking him? He couldn't reason out those answers, but he did know one thing. That mischievous glint in her eye was very sexy.

"I'm glad you aren't…that kind of person," he said slowly, one corner of his roughly hewn mouth curving upward.

Kathleen was momentarily mesmerized by the dimple in his lean cheek, the glint of his straight white teeth, the amused light in his narrowed eyes.

"I'll just bet," she said, clearing her throat and moving over to the baby.

Seating herself in one of the kitchen chairs, Kathleen took the baby in her arms and offered her the bottle. After a few fumbling attempts, she managed to get the nipple into its mouth, but the baby immediately rejected it with an angry cry.

Kathleen looked up at Ross, her expression a little helpless and even more desperate. "What am I doing wrong? Oh, Ross, what if she won't eat? What will we do?"

The baby's refusal to eat had him just as worried as Kathleen, but he tried not to let her see it. "Don't panic. She'll eat. Just give her a minute."

Kathleen tried again, but the baby spit out the nipple and began to cry again in earnest.

Kathleen wanted to burst into tears along with the baby. "She doesn't want any part of it," she said with a frustrated groan.

"She knows you're worried and upset. Would you want to eat with somebody who was wringing her hands?"

Kathleen glared at him. "I'm not wringing my hands. I'm worried. And I've never fed a baby her very first meal! Here, you do it!"

She stood up and handed the baby over to Ross, who was instantly stunned by the reversal in their roles.

"Why do you want me to try? I don't know what to do!" he practically shouted at her.

Placing her hands on his shoulders, Kathleen pushed him down into the chair. "Neither do I. So you might as well make an attempt," she told him, then handed him the bottle.

Ross carefully positioned the baby in the crook of his arm, then crooned soft, encouraging words to her in his deep voice.

To Kathleen's amazement, the baby began to quiet down. Ross took advantage of the moment and offered her the bottle again. This time the baby got a taste of the milk and latched onto the nipple. Both adults let out a sigh of relief as the tiny girl drew greedily at the warm milk.

"I think she likes it," Kathleen declared.

Ross was aware that she'd taken up a position near his shoulder and was peering down at the baby in his arms.

"I told you she was hungry," he said.

There was such a smug, happy note to his husky voice that Kathleen just had to tilt her head around to look at him. He smiled at her, a smile that made her feel warm and glad.

"So you did, Ross. She must like you better. Or else you have that special touch," she said, smiling back at him.

Her words and her smile pleased him more than she could ever know. "I don't know about that. I just thank God she's nursing. I think she's going to be all right, don't you?"

Kathleen looked at the baby and wondered if this was how it felt to be a real parent. She would never know the answer to that, but she did know that she and this man shared a bond with this new little life. They both wanted her to be safe and protected and cared for. And so far they'd worked together to give her as much of those things as they could under the circumstances.

"Yes. I think she is. She's nursing strongly. She seems to be breathing normally. There doesn't seem to be any fever or congestion. All I can say is an angel must have sent you home just in time."

"You think I keep the company of angels, huh?"

His deep voice was tinged with wry humor, pulling Kathleen's face toward him once again. "I think you had one with you today. Before then, I couldn't say."

Ross couldn't say himself. He considered himself a good guy. At least partially good. He loved old people and children. He paid his bills, and he couldn't stand anyone who was unkind to animals. But there were thousands of people just like him. He wasn't special enough for God to have an angel looking over him. No, he somehow believed that if there had been an angel guiding him home this afternoon, it was for the baby's sake and not for Ross Douglas.

Her eyes met his and Ross felt an unfamiliar tug somewhere inside of him. "I'd like to think I have connections up in heaven," he admitted, "but it's hardly likely."

Kathleen quickly looked away from the warmth of his eyes and to the baby still nursing quietly in his arms. How long had it been since she'd looked at a man and felt like a woman? she asked herself. Years? So why was this man reminding her that it had been ages since a man had held her, ages since a man had made love to her?

She could feel Ross watching her as she stepped away from them and over to the windows that made up one wall of the room. To know that his eyes were on her made her feel warm and strange. She was desperately trying to ignore the feeling when his voice sounded behind her.

"What is it doing out there now?"

Kathleen pulled aside the curtain and peered out at the dark night. "It looks like freezing rain to me. It's really too dark on this side of the house to tell."

"Hells bells, we won't get out of here till spring thaw," he said.

His exaggeration had her glancing back over her shoulder at him. "You Texans think you've gone north if you cross the Red River."

He could see that glint back in her eyes and knew that she was teasing him again. It made Ross wonder if there was something about him that made her do it. Or did she tease all men with her words and her eyes? No. No, he didn't like to think that. He fancied the idea that he was the only one who'd seen that mysterious grin on her face.

"I know it looks bad right now," she said again. "But maybe by tomorrow the road graders will be able to push most of it off. If we're not able to drive down tomorrow, we'll surely be able to by the next day."

Ross thought of the lone package of lunch meat on a shelf in his refrigerator. He'd intended to buy more groceries, but he'd gotten busy moving furniture and cardboard boxes filled with clothes and other bits of junk he'd collected through the years. The chore of getting in groceries had been put aside.

He watched the baby nurse and the measure of milk slowly drain out of the bottle. "Well, I suppose I can survive on pastrami for a couple of days," he said with a good-natured shrug of one shoulder. "I'm not much of a cook anyway."

Kathleen's eyes felt glued to the man. His legs were long, she noted, the hard muscles of his thighs visible through the blue jeans. He was wearing a pair of brown cowboy boots, the high-heeled kind her brother Sam wore. She'd noticed earlier that he moved gracefully in them. When he'd paced around the kitchen with the baby in his arms, his footsteps had barely been audible on the tile floor.

Her eyes moved from his boots to glide up the length of his legs. The sitting position he'd taken had the denim jeans straining against his body in places Kathleen knew she shouldn't be looking at. But she did, anyway.

"You're not going home," she told him.

Chapter Four

Ross stared at her, his expression dazed. "I beg your pardon?"

Realizing just how blunt she must have sounded sent dark color spreading across Kathleen's ivory complexion.

"I only meant that it's a solid sheet of ice out there. It would be crazy for you to try to get to your house. At least for tonight, anyway. Besides, you didn't just intend to leave the baby with me, did you?"

"I hadn't had time to think that far ahead," he said, wondering how she would feel about him staying the night. She might be dead set against having a strange man in her house.

His hedging angered her. Unjustly, she supposed,

but she couldn't help it. She'd been on her way to thinking that he was a man who really cared about people. She didn't like to think that she'd judged wrongly. Again.

"Oh," she said carefully, "I thought you were concerned about this baby. You certainly seemed to care awhile ago when you came to my door."

He made a frustrated sound under his breath. "I do care about her! How could you doubt that?"

Ross noticed that the baby had quit nursing. He pulled the nearly empty bottle from her mouth and motioned for Kathleen to approach. "She needs to be burped, doesn't she? I don't know how to do that, do you?"

Kathleen walked back over to him and the baby. "I think so," she said, taking the chair across from his.

Ross carefully handed her the baby. Kathleen put her on her shoulder and began to pat her back.

After a few moments passed and she didn't say anything else to him, Ross decided she must be angry with him. He also decided that he didn't like it. Whatever Kathleen Hayes thought of him, he didn't want it to be that he was an insensitive clod.

"Look, Kathleen, I want to stay here tonight and make sure you and the baby are okay. I just didn't know what *you* wanted me to do."

She stared at him as though he were crazy or close to it. "You think I'd want to be left alone with a newborn, without any means of transportation? The closest neighbor I have is you, and even if I stuck my head out the door and yelled my head off you'd be too far away to hear me.'' She stopped long enough to draw in a breath. ''Good Lord, I've only just now stopped shaking. And we haven't even talked to the authorities about all of this yet.''

Ross realized all that. Yet he was also aware of the fact that he was a man and she was a woman, and she didn't know him. At least she didn't know him well enough to share her home with him.

He looked at her. ''This is your home. I didn't want to frighten you by insisting that I stay. You don't know me, and you're obviously here by yourself.''

Suddenly Kathleen could see that Ross had been worried that she might have fears of being alone with him in the house. Surprisingly, the only fear Kathleen had was the fear of him not being here with her.

''I think you'll have to agree that this is an unusual circumstance. So don't worry about it. I trust you,'' she assured him.

Relief swept over his face. ''Thank you. I assure you I'm a true Texas gentleman. You don't have a thing to worry about.''

Just then the baby gave a loud, unladylike burp. Kathleen smiled down at her. ''I don't want you to be a gentleman,'' she said to Ross. ''I want you to be my friend. One that I can count on when this little girl wakes up crying in the night.''

"She's going to wake up crying? I thought she'd sleep again now."

"I expect she will. For a while. But I do know that babies wake up frequently and want to eat. Haven't you ever been around a baby before?" Kathleen asked him.

Ross shook his head. "I'm an only child. Sorta."

Kathleen dabbed the milk away from the corners of the baby's mouth with a towel, then held her in the cradle of her arms. "What does 'sorta' mean?"

She was looking at the baby and didn't see the grimace on Ross's face.

"I have half brothers and sisters. Two sets of them, in fact."

Curious, she looked up at him. "Two sets?"

"Yeah. My parents split when I was ten years old. Both of them remarried and had other kids."

"Oh. I...see."

Ross flexed his shoulders while wondering if she really did see. He doubted it. A woman like her didn't know what it had been like as a child to be shuffled back and forth from one home to the other. He'd grown up not knowing where he belonged.

Now he avoided family contacts on either side. Both his mother and father had made their lives with someone else. They each had children of their own.

Ross was the odd one out. He was a living reminder to his parents of the mistake their marriage had been.

"I doubt it, Kathleen. Something tells me you grew up in one house, with your real parents."

Kathleen was surprised by his assessment. Surprised that he'd taken that much notice of her in the first place, and surprised that he'd come up with the right deduction when he had.

"Yes, I did. On a farm not more than twenty miles from here. And I'm happy to say that my parents are together and healthy and still very much in love."

"Lucky you," he said.

Kathleen couldn't quite decide if it was wistfulness or cynicism she heard in his voice. Maybe a little bit of both. "Yes, I guess I have been," she said, then looked down at the sweet, angelic face pressed against her breast. "I wish we could say the same for this innocent baby. What in the world is she going to be able to say about her childhood when she looks back on it at my age?"

His expression quickly changed to a grim one. "We can't predict what her future is going to be. But I do know one thing. I'm going to make damn sure that the people who dumped her will never get her!"

His vehemence took Kathleen by surprise. Although it shouldn't have, she thought. Ross Douglas was a man who obviously had strong ideas about right and wrong. Just like her two brothers. And God knows, both Sam and Nick would fight till their dying day to see that justice was done. Especially where a helpless child was concerned.

"I agree. They obviously didn't want her. And she deserves to be loved. Just as every child in this world deserves to be loved."

A private little ache rushed through Kathleen's heart, compelling her to bend her head and kiss the baby's smooth cheek.

As she looked up, she realized Ross was watching her, his gray eyes filled with something that reminded Kathleen that the two of them were a man and a woman, alone.

She drew in a long breath, then let it out slowly before she spoke. "The baby seems to be fast asleep now. I think I'll take her back to the living room. The fireplace has probably made it nice and warm by now. And we need to see about calling the sheriff."

Ross was quickly on his feet. "Do you want me to carry her or can you?"

She smiled her appreciation at his offer. "I can manage her if you'll carry those blankets for me," she said, nodding toward the stack on the table.

Ross grabbed up the blankets, thinking there was nothing left for him to do but stay the night.

A quirk of a smile moved his mouth as he followed Kathleen and the baby out of the kitchen. Well, Ross, he asked himself, just how bad could it be to spend New Year's Eve with a beautiful woman and a newborn baby?

"This feels wonderful," Ross said when the three of them entered the living room. "During the climb to your house, I didn't think I'd ever be warm again."

A long striped couch flanked by two overstuffed chairs created a sitting area in front of the fire, which was now burning brightly, filling the room with delicious heat. Kathleen placed the baby at one end of the couch and covered her with a light blanket.

"If this baby could talk, she'd probably be saying the same thing." Straightening away from the infant, she saw that Ross was standing on the hearth, his back to the fire. He was raking his fingers through the loose waves of his hair as though he were fighting fatigue.

Now that the baby was cared for and Kathleen had time to think, she was beginning to get a picture of what Ross Douglas had gone through this evening, and she had to admit she admired the man for his efforts. No doubt finding the baby had been a shock to him, Kathleen thought. Having to carry her in the freezing rain up a steep mountainside couldn't have been a picnic, either.

"You must be exhausted. Why don't you sit down and rest while I call the sheriff's department?" she suggested, heading to the phone.

He took a seat in one of the armchairs. "You're

right. I am tired. That mountain out there is covered with a sheet of ice. For every foot I climbed, I slid back two.''

''I can't imagine how you made it with the baby in your arms,'' she told him.

''Well, that wasn't as bad as trying to get up the highway in my pickup.''

Kathleen had just reached for the phone, but his remarks arrested her hand in midair. ''You didn't try it, did you? For heaven's sake, tell me you didn't.''

Frowning, he nodded. ''Now that I've calmed down enough to be able to think, I can see I was crazy to attempt it. I came close to sliding over the edge of the mountain.''

The thought of him and the baby tumbling into a cold, dark ravine made her shudder with fear. ''Well, thank God you didn't.''

Feeling foolish even though he had no real reason to, he said, ''I had to ram my truck into the ditch. I only hope it will stay there until tomorrow, or whenever I can get it out.''

''If the highway workers make it up this far tonight they might push it out for you. I wouldn't worry about it,'' she said as she lifted the receiver to her ear. ''Stranded vehicles are pretty common up here in the wintertime.''

Her fingers automatically reached to punch the emergency number of the sheriff's department, then stopped as she realized there was no dial tone.

"What is the matter with this thing?" she asked aloud, clicking the receiver up and down.

"Try getting the operator," Ross suggested, seeing she wasn't having any luck.

Kathleen did, but to no avail. "Oh, brother! Now what do we do? We can't tell the authorities about any of this without a phone!"

Ross held up a calming hand. "Don't get upset. The line may start working again before long."

"But what if it doesn't? What if the sheriff thinks we kidnapped—or stole!—the baby? What if they think we deliberately avoided calling them? They might try to charge us for not reporting a felony! Oh, Ross..."

Seeing how shaken she was becoming over the whole thing, Ross went over to her. "Getting all worked up isn't going to help a thing." He took her hand in his and found her fingers cold and stiff. Instinctively, he rubbed them with his warmer ones. "And no one is going to charge us with anything. Come on now, forget it. We'll try again in a little bit."

She let out a jerky sigh as he led her over to the couch. "I know you're probably right. I guess...I don't know. Now that the urgency of caring for the baby has passed, I'm beginning to feel the shock of it all."

Ross sat down beside her on the long couch. "Believe me, I know what you're saying. I was feeling the same way when you first let me and the baby into the house." He gave her an apologetic smile. "I know I probably came on a little strong, but I'm not usually like that."

There had been a couple of times Kathleen would have taken satisfaction in slapping his face. But now that the initial crisis had passed, she understood he'd only been acting out of concern for the baby.

"I'm not usually like this, either," she told him. Realizing he was still holding her hand, she gently pulled it away. "So you're forgiven. Am I?"

He wished she hadn't withdrawn her hand. He'd liked the feel of it—the soft skin, the long, delicate fingers against his.

"There's nothing to forgive," he assured her.

"Well, now that the baby has been fed, maybe we should feed ourselves. Before you arrived I was putting a few snacks together. Have you eaten this evening?"

He looked so relieved at her question that Kathleen could hardly keep from laughing.

"To be honest with you, I'm starving," he admitted. "I haven't eaten since this morning."

"You should have said something earlier," she scolded, though her voice was softened by the smile on her face.

He shrugged, as though his physical comfort were of little importance. "I didn't even realize I was hungry until now. All I could think about was the baby."

"Me, too. But she's sleeping peacefully. So why don't you stretch out there on the couch with her, and I'll find us both something to eat."

Ross watched Kathleen leave the room. Then, as if the woman had put some sort of hypnotic spell on him, he did as she'd suggested and stretched out lengthwise on the couch, careful to keep his boots off the cushions.

He wasn't hypnotized, Ross told himself, as he shifted his legs to a more comfortable position. He was only tired, and the events of the past couple of hours had left him rather shell-shocked. After all, it wasn't an everyday occurrence to find a baby on his doorstep. Neither was it common for a woman to have a man come bursting into her house with a new-born baby on his hands. It was no wonder they were both rattled.

His thoughts had him glancing to the end of the couch where the baby lay sleeping. Her face was red and puffy, her nose pugged, her mouth a puckered little bow. Yet when Ross looked at her, he could easily picture an endearing, freckled-face fourth grader, a beautiful young lady dressed in a prom gown.

It was strange, he thought, that he'd never felt as connected to his half brothers or sisters as he did to this child whom he'd first seen only hours ago. Maybe he should feel guilty about that. But he couldn't. This baby didn't have parents or a home. His half brothers and sisters had both.

Leaning his head against the couch, he closed his eyes and breathed a long sigh. Kathleen Gallagher Hayes. Her name swept through his mind, bringing with it strong images of the woman. She was nothing like what he'd expected her to be when she'd first let him and the baby in the front door.

Ross had expected her to be cool, proper, and probably more than a little helpless. So far she'd proven to be nothing like that, and he had to admit he was intrigued by her. And it wasn't like Ross to be intrigued by a woman. He enjoyed female company, but he wasn't a man who allowed his head to be turned a second time.

Love and marriage were for all those other guys out there. The ones who wanted the two-story house and the station-wagon-in-the-driveway kind of life. That life wasn't for Ross Douglas. He'd seen what really went on in those two-story houses, and as far as he was concerned, he'd do better without it.

Chapter Five

"I hope you don't mind leftovers."

Ross opened his eyes to see Kathleen had returned and was placing a tray of food on the low coffee table in front of him. Suddenly he didn't know which he found more tantalizing, her faint scent of jasmine or the smell of hot beef stew.

"I'll eat anything that resembles food," he said, rising to a sitting position.

She handed him a napkin and spoon. "Do you drink coffee? Or would you prefer something else? A soft drink?"

Ross realized she expected him to eat where he sat, and he glanced doubtfully at the beige-and-white sofa and the equally light-colored carpet beneath his boots. "Er—coffee is good, but my eating and this sofa may not be so good."

Kathleen began pouring two cups of coffee from an insulated pot, while the adamant shake of her head told him exactly how much she was worried about the furniture. "Don't worry about it. This is a place to live in, not to look at."

Her attitude surprised him. But then the woman had been surprising him all night, Ross realized.

She handed him the bowl of stew, then took a seat on the cushion beside him. Now that the baby wasn't distracting him, he found his senses consumed by this woman, a fact that made him feel young and foolish, and edgy. He'd never been around a woman who made him feel things without even trying, and he wasn't sure he liked it.

"So tell me," Kathleen said, "how do you usually spend New Year's Eve?"

He chuckled with wry disbelief while dipping his spoon into the bowl of stew. "Well, I don't usually go around finding abandoned babies. Thank God," he added in a more serious tone.

Kathleen took a bite of her stew, then chewed it thoughtfully before she said, "Before you arrived I was really feeling sorry for myself. Tonight my family is having a very special party. My brother Nick has just become engaged and my brother Sam arrived home this morning from his honeymoon."

"So they were expecting you. Do you think they're worried because you haven't arrived?"

Kathleen shook her head. "I talked to Nick shortly

before you showed up. He ordered me not to try driving down the mountain. And when Nick orders, I mean he orders. He's a drill sergeant, you see. But he did promise to call me back.''

"With the phones out, it's unlikely he'll get through to you now," Ross said.

Kathleen shrugged good-naturedly. "He's probably forgotten all about it anyway. He's so in love, he's absolutely soppy. If you know what I mean.''

No, he didn't know what she meant, because Ross had never been in love. A little infatuated at times, but never in love.

"Sounds like Cupid has hit your family," he told her.

Kathleen smiled fondly. "It was about time, too. My brother Sam is a little older than me and has never been married. Nick's two years younger, but I didn't think he'd ever settle down. I'd practically given up on them." She took another bite of stew, then added, "I can say one thing, the holidays have been anything but boring this year.''

Ross had barely noticed Thanksgiving. He'd spent the day alone watching football on TV. And Christmas had passed uneventfully, too. Most of his friends were in Texas. And both of his families he'd simply ignored. They each had their own children and circle of friends to celebrate the holidays with. To Ross, being alone was better than being with them and feeling like an outsider.

"I'll have to admit this tops anything that's happened to me on New Year's Eve," he said.

"I thought I was going to be spending a quiet, lonely evening alone. My family is not going to believe this!"

There was an assortment of cheese and crackers on the tray in front of him. Ross leaned forward and selected a thick slice of Muenster.

"Is going to your parents what you usually do on New Year's Eve?"

When she didn't answer promptly, Ross glanced up to see the soft smile fading from her face to leave a shadow of sadness.

The sight of it took Ross by surprise. Was she still grieving over the death of her husband? he wondered. Had they spent special, happy times together on past New Year's Eves, and did the memories still haunt her?

"To be honest with you, last New Year's went by in a fog. I don't really remember what I was doing. You see, after my husband…well, it was a long time before I could even venture out of the house." She deliberately kept her eyes away from him as she dipped her spoon into the thick stew. "But in the past, well, some New Year's Eves were spent with my parents and some of them were spent at parties given by my late husband's business associates."

"And what kind of business was that?"

As soon as the question was out, Ross knew he

shouldn't have asked it. He didn't know why he had, except that he wanted to know more about this woman, and asking questions was the easiest way to go about it.

"Sorry, Kathleen. You don't have to answer that," he said quickly. "My nose is really sticking itself where it doesn't belong tonight."

Reaching for her coffee, Kathleen said, "Don't apologize. I asked you personal questions."

But she'd had a reason to, he thought. She was a woman alone, living in a secluded area. It was only natural that she'd want to know something about the man she'd allowed into her home. As for himself, Ross could only explain his interest in her as purely selfish.

Kathleen glanced at him, wondering if he had any idea what a chord he'd struck in her. One of the reasons she'd been looking forward to tonight was because for the first time in a long time, she was going to get to spend New Year's Eve with her own family, not with Greg's business cohorts. She wasn't going to have to endure their boasting and swaggering, the rooms full of tobacco smoke, the free-flowing alcohol that loosened too many tongues, the loud music and raucous laughter. No, this man couldn't know any of that.

"Greg was in the business of finding gas and oil."

"A wildcatter?"

She shook her head. "No. Actually, he was a ge-

ologist, but he ended up running the business end of
things rather than doing exploration work in the
field.''

His expression thoughtful, Ross took a sip of his
coffee. ''He must have been a smart guy.''

Kathleen cleared her throat and gave her bowl of
stew an unnecessary stir. ''Yes. Greg was well educated. He knew everything there was to know about
geochemistry.''

Something in her voice gave Ross the impression
she was saying one thing, but feeling another. Or
maybe it was just that she didn't want to discuss her
late husband with him, he thought.

Either way, Ross decided he'd asked enough questions for the time being, and turned his attention back
to his stew.

''I never was too much of a scientist myself,'' he
admitted after he'd eaten a few bites. ''But put a
history book in my hand and I get excited.''

Memories of Greg evaporated as Kathleen struggled to imagine this strong, virile man getting excited
over a history book. The image left her chuckling.
''I didn't know anyone got excited over history. Except maybe a college history professor, or an archae-
ologist.''

Ross cast her a reproving glance. ''Don't tell me
you're one of those people who think things in the
past have nothing to do with the future. Don't disappoint me like that, Kathleen.''

She gave him a wry smile. "No. I'm not one of those people. Actually, I like history, especially early American. But I can't see a man like you enjoying it."

Ross wondered what she could see him enjoying. A bottle of beer and a woman hanging onto his arm? "I look that redneck, do I?"

Kathleen flushed scarlet at his question. "Of course not. I just meant that you look more like an outdoor man."

Ross placed his empty bowl on the serving tray, then, with his coffee in hand, relaxed back against the couch. Heat from the fireplace was seeping into him, making his muscles relax, his eyelids droop. "I am an outdoor man when I'm coaching baseball," he told her.

She glanced at him, her gaze quickly taking in his dark hair, thick, sooty-colored lashes partially hiding his gray eyes, the faint shadowing of beard beneath his tanned skin. He was a strong-looking man. And one who seemed totally unaware of the sensuality that exuded from his every pore. But Kathleen was aware of it. Far too aware.

"Have you always liked the game of baseball?"

After taking a sip of coffee, he answered, "Ever since I was big enough to hold a glove on my hand."

"Did you ever try to play professionally?"

His smile was lazy as he glanced over at her. "I went to the University at Austin on a baseball scholarship. Then went on to play for a minor-league team.''

Ross Douglas more than liked the game, she realized. He'd been very successful at it. Her eyes continued to scan his face. "What happened? Why aren't you still playing?"

Kathleen watched his smile grow a bit wan. "The thing that happens to a lot of players—an injury. In my case it was a knee injury. Even after surgery and all sorts of therapy it couldn't hold up to the strain of the game. I was forced to retire." With a shrug he leaned forward to place his coffee cup alongside the empty bowl. "But that's all in the past now."

How sad, Kathleen thought, that his career had been cut short. But learning all about Ross Douglas's life wasn't something she should be indulging in, Kathleen told herself. She was just beginning to feel like a woman again. She had just started wanting to live again. She wasn't going to allow any man to change the course she'd set for herself. She would become an independent woman in charge of her own destiny.

"That must have been quite a blow for you. You're still very young. You could have probably played many more years. You might have even become another Nolan Ryan."

Low laughter rumbled up from his throat, making Kathleen frown with irritation.

"What's so amusing about that?" she asked.

"You comparing me to one of the greatest base-ball pitchers to ever come along."

Tilting her chin up, she said, "Well, everyone has some greatness in them. As a teacher you should know that and instill it in your students."

He grinned openly. "I was laughing, Kathleen, because I played catcher."

Finding his laughter contagious, she chuckled along with him. "So he throws the ball and you catch it. I was simply trying to say that you might have become as famous as him if you'd continued to play."

He shrugged. "Maybe. I like to think so."

"Was it terribly hard for you to give up the game?" she asked, watching him closely.

"I'd be lying if I said I wasn't a bit lost at first. But I'd always planned to teach someday. So I went back to college to finish getting my teaching degree. And I can truthfully say that I'm as proud of it as I was of my baseball career."

"My daddy always said that being successful wouldn't be nearly as much fun if a person didn't experience a few failures along the way."

"Your daddy sounds like a philosopher."

Kathleen's smile was full of affection. "My daddy is a little bit of everything."

And she admired him; Ross could see it all over her face. He wished he could speak of his own father and know that his face had that same look of love and admiration. But it didn't, and he knew it. Sometimes Ross felt very guilty about that.

"Well, as far as baseball goes, teaching teenage boys how to play the game is very rewarding for me."

Kathleen's gaze traveled from his muscular thighs all the way to where his boots crossed at the ankles as she easily imagined him in a tight-fitting baseball suit. She liked his legs. Liked them far too much, she thought with a little self-disgust.

"I'm sorry that you had to retire, but I'm glad you like teaching. It's an important thing that you're doing," she said.

For long seconds, his gray eyes probed hers. "Thanks for that, Kathleen. And for saying I might have been great."

It was only a simple thank you, she told herself. So why did she feel as if he'd reached out and touched her? Why did she feel like the room was growing smaller and Ross Douglas was only a breath away?

Desperate to break the tide of her thoughts, she practically jumped to her feet and began gathering the dirty dishes. "I'm going to take these back to the kitchen."

His expression quizzical, Ross watched her leave the room. Was he imagining it, or had she suddenly grown cool with him? He couldn't think what he might have said to offend her. They'd been talking about baseball. Or had they?

The question had him muttering a silent oath. He couldn't recall a woman ever rattling him so. While a third of him conversed with her, the other two parts were soaking up the sight of her luscious body, her long, midnight black hair, her ivory white skin. It was no wonder he could remember only a small portion of what they'd been talking about.

With a snort of self-disgust, Ross left the sofa to go stand by the fireplace. At the same time he noticed another telephone sitting on a glass-topped table beside one of the chairs.

Even before he got the instrument up to his ear, Ross sensed that it was dead. Which didn't surprise him. He couldn't imagine anyone being able to work on telephone lines in such bitter weather.

Hanging up the useless phone, he walked around the room, until the sight of the sleeping baby drew him to the couch, where he squatted on his haunches for a closer look at her.

Ross still found it difficult to believe that she'd been left on his porch, that someone had actually meant for him to find her. He didn't believe it. Whoever had left the baby didn't know him. Otherwise, they would have known he didn't have the makings of a daddy, even a temporary daddy.

As though she were picking up on his doubtful thoughts, the baby squirmed and frowned. Ross reached out and gently stroked the top of her head. After a moment the squirming stopped and she made nursing movements with her mouth. Ross smiled, remembering the way she'd gone after the condensed milk. Seeing the baby eat had given him a sense of relief and joy, a feeling that had taken him by complete surprise. He didn't like to think of any child suffering, but this one, he realized, was already winding herself around his heart.

Back in the kitchen, Kathleen was certain she'd gotten herself under control. As she rinsed the dirty dishes, she tried to convince herself there was nothing different about Ross Douglas. Maybe he did happen to be young and handsome. And maybe he did have more than his share of sexuality, but that didn't mean anything to her. Moreover, any normal man would have shown the same concern over a helpless baby. He wasn't a hero. He wasn't special. He was just a man, doing what any man would have done under the circumstances. There was no reason at all for her to be feeling so drawn to him.

That idea flew straight out of Kathleen's head the moment she stepped through the opening to the living room. Ross was kneeling beside the baby, his fingertips gently brushing the top of her head. And no matter how she'd just lectured herself, her heart went soft at the look of awe and tenderness on his face.

"I hope you like German chocolate cake," she said brightly as she moved into the room.

At the sound of her voice, Ross looked up to see she'd returned. This time the tray she was carrying held a cake and dessert plates.

"I have a horrible sweet tooth. Especially for chocolate of any kind," he admitted, watching her take a seat on the floor beside the coffee table.

As she sliced into the multilayered cake, Kathleen could feel the touch of his eyes gliding over her. The subtle awareness produced a tremble in her hands, a huskiness in her voice as she spoke. "Does the baby seem all right?"

"As far as I can tell," he said, moving away from the couch and back to the fireplace. He felt restless, an unusual condition for Ross. Normally he was a laid-back person who could adapt himself to any given situation. But there was something about the quietness of this house, and the woman sitting a few steps away from him that was slowly drawing his nerves into tight little knots.

"I tried—"

"When I—"

Kathleen's laugh was short and breathy. "You go first."

"I was only going to say I tried the phone. It's still dead," he told her.

Nodding, Kathleen glanced over her shoulder at

him. "I know. I tried the one in the kitchen. That's what I was going to tell you."

"We'll just have to make it without one," he said.

Kathleen turned to the table to refill Ross's coffee cup and then her own. "If it weren't for the baby, I wouldn't care that much whether it was working or not. As it is, I wish the da—darn thing was working."

Her near slip of the tongue made him smile. "Well, I'm not trying to be overly confident. I was only trying to reassure you."

At the moment, Kathleen wasn't quite sure what was making her need reassurance, the baby or Ross Douglas. If the baby should need more attention than she or Ross knew how to give, having a phone would be a big help. In fact, if the phone was working, she might even be able to manage caring for the baby on her own, and not have to rely on Ross Douglas.

With him in his own house, she wouldn't have to deal with the awkward tension she felt every time he looked at her. She wouldn't have to think about the carnal urgings she felt every time she looked at him!

But the phone wasn't working, she quickly reminded herself, and she needed him to stay for the baby's sake. And even if the phone was working, would she really want him to leave?

Carrying a slice of cake and a cup of coffee over to him, she had to admit that she was beginning to like the company, and the man.

"I just wish I could feel as calm as you do about the situation," she said with a sigh.

Kathleen believed he was calm? He must be quite an actor, Ross thought. Otherwise, she could see that every time she got within five feet of him, his senses crackled like electricity jumping from one frazzled wire to another.

Murmuring his thanks, he took the dessert plate from her. "Did you bake this?"

"Yes. This morning. I made it for the party tonight."

"Your brothers are probably missing this." Lifting a bite to his mouth, he forced his eyes to shift away from her.

Kathleen laughed softly as she went back to her seat on the floor. "If you knew my mother, you would know the place will be running over with food. Besides, I really doubt Sam or Nick will be thinking about food tonight."

So love and marriage had put her brothers on a cloud, Ross thought with grim amusement. It probably wouldn't be long before both of the poor saps hit the ground with a thud.

But when Ross spoke again he was careful to keep that opinion to himself. "You said that Nick was a drill sergeant. What does your other brother do?"

"He's a farmer. In fact, now that my father has retired, Sam has taken over the Gallagher farm."

"Sounds like both of your brothers are smart, ambitious men."

"Handsome, too. To tell you the truth, I don't know how either of them stayed bachelors for as long as they did."

Ross didn't know how old her brothers were or how long they'd avoided marriage, but so far he'd found it very easy to stay away from the altar. He never allowed any relationship go beyond two or three dates, and if the woman of the moment persisted, he'd find a reason to back away.

"How did they manage?" he asked.

Kathleen shook back her long hair as she thought about his question. "Actually, Sam's true love was in Africa for four years. She was a relief worker in Ethiopia, a whole story in itself. But it wasn't until she came home this Thanksgiving that they reconciled their differences and realized they were both madly in love." She smiled at the memory, then glanced over to see that Ross was watching her intently. She felt herself blush like an innocent teenager.

"As for Nick," she went on, trying with all her might not to be affected by this man and his cool gray eyes, "it's still difficult for me to believe he's headed for the altar. He's always loved women as much as he loves to bark orders. But—" she shrugged as a wistful smile transformed her features "—Allison seems to have changed all that. I've never seen him so dotty over a woman. Of course, you'd probably be dotty over her, too, if you could see her.''

''Pretty, huh?''

''Exquisite. Strawberry blond hair below her shoulders. Skin like milk and one of those tiny waists that most women have to kill themselves in a gym for. But not Allison. Hers is natural. And Olivia is a dream, too. She and I were best friends in college and I always felt dowdy compared to her.''

Ross smiled to himself as he watched her cut a sliver of cake for herself. He could have told Kathleen Gallagher Hayes that she had nothing to worry about in the looks department. He couldn't imagine anyone looking more beautiful than she did at this moment, sitting on the floor, her image bathed in fire glow.

''So you like both of them?''

''Oh, I love them. They're both like my sisters. Of course, I've known Olivia for years, but it didn't take me long to get close to Allison. As a matter of fact, we were friends before Nick was ever introduced to her. She's a strong young woman. There's not many of them out there who could raise a child alone, without help from anyone, the way Allison has.''

Ross was silently speculating over Kathleen's remarks when she shifted around to face him.

''She's an unwed mother,'' Kathleen felt compelled to add. "So you see, I admire her as well as love her."

"What happened to the father?"

Her lips pursed ruefully. "You're being kind, calling him a father. In my dictionary, he's described by a totally different term. You'll find it listed in the *B*s."

One thing was certain about Kathleen Hayes, he concluded; she certainly wasn't shy about voicing her opinions. "I take it he didn't live up to his responsibilities?"

Kathleen shook her head as she sipped her coffee. "He skipped out as soon as he discovered she was pregnant. Allison's own father wasn't any better. He washed his hands of her, too. Because she'd behaved immorally, or so Allison says. Frankly, I believe the old man just didn't want to be bothered with helping her."

"Sounds like your future sister-in-law has had some tough knocks," Ross said.

Kathleen nodded, then her features suddenly brightened with a smile. "Well, I can safely say that's over with. Nick adores her and Allison appears to worship him. I can't see them having anything but a wonderful life ahead of them."

It was obvious to Ross that Kathleen was a romantic. Apparently the loss of her husband hadn't sullied her belief that love and marriage always equaled happiness.

"So when did Sam get married? Obviously sometime between Thanksgiving and now."

She groaned good-naturedly. "We had a big wedding at the farmhouse on Christmas Eve. I didn't know if we were going to live through it and Christmas together. On top of that, Nick and Allison didn't meet until two days before Christmas. Keeping up with this?" she asked with a chuckle.

He shook his head wryly. "Must have been instant combustion."

"Instant," she agreed. "They became engaged before Sam and Olivia returned from their honeymoon in Telluride."

His brows lifted at this news. "I'd call that a cold honeymoon."

Kathleen couldn't know her low laughter shivered over Ross's skin. He drew in a long breath and told himself to quit looking at her. But his eyes refused to obey. They fastened on her cherry-colored lips, which had him instantly wondering what it would be like to taste them instead of the chocolate cake he was eating.

"I doubt it," she said. "When you're madly in love you don't get cold. Or didn't you know that?"

Chapter Six

That teasing lilt was back in her voice, but the little smile on her mouth was definitely an enigma, making him unable to decide if her question was a challenge or an invitation. He liked to think the latter. But thinking like that had gotten Ross into trouble more than once in his life.

His gaze dropped from hers, but not before Kathleen saw a slow grin spread across his face. He couldn't know how boyishly endearing he was to her at that moment.

"I guess it's true that a man can learn something everyday," he said.

Kathleen had to struggle to keep from laughing aloud. Who was he kidding? she wondered. A man who looked like him had to have had women in his past. More than likely several of them.

Kathleen, she silently scolded herself, even if the man has had women in his past doesn't necessarily mean he's been in love. Greg had clearly and painfully proven that to her. A man was usually in lust, not in love.

"Well," she said, her voice suddenly losing its warmth, "then I guess you consider yourself lucky."

Ross supposed he did think himself lucky for eluding that condition called love, so why did it bother him to admit it to this woman?

"Are you trying to ask me if I've ever been on a honeymoon?"

His bluntness brought pink color to her cheeks, but she continued to meet his gaze in spite of it. "No. I don't have to ask. You have that unattached look."

Instinctively Ross glanced at himself, as if there was something on the outside that he'd failed to see. "What is it about me that doesn't look attached?" he asked, his expression quizzical.

Kathleen had never intended for their conversation to stray this far, but now that it had, she decided the best thing to do was handle it lightly. Giving him a smile, she said, "Just about everything."

To know that she'd looked at him that closely, even in a dispassionate way, heated his blood with sexual thoughts. "Well, I haven't been married. I came close once. Or at least I thought the relationship was heading toward marriage. But it didn't happen," he said, thinking about the woman who'd turned her back on him once she'd learned his baseball career had ended. "That experience opened my eyes," he went on. "I don't ever want to permanently attach myself to a woman. By marrying her or any other way," he added for good measure.

So he'd had a broken relationship, too, she silently mused. It was no wonder that he'd wanted to leave Texas and start a fresh life in a new place. "I know what you mean," she told him with unwavering certainty. "Because I don't want to be married, either."

She rose to her feet and moved to the baby. Ross watched her bend over the child and brush her fingers over her brow. "I don't understand," he felt compelled to say. "You seem ecstatic about your brothers getting married."

Satisfied that the baby was sleeping normally with quiet, regular breathing, Kathleen straightened, then looked over her shoulder at Ross Douglas.

"I am ecstatic. I'm thrilled to high heaven for them. And Olivia, that dear woman, deserves every bit of happiness my brother Sam can give her."

"Hmm. I guess I'm missing something, or I just don't get it," Ross told her. "You're obviously thrilled about your brothers getting married, and you believe they'll both be happy. But you don't want marriage for yourself."

"That's right. See, you didn't miss a thing." She walked across the room to the windows and parted the drapes with her hand.

Ross stared at her, still not quite sure he'd heard her right. Although he didn't know why her response had shocked him so. Not every woman wanted to be married. Many of them had careers to think of, and others merely valued their independence, like he did. So why did it surprise him to hear that Kathleen Hayes was one of those women?

Because she was obviously a romantic. Her eyes had a special glow when she'd talked about her brothers marrying the women they loved. It only seemed natural that she would want the same thing for herself—eventually.

Kathleen continued to look out the window. The sleet had turned to snow. Already the ground was covered with a thick white carpet. If the weather had been anything other than this, she mused, she would have been partying with her family tonight. And more than likely she would never have met Ross Douglas. She would have read about the baby being found on his porch in the morning newspaper. Was fate playing some sort of trick on her? Had it sent the ice and snow just so she would be home tonight?

She glanced around to see he was watching her, his expression quiet and contemplative. "I've been married once," she told him. "And I don't believe I could find happiness in marriage again."

Ross realized there were all sorts of things he could read from her words. But he quickly told himself to forget them. Kathleen Hayes's personal life was really none of his business. In fact, it would be a big relief if he could walk out the door right now and pretend he'd never met the woman. She was trouble. He could feel it as easily as he felt the heat from the fireplace. But there was the baby to think about. He didn't want to leave her, and he didn't want to leave Kathleen alone with her.

"I guess losing a spouse would disillusion a person," he said.

He couldn't know how disillusioned, she thought. Because Ross Douglas didn't know that she'd lost her husband long before the accident that had taken his life.

"He was killed in weather like this," she found herself telling him. "In a plane over the Boston Mountains. Greg was a good pilot. But apparently the flight instruments failed and the snow was so heavy there was no visibility."

Ross's eyes fell from her pained expression to the toes of his boots. "I've never lost anyone close to me," he said quietly, "but then there's not too many people that want to be close to me."

Rubbing her arms to chase away the chill, Kathleen moved from the window and came to stand a few steps away from him. "I really doubt that. With two sets of families you must have lots of close relatives."

With a wry twist to his mouth he said, "Let's just

say I have relatives. The closeness part...I'd call questionable.''

He leaned forward and placed his empty dishes on the coffee table. ''While you were in the kitchen, I was thinking about the baby.''

''What about her?''

''She needs a name. Or are we just going to keep calling her 'the baby'?''

Kathleen met his sidelong glance with a questioning one. ''We don't have a right to name her. Do we?''

''Who has a better right? At the moment we're her parents. Besides, I'm not talking about a legal name. We can consider it our right to name her. For the time being.''

Kathleen's eyes slipped away from his face and over to the baby, who'd started to squirm and wake. ''Well, I suppose it wouldn't hurt. If the authorities had her they'd probably tag her Baby Doe or something equally awful.''

''You're right. So what should we call her?''

A smile softened Kathleen's features as she took a seat beside the newborn baby. ''I don't know. Naming a child is something I've never done.''

Ross looked down at both of them. ''Neither have I,'' he admitted. ''Don't people usually name babies after their relatives?''

''Some do. I was named after my aunt on my mother's side. What about you?''

"My paternal grandfather. He was a World War 1 veteran and hell with the ladies."

Kathleen could hear a hint of fondness in his voice. Looking up at him, she said, "I take it he was one relative you were close to."

Ross nodded. "Yeah. He lived to be ninety. He drank a cup of hot water every morning and read the Bible every evening after supper. And he never went to bed without having a shot of bourbon. For medicinal purposes, of course."

"Oh. Of course," Kathleen said with a knowing laugh.

"Well, it's a cinch our little gal doesn't have any relatives to be named after—at least that we know of."

Kathleen studied the tight grimace on his face. "I take it you're not a forgiving man."

His eyes widened as he realized she *expected* him to be forgiving. "Let's put it this way. I find it very hard to understand how someone could leave a baby out in the cold."

"I understand how you feel. I feel the same way. Even though I'm trying not to."

He narrowed his eyes. "Why are you trying not to?"

Kathleen shrugged as she tried to come up with a reason why someone would leave a baby on a doorstep. "It's not good to be judgmental of other people.

Especially when we don't know anything about the circumstances.''

His sardonic expression disappeared as he considered Kathleen's words.

"You're obviously a kind-hearted woman. But you are right about being judgmental. I don't want to condemn whoever left the baby. But I would like to know why.''

He came over to the couch and squatted down beside them.

Kathleen allowed herself a moment to study him at close range. With his head bent down toward the baby, she could see that his dark hair had dried after his icy trek up the mountain. For the most part it was cut short, except for the top, which fell to one side of his forehead in undisciplined waves. His skin was smooth, but coarsely textured, and a startling contrast against his white teeth, although she supposed he'd lose the dark tan now that he'd moved north.

"So, back to the baby,'' she said, in an effort to halt her straying thoughts. "Do you have a name in mind for her?''

One of his shoulders lifted, then fell as his eyes drifted down to the baby's face. "Not really. Every time I look at her I keep thinking how shocked I felt when I discovered her in that box.''

"She certainly arrived under unusual circumstances. Not to mention in one of the worst ice storms I can remember.''

"Hmm. Forget the ice and snow. This little girl created a storm all by herself. She just doesn't know it yet."

"Then maybe we should call her Stormy," Kathleen suggested, her gaze encompassing both him and the baby.

Ross looked at Kathleen, then a grin spread slowly across his face. "Yeah. Stormy. I like that." He glanced down at the baby. "What about you, little one?"

At the sound of his voice, the baby's face scrunched up and grew even redder. In a matter of seconds she was crying lustily.

"Good Lord, she must hate the name," Ross said with a faint chuckle.

Kathleen pulled back the blanket and quickly discovered that the new little Stormy needed changing. "She doesn't understand a thing you're saying. Right now she doesn't care what you call her. She's trying to tell you to change her diaper."

"Me?" Ross asked with amazement. "What about you? You're the mother here."

"And you're the father. Nowadays fathers change diapers, too."

"Whoa, now," he said, thrusting his palms up. "You can't expect me to be an instant father, and— and know about these things."

"Why not?" Kathleen asked, finding his reluctance more amusing than anything. "You expected me to know about these things."

He cleared his throat. "Well, yes. But that's different. You're a woman. This kind of stuff comes natural to you."

Dimples appeared on either side of her mouth as she tried to hold back a smile. "I'm certain it will come naturally to you, too. Just watch her while I go get a diaper from the kitchen."

Ross rose so quickly to a standing position that his knees made a loud popping noise.

"My catcher's knees," he explained, seeing Kathleen's quizzical look. "They're getting stiff. Uh, let me go get the diaper for you."

He left the room in a quick stride. Kathleen laughed softly, then said to the fussy baby, "Men won't always run from you, Stormy. When you're all grown up, you'll be so pretty they'll be running to you. As far as that goes, I've got a daddy and two brothers you could easily wind around your finger right now."

The thought of her family made the smile fade from Kathleen's lips. She'd used to dream of giving her parents a grandchild, her brothers a niece or a nephew. These past few years she'd had to face the fact that those dreams would never come true. She'd thought she had adjusted to the reality of being childless. Until now. Having this newborn baby in her home and in her arms was bringing all the old yearnings back to her.

"Here. I brought the whole stack."

Kathleen looked around to see that Ross had returned with the diapers. Realizing her eyes had misted over, she blinked them and did her best to smile.

"Thank you," she said taking one of the squares of sheeting. "Did the trip to the kitchen stretch your legs?"

"My legs?"

"You know. The problem with your knees," she reminded him. "I hope you didn't hurt your injured knee when you were climbing the mountain."

He took a seat in the nearby chair that sat at an angle to her and the baby. "Oh, no," he said, oddly touched by her concern for him. "The knee is fine. It's just that from the time I was eight years old I spent every summer in a squatting position. Sometimes the knees balk when I tell them to straighten out."

She spread the sheeting out on the cushion to her right and folded it into a small rectangle. "I've often wondered what keeps my brother Nick's legs going. He does so much marching and running with the troops." She glanced over at him, then smiled impishly. "Are you watching this closely? Next time it's going to be your turn."

From the corner of her eye, Kathleen could see

Ross crossing his legs at the ankles and resting his head against the back of the chair.

"The only diaper I ever changed was the kind with tapes on it. I couldn't pin that thing. I'd stick her."

Kathleen removed the damp towel from the baby, then slipped the dry diaper beneath her bottom. "No, you won't," she said, then motioned for him to come close. "Here, I'll show you."

Ross went over and squatted beside Kathleen and the baby. "Are you sure I'm going to need to learn how to do this?"

Kathleen turned her head to find his face was dangerously close to hers. And when their eyes collided, her heart reacted with a strange little thump that quickly turned into a wild gallop.

"We, uh, don't know how long the snow and ice will last. For all we know we may have to be her parents for several days."

Several days? Ross didn't know if he could survive being around this woman for several days. She already had him thinking things he shouldn't be thinking, and wanting to do things he shouldn't want to be doing.

"I don't know anything about being a daddy," he said, his eyes skimming over her pale features. She had thick black lashes that were long enough to be false, but Ross knew they weren't. Everything about this woman was genuine and beautiful.

Her full lips curved into a wan smile. "I don't

know how to be a mother, either. I guess we can learn together.''

''Let's hope we do it right,'' he said, his eyes dropping to the curve of her moist lips.

Suddenly breathless, Kathleen turned back to the baby. ''See,'' she said, hoping her voice didn't betray her runaway heart. ''You put your fingers between the baby and the diaper, then you use your other hand to pin with. That way if you stick anything, it will be yourself.''

She pinned one side of the diaper to show him how, leaving the other side. He looked at her skeptically as she held the pin out to him.

''You must have been hell on wheels in the classroom. I'll bet your students learned a lot. Even the ones that didn't want to,'' he said wryly, taking the pin from her fingers.

''I like to think they did.''

Ross reached for the diaper, and from the corner of his eye he could see Kathleen smile. His attempts to help care for the baby obviously pleased her, and that gave Ross a strange feeling of satisfaction. What man alive wouldn't like to believe he could please a beautiful woman like Kathleen? he asked himself. But to be doing it by pinning a diaper on a baby was certainly a new one for Ross.

Kathleen watched his fumbling attempts for a moment before she reached for his left hand. ''Put your thumb here, and three fingers back here,'' she said, positioning them on the piece of white cloth. "Now lap this over with your other hand, hold it down with this thumb, and pin."

Ross did as she instructed, but his mind wasn't on the job. She was so close to him that her scent filled his nostrils, and the gentle touch of her hand on his only had him thinking of how soft and smooth the rest of her must feel.

"There you are," Kathleen told him. "I knew you could do it. You're going to be a natural."

"You think so?" he asked, his eyes back on her face.

Even though the job was finished, Kathleen realized her fingers were still curved around his, and for one wild second, she wanted to tighten her hold on him, to lean forward and taste his lips.

What was she thinking? Why was she feeling these things? The questions shot fear into her, one that had nothing to do with the ice storm or the baby. She quickly jumped to her feet.

"I think...uh, if you'll watch the baby, I'll turn on the TV and see if we can get a weather forecast."

With a puzzled frown, Ross watched her cross the room and switch on a large set that was built into an entertainment center. He'd felt for certain that she'd been about to say something else. He'd even thought for one split second that she might kiss him.

Ross, have you totally lost your mind? he asked himself. Well, maybe she hadn't been about to kiss him, he argued. Maybe she'd been going to let him kiss her. That's just as crazy, Ross, he fiercely told himself. Forget it. Forget about kissing. Think about the storm, the baby, anything but Kathleen Hayes.

Chapter Seven

The TV weatherman predicted snow through the remainder of the night, with clearing skies in the morning and high temperatures for tomorrow ranging in the twenties.

When the station broke for a commercial, Ross looked at Kathleen, who'd taken a seat on the floor by the fireplace.

"What kind of shape will that leave us in?" he wanted to know. "If it snows all night, we might not be able to get to the highway, much less to the city."

Kathleen glanced away from the TV screen and over to where Ross sat closely watching the baby. Even though Stormy was asleep, it was obvious that he wanted to be near her, as though somehow their trek together through the snow had bonded him to her.

"I don't know. But we do have a good highway department and they'll be out working round the clock, so that if people are stranded it won't be for long."

Kathleen rose to her feet and went over to the phone. Lifting the receiver to her ear, she found no dial tone, and she wondered what her family would say when she was finally able to reach them with the news of little Stormy. It was going to be a shock, to say the least.

"It's still dead," she told Ross, seeing the expectant look on his face.

Groaning, Ross passed a tired hand over his face. "What time is it, anyway?"

Kathleen pushed back the sleeve of her sweater to glance at her wristwatch. "Oh, my! It's almost twelve. The new year is almost here!"

The approaching midnight hour suddenly reminded her of the champagne she'd left chilling in the refrigerator. "We've got to celebrate!" she said, quickly heading out of the room. "I'll be right back."

Ross was still on the couch with the baby when Kathleen returned, but he got to his feet the moment he saw she was carrying a bottle of champagne and two long-stemmed glasses.

"When you say celebrate, you really mean celebrate," he said.

She laughed at the surprised look on his face.

"Actually, I'd bought this for Nick and Allison. But what the heck. If they can't enjoy it, we might as well."

She placed the glasses on the coffee table, then handed the bottle to Ross. "Would you do the honors of opening it?"

"Sure. But maybe we'd better move away from the baby. I don't want to spray her with champagne after all she's been through tonight."

At the other end of the room there was a love seat positioned in front of the TV, and Kathleen motioned to it. "Let's go over there. Maybe one of the stations will be having a countdown to midnight."

While Ross worked the cork in the champagne bottle, Kathleen switched television channels.

"Oh, look, this one is showing the scene at Times Square in New York City!"

She'd barely gotten the words out when the cork popped and the pale gold liquid erupted from the bottle. Laughing, she held the glasses out to Ross, who managed to fill them without losing too much onto the floor.

"I wasn't expecting to have champagne tonight," he told her, his gray eyes warm on her smiling face. "Especially not with a beautiful woman."

Her green eyes sparkled back at him. "Oh, don't tell me you're a flatterer, along with being a savior, too."

A touch of color swept across his dark face. He

didn't know why he'd let that last little bit slip. But at the moment he didn't care. Kathleen was beautiful, and the way she smiled was like no other woman had ever smiled at him. "I'm hardly a savior. Just a man who found a baby."

Kathleen shook her head. "You're being too modest. And as for expecting things, I never expected to see a strange man and a baby in my house tonight!"

And he'd never expected to find a woman like her in this house, or any other place. But he kept the thought to himself. "So are we going to make a toast?" he asked.

"Of course! We have a wonderful reason to make a toast. To our new little Stormy. She wasn't born on New Year's Day, but very close to it." Kathleen softly clinked her glass against his. "And if it weren't for you, Ross, she wouldn't be starting life in this new year. God bless you for saving her life," she whispered, her eyes suddenly brimming with tears.

His eyes were riveted on her face as pride, joy, desire all rushed through him, bubbling and fizzing like the champagne in his glass. Never in his life had Ross felt like he did at this moment. And before he knew what he was doing, he'd reached out and pulled her against him.

"Happy New Year, Kathleen Gallagher Hayes," he whispered before bringing his lips down on hers.

Kathleen didn't know which stunned her more, the

fact that he was kissing her, or the fact that it felt so good.

But as the kiss went on, both thoughts flew off into oblivion. Because he'd gone beyond just kissing her. He was tasting her, luring her, silently asking her to kiss him back. And Kathleen found it impossible to refuse him. For long moments, she stood on tiptoe and kissed him with a passion she'd never expected to feel.

The moment he finally lifted his mouth away from hers, she whispered breathlessly, "Happy New Year, Ross Douglas."

Ross looked down at her and knew he couldn't have been more intoxicated than if he'd just drunk a whole bottle of champagne.

"I think it's midnight," he said unsteadily.

Kathleen glanced at the TV, where people were shouting and kissing and singing "Auld Lang Syne." "Yes, an old year is gone and a new one begins. Shall we drink to it?"

Ross would rather kiss to it, but he wasn't going to act on his impulses again. One taste of her had been like a wham in the head with a sledgehammer, and Ross wasn't a man who went around deliberately asking to be hurt.

"Sure," he said, bringing his glass up to his lips. "To the new year and to Stormy."

Grateful for the diversion, Kathleen took a long sip of the bubbly liquid, then another.

She didn't know what was happening to her, she thought, as she sank weak-kneed to the love seat. She'd never experienced such a strange mixture of feelings in her life. She was happy and excited, scared and shaky. And even more, she felt drawn to Ross, connected to a man she'd never seen until tonight. It was all happening too fast, she thought. Her emotions were whirling around inside her like a ray of multicolored lights.

"Would you like some more?"

She glanced up to see that Ross was holding up the champagne. "Er, no, one glass is enough for me. I don't want my senses to be dulled. Stormy might wake up and need another bottle."

He could sense she was drawing away from him. Probably because she was regretting that kiss. Well, he was regretting it, too. Because Ross knew that one kiss was going to be hell to forget. "It's getting late, and you must be exhausted. Why don't you go to bed?" he suggested. "I'll sit up with the baby. I know what to do now. I think."

Kathleen quickly shook her head. "No. I couldn't leave you with her. You go to bed. There're four bedrooms down the hall—just take your pick, except for the last one on the right. That one is mine."

Ross shook his head in turn. "I couldn't. But you suit yourself."

Even though Kathleen was exhausted, she knew if she went to bed, she wouldn't be able to sleep a wink. Not with him and the baby in here. And definitely not with everything that was going on in her head.

She finished her champagne, then carried her empty glass over to the coffee table. Stormy was still asleep, her tiny little fist drawn up to her mouth. With a surge of protectiveness, Kathleen tucked the blanket closer, then whispered, "Good night, little one. Ross and I will be here to watch over you."

Kathleen didn't know what woke her first, the baby's cries or the ringing of the telephone. But by the time she managed to open her eyes and push herself to a sitting position, Ross had picked up Stormy and was carrying her toward the kitchen.

"You get the phone. I'll heat her bottle," Ross tossed over his shoulder.

Kathleen hurried over to the phone, half afraid the caller would hang up and she'd lose all connection to the outside world.

"Hello."

"Good morning, Kathleen. How are things on the mountain?"

"Sam! Oh, Sam, it's so good to hear your voice. You're not going to believe what's happened!" She quickly began to relate the whole story, finally ending with, "Ross has just now taken her to the kitchen to feed her."

"Ross? You mean the man is there with you now?

You let a strange man you don't even know spend the night in your house? Kathleen, have you gone crazy or what? You don't know where he found this baby! He could have kidnapped it, for heaven's sake!''

How strange it sounded for her brother to be saying she didn't know Ross. He already seemed so much a part of her. But Sam wouldn't understand that. Sam took a slow approach with everything. ''Sure, Sam, he probably did, just so he could bring it up here to me,'' she said dryly.

Her brother let out a sigh of resignation. ''I guess you're right, sis. But I thank God we didn't know about this last night, or I would have been worried.''

''Of course I'm right. Besides, Ross is my neighbor. He's moved into the old Mabry place down the road from here. Remember?''

''Yes, I remember. So what are you going to do now?''

''Well, we've tried to call the authorities to report everything, but my phone has been dead. I guess now that we can do that, we'll see what they have to say.''

''Yes, do that, pronto. And Kathleen, maybe you'd better get in touch with Parker Montgomery. You might need some legal advice—you never know about these things.''

''You're right,'' Kathleen said, shoving her tousled hair off her forehead. ''I'll call him first. Once we talk to the authorities and get things straightened away, I'll call you back and let you know what's happening.''

''Well, don't keep us waiting long. As soon as I get off the phone and tell this story, the whole house is going to be in an uproar.''

Kathleen could very well imagine. ''I'll call as soon as I can,'' she promised, then hung up and hurried out to the kitchen.

She found Ross still feeding the baby. There were lines of fatigue on his face, but he looked more rested than he had last night after midnight, when he'd fallen asleep on the floor by the fireplace.

Rather than wake him, Kathleen had covered him up with blankets, then had lain down on the couch with the baby. It was the last thing she remembered before waking up this morning.

''Who was that calling at this hour? It's only five o'clock!''

Kathleen went straight to the coffeemaker and began filling it with cold water. ''It was my brother Sam. I told you he's a farmer. Five o'clock in the morning is late to him.''

Ross's eyes ran up and down the length of her. As he noticed her feet, he began to smile. ''I see you finally took your high heels off.''

Groaning, she looked down at her stockinged feet, then back up at him. She knew she probably looked horrible. Her hair was tumbled and tangled, her face without makeup. ''I decided the party was over.

Want some breakfast? Looks like Stormy is getting hers.''

"She was definitely hungry. And so am I. But maybe we'd better talk with the police before we do anything else."

She nodded as she quickly finished putting the coffee makings together. "You're right. While the coffee drips, we'll make the call."

For the next few minutes Ross related his part of the story, then Kathleen took the phone and related hers. When they were finally allowed to hang up, Kathleen said, ''They didn't act nearly as surprised about this whole thing as I thought they would.''

"They're police officers. They're used to hearing and seeing shocking things.''

"I guess you're right, but I wish we didn't have to go down to the station. We've already told them everything we know."

Ross shrugged as he took a seat at the kitchen table. ''They do need to see the baby, so they'll know we haven't just fabricated this whole thing. And I'm sure they'll probably want us to hand her over to them.''

Kathleen stared at him in horror. ''Are you crazy? I'm not handing Stormy over to them!''

Ross looked across the table at her and was amazed to see that she was visibly shaking. ''What do you mean?'' he asked. ''Right now she's an orphan. A ward of the court.''

Kathleen shook her head vehemently. "No! I don't want her to be a ward of the court. They'll send her off to some crowded orphanage, or to some foster parents she won't even know! She's just been born, Ross, and all she knows is you and me. It would be better if we could keep her, for a few days at least. Don't you think so?"

If we could keep her. Ross couldn't help but notice how she included him, as though he were going to continue to be a part of this whole thing.

Before he'd fallen asleep last night, Ross had told himself that the best thing he could do was get the baby to the right authorities, and then back away and go on about his own business. Forget Stormy and forget Kathleen. But in the light of day, with the now-familiar weight of that little being in his arms, he knew deep down that he didn't want to hand the baby over any more than Kathleen did.

Dear Lord, Ross, you're thinking with your heart now, and that kind of thinking will get you into trouble. You know that! "I don't know, Kathleen. In the case of a child, I don't think you can apply the rule of Finders, Keepers."

Kathleen suddenly snapped her fingers and jumped to her feet. "I haven't called Parker yet. He can fix things. He'll know exactly what to do."

"Who's Parker?"

"Parker Montgomery. He's an old friend of mine, who also happens to be a lawyer. He handled all my legal affairs when Greg was killed,'' she told him as she headed for the phone on the breakfast bar. Quickly she began punching out his number. ''And he has friends in high places.'' She glanced over her shoulder at him. ''So keep your fingers crossed. Stormy isn't going to become a Baby Jane Doe yet.''

By noon the sun was shining brightly and the road crew had managed to clear the highway enough to make it passable. Ross got his pickup out of the ditch, then stopped by his house long enough to take a shower and change into clean clothes. By the time he returned to Kathleen's house, she had herself and the baby ready to go into Fort Smith and the police station.

She'd changed into a pleated corduroy skirt and matching long-sleeved shirt. The outfit showed off her small waist and the red color looked luscious against her dark hair. She was wearing red lipstick, too, Ross noticed. And he found he was having trouble keeping his eyes off her. Especially her lips, which seemed to be smiling at him more often than not.

''I'm glad to see you made it back in one piece. Is the highway clear enough to make it down safely?'' she asked.

''There's still a lot of snow in places, but the road crew has spread sand on it. Plus there's traffic moving now, so it must be passable,'' he told her.

"Maybe we should take my car. It has front-wheel drive," she suggested. "I certainly won't mind, if you promise to drive. I'm not very good on ice."

He gave her a wry grin. "You think I am? If you'd seen me last night, you wouldn't be asking me to get behind the wheel of your car."

She fished the keys out of her purse and tossed them to him anyway. "I trust you. I'll bring Stormy out when I think the car has had time to warm up."

They left the house a few minutes later. Ross wasn't that keen on driving. One wrong slip and he could cause Kathleen or the baby to be hurt, and that thought kept a knot of fear in his stomach as he slowly maneuvered the car down the winding highway. On the other hand, Kathleen seemed to be completely relaxed, absorbed with the beauty of the snow and the baby in her lap.

"I wish I'd had something to dress Stormy in," she told Ross, after they'd traveled a few miles. "The only thing I could find was a shrunken T-shirt of mine. It was far too large, but I thought it would serve the purpose of a gown."

"We'll get something for her when we're finished at the police station," Ross told her as he carefully steered the car over large patches of snow and ice.

"I know I'm not supposed to be holding her in my lap while we're traveling. I should have strapped her into a car seat." She tapped her finger thoughtfully against her chin. "Maybe I should get one of those, too. And some bottles and diapers.'' She looked over at Ross. ''Gosh, I never realized how many things a newborn needs!''

Ross knew he should probably remind her that she was going to have the baby with her for only a brief time, if any time at all. But he couldn't bring himself to. He could see the way she was cuddling the baby to her breast, the tender love on her face each time she looked at it. She didn't want to give her up now, and he was beginning to doubt that she ever would.

Kathleen's lawyer met them at the police station. He was somewhere around forty, Ross figured, with a head of sandy-colored hair and brown eyes that kept sizing Ross up and smiling at Kathleen.

Ross didn't know whether he liked the man or not, but Kathleen seemed to trust him implicitly, so he figured that was all that really mattered.

Once the interview with the police was over, the lawyer walked with the three of them out to the parking lot.

''You don't have anything to worry about,'' he told Kathleen. ''I've already talked with Judge Lawton and he's agreed to let you have temporary custody until a suitable foster home can be found for her.''

Kathleen cringed inwardly. ''And how long will that be?'' she asked.

The lawyer shook his head. ''That will be up to

the child-welfare department and how quickly they'll be able to find a home for her. At any rate, someone will be contacting you soon. So don't worry.''

Nodding that she understood, she thanked him for taking time on New Year's Day to help her.

It wasn't until they'd said goodbye and gotten back into the car that Kathleen turned to Ross and said, ''I don't want Stormy to go to some couple who already have a houseful of children! I want her to get the care and attention she needs.''

''You should have made that clear to Mr. Montgomery,'' he said, as he reached to start the car.

Kathleen shrugged, a worried frown on her face. ''I know. But I don't think he understands how I feel. And I know that you do.''

''I do?''

She gave him a sidelong glance while arranging the blanket around the baby's face. ''Yes, you do. You know that I love her and that I want her to be in a loving home. And you feel the very same way.''

''Yes, I do,'' he said, his expression somber.

He steered the car out of the parking lot and onto the street. As he did, he noticed Kathleen was pressing her cheek against the baby's, and there were tears glistening in her eyes. The sight tore at his heart.

''Oh, Ross, when we were being questioned by those policemen and they kept talking about the real mother, I just wanted to scream at them that there was no other mother. That I was her mother! Is it crazy for me to feel this way?''

Her voice was quavering and he knew the past hour had shaken her more than she was letting on. ''No, it isn't crazy. But...'' He glanced at her, then wished he hadn't, because her tearful green eyes were looking at him, begging him for some kind of reassurance. He drew in a long breath, then let it out slowly. ''Look, Kathleen, I think you're going to be hurt if you let your emotions get involved with this child. Pretty soon you're going to be telling me that you want to keep her for your own.''

That idea had crossed Kathleen's mind more than once last night. She'd wanted a child for such a long time. Now it seemed as though God had intentionally placed one in her lap. This child needed a home. And this might be Kathleen's one and only chance of having a baby.

''I don't suppose I told you this, but I've wanted a child for a long time.'' She smoothed her fingertips over the baby's dark hair. ''Why shouldn't I want to keep this one?''

''I don't know, Kathleen. But I imagine the fact that you're single would make it extra hard for you to permanently adopt her. Besides, it might turn out that she has other relatives around here who might want her.''

Horrified, Kathleen tightened her hold on the baby.

"Oh, Ross, you don't think they'd let them have her, do you?"

"Kathleen, I'm only wanting you to look at all possibilities. I don't want you to be disappointed."

Kathleen fished a tissue out of her purse and carefully dried her eyes. "I know, Ross. And I'm sorry for becoming emotional. I guess these past twenty-four hours have been more of a strain on me than I thought."

"Look, why don't you forget about all this for right now. You have custody for the time being. So let's take her to a doctor for a checkup and then we'll see about buying her a few things," he suggested.

"You're right. Today is the beginning of a brand new year. Let's enjoy what's left of it."

"Good. I might even take you out to eat later. To repay you for the breakfast you cooked for me," he added.

As she looked at him, her spirits began to lift and a smile curved her lips. "You've got a deal."

Chapter Eight

Stormy weighed six and a half pounds and the doctor pronounced her healthy and fit. He clamped off her umbilical cord, and gave Kathleen the name of a formula to start her on, plus several small booklets of information he felt would be helpful to her. Kathleen and Ross left the twenty-four-hour medical clinic feeling happy and relieved about the baby's physical condition.

They found a discount store that was open in spite of the day being a holiday, and the two of them quickly began to fill a shopping cart with baby formula, diapers, bottles and a baby carrier.

When they came to the clothes, and Kathleen started tossing in all sorts of garments, Ross didn't say a word to discourage her. He'd already seen her tears once today. And if buying the baby clothes made her happy, he wasn't going to be the one to spoil it for her.

They chose to eat at a nearby restaurant that specialized in home-cooked meals. Since it was New Year's Day, black-eyed peas, hog jowls and corn bread were offered with all the main courses.

"We have to eat black-eyed peas," Kathleen insisted, "so our year will be filled with good luck. Don't you believe that?"

While the waitress stood waiting for them to make up their minds, Ross gave Kathleen an indulgent smile. "If you believe it, Kathleen, then I'll eat them."

He handed the menu back to the waitress. "I'll take mine with fried catfish."

Kathleen decided on the same thing, then asked the waitress if she could prepare a bottle for Stormy. The woman kindly obliged, and while they waited for their meal, Kathleen fed the baby.

As she sat in the booth across from Ross and held the baby in her arms, she wondered if this was how it felt to have a real family, the family she'd always wanted. The baby wasn't hers. Neither was Ross, but just for tonight she wanted to pretend that she was a woman loved by this dark handsome man across from her. And in return for that love, she'd given him a beautiful daughter.

"You know, there really was an angel on your

shoulder last night,'' Kathleen told him. ''Because you came home and found the baby before the cold temperature had a chance to harm her.''

Ross looked at his shoulder, then grinned at Kathleen. ''An angel, huh? Well, I only hope she didn't hear all that cursing I did when I was trying to make it up the hill to your house.''

''I'm sure in this case you've already been forgiven.''

Since Stormy had now finished the bottle, Kathleen put her back in her new carrier. Even though she weighed next to nothing, Kathleen's arms were beginning to grow tired, and she knew it was better for the baby's neck and back to be well supported.

Their meal arrived just as she'd gotten the baby settled. While the two of them ate, Kathleen encouraged Ross to tell her about himself. ''I feel as if you know all about me and my family,'' she told him. ''So tell me something about you. Did you grow up in San Antonio?''

He nodded. ''Just outside of the city. Have you ever been there?''

Kathleen shook her head. ''No. I've been to east Texas. That's where my mother and father are going to retire this coming spring.''

''Oh, well,'' he said, slicing into the filleted catfish, ''then you should go down there sometime. It's beautiful. Everyone should go down the Riverwalk and see the Alamo.''

Her eyes glided over his face, then down to his broad shoulders. He was wearing a beige shirt with tiny black stripes running through it. On any other man it would have been plain, she thought, but on Ross it was downright sexy. She found that her eyes kept returning to the dark column of his throat and wondered if he was that same tanned color all over.

Good Lord, she hadn't thought about a man like this since—well, not since she'd first fallen for Greg. And look where that had gotten her, she quickly reminded herself.

"Maybe I will," she told him. "Sometime."

Ross wanted to tell her that he'd take her to Texas, but stopped himself short. He'd already let himself get more involved with this woman than he'd intended to. He wasn't about to make promises for the future, no matter how much he would enjoy taking Kathleen down the romantic Riverwalk in San Antonio.

"So what really made you move up here?" she asked him. "Other than the chance to take over your friend's coaching position."

Ross shrugged. "Since I graduated late last fall, it was hard to find a teaching position. So when this one presented itself, I decided it was just what I was looking for."

"And what were you looking for?"

His gray eyes met hers across the table, and even though she'd been with him all day, she felt just as jolted by them now as she had this morning over breakfast.

"A school where academics are as important as sports. A school that took not only my baseball, but also my teaching ability seriously. Sports are a great part of learning, but knowledge is vital for success."

"And you should know. I'd say you've come full circle." He was a man who was obviously passionate about his work, Kathleen thought, and one who stood by his convictions. Her father and brothers were like that, too. Unlike Greg, who'd been easily swayed to change his beliefs, especially when he thought money was going to change hands.

"A lot of people think I'm crazy for being a teacher instead of picking a career that would have earned a lot bigger salary."

Kathleen shook her head. "Money isn't everything. My late husband made plenty of money, more money than I was certainly ever used to having. But he wasn't happy. At least not with me."

Her words shocked him. He hadn't expected her to tell him something so private. And now that she had, all he could think about was how happy it made him just to look at her, to be with her.

"I—I'm sorry," she said in an embarrassed whisper. She dropped her gaze to her plate. "I shouldn't have said that to you. I don't even know why I did."

Ross reached across the table and took her hand in his. "Kathleen, look at me."

She did and her heart surged with a feeling so warm, so achingly sweet that tears burned the back of her eyes.

"You can say anything you want to me. No matter what it is." His mouth curved into an encouraging smile. "We're friends now. Aren't we?"

Kathleen had never realized how special that one word was until now. "Yes, we are. And I'm glad."

It was dark by the time they left the restaurant. On the way back up the mountain Ross decided he had to stay in his own home that night. He knew he could no longer trust himself or his feelings where Kathleen was concerned. Alone with her, he'd be more than tempted to make love to her, and right now that was the last thing either of them needed.

When they reached Kathleen's house and he told her he was going home, she looked at him in surprise. "Oh, Ross, are you sure? I was planning on you staying here with me and Stormy tonight."

Ross felt cut to pieces by the disappointment on her face, but held fast to his decision. "I know you were. But now that Stormy has been checked by the doctor and you have everything you need, you'll be fine."

Kathleen had never been a weak, clinging vine and she certainly didn't want Ross to think her one now. "Of course I'll be fine. Why, there's thousands of single mothers out there. I can do it. And anyway, it was my choice to keep the baby. She's my responsibility, not yours.''

Ross should have been relieved by her independent attitude. But he wasn't. He felt like a heel. And more than that, he felt left out, separated from the instant family he'd been a part of this past night and day.

But that was the way it had always been for Ross. His mother had shoved him off on his father; then, when his father had remarried and started having children, he'd shoved him back to Ross's mother. Then *she'd* remarried, and her new life and new children hadn't included him, either. By the time he'd graduated from high school he'd left home, vowing that he would never again stay where he wasn't wanted or needed.

"Yeah, well, if you need me, you know where I am. Goodbye, Kathleen."

"Goodbye," she told him, then watched with a puzzled frown as he hurried out the door. In the last few minutes he'd suddenly changed from a warm, caring friend to a distant stranger. What had she done or said? Or was he simply telling her he'd done his part—he'd saved the baby's life—and his involvement was over?

The idea filled her with loneliness. And even though she had the baby to care for she couldn't shake the sad feeling, or Ross Douglas, from her mind.

* * *

"Kathleen, are you sure about this?" Ella Gallagher asked her daughter. "Adoption is a big responsibility for a couple to consider. And you're single. You wouldn't have a father around to help raise the child. Believe me, honey, this is something you need to think about."

Kathleen switched the telephone receiver to her other ear, then said, "I have thought about it, Mother. I've thought about it ever since I first held her in my arms. Oh, Mom, she's just so precious and beautiful."

Ella let out a knowing sigh. "Yes, I know, Kathleen, all babies are precious and beautiful. Then they grow up into precocious teenagers. Raising a baby to adulthood is not a snap, believe me."

Kathleen frowned as she tried to butter her breakfast toast with the phone jammed between her shoulder and her ear. "So you're trying to discourage me. You think I'd be making a mistake. Mother, you know how much I've wanted a child!"

"I do know, Kathleen. So does your father. And we want you to have a child just as much as you do. It's only that we wanted you to have it with a husband."

"Well, I wanted it that way, too. But it just didn't happen." She paused and took a deep breath. "Look, Mom, I might as well tell you that I called Parker

Montgomery first thing this morning and told him my decision to try to adopt Stormy.''

''And what did he say?''

''Basically, that the circumstances of her real parents will have to be dealt with. If the authorities can find them. And also that my being single won't help matters. But he also said that it doesn't rule out my chances, either.''

Ella was silent for so long that Kathleen wondered if she'd fallen over in a faint. ''Mother! Are you still there?''

''Yes, yes, I'm still here. I was just thinking.''

''Thinking what?'' she asked urgently. If there was one thing Kathleen needed now it was the support of her family, and she was praying they'd give it to her.

''That if this is what you really want, then you know your father and I will help you all we can.''

Tears stung Kathleen's eyes. ''I love you.''

''If you do, then you'll come over tonight for supper and bring the baby. We're all dying to see her. And bring that young man who found her, too. We'd like to meet him.''

''How do you know he's young? I didn't tell you that.''

Ella laughed. ''I knew he had to be young, because an old man certainly couldn't have carried a baby up that mountain in a snowstorm. Except maybe your daddy,'' she bragged, then laughed impishly.

Always amazed at her mother's deductions, Kathleen smiled and rolled her eyes. "You're right, he's young and he's handsome. And I'll try to get him and the baby there before you all sit down to eat."

"We'll be looking for you," Ella said, then after a quick goodbye, hung up the telephone.

By three o'clock that afternoon, Kathleen didn't know what to do about inviting Ross to dinner at the farmhouse. She'd been sure that he'd be back to check on her and the baby today, but so far she'd seen nothing of him. Since it was Saturday, she knew he wouldn't be at school teaching. And since he was new in the area, she really doubted he was visiting friends.

Well, if he didn't show up soon, she thought, she'd get in the car and drive to his house. He might not want to see her, but she wanted to see him. And since Kathleen had never been bashful, she wouldn't mind telling him that, or inviting him to have dinner with her and her family.

Ross stood by the picture window in his front room and absently lifted the coffee cup to his lips as he stared at the wooded hillside that led up to Kathleen's house. All day long he'd kept himself busy, unpacking boxes and putting the last of his things away. And all the while he'd worked, he'd thought about Kathleen and the baby. He missed them both,

and the more he told himself he didn't need to see
them, the more he wanted to see them.

Damn it, Ross, you're twenty-nine years old, he
silently argued with himself. You've gone this long
without letting a woman get under your skin. Just
because Kathleen looks like a black-haired goddess
and tastes like a piece of heaven doesn't mean you
need her in your life.

But he did need her. He felt as empty as hell without her around him. So why was he fighting it? Why
didn't he drive up the mountain and see her?

Because he had this crazy feeling that once he saw
her again, he wouldn't be able to stop himself from
falling in love with her. If he hadn't already.

Kathleen had just changed into a long, plaid wool
skirt of deep browns and russets, a white blouse and
a pair of fawn-colored dress boots when she heard
the doorbell ring. Tossing her hairbrush aside, she
hurried to answer it.

The moment she opened the door and saw Ross
standing there with a wry grin on his face, her heart
leaped with joy.

"Ross! I've been looking for you all day. I was
about to think you'd forgotten all about me and
Stormy."

As if he could, Ross thought, as she took him by
the arm and led him into the house.

"No. I hadn't forgotten. I've been working—trying to get my things unpacked and put away." He wasn't going to admit he'd only now decided to come see her. And maybe that decision had been a mistake, he thought. But he didn't think so. Now that he was here, seeing the smile on her face, he felt good inside. He felt some unexplainable joy that he'd never felt in his life.

"How's the baby? Did she keep you awake last night?"

Kathleen led him over to the couch where Stormy lay sleeping. "She's fine. And no, she only woke up once during the night."

Kathleen wasn't going to admit to Ross that *he* was the reason she'd lost sleep last night, not the baby. She'd lived alone for more than a year now, but she couldn't remember a time when the house had seemed so quiet and empty. Even the baby's presence couldn't make up for Ross not being with her. But she couldn't tell him that. It would make it sound like she was falling in love with him. And she wasn't, was she?

Ross took a seat beside the baby and found he couldn't stop himself from touching her fine baby hair and the soft little curve of her cheek. Kathleen had put a dress on her. It was white, with little red bows and hearts embroidered across the front. She looked like a little dark-haired cherub.

"She looks all dressed up now. Nothing like the pathetic little mite I found in that cardboard box."

Kathleen smiled down at both of them. Now that Ross was with them, she felt complete. "I just changed her clothes a few minutes ago. I'm taking her over to meet my family. That is, *we're* taking her over. You're invited, too."

His head jerked up. "Me? Oh, no—no, I couldn't be invited. Your family doesn't even know me!"

Kathleen laughed at his shocked expression. "Of course they don't know you. That's why they want to meet you. You've become a hero, you know."

Ross shook his head in dismay. "Damn it, I'm not a hero. I'm not anything close to it."

"Well, when Stormy grows up, she's going to thank you," Kathleen told him.

He looked back at the baby. Would he mean anything to this tiny little girl when she grew to be a woman? Would she even be a part of his life? The questions made him realize what a loss it would be not to have children in his life. And even more, what a loss it would be not to have a part in this child's life.

"Are you sure your family really invited me? You're not just pushing me on them?"

Kathleen laughed. "You can't push anyone on the Gallaghers, believe me."

"Well, I'm not exactly dressed for a family dinner."

Her gaze quickly took in his jeans and boots, and

black-and-red letter jacket. "You're not naked under that jacket, are you?" she asked impishly.

With a crooked grin on his mouth, he pulled back one side of the jacket to show her he was wearing a plain black T-shirt.

"You're perfect," she assured him with a wave of her hand. "So I'll get Stormy's carrier and diaper bag and we'll be off."

Ross had never been invited by a woman to meet her parents or family before, and he wasn't quite sure he wanted to go. But since Kathleen was with him and they were already halfway to the farm, he could hardly turn around and run for his life.

"My brother Sam is the quiet, serious one of us. Nick is the teasing prankster who's been pestering me ever since he was old enough to try," Kathleen told him as they turned into the lane leading up to the farmhouse.

"And your serious brother Sam always came along and stood up for you."

She laughed. "How did you know?"

Ross could hear the fondness in her voice as she spoke of her brothers, and he wondered what it would be like to hold such a place in her heart. She was a special woman. And the man she loved would have to be special. Not someone like him.

"Just a guess," he answered.

Kathleen glanced over at him, her eyes sliding appreciatively over his strong profile. "Oh, you probably have a brother or sister just like that, don't you?"

A faint frown passed over his features. "I don't have any brothers or sisters."

Clearly puzzled, she stared at him. "But you said you had two sets of half brothers and sisters."

He nodded, his expression stoic. "I do. Two brothers. Three sisters. But I don't consider them real brothers and sisters. They were just kids I grew up around, some of them for longer periods than others."

How terribly sad, Kathleen thought. She couldn't imagine her life without Nick or Sam, or the love and companionship they shared with each other. And it hurt her to think that Ross had never known that kind of love and closeness.

When Kathleen and Ross entered the house, they found the whole family in the den. Even Jake and Leo, Sam's two collies, were stretched out asleep on the fireplace hearth.

"Here they are," S.T. boomed when he spotted his daughter coming through the doorway.

S.T.'s announcement caused a stir of commotion, and Ross suddenly found himself, Kathleen and the baby surrounded. As his eyes quickly darted over the group, he registered three tall, strongly built men and three very attractive women.

"Okay," Kathleen said as everyone started to talk

at once. "This is Ross Douglas." Smiling, she looked at Ross who was still close to her elbow. "Ross, this is my mother and father," she said proudly.

Ross nodded at the older, but still-handsome couple. "Nice to meet you, ma'am. Mr. Gallagher."

"Same here, Ross. And it's Ella and S.T. We don't go for that formal stuff around here," S.T. told him.

Kathleen continued to introduce the rest of the group to Ross. "And this stony-faced one in the flannel shirt is my brother Sam. And the beauty he's hanging onto is his new wife, Olivia."

"Hello, Sam, Olivia," Ross greeted them both.

Kathleen motioned her hand to the last two adults. "This handsome thing is my brother Nick, the rebel. And of course, that's his sweet fiancée, Allison. Oh, and over by Jake and Leo is little Ben, Allison's son."

Ross's gaze circled the whole group. "It's very nice to meet Kathleen's family. I only hope I'm not intruding."

"Nonsense, boy! We Gallaghers always like to see an extra face around here," S.T. told him.

"That's right, so let's see the baby," Nick told Kathleen. "You've got her hidden under all those blankets. Are you trying to suffocate her, sis?"

Kathleen rolled her eyes at her brother. "Not hardly. It's cold outside, or do you realize that, now that you're in love?"

Grinning wickedly, Nick looked at Allison. "Did you know it was cold outside?" he asked her, then looked back at his sister, his expression an exaggeration of innocence. "We didn't know, sis."

"Give me that baby! I'll not stand around and wait while you two bicker," Ella said. She took Stormy from Kathleen and carried her over to the couch.

Everyone followed, and as Ella peeled back the baby blankets, they crowded around for a look.

"Oh, my. Look at her, Sam," Olivia said in a hushed voice. "Isn't she precious?"

"And look at all that dark hair!" Allison exclaimed. "Benjamin was nearly bald when he was born."

"We can have that buzzed off in no time," Nick teased, making the women groan.

"She's not one of your soldiers, Nick," Kathleen scolded him, although her voice was filled with affection.

"I can't believe someone left her in a storm," Sam said, his voice full of disbelief and outrage.

"Neither can I," S.T. put in. "Whoever did it ought to be strung up by the heels and hung out to dry."

Ella, who had yet to say a word, looked up at her husband, her eyes glistening with tears. "S.T., she looks just like Kathleen did when she was born."

S.T. patted his wife's shoulder. "Now, honey, you know that can't be."

"S.T., don't argue with me," she said with a sniff. "I ought to know. I suffered through twelve hours of labor to get her born. I should know what she looked like when she finally did come out. And it was just like this. A mass of black hair. And those eyes—they'll turn green before she's a year old. I'll bet you anything they do."

S.T. chuckled fondly at his wife's prediction. "I can see you've already christened her a Gallagher."

"Well, she will be a Gallagher if Kathleen is able to adopt her."

Adopt her! Ross went rigid with shock. Was Kathleen going to try to adopt Stormy?

Chapter Nine

"I think this calls for a toast," S.T. said. "Sam, you and Nick go pour everybody a round of that wine your mama had left over from New Year's Eve."

Wine was passed around and glasses were raised to the new baby. Ross looked at Kathleen, to see her face was glowing with joy as she watched her family fuss over Stormy.

"Kathleen?"

When she turned to answer, he took her by the arm and led her across the room, away from the others.

"What is this about adopting Stormy? You didn't say anything to me about adopting her."

Kathleen suddenly felt incredibly guilty. She'd

wanted to tell Ross of her decision. In fact, she'd wanted to tell him before she'd told anyone else. But a part of her had been afraid he'd try to dissuade her. "I know. I was going to, later."

Why did he suddenly feel so left out? Her family had obviously already learned of her decision to adopt the baby. But he hadn't. Hell, Ross, he scolded himself, she loves her family. You didn't expect her to treat you the same way, did you?

"So you have decided to adopt her?" he asked.

Wanting and needing to feel the reassurance of his touch, she reached for his hand and threaded her fingers through his. "I know that I'm single and that I might have trouble getting her. But I have to try, Ross. I've fallen in love with her. I can't just let her go."

And Ross had fallen in love with Kathleen. He didn't know when, or how it had happened. But it had. And as he looked at her now, surrounded by this big, loving family, he wondered where, if at all, he could possibly fit in.

Dinner was a big meal of plain, home-cooked food and boisterous conversation. Ross was told all sorts of stories that ranged from farming incidents, to childhood pranks, to Allison's account of how she'd accepted Nick's engagement ring only because she'd been afraid he'd throw it into the hog pen if she refused.

Ross enjoyed all the anecdotes, and even more, he enjoyed being with Kathleen's family. They were an open bunch who said what they thought, and whatever they were curious to know about him they asked outright, instead of digging at him with sly innuendos and subtle questions.

After supper the men took their coffee to the den, while Olivia and Allison insisted Kathleen go upstairs with them to look at a dress in a brides' magazine.

"But what about Stormy?" she protested, as the two women urged her up the stairs.

"Ella is already in there changing her diaper," Olivia assured her. "She'll be fine."

When they entered Kathleen's old bedroom and shut the door, she looked around the room. "Okay, where's the magazine? Is the dress short or long?"

Allison looked uncomfortable, while Olivia giggled. "There is no magazine. I mean, there is, but Allison is still trying to decide about a dress for herself, first. We wanted you up here for other reasons."

Kathleen looked at both women. "What other reasons?"

Allison smiled. "We've heard all about the baby. We sorta—well…"

"There's no 'sorta' about it. We want to know about Ross," Olivia finished for her.

Kathleen's brows arched upward. "You've already asked him everything. I'm surprised Sam didn't ask him for his Social Security number!''

Olivia and Allison burst out laughing, but Kathleen merely glared at the two of them. ''What's so funny about it? I imagine Ross feels like he stepped under a microscope instead of into a farmhouse!''

''Oh, I'm sure he doesn't feel that way at all,'' Allison put in. ''He seems to be enjoying himself. Especially when he looks at you, Kathleen.''

Kathleen could suddenly see where the two women's thoughts were heading and she threw up her hands to quickly put a stop to it. ''You're imagining that. Besides, I met the man less than three days ago!''

Allison looked at Olivia. ''Remember when I was saying the very same thing about Nick?''

Olivia nodded smugly. ''I remember it vividly. It was on my wedding day. And now you're happily engaged and soon to be married.''

''Okay, okay,'' Kathleen conceded, as she sank down into a wooden rocking chair. ''So I did badger you two about your love lives with my brothers. But this is different. Ross is…well, he is special. And I…really like him. A lot. But, well, it's not like what you two have with Sam and Nick. Ross isn't thinking that way toward me. Why, he so much as told me that he's purposely steered clear of love and marriage.''

''Hmm. That's just what Nick told me,'' Allison

said as she exchanged a knowing little smile with Olivia.

"So are you thinking that way toward him?" Olivia asked.

Kathleen's mouth formed a surprised O. Was she thinking about Ross in those terms? "Olivia, you know what I went through with Greg! Our marriage was horrible. He cheated on me and I...well, I've just gotten my life back together again. Why would I want to become involved with a man?"

"Some of us can't seem to help it," Allison said softly, then glanced once again at Olivia.

"Well, from what you've told me, I can't see where Ross is anything like Greg." Olivia walked over and took a seat on the side of the bed, then looked back at Kathleen. "In fact, I think the whole family likes him."

"I'm glad," Kathleen told her. "As I said, I like him, too."

"You know," Allison put in, "you did catch Olivia's wedding bouquet. I think that really did mean something."

Kathleen's laughter was full of disbelief. "What makes you think so?"

"Well, a tall, dark man has come into your life. Plus a baby. I can't think of a better sign."

"You know," Olivia added impishly, "Ross reminds me of a black-haired James Dean. He has that roguish sort of charm, I think. And when he smiles, that little dimple next to his mouth...well, he's anything but ugly, Kathleen.''

"Shame on you! I'm going to tell Sam you have roving eyes already!''

Olivia laughed like a woman who was sure of her man and her marriage. ''Sam knows I love only him. And that's the way it will always be.''

Kathleen looked at her sisters-in-law and felt a pang of envy. These two women had men who loved and adored them. And more than likely they would soon have children. Kathleen might never have either.

"Kathleen, why don't you and Ross come back tomorrow and have Sunday dinner with us,'' Ella said later that night as Kathleen and Ross were preparing to leave. ''I haven't gotten to hold this baby nearly enough.''

"Good idea,'' Nick spoke up. ''Come on back, Ross. Sam has this idea that we *have* to cut firewood tomorrow. He'll put you to work.''

Later, when Ross pulled his pickup to a stop in front of her house, Kathleen said, ''You don't want to go to the farm tomorrow. I can tell.''

"Why do you say that?''

Kathleen looked at him. He'd been so quiet and withdrawn on the way home. Kathleen could only imagine that he was regretting spending the evening with her and her family. "I don't know. Just a feeling."

He let out a tense breath. All the way home, Ross had felt her beside him. He wanted more than anything to touch her, to kiss her again, and he wondered what her reaction would be if he did.

"Your family was crazy about Stormy," he said, reaching to switch off the motor.

Kathleen smiled at the baby who was strapped in her safety seat. "Yes, they were." She glanced back at him. "They liked you, too."

He made a sound of disbelief. "Oh, yeah? How could you tell?"

"I just could. You know what Olivia said about you?"

He gave her a wary look from the corner of his eye. "No. What?"

"She said you reminded her of a black-haired James Dean."

Ross threw back his head and laughed. "I guess that's a compliment."

"She meant it as such," Kathleen said as she reached to unstrap the baby carrier.

"Here, let me carry Stormy into the house for you," Ross offered. "I don't want either of you to get hurt on the ice."

Kathleen handed him the baby, then quickly gathered her purse and diaper bag from the floorboard of the pickup. Once they made it into the house, Kathleen had him carry the baby on to her bedroom.

"Since the bed is king-size, I let her sleep with me," Kathleen told him as they walked down the hall. "That way I can hear her if she cries."

A dim shaft of light from the hall slanted across the large room, showing Ross the way to the bed. Kathleen followed closely behind him and switched on a small table lamp as he gently placed the baby on the bed.

Since Stormy was already wearing footed pajamas, Kathleen carefully covered her with blankets, then placed pillows on either side of her. "I know she won't be able to roll for a long time yet, but it gives me a sense of security to have them there just in case," she told Ross.

Straightening up from her task, she looked at him and smiled. "Maybe I should look into getting a baby bed."

"Kathleen..."

She could see all sorts of doubts crossing his face and knew what he was going to say. "I know, Ross. You're going to tell me I shouldn't get my hopes up."

She was only a step away. Ross closed the distance and put his hand on her shoulder. "You'll be hurt if you have to give her up. And I don't want to see that happen to you."

Kathleen's eyes searched his face, and as she did,

her heart began to hammer in her breast. The look in his gray eyes wasn't just one of concern, it was also a look of desire.

"Then I hope you'll keep your fingers crossed for me," she said, unaware that her voice had dropped to little more than a whisper.

In that moment, as Ross gazed down at her, he realized he'd do anything to make this woman happy. "I will."

His hand was warm upon Kathleen's shoulder and the subtle scent of his masculine cologne teased her nostrils. Except for the baby, they were completely alone. And her whole body began to quiver with anticipation.

"About going back to the farm with you tomorrow," he murmured, "I'd like to. If you want me to."

His words pleased her far more than she wanted to admit, and before she realized what she was doing, she rose up on tiptoe and kissed his cheek. "I'm glad. I do want you to go."

The moment her lips touched his face, Ross was lost. His hands meshed in her thick hair and held her cheek close against his.

"Oh, Kathleen, you are the most beautiful woman I've ever seen," he whispered fervently. His fingers moved to her face, where he touched her eyes, her nose, her cheeks and finally her lips. "Do you know how much I want to kiss you? Hold you in my arms?''

His words and the urgency of his fingertips on her face echoed Kathleen's own feelings, and she was helpless to resist him or the desire coursing through her body. His name rose up in her throat, but before it could pass her lips, he'd taken her into his arms and covered her mouth with his.

Kathleen had forgotten nothing about the kiss they'd shared on New Year's Eve, and as she surrendered her lips to his, she found she didn't have to go looking for the same passion she'd felt that night. It was already there, burning like a flame between them.

Ross had never been so lost in his life. He forgot where he was, or the long minutes slowing ticking by. He forgot everything as his senses blurred and became consumed by the woman in his arms. She smelled like red roses in the hot sun, and her lips were soft, velvety and achingly sweet. The feel of her ripe curves pressing into him made him shake with the need to make love to her.

''Kathleen!''

Her head spun dizzily as he breathed her name and scattered kisses across her cheek. By the time his teeth sank gently into her earlobe, she was clinging desperately to his waist.

''Oh, Ross, this is madness! I don't think—''

"No. Don't think," he said thickly, "just let me kiss you."

His lips were on her face, pressing kisses along the curve of her jaw. With a tormented groan, Kathleen's head fell limply back, allowing him access to the smooth column of her throat.

His lips quickly followed the V of her blouse until he reached the button above her heart. Then his fingers quickly went to work, until finally the fabric fell away to expose her creamy breasts encased in white lace. A low, guttural sound was torn from Ross's throat as he bent his head even lower.

Katherine wanted him to make love to her. She'd never wanted anything so badly in her life. So why shouldn't she give in to this magic he was working on her? she asked herself. Why shouldn't she let his body appease this burning ache within her?

The answer to that question left her groaning inside. She wanted this to be lovemaking, not just a sexual encounter. And it *would* be making love on her part. She realized that now. She loved this dark-haired man with his crooked smile and cool gray eyes. And she wanted him to love her back. Not just with his body, but with his heart.

"Ross, I can't. I—this is too soon," she whispered brokenly.

Her fingers threaded into the dark waves of his hair and urged his head up to hers.

"My God, Kathleen! Don't ask me to stop now! Do you know how much I want you?"

Yes, she knew it. Because she wanted him just as badly. "I know. But I'm…just not ready for this."

Drawing in a ragged breath, he turned away from her. "No, I guess you're not," he said huskily.

"Please don't be angry with me," she whispered.

"Don't apologize, Kathleen," he said in a tormented voice.

Sensing she'd hurt him more than angered him, Kathleen placed a tentative hand against his back. "Whatever you might think of me, Ross, I don't go around tempting men to make love to me."

He knew that. In fact, he doubted she'd ever made love to a man outside the sanctity of marriage. "Well, whatever you might think, I don't go around trying to make love to every woman who gets within a foot of *me*."

She sighed wistfully. "I don't imagine you do."

He turned back to her. "I guess after this…well, if you want to cancel tomorrow, I'll understand."

Wide-eyed, she stared at him. "Cancel? No. I don't want to cancel anything!" Reaching for his hands, she threaded her fingers through his. "Ross, I still want us to be friends! I mean, we can forget about this and still be together, can't we?"

She expected them to be together, like friends? After what they'd just shared? She must think he was superhuman! How could he resist her? How could he look at her and not remember what it felt like to hold her, kiss her?

"I don't know, Kathleen. I—"

Hearing the hesitation in his voice, she said, "Look, Ross, you told me you wanted no part of marriage. And I can certainly understand that. That's why I think...well, I guess I'm old-fashioned, because I realize I couldn't make love to a man unless he was committed to me. And I'd never ask that of you. Anyway, I've vowed a thousand times I'd never marry again."

Ross had said all that, and he respected everything she was telling him. But the truth was, he no longer felt that way. He wanted to tell Kathleen that he was committed to her. And that if she wanted it, his heart was hers.

But Ross had been shut out so many times before that he was afraid to expose his true feelings. And from what she was saying to him now, it was all for the best that she didn't know how he really felt. She wanted no part of him, or any man.

"I, uh, I gotta get out of here. I'll see you tomorrow," he muttered.

Feeling wounded but not really understanding why, Kathleen watched him leave the room. Moments later, she heard a door slam and knew he'd left the house. Maybe forever, she thought sickly.

"Damn it! Damn it all," she whispered fiercely. Why had this happened? Why couldn't they have kept their hands off of each other? she asked herself, tears forming in her eyes. Now everything had changed. Everything! And she was terrified of what this change might do to her already scarred heart.

The next morning, while Kathleen was getting ready to go to the farm for Sunday dinner, she wondered how she would be able to face Ross and act as though everything was normal.

Everything was far from normal, she thought; in fact, she was a wreck and she looked it. She'd slept little, if any. Not because Stormy had awakened twice in the night. No, it had been a little more complicated than that. She hadn't been able to get Ross out of her mind. Every time she'd closed her eyes, his image had been right there in front of her, tempting her, troubling her with all sorts of thoughts.

She didn't know how she'd let herself fall in love with him. Since her disastrous marriage to Greg, she'd believed she would never be capable of loving again. But on New Year's Eve, Ross had walked into her house and into her heart.

Sometimes we can't help ourselves. Allison's words about falling in love were coming home to Kathleen. Because now she understood that loving a person wasn't something you could make happen, or something that you could prevent. Good or bad, it just happened.

When Ross arrived a few minutes later, Kathleen

felt her heart stirring in spite of herself. He had come back.

"Good morning," she said as she shut the door behind him.

"Good morning," he said, his gray eyes slipping over her face. She looked tired this morning, and he wondered if the baby had kept her awake. "How did it go with the baby last night?"

Smiling briefly, she motioned for him to take a seat. "It went fine," she said, which was true enough. It just hadn't been fine without him. She'd missed him. Every waking minute she spent without him, she missed him. It was crazy. She knew having him near was a dreadful temptation, but it was equally dreadful for her when he was gone.

Ignoring the couch, Ross went to stand by the fireplace. "She didn't wake up?" he asked.

"Only twice."

He should have been here to help her, Ross thought. A woman shouldn't have to care for a baby without the help of a man. Even though Stormy hadn't been born to them, he felt as though Kathleen was her mother and he was her father. And parents needed to live under the same roof together. They needed to share the same dinner table, the same bed. Ross knew that better than anyone.

"I woke up last night thinking I heard her cry," he admitted. "I couldn't go back to sleep."

Something akin to pain wound around Kathleen's

heart. She knew he'd grown close to the baby. It was probably hard on him to be away from her, not to be able to hold her or see for himself that she was all right. As this thought passed through Kathleen's head, it dawned on her that she and Ross were almost like a divorced couple with a baby in between. It was no wonder that Ross didn't want to have a family, she thought. He knew firsthand what kind of pain went along with torn marriages.

"You shouldn't have worried," she said huskily. "You knew I'd be here to take care of her."

He looked at her, taking in her long black hair, her ruby red lips, her tall, lush figure beneath the shirtdress she was wearing. She was achingly beautiful and Ross knew it was a good thing they were going to be around her family today. Otherwise, all he could think about was going over to her and unbuttoning the long row of black buttons on her dress, kissing her mouth and carrying her to bed.

Dragging in a heavy breath, he looked away from her. "Yes, I knew you were here to take care of her," he said quietly, "but I worried just the same."

Kathleen crossed the room to him and instinctively put her hand on his arm. "I don't want you to worry about Stormy, Ross. You can come check on her anytime. Even if it is the middle of the night."

His gaze went from where Kathleen was touching him up to her face. "I don't think that would be a good idea, Kathleen."

Stabbed by his words, she quickly dropped her hand and tucked it behind her back, as though keeping it hidden would help her to quit touching him.

"Maybe you're right," she murmured, unaware of how sad she sounded. She didn't know why she felt so hurt and rejected. She'd made it clear to him last night that she didn't want anything physical between them. What was she going to do? She felt torn up inside.

After several tense moments passed and Ross didn't say anything, Kathleen let out a long breath and said, "So, if you're ready, maybe we'd better be going. Mother usually fries chicken on Sunday. We don't want to be late."

After dinner, S.T. turned on a football game and the women took the baby upstairs. Nick and Sam invited Ross to help them cut firewood.

"We don't usually make our guests work," Nick told him, as the three men drove across the east pasture in Sam's pickup, "but you've been promoted from guest to friend of the family now. So that means you *have* to work."

"Just keep a close eye on Nick," Sam warned Ross, "or he'll be sitting on the tailgate, while you and I do all the work."

Ross smiled, enjoying the companionship of Kathleen's brothers. "Maybe I'd better warn y'all that I haven't done much woodcutting. Where I come from, we didn't need much heat.''

Nick laughed and slapped him on the shoulder. ''Boy, have you come to the right place to learn about using a chain saw. Sam thinks a man hasn't lived until he's had a chain saw in his hands.''

''It's a damn sight safer than that M16 you tote around,'' Sam said dryly. ''And more useful, too.''

''Is that so? Well, who had to go get ten stitches in his leg last winter? It wasn't me and my M16,'' Nick said, sharing a wink with Ross.

An hour later, all three men were sweating in spite of the cold weather. They had the pickup half-loaded with cut hardwood and had decided to take a little breather. Sam had brought a thermos of coffee and he passed cups to Nick and Ross, who were sharing a seat on the open tailgate.

''You know, Ross,'' he said, ''Nick and I are both glad to see you with Kathleen. She's had a hell of a time of it this past year.''

Ross looked down at the brown liquid in his cup. ''She told me about her husband being killed. I guess it's been hard for her to get over.''

Nick shook his head. ''Hard? I was honestly beginning to think she was going to grieve forever.''

Sam frowned. ''I don't really think she was grieving. I think Greg left her downright sick.''

Nick nodded. ''You're right about that. He made her life miserable.'' His eyes narrowed with recollection. "You know, the first time I ever laid eyes on the man, I knew I didn't like him. He was a self-absorbed son-of-a—" He glanced at Ross. "Well, you get the picture, don't you?"

Ross nodded. He got the picture all too well, and it made him sick to think of Kathleen being hurt by a man, or hurt by anything, for that matter.

"Anyway," Sam said, "we're glad she's taken to you. We didn't think she'd ever look at another man. You're just what she needs."

Kathleen's brothers thought she was looking at him like that? They thought Kathleen needed him? He'd never been needed in his life. "You two have it all wrong if you think Kathleen is taken with me. It's not like that at all."

Nick and Sam exchanged knowing glances. "Oh," Nick said, "I guess we were wrong. We just thought from the way she looked at you that you and she were...well, getting close."

Maybe they had gotten close, but Kathleen was seeing to it that they didn't get any closer. "Kathleen is all caught up in the baby. She's not thinking about me."

Sam exchanged another look with his brother. "Yeah," he said to Ross, "Kathleen has wanted a baby for a long time. But just between the three of us, I don't think she has a prayer in hell of adopting Stormy."

"I agree," Nick said grimly. "I can't see a judge

handing that baby over to Kathleen when there are plenty of two-parent families out there just begging to adopt a child.''

Ross looked from Nick to Sam, then back to Nick. ''It will kill her if she doesn't get to keep that baby,'' he said.

''We know. That's why we're glad she has you,'' Sam said. ''She's going to need you to help her get over the disappointment.''

Chapter Ten

That's why we're glad she has you. Sam's words haunted Ross through the remainder of the day. And that night, on the drive home from the Gallaghers', he came to a decision.

"Do you mind if I come in, Kathleen?" he asked when he pulled the truck to a stop in Kathleen's driveway. "There's something I want to talk to you about."

For the bigger part of the day, Ross had kept his distance from Kathleen, so his request surprised her, to say the least. "What is it?" she asked him after they'd gathered Stormy and her things and gone into the house.

He motioned toward the baby. "Let's get her into bed first," he said.

"All right," she agreed, wondering at his serious tone. What was it? Was he going to tell her that he thought it would be better if he didn't see her or the baby anymore? The mere thought shook her.

Once Kathleen had Stormy settled in bed, she kicked off her shoes and went to the kitchen to make a fresh pot of coffee. Ross followed, wondering how he was going to manage talking to her for more than five minutes without putting his hands on her.

"I hope my family hasn't hurt you in some way. Mother and Nick can be so direct at times. I hope neither of them said anything that angered you."

He waved away her suggestion and leaned against the counter a step or two from her. "It's nothing like that. Your family is wonderful. They've gone out of their way to be nice to me," Ross said. Then, deciding it would be better if he put some distance between them, he took a seat at the table in the middle of the room. "But your family is not what's on my mind. I've been doing a lot of thinking these past two days...."

Kathleen switched on the coffee machine, then turned and rested against the counter. "About what?" she asked, hoping she didn't sound as nervous as she felt.

"About me and you, and Stormy."

Kathleen's heart began to thud so hard she felt light-headed. "What about us?"

Unable to keep his distance, Ross got up from the

table and came to stand in front of her. There was a strange lump in his throat as he looked at her. "I think you and I should get married."

Kathleen was so stunned her knees threatened to buckle beneath her. "Married! What are you saying, Ross?"

He wanted to sound casual and unaffected, but he knew he couldn't keep the emotions he was feeling out of his voice. He'd never loved a woman before. He'd never been brave enough to let himself. But his heart was on the line now and he'd never been more afraid.

"I'm saying that if you really want to have a chance of adopting Stormy, we need to get married. Of course, it would be in name only, but the courts wouldn't have to know that."

Dazed, Kathleen stared at him. "You mean you'd do that for me? For her?"

He nodded, and Kathleen realized if she hadn't been leaning against the counter, she would have fallen. Ross was willing to marry her for her and the baby's sake. It was one of the most unselfish gestures Kathleen had ever heard of. But on the other hand, she realized a part of her was deeply wounded because he wasn't proposing to her out of real love.

"I can't imagine—" She broke off as her eyes searched his. "Are you really serious?"

His hands curved around her shoulders. "I'm very serious. I want you to have Stormy." He wanted that almost as much as he wanted her to be his wife. And he'd do anything to make both of those things happen.

Kathleen turned away from him. She knew she had to. Otherwise, she might become so mesmerized by his touch, she'd be tempted to say yes.

"I'm sorry, Ross. I couldn't marry you under those circumstances. I couldn't marry you under *any* circumstances."

Without looking at him, she turned and left the room. Ross followed her down the hallway and out to the living room. "Why can't you?" he asked. "What could it possibly hurt? You could get the baby you've always wanted. And I'd know she was where she belonged. Then later on—if you wanted—we could get a divorce."

A divorce! How many times had Greg flung that word at her? she wondered hysterically. She hadn't been able to give him the child he wanted. She hadn't been able to make him happy. He'd wanted a divorce so he could find a woman who could do both of those things.

Now the thought of Ross using that same word with her made Kathleen feel like she'd been cut with a dirty knife. "I don't want to be married! Don't you understand that, Ross?"

She walked rigidly to the windows overlooking the front lawn. Ross followed and stood just behind her. "I understand that you had a bad marriage. Your brothers told me what a bastard Greg was. But that has nothing to do with you and me. You wouldn't be marrying me for love.''

Kathleen felt like a lance had been thrust through her heart. She *would* be marrying Ross for love. That's why she couldn't marry him. She'd be setting herself up for all kinds of hurt. She wanted Stormy desperately, but she couldn't risk that kind of involvement just to help her chances for adoption.

She let out a brittle laugh. ''I had something worse than a bad marriage, Ross. And the crazy thing about it, I didn't even realize how bad it was until Greg was killed. I guess for the three years we were married I closed my eyes. I wanted to believe that everything was all right. But when he died...I had to finally face facts.''

Before he could say anything, Kathleen whirled around to face him. ''What did my brothers really tell you? Did they tell you that when my husband went down in that plane, his mistress was with him?''

Ross was sickened by the dark image Kathleen was painting for him. ''You mean...she died with him?''

Her features stiff, Kathleen gave one nod. ''Yes. Poor thing. Sometimes I think fate dealt her a kinder hand by taking her life instead of letting her live and continue to love Greg Hayes. He would have only wound up hurting her, too.''

"Oh, Kathleen, what a thing to live with! Did you know about her before the accident?"

She made a little sound of self-mockery. "I had my suspicions, but I turned a blind eye to them. I kept thinking…"

Unable to go on, Kathleen looked away from him. She couldn't tell Ross that she'd continued on with Greg, hoping and believing that if she could become pregnant and give him a child, their marriage would turn around and become the family she'd always wanted. She couldn't bear for this man to know that she was infertile, something less than a woman.

"It doesn't matter what I thought. I can't marry you, Ross. I'll never marry anyone!"

Ross shook his head with frustration. "But this would be different, Kathleen. This wouldn't be a real marriage where hearts and emotions are involved. It would just be a legal convenience, that's all."

A legal convenience! How could he talk about something as sacred as marriage in such a way? She'd thought he was different from other men. She'd thought he had moral dignity, but apparently he viewed marriage the same way Greg had. It was just a convenience for whatever served their purposes.

"How could you say that to me?" she whispered fiercely. Hot tears spurted from her eyes. "You're just like Greg was. Marriage means nothing to you! It's only a way to get what you want at the time you're wanting it. And if it doesn't work out—well,'' she said with a bitter laugh, ''what the hell, there's always divorce. It doesn't matter that marriage is supposed to be holy, that it's supposed to last for life!''

With a little sob she turned away from him and covered her face with her hands. ''I don't want to talk about this anymore, Ross.''

Ross had never felt so bewildered as when he watched her slumped shoulders shake with silent sobs. He hadn't expected her to react this way. Before he'd asked her to marry him, he'd tried to steel himself against a rejection, because he'd expected one. But Ross hadn't expected such an emotional one, and he couldn't understand it. He wasn't asking her to love him, though he knew how much he wanted her love. He was trying to help her. Couldn't she see that?

He ventured closer and touched her arm. ''I didn't ask you to marry me as a way to hurt you, Kathleen,'' he said gently, in hopes of reassuring her.

With her back to him, she shook her head. ''Please leave, Ross,'' she said, her voice broken by tears. ''I can't bear this now. Please.''

Ross knew what it felt like to be shut out. It was something he'd been experiencing all his life. But being shut out by Kathleen was something altogether different. As he went out the door, there was an ache in his heart such as he'd never known.

* * *

The next morning Kathleen had to drag herself out of bed. She felt dead, physically and emotionally dead. After Ross had left the house she'd cried a storm of tears, and finally, when no more tears would come, she'd lain awake in the dark, thinking and hurting, agonizing over every word Ross had said to her and regretting every word she'd said to him.

He hadn't deserved the outburst she'd laid on him. He was only trying to help her get Stormy. He didn't know that Kathleen had fallen in love with him. And last night, when he'd proposed, that love had gotten tangled up in everything he was saying and everything she was feeling.

He must be thinking she was a hysterical wreck of a woman, she thought with a groan of self-disgust. But when he'd talked about a marriage of convenience, Kathleen's heart had been torn right down the middle. She didn't want that from him. She wanted more. But she was going to have to forget all of that. She was going to have to completely forget this whole marriage thing.

She couldn't marry Ross. Living with him under the same roof would make it impossible for her to keep her true feelings hidden. And when he discovered that Kathleen loved him, he'd feel caught, maybe even obliged to stay in the marriage. No, she couldn't have that. It would be like reliving her nightmare of a marriage to Greg all over again. Ross didn't love her, and sooner or later he would find a woman he did love and want to have children with. And then she'd have to let him go.

Kathleen had just finished giving Stormy a bath and had dressed her in a pair of footed pajamas when the telephone rang. As she hurried to answer it, she realized she wanted it to be Ross's voice she heard on the other end of the line.

To her surprise, it was the police sergeant she and Ross had talked to about Stormy.

"What can I do for you this morning, Sergeant?" she asked quickly.

"I'm calling to tell you that we've found the person who left the baby on Mr. Douglas's porch."

Kathleen couldn't contain her gasp of surprise. "Who was it? Was it someone local?" Her heart began to race with dread. "What about the mother?"

"I think, Mrs. Hayes, it would be best if you'd come down to the precinct this morning. As soon as possible. We'll answer your questions then, okay?"

Kathleen was suddenly shaking with fear. Were they going to take the baby from her now? She needed Ross with her. "Yes, all right. I'll…be there shortly."

A week ago, Ross had been looking forward to getting back in the classroom, but this morning, his first day on the job, had been especially rough for him. Not because of rowdy or lethargic students, but rather from his lack of concentration. With half his thoughts on Kathleen, he couldn't make a lecture on American history interesting to a class of teenagers.

He feared his marriage proposal to Kathleen had driven a wedge between them, one that he might not ever be able to tear down. But Ross couldn't think about that now. He had another class in thirty minutes. He planned to lecture them on the Monroe Doctrine, and he didn't intend to have students leave the room yawning.

A click of high heels on hard tile caught his attention and he turned his head toward the doorway, expecting it to be a fellow teacher coming to welcome him aboard. Instead, he was shocked to see Kathleen walking into his room.

"I hope I'm not interrupting. The principal said I could probably find you here," she said.

He shook his head, thinking how gorgeous she looked. She was dressed in a black coat dress that buttoned all the way down to her knees with large gold buttons. A black-and-gold patterned scarf had been twisted, then tied around her head to hold her black hair away from her face.

Ross realized her beauty stunned him almost as much as her being here. Then he realized something else. The baby wasn't with her. "Where's Stormy?" he asked quickly. "They haven't taken her, have they?"

She held up her hand to allay his fears. "No. She's with Mother at the farmhouse."

She walked farther into the room, and Ross rose to his feet as her shaken state became apparent to him.

"Is something wrong, Kathleen?"

"I don't know. I mean, yes. It is."

He waited for her to go on. When she didn't, he skirted around the desk and took her by the arm. "Kathleen, you're pale and you're shaking like a leaf. Has something happened?"

Funny, she thought, how just hearing Ross's voice was enough to make her feel better. She looked up at him and tried her best to smile. "First of all, I want to apologize to you for last night. I said some awful things to you. Things that I know aren't true. You aren't like Greg. God forgive me for ever saying you were."

He reached out and touched her cheek. "You don't have to say this to me, Kathleen."

"Yes, I do. Because I don't want to hurt you. And I don't want you to be angry with me."

He groaned at the thought. Angry was the last thing he could ever be with Kathleen. "If you came all the way down here to ask me not to be angry with you, then you've wasted your time. I wasn't angry with you last night. I'm not angry with you now."

His voice grew soft on the last words, and Kathleen was suddenly reminded of that same low voice telling her he wanted to make love to her. It had sent shivers down her spine then, just like it was doing now.

"I'm glad about that, at least," she said, then sighed and passed a shaky hand across her brow. "I just came from the police station. They found the person who left Stormy on your porch."

Ross grabbed both her shoulders. "Who was it? Have they locked him or her behind bars?"

Her expression grim, Kathleen nodded. "Yes. But I don't really see what good locking him behind bars is going to do now."

"Him? It was the father? What a bastard!"

"No, it wasn't the father of the baby, although I think he did know about it. But since he didn't want any part of the child, it didn't matter to him what they did with it." Feeling her knees growing spongy, she reached for his arm. "I'm sorry, Ross, I've got to sit down."

Ross led her over to a long wooden bench next to a plate glass window. Sunlight streamed down on them and bathed Kathleen's pale face with warmth. Ross waited patiently while she drew in several long breaths and tried to collect herself.

"Actually," she told him, "it was the grandfather who left the child. Apparently the whole family is poor and uneducated. A daughter became pregnant out of wedlock, and since she was far too young to be able to keep the baby, they decided to give it away.''

Ross's head shook back and forth as though he couldn't believe what he was hearing. ''But why? And why give it to me?''

''That part is—'' unable to stop herself, she clutched at his hands ''—I think the strangest and saddest part of all. None of them wanted the baby. They all considered her just another mouth to feed. But the mother wanted me to have her.''

Ross was stunned. ''You! It was someone who knew you?''

Kathleen shrugged, as though she were just as lost as he was about the whole thing. ''I scarcely remember the girl, Ross. From what I can recall, she was in a reading class of mine. And I do remember that she would only show up for school maybe two days out of the week. I tried to give her special attention. I guess she must have remembered that, I don't know. Anyway, she told the police that her father had meant to take the baby to my house, but apparently he got the houses mixed up and she wound up on your porch.''

''Oh Lord, this is unbelievable!''

Kathleen nodded. ''I know. Unbelievable and sad.''

He looked at her as new thoughts struck him. ''So what does this all mean? What's going to happen to Stormy?''

"The girl and her parents have signed all rights to the child over to the state. She'll be placed on an adoption list."

"And that terrifies you, doesn't it?" he asked softly.

She nodded, her eyes brimming with tears. "You can't imagine how much," she whispered.

A tear rolled onto her cheek and Ross wiped it away with the pad of his thumb. He wanted to help her. He'd do anything to make her happy, if only she'd let him. "That's why we should get married, Kathleen. If the courts saw us as two parents, a mother and a father, then the chances of us getting her would be far greater. You know that."

She knew a lot of things. Mainly that she couldn't marry this man, even at the risk of losing Stormy. Rising shakily to her feet, she said, "I know, Ross. But I haven't changed my mind."

Groaning with frustration, Ross pushed his fingers through his hair. What was he going to do? What could he say to her to make her see reason?

A group of teenagers was now milling about in the hall outside the classroom. Seeing them, Kathleen figured lunch hour was nearly over and the bell was about to ring. "I'd better go," she said.

"Kathleen, we've got to talk about this," he said, desperately catching her arm as she turned to go.

Her eyes pleading with him, she shook her head. "It's wrong. It's all wrong, Ross."

There was nothing wrong with loving her and wanting to marry her. But how could he tell her that when she was so obviously embittered over her past? She didn't want his love. She didn't want to be his wife. All she wanted was the baby. It was something he'd known from the very beginning, but that didn't make it hurt any less.

Suddenly the bell rang and students began to pour into the room. Ross was forced to release his hold on Kathleen's arm. The minute he did, she shot out of the room, leaving him no opportunity to say anything else to her.

It was just as well, he thought dismally, as he turned back to his desk and began to gather up his history notes. Right now he didn't know what to do or say that would make a difference between them. Maybe he never would.

Chapter Eleven

When Kathleen returned to the farmhouse to pick up Stormy, the whole family was amazed to hear what she'd learned at the police station. They were also concerned about Kathleen's growing involvement with the baby and afraid of what it might do to her if she lost her.

None of them was more worried than Sam, who followed his sister out to the car as she prepared to leave.

"Kathleen, why don't you spend the night with us?" he suggested as he handed the baby over to her.

She smiled wanly as she took Stormy from him and strapped her safely in the car seat. Sam had always been her protector. Anytime she'd ever been in trouble or needed help she'd been able to come to him, and he would do anything humanly possible to help her. But this time she was afraid there was nothing anyone could do.

She'd made the mistake of falling in love with a man she couldn't have and a baby she couldn't keep. How could anyone possibly help her?

As she settled herself behind the steering wheel, she looked up at her brother. "I don't think so, Sam. I need to be home in case the child-welfare people try to get in touch with me."

"Do you think that will be soon?" he asked, shutting the car door, then leaning his head into the open window.

She nodded glumly. "I'm afraid so. Parker Montgomery said the temporary custody would only last a few days at the most. Or until a foster home could be found. I'm sure I'll have to turn her over in the next few days."

He placed his hand on her shoulder. "Kathleen, I can't stand to see you so torn up like this."

Kathleen pressed the heels of her palms against her aching eyes. "This might be my only chance of ever having a baby. Oh, Sam, I'm terrified of losing her." She dropped her hands and looked back at her brother's worried face. "Ross has asked me to marry him. He says it might help my chances of adopting Stormy."

Sam didn't say anything for a moment and Kathleen watched his face for a reaction. However, with her brother it was always hard to tell what he was thinking. The only thing about his expression that changed was the faint arch of one dark brow.

"It probably would," he said after several moments had passed. "What did you tell him?"

His question had Kathleen gasping audibly. "What do you mean, what did I tell him? Good Lord, Sam, you know I had to say no!"

"Why? Because of what Greg did to you?"

It was true that her bad marriage to Greg had left her wounded and scarred, and more than a little wary of men and marriage. Yet Kathleen knew the biggest reason she couldn't marry Ross was because she loved him. But Kathleen couldn't tell her brother that. What she felt for Ross was too fresh, too private and precious a thing to share with anyone.

"Isn't that reason enough?" she answered.

He frowned. "What are you going to do, let his memory ruin your entire life?"

Anxious now to end their conversation, Kathleen put her hand on the key. "It's not that simple, Sam. Believe me."

He gave a lock of her hair an affectionate tug. "Just remember, sis, that I know what it's like to suffer. I lived my own private kind of hell until Olivia came back from Africa. We all need someone to love us. You included."

Yes, she did need someone to love her, Kathleen thought as she drove home. But she couldn't make Ross love her, anymore than she could marry him just for legal purposes.

When Ross arrived home from school, he drove straight to Kathleen's, only to find she wasn't home.

Frustrated, he went back to his own house and told himself to calm down. Even if she had been home, Ross doubted he could have reasoned with her any better than he had earlier today.

Still, he couldn't shake this helpless, desperate feeling that had settled over him, as if a bomb were tied to him and was ticking away. If he didn't do something to stop it from exploding, he would lose Kathleen, they'd lose the baby, and the family he wanted so badly would be lost to him forever.

For the next hour Ross paced the house and watched the highway for the sight of Kathleen's car. When he finally spotted it, he threw on his jacket and hurried out to his truck.

Kathleen had just gotten into the house and placed Stormy on the couch when she heard Ross's pickup pull into the driveway. As she went to the door to let him in, her heart leaped in spite of the misgivings she had about being with him.

"May I come in?" he asked.

How could she turn him away when everything

inside her ached to be with him? She pushed the door wider and stood aside to allow him entry.

"I just got home," she told him, noticing he was still wearing the jeans and boots he'd been wearing at school, but his tweed sports coat had been replaced with the well-worn letter jacket, a garment she was beginning to associate with him.

"I know. I've been watching for you," he said.

As Ross moved into the room, he spotted the baby on the couch. It was a relief to see her again and he took her out of her carrier and held her close to his chest.

Kathleen didn't say anything. She was too busy watching him with the baby. It was obvious he loved her, and Kathleen wondered if the real reason Ross wanted to marry her was so he would have the chance to be Stormy's father.

"You were watching for me," she repeated. "Why? Was there some reason you needed to see me? Did the police contact you about anything?"

With his hand carefully cradling the baby's head, he lifted her against his shoulder and pressed his cheek against hers. She smelled powdery soft and sweet and innocent. He'd never known that babies smelled that way. He'd never known he could feel such fierce protectiveness toward such a tiny being. He'd never dreamed he would ever want to be a daddy. But he did. He wanted it almost as much as he wanted Kathleen to be his wife.

"No. They've probably tied up all the loose ends of the case by now," he told her.

"Then why did you want to see me?"

He put the baby back on the couch, but she immediately began to cry, so he picked her up again.

"I imagine she's hungry," Kathleen said as she went to her diaper bag for a bottle. "I'll go heat this and be right back."

A couple of minutes later, Kathleen returned with the warmed bottle. Ross took it and settled himself and Stormy in one of the armchairs.

While Ross gave Stormy her bottle, Kathleen went to the kitchen and prepared a pot of fresh coffee and a tray of sandwiches. She wasn't hungry, but she figured he was. And she needed something to keep her busy and away from him as much as possible.

"You didn't have to do that for me," he said, motioning his head toward the sandwiches she'd prepared.

Kathleen glanced around to see Ross had entered the kitchen. Nervously, she reached for a tea towel and wiped her hands. "I figured you hadn't eaten anything this evening. Have you?"

He shook his head. He'd been too wired up to eat. "I didn't come up here to have you fix me something to eat."

She carried the sandwiches over to the breakfast bar. "I didn't expect you did," she said, then looked at him as he took a seat on the bar stool next to her. "Where's Stormy?"

"She's asleep. I put her on your bed. And yes, I covered her up and put pillows beside her," he added before she had the chance to ask.

"You remembered," she said quietly, her green eyes going soft as she looked into his face.

"I remember a lot more than you think," he said in a low voice.

Kathleen remembered, too. She recalled every moment she'd spent in his arms. She remembered the rough texture of his hands against her skin, the eager warmth of his lips. She remembered every sigh, every kiss, every word he'd said to her.

It was all burned into her mind. As though he'd branded his mark on her without ever fully possessing her. The thoughts caused heat to seep to the surface of her cheeks, forcing her to look away from him.

She handed him a mug full of coffee. "I told my family what the police had to say. And I talked to Parker Montgomery about it."

Ross took a bite of sandwich, but for all he knew he was chewing wood chips. "And what did he have to say?"

Still unable to meet his eyes, she shrugged. "He

can't really give me any kind of reassurance. Though he does know my temporary custody will end any day now.''

She sounded resigned to the fact, which only made Ross want to reach over and shake her. ''That's why we can't wait around about this, Kathleen. We have to get married. Now, tomorrow, or as quickly as we can!''

Kathleen didn't answer him. Instead, she stared unseeingly at the other end of the room and wondered what her life would be like once Stormy and Ross were no longer in it.

''Kathleen? Did you hear what I said?''

She turned her head to look at him, and as she did, she tried to steel her heart against him. ''Ross, why are you badgering me about this? I told you no, and I meant it. I'm not going to marry you. Not now. Not ever.''

Tossing down the sandwich, he wearily scrubbed his face with both hands. ''Then all I can say is you must not want Stormy very badly.''

Kathleen wanted to strike at him with both her fists, to scream how wrong he was. But all she could manage to do was stare at him as a chilling pain swept over her.

''How dare you say that to me! You could never know how much that baby means to me,'' she said in a low, fierce voice. "You could never know how much I want her!"

All the doubts and uncertainty she'd felt these past few days suddenly welled up in her throat, choking her with fear. With a strangled sob, she slipped off the bar stool and ran out of the room before he had a chance to stop her.

A few moments later, Ross found her in one of the spare bedrooms. She was sitting on the side of the bed with her back to him. Her shoulders were slumped, her head bent downward. When he sat beside her and lifted her face to his, he found tears on her cheeks.

The sight of them cut him to the core and he wanted more than anything to draw her into his arms and kiss them away.

"I'm sorry, Kathleen. Maybe I was wrong—"

"You were wrong!"

His hands lifted, then fell helplessly back to his knees. "I don't understand you, Kathleen."

She began to quiver like a trapped animal doomed to a fate it couldn't control. "No, you can't understand, Ross. Because you don't know. And if you did, you could see why I do want Stormy so badly."

Reaching out, he cupped the side of her face. "Then tell me, Kathleen. This is tearing me up. I want to help you, but I don't know how."

Something in his voice prompted her to look at

him, and as she did she realized that she could no
longer think just about herself, her feelings and
wants. She had to think about Ross and what all of
this was doing to him. "The reason I—" With a
shake of her head, she stopped, then started again.
"The truth is, Ross, I can't have children."

Ross felt as if he'd been whacked in the chest and
had lost his air. Kathleen. His beautiful Kathleen,
unable to have children? He couldn't believe it! He
didn't want to believe it!

"Kathleen, I...dear God, why didn't you tell
me?"

Amazed that he had to ask why, Kathleen's eyes
searched his face. "Because I couldn't! Because I
didn't want you to know! Do you think it's something a woman is proud to announce? Something she
can go around telling a man who—" She broke off
abruptly, appalled at what she'd been about to say.
A man who she loves. She'd almost told Ross that
she loved him!

Drawing in a desperate breath, she turned her head
away and stared across the bedroom, which was
quickly becoming dark now that the sun had set.

"Kathleen, look at me," he said, his thumb and
forefinger dragging her chin back around to him.
"Didn't I make it clear that you could tell me anything?"

She nodded stiffly as she recalled the conversation they'd shared over dinner on New Year's Day.

"Well, that means anything and everything." His hold on her chin eased, but his fingers remained on her face, to gently trace her cheek. "I would have understood. I understand now," he said softly.

His touch and his kindness brought a bittersweet ache to Kathleen's heart. "I'm glad you understand, Ross. So now you can see why I can't marry you."

Bewildered, he shook his head. "No, I don't see that. You not being able to bear children shouldn't stop you from marrying me. It should make you want to marry me even more—seeing that Stormy might be the only child you'll have."

"Might have," she reminded him wearily, then rose to her feet and walked across the room. A framed picture of Sam, Nick and herself was sitting atop a dresser just to her right. She picked it up and studied it for long minutes before she said, "You're not thinking about this, Ross. Not really thinking."

He went across the room to stand at her shoulder. "And you're thinking too much," he told her.

Her head twisted up and around in order to see his face. "One of us needs to. I've already gone through this once, Ross. Greg wanted a family. I don't really know why—he wasn't a family-type man. Maybe it was an ego thing, I don't know. And I guess that part of it no longer matters. What does matter is that I couldn't give him one, and he became very unhappy in our marriage.''

''Kathleen—'' he began, only to have her interrupt.

''Don't tell me it doesn't matter, Ross. Because I know that it does! I know how dissatisfied and trapped he felt by our marriage. And it would be the same way with you.''

He lifted her long hair in his hands, relishing the silky texture and the flowery scent that rose to his senses. ''It wouldn't be the same at all. I'm not asking you to marry me to give me children. I don't expect you to give me any.''

Jut having Ross so close to her, having his chest brushing against her shoulders, his hands in her hair, made her nearly weep with longing. She knew he desired her physically, and she knew all she would have to do to have him was to turn and invite him into her arms.

But she knew in the end a physical relationship between them would only complicate matters even more. And a marriage based solely on physical desire would be even worse than marrying to adopt Stormy.

''I know that you only want a marriage of convenience,'' she said, her voice growing thick. ''But what if you fell in love with someone and wanted to have children with her? Do you know how guilty that would make me feel?''

How could he tell her that her fears were ground-
less? How could he tell her that he would never fall
in love with someone else because he'd already
fallen in love with her? And that he would love her
forever? He couldn't.

More than likely she would think he was making
it up just to allay her fears. But on the other hand, if
she did believe him, he had no doubts that she would
run as fast and as far away from him as she could
possibly get.

Groaning at the hopelessness of it all, he said,
"Kathleen, you're getting way ahead of yourself. Besides, if that should ever happen, we could get a divorce. Like I first suggested."

She whirled on him, her face rigid with anger.
"That would really be nice, wouldn't it," she hurled
at him. "Give Stormy two parents and let her get
used to having both a mother and a father, then get
a divorce and split her family apart. How could I
explain that to her? Tell her that she wasn't important
enough? That her daddy had to move on and make
himself another family?"

Ross wanted to curse at the top of his lungs. But
rather than give in to the urge, he drew in a steadying
breath and said, "It wouldn't be like that, Kathleen."

Shaking from head to toe, she stepped around him.
"This is it, Ross! I'm not discussing this any further.
In fact, I'd prefer it if I never saw you again!"

Ross stared at her retreating back, knowing he couldn't have felt any more pain if she'd pushed a lance right through his heart.

"What about Stormy? You'd keep me from seeing her?"

At the doorway to the bedroom, she turned and looked back at him. She saw the raw pain on his face and realized how much she was hurting this man, and she hated it. But she was doing it out of love. She had to keep telling herself that, or she was going to shatter into a thousand pieces.

"No. I wouldn't do that. You can see her whenever you want. But this—this thing between us is over. Don't ever mention the word marriage to me again!"

"Okay, class, tomorrow we're going to be discussing amending the Constitution. Who can tell me what the first ten amendments to the constitution are called?"

Ross turned away from the blackboard to see several hands raised in the air. He pointed to a blondheaded girl in the back.

"The Bill of Rights, Mr. Douglas," she answered.

"That's right, Cynthia," he said, then turned back to the blackboard and began to write. "So, your assignment for tomorrow, class, is to write a brief description of each amendment that makes up our Bill of Rights.''

The bell rang and noise filled the room as students called to each other and made a quick race to the door.

Ross was gathering up a stack of papers to take home to grade when he realized someone had returned to the room. Looking up, he saw it was one of his history students.

''Did you forget something, Matthew?''

''No, Mr. Douglas,'' he said, taking a tentative step toward Ross. ''I just wanted to ask you—well, the rumor has been going around school that when you played baseball in college, a major-league team offered you a contract.''

Apparently Matthew was going to be one of his baseball players, he thought wryly. ''Well, I don't know where you heard the rumor, but it's true.''

The tall, lanky boy was obviously impressed. ''Wow! So why aren't you still playing? I mean, you're not too old to play baseball.''

Smiling, Ross dropped a friendly hand on the boy's shoulder. ''No, I'm not too old. I had a knee injury. That's fatal for a guy who plays catcher.''

''So you had to retire,'' Matthew said, his expression as miserable as if he'd suffered the injury himself. ''I guess teaching must be boring after playing in a minor-league club.''

Ross chuckled. "It's not boring at all. I enjoy making sure boys like you know what the Bill of Rights is."

"Aw, shoot. Is that really the truth?"

"It's really the truth," he told the boy. And it was the truth, Ross realized. Teaching wasn't just something he'd taken up because he could no longer play baseball. It was what he wanted to do with his life. He wanted to be with children. To try to make a difference in their lives. There were too many of them out there with only one parent or no parents at all. He wanted to be there for as many of them as he could be. He wanted to see that his students never felt as left out as he had.

"Boy, you must really like kids," Matthew said.

When Ross left the building a few minutes later, he was still thinking about Matthew's comments. The boy's words had made him realize just how much he did like kids. Even though he'd always told himself he liked his freedom better.

However, that had all changed when he'd found Stormy on his front porch. In spite of his fears about marriage, he wanted to be Stormy's father. And he couldn't be Stormy's father unless he married Kathleen and they tried to adopt her together. But he could hardly see that happening now. Kathleen didn't care if he ever showed his face in her life again. In fact, she would probably be happy if he didn't.

Well, he thought grimly, he'd left her alone last night, although it had very nearly killed him to stay away. But tonight he was going up to see her and the baby. He wouldn't mention marriage. But he would let Kathleen know that he hadn't forgotten about it, either.

"Ross?"

At the sound of his name, Ross turned to see Nick Gallagher jogging toward him.

"Nick! How on earth did you find me here?"

"I remembered you telling Mom and Dad where you'd be teaching. Are you on your way home?"

Ross nodded, wondering why Kathleen's brother had gone to the trouble of looking him up. "Is…something wrong? Has something happened to Kathleen?"

Nick shook his head, but from the frown on his face Ross could see something *was* wrong.

"It's not—she hasn't had an accident or anything. But she's in awful shape, Ross. She had to turn the baby over today. A child-welfare worker took Stormy to a foster home."

Ross felt like he'd been hit with an ax. "Where is she now?" he asked, a sick feeling in the pit of his stomach.

"You mean Kathleen?"

Ross nodded soberly.

"She's at the farm. She was so torn up, Dad

wouldn't let her drive home.'' He made a helpless gesture with his hand. "I thought if you'd come over to the farm and see her, it might help.''

Ross was more than surprised at Nick's request. "I, uh, don't think Kathleen wants to see me. She didn't ask to see me, did she?''

Nick frowned. "No. But right now Kathleen doesn't know what she's doing or saying. She only knows her baby has been taken away from her.''

Lifting his face to the sky, Ross drew in a long breath in hopes of easing the pain in his chest. "This is all my fault. If it wasn't for me, Kathleen wouldn't be in this shape now!''

Nick folded his arms. "You sound about as crazy as Kathleen does. It isn't your fault she wants that baby so badly. Didn't you know about…well, Kathleen can't have children.''

"I know. She told me.''

Nick couldn't keep his surprise hidden. Ross could see his shock and realized that other than the family, Kathleen hadn't told anybody about her inability to conceive. Until now. Ross thought about that as Nick continued, "Then you can understand why she's hurting so badly.''

"I do understand. I just can't see that I could do anything about it. I tried.'' He groaned with frustration. "Oh, hell, I should never have taken the baby up to Kathleen's house that night. I should have gotten her down the mountain somehow.''

Nick slung his arm around Ross's shoulder. "You did the best you could for the baby. Don't be feeling guilty now. Just come talk to Kathleen.''

"She has all of you, Nick. You're her family.''

"Yes, she has all of us. But you're the one she needs.''

No one had ever needed Ross. It was incredible to him to think that Kathleen did.

"I do want to see her,'' Ross admitted.

"Good.'' Nick gave his shoulder an encouraging shake. "She doesn't know I came over here to find you and I won't tell her you're coming. But I can tell you that the whole family is going to give a sigh of relief when they see you.''

"Why is that?''

Nick's expression was suddenly wry. "Can't you see that Kathleen loves you? We all can.''

Chapter Twelve

Kathleen loves you. Kathleen loves you. As he drove to the Gallagher farm, the words played over and over in his head like a litany he couldn't shut off.

Could Nick be right? Did Kathleen love him? She'd responded to him physically, but she wouldn't make love with him. Moreover, she completely refused to marry him. That didn't sound to Ross like a woman in love.

When Ross arrived at the farmhouse, Nick met him at the door and led him through the kitchen and into the den.

Olivia, Allison and Ella were all sitting on the couch going over brides' magazines. Kathleen was sitting on the floor with Benjamin, who was showing her the new eyes Ella had sewn on the stuffed basset hound Kathleen had given him.

"I'm sure Buddy can see a rabbit a mile off with those eyes," Kathleen told the boy.

Ben giggled. "Will he chase the rabbit and eat him?"

Kathleen smiled wanly. "Buddy only chases rabbits. He'll come home and eat dog food for his supper."

Benjamin giggled again. "Buddy won't do that, Kathleen, 'cause he don't eat dog food."

"Ben," Nick called out fondly, "come here, son. Let's go with Uncle Sam to feed the hogs."

Always ready to go with Nick, Ben jumped to his feet and followed Nick out of the room. The three women on the couch rose to their feet also.

"Girls, I think it's about time we started supper," Ella said. "And S.T. wants ribs tonight. We'd better cook up some barbecue sauce."

Ross hardly noticed as the women quietly filed out of the room. He was too busy looking at Kathleen, who was still sitting on the floor, staring up at him.

He moved closer, and as he did, Ross could see that she'd been crying long and hard. Her face and eyes were swollen, her hair disheveled. She looked terribly sad, and terribly beautiful.

"What are you doing here?" she asked him.

"I heard about Stormy," he said quietly.

She looked away from him and Ross knew she was struggling to keep more tears from surfacing.

"You shouldn't have come. There's nothing you can do."

Her voice was flat, as though every bit of life had drained out of her. Ross realized she didn't want to see him. All she wanted was to get her baby back. It was a painful fact. Nick might know all about Allison's heart, but he didn't know about his sister's. She didn't love Ross. He'd been crazy to ever hope she would. He'd been even crazier to think he could compete with Stormy and the Gallagher family for her affection.

"It's not over, Kathleen. She hasn't been adopted. She's only gone to a foster home." He knelt beside her, trying to comfort her.

She looked back at him and her face crumpled as fresh tears filled her eyes. "They just took her, Ross. Like it was nothing. They took *our* baby! She was mine and yours, not theirs. She belongs to us!"

Ross drew her into his arms and pressed her cheek against his chest. "I know, Kathleen. It hurts me, too," he said, his voice rough with emotion.

Sobs were torn from her throat as she buried her face in the folds of his shirt and clung to him desperately. For long moments Ross stroked her hair and back and prayed for her tears to subside. He couldn't bear for her to be hurting this way. And though he'd never believed himself capable of loving any woman, he knew Kathleen meant more to him than his very life.

Eventually Kathleen pulled away from him and wiped her eyes with the back of her hands. She hadn't meant to break down in front of Ross. But the moment she'd looked up and seen him, she'd been struck by how much he'd become a part of her life. She'd been struck by the memory of him carrying Stormy into the house that first night. He'd been half-frozen and covered with snow. But his only thoughts and concern had been for the baby. She'd loved him for that. And for so many more reason, she loved him now.

That was why her heart was breaking. She not only had to give up Stormy today, she knew she had to give up Ross, as well. He was a man who deserved to have children of his own. And since she couldn't give him any, she wanted him to be free to marry someone who could.

"I'm sorry," she said, rising to her feet and pushing her tousled hair out of her face. "I didn't mean to get so emotional. I guess you think...I'm one of the weakest women you've ever seen."

"I don't think you're weak. I think you're human."

Swallowing the lump in her throat, she turned and walked over to the fireplace. She couldn't remain close to Ross, otherwise she might just fling herself into his arms. "Yes, well, I don't feel very human now. I feel dead inside."

Her defeated expression had Ross slowly shaking his head. "Kathleen, you can't give up now. You can't just say it's over, they took her and I'll never get her back. We've got to fight to get her back. The real mother wanted you to have her. Maybe there's a way she could simply sign the baby over to you."

Kathleen shook her head. "I don't think so. The mother is a minor. And even if she wasn't, I'm sure I'd still have to go through adoption procedures to get her."

"We're going to get her," he said firmly.

Her hands lifted, then fell back to her sides. "And how do you propose to do that, Ross? There's no telling how many couples are out there on a waiting list. Waiting for a newborn like Stormy to come along. My name will be way down at the bottom."

Fresh determination made Ross go to her and take her by the arm. "We had Stormy first. We were the ones who rescued her in that ice storm—that should count for something. We can talk to that lawyer of yours and tell him that we're going to be married. We can let him and the child-welfare department see how much we want her!"

Anger gave Kathleen the strength to jerk her arm away from his grasp. "I told you not to ever mention that word to me again! How could you...bring it up now? What are you trying to do, rip me completely apart?''

It was obvious that he'd angered her. But Ross didn't care. Anger was much better than tears. And now was the time for her to see how things really were, not after it was too late to do anything.

"You keep telling me how much you want the baby. So why don't you prove it? Why don't you quit trying to hide behind a bunch of excuses and prove how much you want her?''

Incredulous, Kathleen opened her mouth to protest. "I don't have to prove anything!" she spluttered, her eyes suddenly snapping with fire. "And I'm not trying to hide behind anything, either!''

"Yes, you are! You have all sorts of reasons and excuses not to marry me. But we both know they're not the real reason you're fighting me!''

Everything inside of her went stock-still. Did he know? Had he guessed that she loved him? She looked away from him and into the fire. "What are you saying?''

"I'm saying that you don't want to marry me because you're too afraid.''

"I'm not afraid! I'm—''

His hands closed around her shoulders, forcing her to turn her head and look at him. "Don't lie to me, Kathleen. The fear of living is more frightening to you than the fear of losing Stormy.''

"That's not true!" she cried, her whole body beginning to tremble.

His fingers bit into her shoulders as frustration drove him on. "It is true, Kathleen. When you look at me and Stormy, all you can think about is your husband and the baby you couldn't give him. You're not really thinking about me, or her, or what might be best for us! You're thinking about yourself!"

Her eyes were suddenly hard green rocks. "You—you cruel bastard!"

Before Ross realized what he was doing, he'd jerked her into his arms and captured her lips with his.

Instinctively, Kathleen raised her hands to push him away, but by the time they reached his chest, the anger inside her had been swept away by his kiss. Her fingers curled into his shirt, her lips clung mindlessly to his.

Ross had to force himself to tear his lips away from hers. "Goodbye, Kathleen. When you decide what it is you really want, you know where to find me."

Kathleen watched him walk away, wondering how long it would take for this ache in her heart to subside. And wondering, too, how long, if ever, it would take her to forget him.

"Kathleen, what do you think about this one?"

Kathleen looked at the pearl pink dress Olivia had

zipped Allison into and tried her best to look interested. "It's pretty. But it's too glamorous for a wedding."

Frowning, Olivia went over and pulled Kathleen off the dressing-room chair. "All right, you came with us to be a help. So you're going to help, not sit there on your butt and mope."

"I'm not moping," Kathleen argued with her sister-in-law.

"She is, isn't she, Allison?"

The youngest of the three women nodded in agreement. "I'm afraid you are, Kathleen. You haven't said more than three sentences since we came into this bridal shop."

Olivia shook her head. "I thought you were excited about Nick and Allison's wedding."

"I am. I couldn't be more thrilled about it. Allison knows that."

"Well," Olivia said, throwing her hands up in the air, "then act like it. The wedding is on Valentine's Day, remember? That gives us only a short time to get everything ready. And we've got to find the perfect dress, one that will knock Nick right off his feet the moment he sees Allison in it."

"That shouldn't be too hard. Nick is still walking on air."

Allison shook her head and Olivia groaned.

"Okay, I'll try to have a bit more enthusiasm, if

that's what you two want," Kathleen said. She gave them a broad smile. "There. Is that better?"

"It would be if it were real," Olivia told her.

Sighing, Allison stepped out of the pink dress. "Maybe I should just wear the dress Nick bought me. The one I wore at your wedding, Olivia."

Kathleen felt awful. She loved Allison and wanted her to have a wonderful wedding, but it was hard to put on a happy face when she felt dreadful. "Don't be silly. You deserve a beautiful wedding dress." She went to Allison and put her arm around her shoulders. "Don't mind my moodiness, Allison."

The younger woman put her hand on Kathleen's cheek. "We only want you to be happy."

"Yes, I know. And I will be. Just give me a little time, that's all I need. But for right now I'm going back out to the front to see if I can't find you another dress to try on."

As soon as Kathleen stepped out of the dressing room, Olivia and Allison exchanged worried looks.

"We've got to do something about this," Olivia said.

Allison nodded grimly. "You're right. But what?"

The women did find a wedding dress. It was made of antique ivory lace with a high collar and leg-of-mutton sleeves. The romantic style suited Allison beautifully, as did the color, which was a perfect foil for her tawny red hair.

Pleased with their success, the women decided to splurge on lunch at a nearby restaurant that served delicious Mexican food.

"I miss Nick so much since he had to go back to Fort Sill," Allison said.

The three women were sitting at a booth by the window, sharing a basket of tortilla chips and salsa while they waited for the main course to be brought to them.

"I know you do," Olivia said. "But at least we now know his transfer has come through and he'll be moving back here to Fort Chaffee next month. Having him home to stay will be worth the wait."

Smiling, Allison nodded in agreement. "Grandmother Lee was so happy to hear that we'll be living here. I think she would have missed Nick more than she would have missed me."

"We're all happy that you and Nick will be living close to us," Kathleen told her.

"Especially Sam," Olivia said. "He doesn't come out and say it, but I can tell that when Nick's not around, he misses him terribly." She glanced at Kathleen. "And he's also wondering why we haven't seen Ross lately. He'd like for him to come back over for supper one night this week."

Even though her heart lurched at the mention of Ross's name, she gave her sister-in-law an indifferent shrug. "I'm sure he would come if you'd give him a call. Just be sure and warn me so I won't be around.''

Olivia made a snorting noise. "Kathleen, I'm tired of tiptoeing around you. So is Allison. So is the whole family. We understand that you've been upset about Stormy. But what about Ross? We want to know what happened between the two of you.''

"Nothing has happened," Kathleen said, her eyes carefully avoiding the other two women. "Now that Stormy is gone there is no reason for us to be together.''

Olivia glanced at Allison before turning her attention back to Kathleen. "How can you say that?''

"Because it's the truth," she said shortly.

"Sam said that Ross asked you to marry him.''

Kathleen's hand trembled as she reached for her water glass. "Sam has a big mouth.''

"Sam? A big mouth?" Olivia echoed wryly.

"Well, in this case he had one," Kathleen said, "because he shouldn't have told you about it.''

Olivia sighed impatiently and Allison said, "We thought you were falling in love with Ross. Now you don't even want to see him.''

"You're right. I don't want to see him. When I'm—" She had to stop. She couldn't tell them that every time she was in the same room with Ross it tore her apart. Reaching for a chip, she forced herself to continue, "Just believe me when I say it's best Ross and I don't...be with each other.''

"Then you didn't care about Ross? You were just hanging around with him because of the baby," Olivia said.

"No, I..." An annoyed frown on her face, she looked at both women. "I don't have to explain my feelings about Ross to you two."

"No, you don't," Olivia agreed.

"But we care about you," Allison said. "And we know...well, you remember how mixed up and afraid I was when Nick asked me to marry him. You gave me the nudge I needed to make me see things clearly."

"And you surely haven't forgotten how miserable I was when I was trying to come to terms with my feelings for Sam. But even though I was miserable, you kept pushing me toward him anyway."

"Somebody had to," Kathleen said, a grimace on her face. "You didn't know your own mind. Neither did Allison."

"And you know your own mind about Ross?" Allison wanted to know.

Desperate to put an end to this interrogation, Kathleen leaned across the table toward the two women. "You both," she began in a quiet but fierce voice, "want to know how I really feel about Ross? I love him desperately. I'm miserable without him. But that's something I'm just going to have to learn to live with."

Allison shook her head in dismay, while Olivia let out a long, disappointed breath.

"Why?" Olivia asked.

Kathleen tried to ignore the pain in her heart. But it was impossible and it showed in her voice as she began to speak. "Ross doesn't love me. And even if he did, I wouldn't marry him."

"Very sensible," Olivia said with sarcasm. "It might make you happy and we can't have that. That would ruin your plans to be miserable for the rest of your life."

Kathleen kept her eyes fixed on the traffic outside the plate glass window. "You two think it's all so simple. And I guess it is to you. You each have a man who loves you."

"How do you know Ross doesn't love you?" Allison asked. "Have you asked him?"

"No. And I'm not going to. Because whether he loves me or not isn't the issue."

This brought looks of amazement to Allison and Olivia.

"Love isn't the issue?" Olivia repeated. "Come on, Kathleen, love is always the one and only real issue. Don't try to say it isn't."

"Okay," she said, realizing these two weren't going to stop unless she came out with everything. "I love Ross too much to marry him. You both know I can't have children. How could I do that to him?

He's a young man. How could I take away his chances of ever having a family?''

Allison reached across the table and touched Kathleen's hand. ''Maybe he'd rather have you.''

Kathleen's throat was suddenly lodged with tears, making it impossible for her to speak.

After a moment Olivia said, ''You know, when Sam asked me to marry him, he didn't turn around in the same breath and ask me if I could bear children. Women never really know if they'll be able to have children until they start trying to. And when a man truly loves a woman, that doesn't really matter to him.''

Allison nodded in agreement. ''I know I have Benjamin and that makes things a little different in my case. Still, Nick didn't ask me if I could bear more children. I know he would like them. But I know he would marry me even if I couldn't.''

Before anything more could be said, a waitress arrived with their meal. The three women began to eat, and eventually the conversation drifted back to the preparations for Allison and Nick's wedding. Kathleen was relieved, but she remained torn by what Olivia and Allison had said about love and having children.

Maybe she was wanting and expecting things to be too perfect. Maybe if she agreed to marry Ross, he would eventually come to love her, and nothing would matter to him except that they be together. It was more than her weary heart could dare to hope for.

Chapter Thirteen

The following day brought cold, drizzling rain. The dreary weather matched Ross's mood, but he didn't let it interfere with baseball training. Out on the gym floor, he had the boys do a calisthenics routine that would get them into shape before spring weather arrived and they could take to the field.

"Why can't we play catch, coach?" one of the boys in the group called to him.

Ross shook his head. "No gloves or baseball for at least another week. The team that wins the state championship this year will be the team that's the strongest. And I intend for that team to be you guys, so back to work. Ten laps around the gym. Up and down the bleachers," he added, to the consternation of the already tired boys.

As Ross watched the group head to the bleachers, he noticed a familiar figure standing at the edge of the court. All sorts of thoughts ran through his head as he jogged over to him.

"Hello, Ross."

Ross reached for Sam's hand and shook it warmly. "Good to see you. What brings you to school? Decide you wanted to play a little baseball?"

Sam grinned. "Not if I have to do all that," he said, motioning toward the group of boys jogging tiredly around the gym.

Ross laughed. "They don't like it, either."

Sam's expression grew serious again and Ross knew this man hadn't come here to make small talk.

"I'm not going to take up your time, Ross," he said. "I just came by to see why you haven't been over to the farm this past week. We've all missed you."

All of them except Kathleen, he thought ruefully. "Getting settled into this new position has kept me busy."

Frowning, Sam said, "Look, I'm not going to beat around the bush here. And I don't want you to, either—"

"Has Kathleen heard anything about the baby?" Ross asked quickly before Sam could go on.

"No, I'm afraid not."

"So...how is she? Kathleen, I mean."

Sam looked at him thoughtfully. "She's miserable.

That's why I'm here. I want to know how you really feel about my sister.''

"Sam, I'm not coming over to the farm tonight, so just forget it," Kathleen told him over the telephone. "All I want to do is eat a salad and relax in front of the TV."

"You never watch TV."

"I am tonight," she lied.

"Kathleen, you're making me mad."

"You can get glad in the same shoes," she told him, then hung up the phone before he could say anything more.

Normally, Kathleen loved to spend time with her family, but this past week they'd been smothering her. She realized they were doing it out of love, but what they didn't know was that it made her sadder to be around them. Sam had Olivia. Nick had Allison. Her mother and father had each other. Kathleen didn't have anyone.

Maybe that was her own fault, she thought sadly. Maybe what Ross had said was true. Maybe she was still living in the past, afraid to face the future and take life's risks.

Every night for the past week, she'd stood at the living-room window and stared through the woods toward the lights in Ross's house. She'd wondered what he was doing and how he would react if she were to show up on his doorstep.

Tonight she was staring at them again, the now-familiar ache in her heart weighing her down. At first she'd been so distraught over losing Stormy that she hadn't realized the full extent of her love for Ross. But now, after a week without him, she knew that he meant more to her than anything.

The fact had her turning away from the window and reaching for her sweater. Damn the risks, she whispered fiercely. On New Year's Eve she'd toasted in the coming year with Ross and made a resolution to forget her painful past. Now was the time to meet that resolution.

Ross had never been a man who got nervous. But tonight, as he prepared to go to the Gallagher farm for supper, the thought of seeing Kathleen was tying his stomach into anxious knots.

He'd been hoping, praying that this past week had given her the time and space she needed to see that they belonged together. Yet Kathleen hadn't approached him with a phone call or a visit, and now Sam had asked Ross to go to her. He wasn't sure it was the right thing to do, but he was desperate to make her understand that he needed her in his life.

He was pulling on his boots when he heard a knock at the door. "Just a minute," he called, wondering who could possibly be wanting to see him at this time of the evening.

When he opened the door and found Kathleen on the porch, he stared at her in total surprise.

"Kathleen!"

Her throat was so tight with nerves, she was forced to swallow before she could speak. "Hello, Ross. May I come in?"

He pushed the storm door open so that she could enter the house.

"I guess I should have called first. Is your phone working now?"

She looked around the neat living room, then at him. He was dressed in a pair of jeans and boots, and a white shirt that was unbuttoned and hanging loosely against his chest.

"Yes, it's working now. They hooked it up yesterday," he said, carefully shutting the door behind him.

Kathleen walked to the middle of the room, then stood facing him, her hands clasped awkwardly behind her back. It looked as though he'd just showered. His hair was wet and she could smell the faint scent of after-shave on him.

He began to button his shirt while Kathleen's heart began to race. "I, uh—were you going out? I wouldn't want to keep you."

From her question, she couldn't have known he was going to be at her family's for dinner tonight. Nor did she look as though she was planning on being there. She was wearing old jeans, a cardigan and a pair of ragged-looking flats. Her hair was pulled back into a ponytail and her face was devoid of makeup. In that moment he realized she'd never looked more beautiful to him.

"You're not keeping me," he assured her.

Kathleen moistened her lips with the tip of her tongue. "I guess after I saw you at the farm—" Not knowing how to go on, she stopped and drew in a bracing breath. "I've missed you."

Ross stared down at her, afraid to hope that her feelings had changed toward him. "I've missed you, too," he said.

She looked at him, wondering, aching. "Why didn't you come see me? Tell me?"

"Because you told me you didn't ever want to see me again. Remember?"

She sighed, recalling the day she'd lost Stormy, and then, later, had argued fiercely with Ross about marrying him. She'd been in agony ever since.

"Yes, I remember. But I was hoping you'd realize I didn't really mean it," she said, her eyes dropping away from his.

He continued to look at her. "If you didn't really mean it, why did you say it?"

Her hands lifted helplessly, then fell back to her sides. "Because I was desperate. And like you said, I was afraid." She looked back up at him, and as her eyes roamed his dear, familiar face, she couldn't hold back her feelings any longer. "I was afraid to tell you the truth."

Tentatively, his fingers reached out and touched her cheek. "And what is the truth, Kathleen?"

"That I love you."

Ross had prayed to hear her say those words, but he'd never expected it to happen. Now that it had, he was momentarily stunned.

"Oh, my Lord," he whispered in wondrous disbelief.

Afraid to see the rejection on his face, Kathleen quickly whirled around and away from him. "Now you know why I've been fighting you so."

Bewildered, he put his hands on her shoulders. "No, I don't know why. If you love me..."

She steeled herself to turn her head and look at him. "When I realized how I felt about you, I knew I couldn't settle for a marriage of convenience. And since that's what you want, I—"

His fingers gripping her shoulders, he gave her a little shake. "Kathleen, I proposed a marriage of convenience because I figured that was the only way I could get you to accept."

She shook her head from side to side, as though she couldn't believe what he was saying. "But you said...Ross, that very first night we met, you told me how you never wanted to be married, that family life wasn't for you."

"You told me the same thing," he reminded her.

"I know. But I changed my mind."

"So did I," he said, then drew her into the circle of his arms. "The moment I realized I loved you."

Kathleen clung to him as her whirling thoughts tried to take in what he was saying. "You love me?"

"Like nothing or no one in my whole life."

"I thought you wanted to marry me just because of Stormy."

His arms tightened around her and he pressed his cheek against the top of her head. "I do want to marry you because of Stormy. And because I want you to be my wife. A real wife. A wife I can hold in my arms. A wife I can make love to, and share the rest of my life with. But I was afraid to tell you that, Kathleen. I've never really been a part of a family before. When my parents got divorced, they both shut me out of their lives. That's why I vowed I'd never get married and put myself or an innocent child in such a vulnerable position."

She lifted her head away from his chest, and as Ross looked at her, he could still see doubt in her eyes.

"I understand that, Ross, but…this is all happening so quickly. We haven't really known each other that long."

"I don't need more time to know how I feel about you. Kathleen, this past week without you has been hell for me. Don't tell me we don't belong together. I won't accept that."

Her hands came up and framed his face. "I'm afraid I'll disappoint you. I only have myself to give you."

"Kathleen, ever since you told me you couldn't have children, I've wanted to ask how come you're so certain? Has a doctor told you there's absolutely no chance that you might conceive?"

She shook her head. "The doctors could never find a reason why I couldn't conceive. But since I never did, I assumed that something had to be wrong."

"Something was wrong," Ross agreed, "with your husband. Or was he tested, too?"

Kathleen grimaced. "No. He wouldn't agree to a fertility test. I guess it was an ego thing with him."

Ross's eyes were suddenly filled with hopeful light. "If your husband wasn't tested and you checked out healthy, then who's to say that things might be different with you and me? Maybe *we* could have a child together."

She gripped his forearms, afraid to let herself believe or hope that what he was saying might be true. "Do you really think there's an outside chance that the problem could have been with Greg?"

"I think there's more than an outside chance."

She studied his face, her expression guarded. "Maybe so, Ross. But what if it doesn't happen? What if I can't give you a child? I don't think I could bear it if you thought less of me. You deserve children and—"

"You deserve children, too," he said, drawing her closer against him. "And if we manage to adopt Stormy, we'll have one and it will be wonderful. If we don't, we'll have each other. And that's all that really matters, my darling Kathleen. You and me, sharing the rest of our lives together."

Happy tears filled her eyes. "Olivia and Allison tried to tell me you would feel that way. I was afraid to believe them."

For the first time since Kathleen had entered the house, he let himself smile. "I can see I'm going to have two very smart sisters-in-law."

She smiled back at him, her face an expression of pure love. "And I'm going to have a wonderful husband for the rest of my life."

Leaning his forehead against hers, he said, "Stormy might not be with us now, but she brought us together, and I thank God for that."

"Oh, Ross," she whispered, circling her arms around his neck. "Kiss me. Now, this very minute."

He crushed her to him, hungrily kissing her lips, her face, her throat. Kathleen touched him as if she'd never let him go.

Suddenly headlights swept across the room, warning them that someone had pulled into the driveway. Frustrated, Kathleen pulled away from him.

Chuckling, he said, "I see my smart sisters-in-law have called in the recruits. It's Sam."

"Sam!" Kathleen burst out. "Oh, my! He must

be hopping mad because I hung up on him. He wanted me to come over for supper tonight and now—"

"I know," he said with a sheepish grin. "That's where I was getting ready to go. Then you came and—"

She looked at him with surprise. "You were going to be at the farm tonight?"

Quickly, he went to her and held her in his arms. "Sam asked me to come. And I couldn't refuse. Not when I loved you."

Suddenly she was giggling. "Sam? A match-maker? This is wonderful!"

He bent his head and kissed her lips. "It's pretty wonderful, all right," he whispered as a knock sounded on the door. "Do you think we should let him in and tell him that he was successful?"

Laughing, she reached for Ross's hand, and together they went to give her brother the news.

Epilogue

One year later, the Gallagher farmhouse was ablaze with lights and filled with music, food and laughter, and most of all, family and friends.

It was New Year's Eve and it was also Stormy Douglas's first birthday. However, at the moment the little black-haired, green-eyed girl was crying her eyes out. Her cousin Ben had let the collies into the house so that he and Stormy could play with them, but her Uncle Nick had come along and spoiled all the fun by putting Jake and Leo back outside.

"Stormy," Kathleen said, as she drew her daughter onto her lap and tried to console her, "the dogs are too big to be in the house with all these people.

Besides, you don't want them to eat your pretty birthday cake!''

The child pointed her arm in the direction of the door and sobbed.

"She knows what she wants, Kathleen," Ella said as she moved through the room with a tray of snacks and drinks. "Maybe if you took her outside and let her see the dogs for a minute or two, she'd be satisfied.''

"Mom, that would be spoiling her," Sam put in.

Ella looked smugly over at her son who had Olivia, now six months pregnant, cuddled in the crook of his arm.

"Oh, and I'm sure once yours gets here, you're not going to spoil it at all," she said dryly.

Sam patted Olivia's rounded tummy. "Not at all," he assured his mother, then looked across the room at his brother, who was presently dancing with a pregnant Allison. "You're not either, are you, Nick?''

Laughing, Nick kissed his wife's cheek. "What? Spoil our coming baby? Not at all! We don't spoil Ben, and we won't spoil this one. We'll raise them all with army discipline. Right, Allison?''

This brought a howl of laughter from everyone in the room.

"Right, Nick, that's why Ben sneaked around to

the front parlor and let the dogs in," Allison told him.

Ross reached over and took Stormy from Kathleen's lap, which had become nearly nonexistent these past few weeks. Much to everyone's joy and wonder, Kathleen had not only conceived, she was eight-and-a-half-months pregnant and expected to deliver any day now. Proving to the doctors, and her family, that love was what really made babies.

"Well, Kathleen and I can't say we won't spoil ours," Ross told the group. "Because Stormy is already spoiled rotten."

"She's not spoiled," S.T. contradicted proudly. "She's just a stubborn-minded Gallagher."

"Amen," Ella echoed enthusiastically as she passed glasses of milk to her expecting daughter and daughters-in-law.

Ben suddenly raced into the room and didn't stop until he reached the couch where Stormy sat crying on her daddy's lap.

"Here, Stormy." He pushed a ragged replica of a basset hound at the girl. "You can have Buddy. He's a good dog."

Stormy's tears dried instantly as she gathered the cuddly old toy in her arms and wiggled down to the floor to play.

Her eyes misty, Kathleen looked over at Ross and smiled.

"One stops crying and the other one starts," he said with wry tenderness. "What's a man to do?"

"Pray the next one will be a boy," S.T. joked.

A week later the prayer was answered.

* * * * *

Another Man's Baby
KAY STOCKHAM

To Jessica Bird/J. R. Ward for describing
the many aspects of Garret's job. You *rock*!

CHAPTER ONE

PAIN SURROUNDED her pregnant stomach and sharpened with knifelike intensity. Darcy Rhodes swallowed once, twice, as the threat of hurling abated along with the cramp that had taken her so by surprise.

Sliding into the narrow, Tennessee mountain road's salt-rusted guardrail hadn't been fun, but at least she'd stopped with a fairly light, if jarring, jolt. For a split second mid-skid, she'd wondered if she would plunge right over the edge.

You just had to keep driving to make up for the pee stops, didn't you?

She collapsed against her Volkswagen's seat, barely daring to breathe for fear that the pain would return or, worse, the movement would cause the guardrail to break and send her hurtling down the mountainside. Before the cramp had hit she'd done little more than reassure herself that she hadn't been severely injured—all body parts were still attached—and all four wheels appeared to be on solid, if slippery, ground. But now...

Now what?

The passenger-side air bag had deployed on impact and sagged across the dash like a deflated balloon. Chalky powder filled the air, making her nose itch and her throat burn. Who *wouldn't* tense up and react to what had happened?

She took a deep, cleansing breath, coughing weakly because of the powder. The cramp was just that, a mixture of fright and the need to pee. A normal reaction. As soon as she twisted the keys in the ignition the car would start and she would be on her way once again, slowly but surely. The very first hotel she saw, no matter how dirty, smelly or disgusting, she would stop without a single complaint.

The steady stream of freezing rain quickly changed over to a sleet-snow mix, and she watched, dazed, while the little bits of ice globbed together on her windshield before slowly sliding toward the hood.

Ignoring the weather as best she could, Darcy grasped the keys and turned. Nothing. Not even a stutter. She tried again. And again. *Nothing?*

She stared out the moisture-blurred windshield, her mind too full to think clearly. Mostly because it flashed to the horror flicks she'd watched as a kid. She knew what happened to stranded motorists—they were always the first victims. Back then she'd clamped her hands over her eyes to escape the scary parts, but there was no escaping this. When had she last seen a car? Twenty minutes? Half an hour? "They had better sense and stopped somewhere."

And now you're talking to yourself. Someone will be along soon.

But when? Darcy groaned, all too aware the passenger door was a lot closer than it had been five minutes ago, and shifted to find her cell phone. When she couldn't, she leaned over to peer into the dim abyss of the passenger floor, the shadow she cast negating the illumination offered by the overhead light. At least her air bag hadn't deployed and she hadn't hit the console between the seats. If she had, she could've broken a rib, and her baby—

Not going to go there, she told herself firmly. "Everything is fine." Her thick coat and the pillow she used for comfort had cushioned the impact.

Finally spotting the phone lying near an empty sour-cream-and-onion chips bag, she managed to snag it, only to swear at the illuminated display. She shook the phone, held it up in various spots in the interior of the car, but the little bars indicating signal strength didn't budge.

Her mind chose that moment to flash on an image of the movie heroine having car trouble and a strange man appearing out of nowhere and offering to help, the bowie knife concealed until it's too late.

Stop it!

Darcy turned off the overhead light and stared out at the landscape revealed by her one remaining headlight. At least the battery still worked. It didn't power the heat, but she wouldn't have to sit in total darkness while her mind ran amok.

Cold seeped into the car with every gusty blow of wind, the battered little Bug rocking with the force. *And when the bough breaks?*

"Nothing's going to break. You're not going to—"

Something struck the rear, the *thump* startling her so badly her breath hitched in her throat. What was *that?*

She jerked around to look out the back window, the side mirrors, but saw nothing. The wind in the trees? A twig or branch? The road was littered with them, the combination of the wind and precipitation wreaking havoc on the area. Just her luck, she would have to get lost in the stupid forest.

Darcy double-checked the locks on the doors. If she jumped and tensed at every little sound, she'd be a basket case in no time. Maybe music would help? She turned the knob.

"And now a weather update…" Two seconds after finding a station, she groaned. In typical weatherman style, they'd gotten it wrong. The forecasted dusting of snow was now a full-fledged winter-storm advisory, and she was right in the middle of it with a car that wouldn't start and no cell service.

Where *was* everyone? Surely there was someone out on the roads. "Where's a cop when you actually need one?" She shoved her hair behind her ear, but it sprang right back.

"Be prepared for the worst," the too-chipper radio voice added. "We're in for a doozy. Stay indoors and conserve heat. Power outages are being reported throughout the listening area, and repair crews are running behind. For further updates and information, stay tuned. Up next is everyone's favorite, 'Don't worry, be happy.'"

Darcy rolled her eyes and turned the radio off with an angry twist of the knob. This couldn't be happening. Seriously, how many people got stuck like this?

Bands of muscle began to contract, up her back and around her middle. No, no, no. This was not happening. It was too soon.

She fought the pain, tensing, then just as quickly tried to will the muscles lax. She was fine. *They* were fine. It was only a cramp. The phone in one hand, she rubbed her belly, noted that it was hard as a rock and getting harder, the ache in her back growing sharper and more uncomfortable. "It's just a cramp," she whispered, eyes squeezed tight. Slow, deep breaths. In and out. Calm. Soothing. She gave massages for a living, she knew soothing. She could *do* soothing. It was mind over matter.

"Just calm down. A car w-will be along soon, and

this—" she exhaled, blowing the air out of her mouth "—is just a cramp…. Just an itsy-bitsy cra— *Ohhh!*"

The phone clattered as it hit the floor. Her hands fumbled, finally latching on to the steering wheel. She squeezed hard, a low moan escaping her lips she couldn't have held back if her life depended on it.

Finally the contraction—oh, God help her, they really *were* contractions!—subsided and that's when pure, unadulterated fear kicked in. No cell signal. Lost because of a wrong turn, stranded in the mountains in a snowstorm and—*in labor?*

"Oh, God, please. It's been a while. Okay, I know, it's been a long, *long* time, but please—" She bit her lip, unable to deny the truth any longer. "Help me. I can't do this here. I can't do this *alone.* I need help. *Please,* I need help!"

Time passed, minutes blurring together as contractions came and went. She remained where she was, her grip tight on the wheel, eyes closed during the worst of the pain when it felt as though her body was being shredded from back to front. Oh, please. Please, please, ple—

Bang-bang-bang!

The pounding on Darcy's car roof scared her so badly she shrieked and leaned sideways in the bucket seat to escape. How had she missed seeing the headlights of the vehicle stopped beside her car?

I've told you a million times, child. Ask and ye shall receive. Believe and, if it's His will, you'll be just fine.

She blinked, dazed by the combination of pain, surprise and the memory of her grandmother's voice.

"Hey," a man's voice called, "you okay in there?" *Bang, bang.* "Need some help?"

"Please don't let him have a knife." Her pain-tensed body tightened even more when she spied the large shadow looming outside her window. But what choice did she have?

Hoping Nana was right, Darcy flipped the lock, fumbled with the handle and pushed weakly, but the door didn't budge. She hit it with her palm.

Apparently catching on that the door wasn't opening, the man yanked twice before it gave with a shattering explosion of ice. "Are you all right?"

Unable to respond because the contraction hit its peak, she bit her lip and shook her head because it was all she could manage.

"Are you hurt?" The man's tone was more insistent.

She reached out and grabbed his overcoat to make sure he didn't leave and the soft, expensive feel of the cloth registered at the same time the banded muscles finally loosened their grip on her body. She fell against her seat in relief.

The man bent into the car, effectively blocking the opening and shielding her from the worst of the weather. She caught a brief sniff of his cologne. The dome light above their heads didn't illuminate much, but she was able to make out dark, close-trimmed hair, thick brows, a longish nose and the shaded roughness of lightly stubbled cheeks. He had to be gorgeous, didn't he?

His lips were turned down at the corners in a concentrated scowl, his expression clearly worried and concerned rather than threatening. A little of her anxiety eased, but not all. *If you sent me an angel, Nana, this one has black wings.*

"Where do you hurt?"

"I…I'm p-p— Oh, no." She moaned when another contraction made itself known, and vaguely heard her handsome rescuer mutter something indistinguishable when he realized the lump between her and the steering wheel wasn't just the bulk of her coat.

"You're *pregnant?*"

She managed a nod, imagining she heard his deep voice squeak a bit there at the end.

"Okay, uh— How far apart are the contractions?"

This pain ended fairly quickly and wasn't as intense as before. That was a good thing. Right? She released the air from her lungs in a gush. "They're…c-close together b-but irregular."

A glove-warmed hand brushed the hair off her forehead. He had calluses on his fingers, not thick or abrasive but there; something she wouldn't have guessed him to have, given his expensive appearance.

"How far along are you? Any special conditions? Who's your doctor?"

She struggled to focus on the questions. "I…I don't have a doctor. Not here. I'm on my way to Indiana." Her grip tightened on his coat. "I *can't* have the baby *here!*" She felt herself weakening, the fear she'd barely managed to keep locked away breaking free.

"Hey, no tears. Come on, sweetheart, don't do that to me," the man murmured. He brushed his thumb over her cheek.

The gesture had a calming effect, and even though her body ached and everything had gone wrong, she felt a connection with him.

Because he's the only thing standing between you and self-delivery. Did you even look *for a knife?*

"Stay still, okay? I'll go call for help. Don't move."

Like she could go anywhere else. The guy straightened and the door closed sharply, carried by the wind. The slam caused more ice to crack, and a small sheet slid down the windshield where it wedged beneath the wiper blade, obliterating her ability to see.

This was what it was like to suffocate. To feel hemmed in and confined, surrounded by darkness.

Melodramatic much? Just stay calm. All she had to do was keep it together and ignore the pain spreading along her back. Relax. *Breathe.* But what if the man didn't return? What if he went back to his car and drove away because he didn't want the responsibility of helping her? How many people *would* help her? Had it been someone else by the side of the road and her driving by, would she have stopped?

She gripped the steering wheel so tightly her fingers went numb. Then, as fast as it had come on her, the contraction ended, the tension subsiding to a dull ache.

Darcy huddled in her seat, cold in a hot and shivery, this-really-can't-be-happening kind of way. The baby would be fine. She had to believe that. She couldn't believe anything else because if she did—

She caught a glimpse of movement in her peripheral vision, unable to believe what she was seeing. The man's vehicle was *moving.*

Darcy straightened in the seat, her heart racing out of control the way it had when she'd been the new kid on the merry-go-round the bullies had tried to sling off. She flattened her hands on the window. Pounded on the glass. Her sweaty palms left prints behind. "Wait! Wait, don't leave!"

But the large vehicle drove on.

Images came again. First Stephen, his parents, the storm and the accident. The baby and now this. She dropped her forehead to the cold glass, fighting the cramping sensation as long as she could.

I asked, Nana. I asked! What now?

The contraction leaped from cramp status to uncomfortable, this-really-hurts *pain*. What now?

All she wanted was to give her baby the best life possible, make up for screwing up the beginning of its life. A nice home, someplace safe. Maybe a nice guy somewhere down the line. To *be* the mother—

You don't know how to be?

She wrapped her arms around her stomach and rocked. "*Please*…don't leave me."

CHAPTER TWO

GARRET TULANE DROVE past the little Volkswagen to a straightaway, then carefully began the arduous task of turning his large SUV around on the slippery, narrow road.

The conditions were dangerous no matter how good a driver was and, glimpsing the Florida tags on the newer model VW, he doubted the woman inside had a lot of experience with snow and mountains.

The attorney in him balked at the potential lawsuit she could file if something happened to her or the baby while in his care, but what else could he do? People bit the hand extended to help them all the time. It was a risk he had to take.

With the Escalade in position Garret got out, the blast of cold air actually feeling good on his adrenaline-heated body. Leave it to him to stumble upon a pregnant woman on a night like this.

He pulled open the VW's door and, for the second time that night, he inhaled evergreens and spices he couldn't identify. But it was the quiet sobs tearing out of the woman's chest that broke his heart.

"What's wrong? Did something else happen?" *Don't let her water have broken.* Unheroic or not, he grimaced at the thought of what that would do to his leather seats.

She raised her head and stared at him in surprise, her long lashes spiky with tears. "Y-you came back?"

Back? Humbled, he leaned a shoulder against the roof and reached out to wipe the tears off the cheek closest to him, noting the unbelievable softness of her skin. "Sweetheart, I wouldn't leave you here like this. I had to turn around and I didn't want to do it with you in the car in case I ran off the road."

The woman touched her tongue to her lips, wetting them. What he could see of her expression looked to be a mixture of disbelief, thankfulness and fear.

The stress of the day left him in that instant—work, family problems, the snow and the ridiculously expensive seats. Staring into her tear-streaked face he bit back his questions and anger as to why she was alone, and forced himself to smile. "Tell you what," he told her, grateful his head was being spared the biting shards of ice since he'd ducked beneath the car roof, "I'll forgive you for not believing in me if you'll tell me your name. Deal?"

She laughed abruptly, the gust of sound tear choked and rough. "D-deal." She gave him a wobbly smile, her cheek moving against his hand. "I'm Darcy, Darcy Rhodes."

"Garret Tulane." He dropped his palm from her face and took her fingers in his, squeezing gently. "Nice to meet you, Darcy." Shaking once, he let go but didn't move away. "You're not alone, okay? Not anymore. But we do have a major problem."

Darcy's brave face crumpled for a moment before she pulled herself together with a deep inhalation and a courageous nod. She looked down at her stomach, her hands roaming over the mound in rapid strokes indicative of her state of mind.

"You don't have a cell signal, either, do you?"

"No, but I do have OnStar and I contacted the hospital.

It's small and they don't have an ambulance available right now. Which means even though I'm a stranger, you're going to have to trust me enough to let me drive you there. Think you can do that?"

Fresh tears flooded her eyes, but she blinked rapidly and not a single drop fell. "I don't know where it is."

"Then you're in luck." Admiring her spunk, he bent lower and reached across her to unbuckle her seat belt. "Because I know exactly where it is. I work at the hospital and I could find it in my sleep. You'll be well cared for."

"You're a doctor?"

He saw hope flare in her eyes and hated to disappoint her. "No, but—" A firm little *whack* hit his arm where his coat had pulled back from his wrist. He glanced down in surprise. "Whoa."

Darcy snorted. "Kicks like a soccer player," she informed him, her expression sad and proud at the same time. "But it's too soon. I can't have the baby now because it's *too soon.*"

He stomped down his own fears of what the next hour or so might bring and tried to adopt a reassuring expression. "Hey, stress is only going to make things worse, right? So you can't stress," he ordered gently. "Try to relax and let me get you to the hospital. Concentrate on staying calm."

She sniffled but nodded, then took a deep, shuddering breath. "Hear that, Cameron? We need to destress. Garret is going to take us to the hospital, and you're going to stay put—that's an order."

He noted the way her stroking hands had slowed their frantic pace. "Good job." Once more he leaned over her, pressed the release on the seat belt and then pulled it loose. "Grab your purse and I'll help you. Be careful of the ice."

Darcy gripped his arm and held, her face a scant inch away from his. "My suitcase. Will you get it? I want my things, the baby's things. Just in case. It's in the trunk. Please?"

Garret bit back his impatience, but if he'd learned nothing else in his years working at the hospital, it was to not mess with hormonal, expectant mothers. "I'll take care of it. But let's get you settled first and strapped in, okay?" He braced himself while she shifted to get out. "Careful. That's it, I've got you." He wrapped an arm around her waist and held on while she walked the few steps it took to get her to the Escalade. Her foot slipped on the running board getting in.

Time slowed in that split second. Her foot slipped, Darcy gasped, and he wrapped his arms around her so that her weight fell against him, praying she'd land on him and not the ice. Somehow he managed to keep them both on their feet, his nose landing in her hair from where it spilled beneath a knit cap. Heart thumping wildly, they stood frozen for several long seconds. Finally Garret squeezed her gently to let her know she was safe, and urged her inside.

Grabbing the seat belt, he pulled it out for her to take and got another whiff of evergreen. He'd thought it was an air freshener inside her car, but the smell was too strong. Her perfume? Whatever it was, the scent was natural and earthy and completely unlike the heavy, designer fragrances Jocelyn favored.

The multiple lights over her head and from the dash were brighter than the single one in her small car, giving Garret his first good look at her.

A riot of soft blond curls tangled around Darcy's tear-streaked face. She had a small, straight nose—albeit red and runny—and what looked to be chocolate-brown eyes. But it was her full, wide mouth that held his attention. While she fumbled to latch the seat belt, she sank her teeth into the soft pink flesh of her trembling lower lip. He stared, transfixed until a blast of wind nearly knocked him off his feet, reminding him that now was not the time to be standing around.

Garret shook his head at himself and went for her suitcase, stowed it in the backseat of the SUV before climbing in beside her just in time to see Darcy's face tighten with the onset of another contraction.

"Garret?"

"Yeah, sweetheart?"

"Um…I think we'd better hurry."

DARCY HATED putting more pressure on her rescuer, but she was scared out of her mind. And with every contraction her fears quadrupled. She still had six weeks to go, so now was too early for this baby to arrive.

The vehicle slipped and slid, and maneuvering the ice-coated road required Garret's undivided attention. A good thing, considering how self-conscious she felt about having groaning, hug-the-belly pains in front of a gorgeous stranger. What if he had to deliver her baby?

Times like these called for her to be pragmatic but she hadn't shaved her legs and had worn her most comfortable panties. She didn't want her handsome driver to remember her due to the holes in her underwear. Wouldn't that be a story for his grandkids?

"How far is it?" she asked when the contraction was over and the silence in the vehicle became too much. "Are we close?"

"Very. Just relax."

"Why don't I believe you?"

Garret smiled, his teeth looking impossibly white. Why couldn't she have been rescued by a sweet little old midwife?

"Because you're too perceptive for your own good? The hospital isn't far, less than ten or fifteen minutes on a good day."

But what about a really bad one? "If the baby comes—"

"It won't."

"But if it *does* and you have to deliver it," she continued determinedly, her face growing hot. "I just want to apologize in advance." *For the underwear, the porcupine legs and the mess and trauma birth would cause the immaculate vehicle and you,* she added silently.

She shouldn't have waited so late in her pregnancy to move. She should have known Stephen would never come around and man up to being a dad. She should have moved months ago. In fall, not winter!

"Nothing's going to happen to you or the baby. And there's no need to apologize. You're getting yourself worked up because you're scared. Sit back and relax. Think happy thoughts."

Was he kidding? She closed her eyes and leaned her head against the buttery-soft seat. "I should've been more responsible and stopped for the night before it got dark. Then I wouldn't have made the stupid wrong turn."

"The weather front shifted suddenly. You couldn't have known. Besides, I don't know a single woman who wouldn't be frightened right now. But you've got to remember that stress isn't good for the baby. You're doing fine, Darcy. Just try to stop giving yourself such a hard time."

Easy for him to say. She could mentally kick herself all

the way to Canada and not be satisfied. The move, the weather. And she couldn't have spared five minutes to shave her legs? "Do you do that for a living? Give pep talks?"

Garret chuckled, the sound gravelly and soothing at the same time. "I push paper and placate temper tantrums more often than not. But sometimes pep talks are needed, too, so yeah."

He looked the type. Sort of like the old gentlemen farmers, all proper manners and clothes on the surface, but calloused and hard beneath. "Then I guess I'll listen to you. I mean I'm trying…" Her words trailed to a stop and she shook her head, unable to give voice to the horrible images rumbling through her brain.

What if the baby came? Would it live?

The void of their conversation was broken by the swoosh of the wipers, the heater fan blowing full blast and the crunch of the ice and snow beneath the tires. The SUV slid as they headed into a curve, and she gasped and braced herself to take a bite out of another guardrail. But other than lurching to one side, the big vehicle kept its course, and Garret's cool thinking and reflexes allowed him to maintain control.

He shot her an apologetic glance. "Sorry about that. You okay?"

She nodded, unnerved by the second close call. "It happens fast, doesn't it?"

"Yeah, especially in the mountains. I saw your tags when I turned around. You're from Florida?"

"Miami. I…I've lived in Miami the past four years." No sooner had the words left her mouth than the pain returned. She stiffened in the seat, trying hard to keep quiet. How could something that lasted mere seconds hurt so much?

When it was over, she couldn't stop shaking. "It's too quiet," she whispered abruptly.

"What kind of music do you like?"

"No, not— I…I need words. Music doesn't distract me b-because I can tune it out. Talk to me. I know you need to concentrate, but I keep thinking about all the things that could happen and— Tell me something. Anything. Recite the alphabet if you want to, I don't care. You said you work at the hospital? What do you do?"

Garret could probably feel her desperation, certainly hear it in her voice. While she'd like to have kept a cool head, it simply wasn't possible. What if she had this all wrong? What if something happened to her and the baby survived? What then?

Her stomach threatened to heave at her thoughts.

Stop this. Stop thinking worst-case scenario.

"I'm the administrative chief of staff at the hospital. It's basically a fancy title for a job that means I make sure the hospital runs smoothly. Contract negotiating, staffing, supplies, security. It all falls under a big umbrella that I oversee."

She lifted a hand to shove her hair off her face. "That sounds hectic."

"It can be. But it leaves the doctors and nurses to concentrate on what they do best."

"Another power player." Anger surfaced out of nowhere. Stephen had loved the authority that came with people reporting to him—especially the maids, although she hadn't found that out until after they'd broken up. Realizing she'd said the words aloud, she faltered. "Sorry. No offense."

"I don't take offense easily."

"I only meant that with a job like that you must enjoy… being in charge."

"I still have to report to the president and the board, but who doesn't like a little say-so in some way or another?" He shrugged. "One of my brothers refers to me as the gate-keeper."

A wave of heat swept over her and her heart picked up speed. Steadily increasing pressure tightened her muscles and gathered around her middle. "Is the nickname…appropriate?" *Don't think about the contractions. They're nothing. They don't—*

She must have made some noise because Garret's hands rotated on the steering wheel, like he wanted to twist and grind it into nothing. The sight touched her more than words could. If he could take the pain away, do something to help her, she knew without a doubt he would. How sweet was that?

"I guess I could be called a scaled-back adrenaline junkie. I get my kicks from solving problems in high-stress situations."

"You must be loving this, then."

He reached over the console and placed his hand on her forearm. "No man likes seeing a woman in pain. Hang in there, we're getting closer."

She tried to smile but couldn't. They might be getting closer, but so were the contractions.

CHAPTER THREE

"Focus, Darcy. Don't think about the pain or worry about what's not going to happen. What did you do in Miami? Huh? Sweetheart, talk to me."

Darcy supposed the situation called for a get-to-know-you info dump because if the baby decided to make its debut, he'd get to know her a *lot* better sooner rather than later. He should probably know a few things about her before discovering she preferred hi-cut low riders over the thongs she'd set aside at five months.

"I worked for a couple of privately owned hotels, before that a gym and a hotel chain." She hesitated, glimpsed his expectant expression for her to fill in the blanks and sighed. "I'm an aromatherapist. I use scented oils in massage therapy."

She waited, really not in the mood for a snarky comment about her profession. Would he be like other people? Look at her, her belly, and smirk?

"Are you having another contraction?"

He probably thought so because of the way she was grinding her teeth, but grasping the excuse, she closed her eyes and leaned her head against the seat. Let him think what he wanted. She knew all guys weren't hound dogs, but her experience working in Miami was that *most* guys who dressed like Garret and drove vehicles like this equated her profession to prostitution. Toss in her pregnant, unmarried state and— Well, most men assumed that she'd played sex games with one too many of her clients and was now paying the price.

You're awfully sensitive, there. This guy hasn't said a word.

But how long would it be until he did? Stephen's parents, and Stephen himself, had had plenty to say about the pregnancy. They'd gotten down and dirty in the insult department when she'd refused to do their bidding and abort.

"Have you ever seen snow?"

She wet her lips, relaxing slightly. *Thanks for sending me a gentleman, Nana.* "I'm originally from southern Indiana, so yeah, I've seen snow."

"And you said you're moving back there? How'd an Indiana girl wind up in Miami?"

Darcy nibbled her lower lip, her gaze on her hands as they moved over her stomach. "The Indiana girl thought Miami was warm and a great change of pace."

Another contraction consumed her, heat first, then pain, harder than any of the others. She leaned forward, balling up in an attempt to fight it.

"Easy. Try to breathe."

"C-can't."

"Yes, you can." He put her hand on her back, rubbing gently. "Come on, Darcy. Listen to my voice. Breathe out, slowly. Good. Now inhale."

When it was over, she straightened and glared at him. A man should have to experience childbirth. *Don't be so cocky,* you *haven't experienced it yet.* "Are we close? Please, tell me we're close."

"Getting there. Beauty is a great little town," he added, pride lacing his voice. "Very low crime, everybody knows each other. I went away to college, but moved back once I graduated because I missed it so much. Some guys want to travel the world, but I knew all along I wanted to stay close to my roots. Wait until you see it and you'll understand what I mean."

"It sounds nice. I—I want that for my baby. Roots and stability. That's why I'm moving back home." But it wasn't home. It hadn't felt like home even when she lived there. Was she doing the right thing?

"Families are good to have around, especially when there are kids involved. I have three brothers and a sister, plus the parents and a huge assortment of aunts, uncles and cousins."

One aspect of his story stuck out in her mind. "Your mother went through this *five* times?"

Garret chuckled, the sound a smooth bass. "Four, actually. My younger brothers are twins."

At the mention of his brothers, his expression grew... mournful? Whatever it was, something in his tone kept her from asking for more details, much as she wanted to. She was curious by nature and having no real family of her own, she loved hearing about other people's.

That was the best part of her job. Facedown on the table, some of her clients habitually unloaded their family problems as though she were a shrink. She knew the names of children, grandchildren. Pets. She'd learned when to ask questions and when to keep quiet and let them ramble.

Garret wasn't rambling. "Is the, um, hospital a good one? Nice people and all? And the baby unit? Are they good with preemies?"

Once again he reached over and squeezed her arm. She felt the heat of his touch through her coat and appreciated the comfort it brought. She wasn't her mother. She didn't hang all over men trying to get them to notice her. If anything she kept her distance and waited them out. But Garret's frequent caresses weren't creepy or touchy-feely, just…nice.

"You're not going to have a preemie. We're going to get there and they're going to stop the contractions. We're not far, but I have to go slow or risk driving us over the side of the mountain."

"I know." She rubbed her aching head with her free hand. "I couldn't believe it when I started to slide. I was going *so* slow, but— My car's really screwed up. It wouldn't start after I crashed and I don't know where to get it fixed or when I'll be able to get back on the road. What if they can't stop the labor? What if the baby has to stay in the hospital for a while? I need to get settled in Indiana, find a job and get an apartment, but…I could be a mom tonight."

Or not.

Chills racked her. The baby had to survive. Be okay. But if they couldn't stop the labor and it *was* born tonight— Was she ready for this? The crying and feeding and supporting, *raising*. And later? If she managed to do all those things, no way was her baby going to drive at fifteen. And dating? Yeah, right. Samuel Tolbert had tried to feel her up at that age—and go a lot further. She'd kneed him in the nuts and walked home. No way would her son or daughter be anywhere near the opposite sex before they were twenty—at least!

"I can recommend a great mechanic. There's nothing he can't fix, so you don't have to worry about that."

She made a face. "Hate to tell you this, but if you drive this kind of vehicle and are still going to the shop a lot for him to fix things, your mechanic is a crook."

Another chuckle. The man would make a fortune bottling the sound.

"Not Nick. He's my brother and a good guy."

There it was again. That tone of his was…sad. "Why do you say it like that?"

While he remained staring straight ahead Garret's expression changed to one she couldn't read. "Like what?"

"If he's a good guy, why do you sound sad about it?"

"I guess because the family doesn't see much of Nick even though he owns the garage in town."

"Should I ask why you don't see him…or keep my mouth shut?"

"It's complicated."

She squirmed, unable to get comfortable. Her back was killing her. "You two have a big fight over a girl?" Tension crept in, slow and sure, wrapping around her like a python, squeezing, *squeezing,* until she couldn't breathe.

"It was nothing like that. Long story short, Nick went against the family wishes and dropped out of high school. Our parents, grandparents—everyone got involved from teachers to the guy at the feed store. And the more people talked, the more distanced and angry Nick became. Things have been tense ever since."

"How long ago…was this?" She gritted her teeth and fought to focus on Garret instead of the pain.

"About fifteen years."

"And they're—*oh*—still upset?" She gasped out the words.

The Escalade slid to the left as they started across a bridge, and Garret slowed even more. She wanted to scream at him to go faster, but couldn't take a breath.

Shaking, unable to fight the tears or the pain any longer

and pretend she could do this with dignity, she released a low groan. "G-Garret?"

"Yeah?"

"I don't think we're going to make it."

GARRET GLANCED at his watch when the contraction finally released its hold. That one had lasted forty-two seconds. No way could he deliver a baby. A legal brief he could handle. A crisis involving multiple unions—a friggin' walk in the park. But a *baby?*

Over the crunching precipitation, he heard Darcy moan, and glanced over to see relief etched on her pale, strained features. "Good one?"

"Oh, yeah."

There were tears in her voice, one trickling down her cheek. Considering they were still miles away from the hospital, the sound and sight sent chills through him. Twenty miles an hour on a winding mountain road was getting them nowhere fast.

"Go on," she murmured. "Please, tell me the story about your brother. It helps to focus on someone else."

He looked at the road ahead of him, not liking the subject but willing to go along with the request. Whatever it took to get both their minds off the present predicament. "Nick dropped out as soon as he didn't need our parents' permission. They were disappointed and upset, and when they couldn't get Nick to do what they wanted, they looked to me to get Nick to change his mind."

"Why you?"

"I'm older than him and a good negotiator. Even as a kid, I settled the arguments in my family." He smiled wryly, various scenes popping into his head. "I actually used to hold court about my siblings' disputes. I'd hear the sides and make a judgment on everything from whose box of crayons it really was to who got to ride in the front seat. But this fight— It was huge. In the end Dad got frustrated and lost his temper. He and Nick are a lot alike that way. Dad told Nick he either had to stay in school or get out of the house."

"The perfect words to make a teenager rebel."

"Exactly. So Nick left. He moved out and lived in a storage area above our uncle's garage."

"Poor guy."

He found himself chuckling at Darcy's description, glad to have something to smile about. "Poor, he's not. Nick's done really well for himself. My uncle owns a variety of businesses around town and he gave Nick a job in his garage."

"Then he's okay?"

She was worried about Nick? Garret nodded to reassure her, liking her compassion. How many people in her situation would be thinking of someone else? "He's done better than okay. A few years later Uncle Cyrus had a heart attack and couldn't work for a while. Nick stepped up to the plate and ran the garage on his own." He flashed her a grin. "Picture an eighteen-year-old kid bossing around mechanics two and three times his age—and getting away with it."

"Your uncle didn't mind?"

"Nah, Uncle C. was so impressed by all the compliments about Nick's work and business ethic that he sold out to Nick when he retired. That's why I said Nick's not a crook. He's had years to take advantage of people if he wanted, but I've never once heard someone say that he's ripped them off."

"Sounds like your brother deserves all the praise after working so hard."

"I think so. He bought the building beside the garage not long ago. It was a gym he went to until the owner started going under because of poor management and rumors of cameras in the women's locker room."

"Pervert. So Nick's a real entrepreneur."

"Yeah, despite his lack of education, turns out he's a great businessman. He's a pretty good dad, too."

Normally he wouldn't dream of discussing Nick and his family's situation with an outsider. Garret couldn't remember ever really discussing it with Jocelyn, but something about Darcy made him feel comfortable. She wasn't judgmental; instead she was supportive, acting as though she could relate.

"He's doing all of that and raising a child?"

Garrett nodded. "He's got one kid. My nephew."

"Good for him. He showed the family, didn't he? He struck out on his own and did well, all the while being a dad. That's admirable."

Darcy was obviously a compassionate person, but when she spoke it was as though Nick's achievements were her own. Because she dreamed of doing the same thing herself? Striking out and being a success while raising her baby? While Garrett applauded independence, he couldn't help but wonder where the baby's father was.

Politically correct or not, what kind of man allowed the mother of his child to travel so far alone? He'd noticed her lack of wedding band. How upset would she be if he asked?

It's none of your business.

"You should be proud of him."

He *was* proud of Nick. Once his little brother had gotten away from the family, Nick's confidence and abilities had soared. There was something significant in that.

Garret turned onto the more heavily traveled road leading to Beauty, thankful the salt trucks had already been there. He still couldn't race to get his passenger to the hospital, but he was able to pick up speed. This close, he wouldn't have to deliver anything but Darcy into the welcoming hospital doors. "I don't want to leave you with a bad impression of my family. They're great, and they love Nick. All of us do. Things simply got out of hand and snowballed."

"That's a *really* bad joke given the weather." Her breathing picked up as another contraction hit.

He glanced at her repeatedly, wishing he could do more to help.

"Families d-don't always get along, but th-they should stay close. Don't you think?"

"Yeah, I do. But what about you? Would you like me to call someone for you? The baby's father?"

Her curls stuck to her cheek when she shook her head. "No."

Hurt, anger. Regret or sadness. The multilayered emotions flickered over her face before Darcy's features smoothed into one of grim determination.

"I'm sorry, Darcy. You would've asked if you wanted my help. That's none of my business."

"It's okay. Obviously if I'm in the middle of Tennessee alone, there's a problem, right?" Her mouth turned down at the corners. "The father and I aren't together. He signed away his rights so I would leave him alone. This baby is entirely mine."

Silence followed her words, but he could've sworn he heard her whisper, *If it makes it.*

Knowing she had every right to be worried and angry at the idiot who'd take advantage of her, he grasped her hand, holding it loosely.

After a moment, a sniffle; her fingers tightened around his. "Garret?"

"Yeah?"

"Are we there yet?"

CHAPTER FOUR

NOT LONG AFTER she'd asked the age-old question in an attempt to lighten the intensity of the moment and the effect Garret holding her hand had on her emotions—who knew holding hands could feel so good?—they pulled beneath the hospital's canopied E.R. entrance. He hurried out of the Cadillac to get help.

Darcy watched as he disappeared inside the double doors, sending up a prayer of thanks because they'd made it safely. She'd been found, and not by a knife-wielding psycho.

The doors slid open again and Garret emerged with several smocked individuals. Within moments she was placed in a wheelchair and whisked inside. Her last glimpse of Garret was as he stood beneath the harsh outdoor lights talking with someone, his dark hair and long wool coat very dramatic against the snowy backdrop.

"When are you due?" an aide asked.

"Mid-March. I've got s-six weeks left." They rushed by the waiting area and veered left.

"Have you had any problems before now?"

Forcing herself to focus on one problem at a time, she nodded reluctantly. "Cramping, if I overdid things. But my doctor in Florida ran some tests and said everything was normal."

The woman wheeled her into an elevator that soared to the second floor with stomach-jarring swiftness, and off they went again. Darcy saw a Labor and Delivery sign posted above a set of doors and after keying in a code, the aide pushed Darcy through as another contraction hit.

"Almost there, honey."

She wheeled Darcy into a room and then disappeared, leaving her in the hands of two waiting nurses. The contraction ended and they helped her step out of the wheelchair. While one nurse went to work on removing Darcy's coat, the second nurse shut the door and snagged a cart from its position near a wall, pushing it toward the bed. It was loaded down with supplies and a machine that looked like something off a space ship.

"What's that?" Darcy asked, wishing absurdly that Garret had accompanied her. She could've used a hand to hold.

"Don't worry about anything, hon," the older of the two nurses said. "We're going to get you in a gown and then we're going to start you on some fluids. After that, we'll hook you up to a monitor to get a reading on the baby's heartbeat, and find out what's going on. I'm Betty," the woman added, "and this is Debra. If you need anything and we're not in here, you press that call button right there on the bed. But don't get up, and don't mess with these machines. If something slips or moves, you call us. Got it?"

Darcy nodded dazedly.

"Good. Now let's get you settled in and all hooked up."

She begged a trip to the bathroom, hoping the act would ease the cramping. It didn't. When she emerged, the nurses helped her out of her blouse and propped her against the bed as another contraction built in intensity. While she breathed through it, they stripped her down, guiding her arms into a gown and snapping it closed with minimal fuss. Their impersonal attitude allowed her to set aside her embarrassment over her hairy legs and ratty underwear.

At least Garret's not seeing it.

The nurses wrapped straps around Darcy's stomach, inserted an IV into her arm with surprising gentleness and fired so many questions at her she could barely answer one before the next query came. Finally the nurse who'd been prepping her with needles, blood pressure cuffs and monitors stood back and checked her handiwork.

Betty finished taking notes in the chart, then smiled. "We're all set. Debra and I are going to check on our other patients, but we'll watch the monitors from the desk. You just lie there and relax. Mr. Tulane specifically asked for Dr. Clyde, and you're in luck because she's still here. She's in delivery right now, but soon as she's done, you'll meet her."

"Where's…Mr. Tulane?" She'd almost referred to him as Garret, but here and now the closeness she felt after the rescue didn't seem appropriate.

"I have no idea. You must have been so frightened. Were you stuck out there long?"

She wasn't sure. "A while."

"Well, we'll take good care of you. Don't worry about anything."

She knew they needed to go, that they had other patients to tend to, but she didn't want to be alone. "Wait—please." She made herself meet their gazes. "Am I going to lose my baby?"

Both nurses fussed and smiled at her before they left to get someone to help her with the necessary paperwork. But neither of them answered her question.

When they were gone, Darcy wrapped her arms around

her belly and held tight, ignoring the pull of the tape
holding her IV in place.

Stephen had gone on and on about how people like
them weren't meant to be parents.

Please, God, don't let him be right.

"DON'T YOU EVER LEAVE?"

Garret looked up from his desk to see Tobias Richardson standing in the doorway. Turning so that Toby could
see the phone he held pressed to his ear, Garret reluctantly
waved his friend in and tried to push through his distraction to concentrate on the hospital president's words.

But every time he closed his eyes he remembered the
look on Darcy's face, the feel of her fingers holding on to
his. It had only been a moment, several minutes at most,
but something about it had gotten to him.

"I want something done and I want it done *now*."

Harold Pierson growled the words into Garret's ear and
jerked him from his thoughts. His boss wasn't a patient
man, and the fact it was midnight on a Friday only seemed
to increase Harry's insistence that his demands be met.

Garret rubbed his forehead, pen in hand. "I spoke with
maintenance before I called. The problem's been taken
care of."

"You're sure?"

If Harry would leave well enough alone, then yeah,
Garret was sure. "Yes. I also had the men double-check the
generators and the salt supplies. Everything's taken care of.
Trust me on this and try to enjoy your weekend." *So I can
enjoy mine.*

"What about the meeting Monday morning? Are those
idiots still driving down from Nashville?"

As of January first, Beauty Medical Center had become

a branch location for a much larger university hospital based in Nashville. According to Harry, the merger was the death knell of all they held dear. Garret knew enough to keep his mouth shut about his belief that the change was the best thing to happen to the town and the hospital. "I'll contact you once I know the meeting's status."

"Are you spending the night to keep an eye on things?"

He didn't doubt Harry would like for him to do just that. But having put in nearly eighty hours this week, the last thing Garret wanted to do was sleep here. Bad enough he hadn't gotten any work done until after Harry had left. Once he knew Darcy was okay and the roads had another layer of salt on them, he was out of here. "If there's a problem, I'll handle it over the phone or drive back in."

Toby grunted at his statement, and Garret shot him a warning glare. Garret did *not* need Harry to overhear Toby's mutters. Harry didn't like Toby for the sole reason that he thought Toby had overstepped his humble upbringing by becoming an attorney.

Well, that and the lawn incident. Twenty years ago Toby's mom—Harry's housekeeper for a very brief period of time—had arranged for her son to mow Harry's lawn. He had watched Toby the entire six hours required to mow and weed the yard. When Toby had finished, Harry had refused to pay because he claimed Toby had done it wrong. In retaliation, Toby had dumped the day's accumulation of grass clippings in the pool.

"If that SOB in maintenance spouts his nonsense again—"

"I've taken care of everything." Garret opened the desk drawer and searched through the Tums, Alka-Seltzer and peppermints for something to ease his pounding head.

"Fine, then. You take care of things but keep me posted. I'm counting on you, Garret."

"I know, sir. I won't let you down."

Toby grunted again. "Suck up."

"You're a good man," Harry said. "Jocelyn complained the other day that I'm working you too hard, but I assured her you were only doing your job."

Garret concentrated on Harry's first comment and ignored the second. He was doing his job plus the majority of Harry's. Over the years Harry had piled more and more on Garret's shoulders. Now Harry had a damn good golf swing and Garret practically ran this place without receiving any credit.

Don't get too big for your britches. You do that and you'll end up going naked cause nothin' fits your ego.

Garret pinched the bridge of his nose, a smile pulling at one side of his mouth. Man, he missed Grandpa. "I'll be sure to call Joss tomorrow."

"You do that. She's been working quite a bit herself lately. Her mother thinks it's because she's lonely and missing you with all the hours you're putting in on the merger. But I'm thinking it's something else entirely."

"Something else, sir?" He ignored Toby's impatient glance at his watch. "Is something wrong?"

"Nothing you can't fix. Did you know I proposed to my Charlotte on Valentine's Day? This year will be twenty-nine years. The date's creeping up, you know."

The hint wasn't subtle. Neither were any of the others Harold had dropped over the past year. "I believe you've mentioned that."

Harry's booming voice had to be carrying to Toby's ears. Garret swung sideways in the office chair in a poor attempt to gain some privacy.

"I suspect you'll do right by our girl then. Soon."

"Of course, sir. If there's nothing else, I'll talk to you tomorrow. I've got a few things to take care of before I head home."

"Fine, fine. Go take care of business. When you talk to maintenance again, tell them I expect hospital property to be clear at all times, and that idiot—"

"Understood," Garret said before Harry could go off on another tangent about the Maintenance Department's performance. The team was top-notch, but Harry wasn't satisfied. "Good night, sir." Garret dropped the phone and held up a hand when Toby immediately opened his mouth. "Don't—"

"Comment on that? Yeah, right. The Whipping Boy's getting an earful tonight. What's got the old goat's goat?"

Garret glared at his friend and returned to his search of the drawer. Finding what he wanted, he pulled out some ibuprofen and downed two with the help of lukewarm root beer left over from lunch twelve hours earlier. He grimaced at the flat taste. "What are you doing here?"

"I was wondering the same thing about you." Toby nodded toward the door. "Maria's in labor and Rob's trying to get back from a business trip in this mess so I got elected to drive her and Ma. Labor and Delivery is a busy place tonight."

"Always is when the barometric pressure drops or there's a full moon. Freaky stuff," Garret muttered, referring to all the cyclical and otherwise unexplainable things that happened in a hospital. He'd learned to prepare for these events over the years after being caught off guard the first year or so on the job. Weather changes were nearly as busy as holidays when families turned against each other and the world's most inept chefs decided they wanted to be Emeril and speed chop.

"You can say that again." Toby's agreement was packed with the vehemence of a confirmed bachelor. "I grabbed this on the way out, thinking I'd slip it under your door." He lifted the file and waved it in the air for a few seconds to make his point before dropping it onto the desk. "The Jacobs settled and agreed to no press statements or public discussions regarding the case. Signed and sealed."

"Thank God." Garret rubbed his hands over his face in an attempt to ease the tension and fatigue. At least that was one problem handled with minimal fuss. The doctor at fault had been ordered to seek employment elsewhere months ago. But keeping the hospital's name out of the papers because of a surgical accident hadn't been easy. Or cheap.

"You know," Toby said, "we could always go through with our plan from law school."

"Beauty would never be the same with the two of us in practice together."

"Just an option to think about. Gotta admit we'd set the white shoe boys on their asses if we did."

Garret nodded as he always did whenever Toby brought the subject of a partnership up, and added the file to the stack he would take home with him—a stack to match the one already in his SUV from his first attempt to leave. He needed to review the settlement before passing the news on to the board at the meeting Monday morning. If there *was* a meeting. Having to reschedule would screw up a whole week's worth of meetings. Was that what life was about? A series of meetings? Was he destined to spend his days listening to Harry complain?

Toby's reminder about their law school ideas left Garret scowling. He'd like to say that opening a practice had been the pipe dream of two idealistic attorneys out to change the world, but that wasn't true.

"You look like hell. Bad day?"

"You could say that." Garret stacked the piles together and stuffed them into his briefcase. He'd told the nurses to call him if things took a turn for the worse and they weren't going to be able to stop Darcy's labor. Did that mean they had? He should've instructed them to update him no matter what.

"I heard that trip to Nashville yesterday scored you a nice ride."

He grimaced. News traveled fast. It had been Harry's responsibility to go to Nashville, but the president had balked at the last minute with a bogus excuse, sending Garret to deal with the university hospital officials instead. Knowing he'd come back to a disaster after a single day away, the visit to the car lot had been a gift to himself. "Always wanted a convertible. It'll be delivered this spring in time for the pretty weather."

He stood and pulled on his coat, piled more files into the already-full briefcase and led the way to the door. Another week gone in the blink of an eye. It wouldn't be so bad if he didn't leave his house before six every morning to hit the gym and arrive at work before the sun did more than brighten the horizon. Why buy a convertible if he could only drive it in the dark? "You'll love it when we take it to the course for the charity golf tournament in June."

Toby waited while Garret locked the office. "Like that'll happen. You'll cancel again. What was it last time? Something to do with the nurses' union?"

"Security upgrade," Garret corrected automatically, his brain clicking through time and events by the problems that had crept up and ruined his enjoyment of them. Toby had a point there, as much as Garret hated to acknowledge it. The odds were against him. "The new system kept going off every five minutes, and it was upsetting all the parents with infants in the nursery." He lifted the leather case and used the worn corner to punch the down arrow at the elevator. "You'll thank me once your niece is in there and all is quiet."

"That law degree must really help with handling that kind of stuff."

Garret twisted his neck, sighing in relief when it popped loudly. "Enough, Tobe. My job may not be one hundred percent law—"

"Or even twenty."

"—but I'm good at what I do and—"

"Your father and grandfather worked hard to get you the position," Toby muttered, his voice reeking of boredom as he made the statement. "Hey, I get that there are perks, and I know guys who'd kill for your pay. But for all the hours and headaches I don't see much in it for you besides a ridiculous salary and a prime parking space. Is the money worth all…that?" He indicated the bulging briefcase.

"Everything's going to be shut down because of the snowstorm. Joss and I are supposed to get together this weekend, but with the snow I thought maybe we could stay in and—"

"Work?" Toby smirked.

"Back off, Tobe. Not now, okay?"

His friend looked away, an apologetic expression on his face. "Sorry."

Knowing he should quit while Toby seemed prepared to drop the subject, Garret sighed. "But?"

Toby hesitated a long time. "But," he drawled slowly, "I think it would take a saint to put up with your plans for a snowy weekend." He grinned. "What happened to 'Bare-it Garret?'"

"It was *initiation*."

"Yeah, well, I still can't believe you wanted to be a part of those drunken idiots."

"Lesson learned. Can we move on? If you've got something to say, spit it out."

"This is perfect weather to get stranded with a beautiful woman. Yet you're planning to *work* for the next forty-eight hours? Give me a break. I'm stuck here, but what's your excuse? When was the last time you spent the weekend in bed with Jocelyn?"

CHAPTER FIVE

GARRET SCOWLED at his friend. "This isn't the high school locker room." He was prepared to deflect the issue rather than acknowledge that Toby was right.

"I'm not asking for details, just trying to make a point."

"Which is that I should take Joss to bed?"

"Yes. No!" Toby shut his eyes and ran a hand through his hair in frustration. "It's just every time I call or see you, you're *here*. It's gotta be hard to have a relationship that way."

The elevator chimed and the doors slid open. Garret stepped on, thankful it was empty. It had been a long, hard week and he was too exhausted to examine his life. That would require brain power he didn't have. He wanted to check on Darcy's condition and make sure she'd stabilized, drive home and go to sleep, all without having to process or think.

"Look, the fact that you're not saying anything says you know I'm on to something." Toby followed Garret into the elevator and punched the button for the cafeteria level.

"You're not on to anything. I'm humoring you by not arguing." Garret punched the L&D floor and hoped his friend wouldn't notice.

"You forget where you parked?"

"I have to stop by the nurses' station and check on something." If he told Toby the truth, his friend would go off on another tangent about how Garret went overboard when it came to his job. To some, simply bringing Darcy in meant his Good Samaritan deed was done. But to him a visit was the least he could do. She was all alone, scared. His right hand curled with the memory of her hand clutching his.

Toby remained quiet, but Garret was aware of his scrutiny the entire time. The elevator chimed and the doors opened once more.

"Remember Michelle?"

He'd known Toby wasn't through. "Why?"

"You pretended to be sick halfway through a date because you said she snorted every time she laughed."

"It was annoying as hell."

"But you didn't tell her that. And what was the other one's name? The one with the big boobs? Rachel? Rochelle? She lasted, what, a month? You ended things with her after you caught her not giving the excess change back to the cashier when she'd given her too much."

"The point, Toby?"

"What are you waiting for? You haven't ended things with Jocelyn, but you haven't moved forward, either. You're in a holding pattern."

Garret glanced around to ensure the hallway was clear before he rounded on his friend. "You know, you're beginning to sound like Harry."

Toby shoved his hands into the pockets of his leather coat. "That's low. Can't we have a simple discussion?"

"You're not looking for a discussion, you're looking for a debate, and so help me—"

"Why haven't you popped the question? You bought the ring."

Garret locked his jaw to keep from swearing a blue streak. "Keep your voice down."

Toby shrugged like a man who knew it wasn't *his* bachelorhood on the line.

Garret stepped closer. "What is this about?" The doors started to close and he shoved the briefcase out to hold them open. He told himself to let it go, to drop the discussion and get out of there while he could. But something wouldn't let him. "What is it you're trying so hard not to say?"

Toby's ears turned red, a sure sign his friend was fast losing patience himself. "I already said it. You bought the ring before Christmas—as a *Christmas present*—but the day came and went and you didn't give it to her. I've kept my mouth shut and waited, thinking you'll tell me what the delay's about. You haven't said a word. *What's going on?*"

Garret wasn't sure. Buying Joss the bracelet had been pure impulse and he'd told himself he was going to give it to her in addition to the ring. But when they exchanged gifts… "Nothing's going on, we're fine. The timing was off. And I'm going to do it. I just haven't gotten around to it."

There was that smirk again. Toby had been his friend for too many years. First as schoolmates, then as playmates when Toby's mom had come to work for the Tulanes. Toby knew what buttons to push, and that smirk made Garret want to plant his fist in Toby's mouth.

"Be still my little ol' heart. That's got to be what every woman wants to hear."

Garret fought for patience. He loved Joss, was going to marry her, no doubt about it. Why was Toby hinting otherwise? "Tobe, I don't—" Garret broke off and swore as understanding dawned. "People know? Is that it? Someone else knows besides you and me?" He and Toby had gone to one of the most discreet jewelry stores in Nashville. A high-end business with nondescript signage and an armed guard who met potential customers at the elevator, walked them through a metal detector before escorting them beyond a bullet-proof-glass-partitioned wall to view the merchandise. How had people found out?

"I haven't said anything, but you know how gossip works and that—" he lowered his voice when a woman in scrubs walked by the far end of the hallway "—was a big-ticket item even if it was one of their less expensive rings. How long did you think it would be before people began to speculate?"

"It's none of their business."

"I agree, but I can't blame them when I'm curious, too. She hasn't *mentioned* it?"

"Joss isn't like that."

"Maybe not, but wouldn't she find a way to let you know she's ready even if she didn't come right out and say it? You know, leave bridal magazines lying around? Something?"

The comment gave him pause. Garret forced himself to unlock his jaw so the pain streaking to his head would ease. "Joss is building a career, just like I am. Timing is everything. You've experienced that enough in court, figuring out when to say just the right thing to sway the juries. Joss and I have plenty of time. Marriage isn't something to rush into."

Toby tugged at his ear. "If you say so."

"I do."

"Fine, whatever. If you see Maria or my mother walking the halls, do me a favor and tell them I went to get something to drink. I'll be up in a few minutes."

Subject apparently dropped for now, Garret nodded. "Sure." He pulled the briefcase from the door, but as they slid shut, he was very aware of the fact Toby didn't look any happier than he had when he'd started the strange conversation. His friend meant well, and Garret tried to remember that despite his irritation Toby's questions had hit home. Joss hadn't mentioned getting married since— When? A long time ago, and she'd made the comment so casually he knew she wasn't hinting.

Toby was feeling the pressure every thirtysomething guy out there felt to settle down and do something with his life. Reacting to it. That had to be the reason behind the inquisition. Tobe was freaking out because his sister was on kid number three while he hadn't made it to first base with a woman in months. Parental pressures to reach certain achievements changed as a kid grew older, but they certainly didn't disappear.

Garret walked toward the nurses' station to check on Darcy, each step longer than the last. He eyed the empty area and set his briefcase at his feet, leaning against the desk while he waited for someone to return. Seconds passed, minutes, his thoughts running rampant but finally becoming centered on the one question he couldn't answer.

When *was* the last time he and Joss had had sex?

"WHAT DO YOU MEAN she isn't here?" Five minutes later Garret bit back the curse that sprang to his lips and wiped a hand over his tired eyes. It was one o'clock in the morning and Darcy had been having labor pains. Where else could she be?

The nurse gave him a chilly stare at his tone. "It's hospital policy to treat and release patients provided their condition is under control, Mr. Tulane."

"She didn't drive herself here. Where did she go?"

The older nurse raised her eyebrows and straightened the multitude of charts in front of her by banging the stack against the counter. "I don't know what to tell you, Mr. Tulane, but she's not here. Try the cafeteria or the waiting area by the main entrance. Now I have to go. We're short-staffed tonight." Her tone suggested the situation was his fault.

That was partially true. The nurses' contract was up for renewal and Harold was balking at the pay raise. Not only were the current wages causing them to lose some of their experienced staff, but also the low rates meant new graduates weren't eager to work here when other hospitals paid more. He couldn't blame them.

Scowling, he grabbed his briefcase and turned to leave, only to stop in his tracks and stare out the nearby window. The hospital appeared to be in the middle of a snow globe. Giant flakes blew in blinding sheets, buffeted by gusts of wind that shook the window in its frame.

Was Darcy out there? Concern overrode every ounce of remaining frustration.

Downstairs, the reception desk was unstaffed, the main lobby empty. The television inside the waiting area was tuned to a local station broadcasting details about the storm he didn't want to consider. Surely she wouldn't have tried to walk? The closest motel was a quarter mile away.

Shaking his head, he hurried to the cafeteria and visually scanned the colorful scrubs and white coats, unease growing when he didn't see her. Where was she?

He'd turned to leave when he spotted her. Darcy sat in the far corner booth with her head propped against her arm. And even though he had no reason to feel the extent of the relief swamping him, he did. Knowing she was all alone and could have easily lost her baby tonight got to him.

Darcy's blond curls were messy and her expression was one of pure exhaustion. But the moment she saw him approach, her brown eyes warmed with welcome. Something twisted inside him at the sight.

She straightened and pushed the small, old-fashioned-looking porcelain doll she'd been staring at into the center of the table. "I was hoping I'd see you again. I didn't get a chance to thank you for all you did for me."

Like kicking her out into the snow? "You're okay?"

She nodded. "Seems so. The contractions were a combination of dehydration and stress. The IVs and medication stopped them almost immediately, and Dr. Clyde said I'm okay. No damage from the accident at all."

"You're not sore?"

She shrugged. "A little in my shoulders and back, but nothing major. Honestly the crash was more like a bumper-car hit because I was going so slow. Taylor and I are fine."

"Taylor? But you called the baby Cameron earlier."

She blushed prettily. "Did I? I like that. I'll have to write that one down."

"Excuse me?"

"I'm trying out names until I find one that fits."

"Okay."

"Don't laugh. How anyone can pick a name out of a book is beyond me. If you really want the truth, I think a parent needs to open the back door and shout it a few times to get the full effect and know if they're going to like hearing it for the next eighteen years or so as they call their kids in for dinner."

This time he laughed outright. "I've never thought of it quite like that, but you might be on to something."

"Thanks for requesting Dr. Clyde. She's very nice. She

wants me to come back if the contractions start again, but otherwise I'm good until my follow-up on Monday."

"I thought she might make you feel more comfortable. She's received good reports during her practice here."

Darcy blinked up at him. "So, what are you still doing here? I would've thought you'd go home after dropping me off."

"I had some things I needed to take care of with the Maintenance Department. I'm heading home now, but I wanted to check on you first."

"That's very sweet. Like I said, I'm fine."

She might be fine, but she looked ready to drop. Inhaling her unique scent, Garret rested the briefcase on top of the table. "You shouldn't have been released in the middle of a storm, not under the circumstances."

"Some rules you can't control. Besides, they did a great job getting the contractions stopped so there's no need to take up a bed. And, being in between jobs like I am at the moment I, uh, don't have a lot of cash to pay for what the insurance doesn't cover. No worries, I promise. They took excellent care of me just like you said they would."

He indicated her suitcase with a nod. "What happens now? Are you staying in town until your car is fixed?"

Darcy looked down and fingered the doll's satin dress. "I'll be here until the storm is over. But after that I don't know. I'm waiting to hear from my mother. I called but couldn't reach her."

Garret hesitated, knew he should leave well enough alone. "Do you mind if I sit down?"

"Oh, of course. Please do."

He seated himself on the opposite bench. "Are you waiting here for a particular reason?"

She tucked the doll into a cloth sack and put it into her

oversize purse. "One of the nurses said if I was still here in the morning, she'd drive me to a motel as soon as her shift was over."

"There isn't another shift change until six. I can't let you sit here for five hours. Come on, you're coming with me."

CHAPTER SIX

DARCY BLINKED at Garret, surprised by the offer. Go with him where? Finding a place to lie down in the lobby had left her feeling too much like a loser, a *cold* loser, so she'd dragged her achy body to the cafeteria. It was warmer here and she could sleep sitting up, thank you. "I'm okay here."

"No, you're not." Garret stood and grabbed her suitcase with his free hand. "I'll drive you to the motel. It's not far from here."

"You've done enough. More than enou—"

"Darcy? Let me drive you. I'd like to know you're safe."

The words flowed over her, through her, and she found herself fighting back pathetic, exhausted tears. Why not? Debra certainly hadn't acted all that thrilled at the idea of having to take her.

Gazing at him, Darcy absorbed all the little details she'd missed during the dark and pain-shrouded trip to the hospital. Details such as the breadth of Garret's shoulders and the sexy angle of his jawline. She was such a sucker for a strong jawline.

"What do you say? Road trip?"

"Thank you. It's not enough, but thank you—I accept." With a smile of gratitude, Darcy took the arm Garret extended and let him help her to her feet.

Maybe white knights did exist. It was just too bad this one had shown up seven months too late.

GARRET ESCORTED HER to the garage where his SUV was parked.

"Here we are again."

"Here we are," she repeated, buckling her seat belt and watching in amazement when he gently tugged on it to check it. Cinderella she wasn't, but she was sure getting the royal treatment. She'd think he was flirting with her if she wasn't big-as-a-house pregnant. Being that she was, it was easy to rule out romance or anything sexual.

Unlike the pelting ice that had caused her accident, big fluffy flakes the size of marshmallow tops now floated to the ground with deceptive grace and speed. The houses near the hospital were decorated with a mixture of leftover Christmas lights and early Valentine's Day decorations. The older homes were layered with gingerbread trim and pretty porches behind yards with thick tree trunks. The odd swing blew crookedly in the wind.

The farther away from the hospital Garret drove, the more modernized the housing became. Another turn brought them into an area of shops with old-fashioned storefronts. Large, black lampposts stood guard on every corner over benches weighted down with snow, and red fire hydrants poked through drifts to add a splash of color. There was even a striped barber shop sign.

It was the best of Norman Rockwell.

Did the townspeople know how precious this all looked? It was a world apart from the glitz and glamour of Miami. Darcy kept her comments to herself and continued her sleepy study of the little mountain town. Finally Garret braked outside a motel with a cottage-style facade. The Hideaway Inn. *Of course.* She only hoped she could afford it.

"Here we are." He got out and grabbed her suitcase, then escorted her to the door with a solid grip on her arm.

Inside a small anteroom, Darcy shivered and wrinkled her nose at the heavy cinnamon fragrance clouding the air. She loved scents and their healing properties, but this was overkill. No doubt an attempt to diffuse the odor of mold making her nose twitch with a sneeze.

Garret rang the bell attached to the wall. No response. Showing the first signs of impatience, Garret hit the bell a couple more times. Finally a light turned on from the other side of a curtained enclosure beyond the reinforced glass entry doors. A buzz sounded and the small speaker beside the bell squawked.

"Sorry. No rooms."

"The sign says Vacancy." Garret growled the words in his deep, ultrasexy voice, and Darcy felt like the biggest pain in all the world.

"The 'no' is busted and I forgot to turn the darn thing off. Try after the snow lets up." With that suggestion, the light went out and all was silent.

Garret scowled. "Come on. The Station House isn't far. We'll try there."

Back to the vehicle they went and Darcy gasped when the bitter cold hit her face. "I'm sorry for all the trouble."

"It's no problem."

She had to wait until Garret crossed in front of the vehicle and climbed in to continue their conversation. "Just take me back to the hospital. It's fine."

"It's not fine," he murmured firmly. "You need a place to rest. Relax, we'll find you something."

The Station House wound up being a remodeled railroad depot that boasted room service and a restaurant. The cars parked outside were newer models than those of the first motel they'd tried, which meant her credit card would take a harder hit. Still, Garret was right. She was desperate for a place to lie down. She'd never felt this tired, so much so she was starting to nod off beside her handsome driver. How embarrassing. The way her night had gone, she'd fall asleep and drool all over herself.

"Stay here and let me check it out, okay?"

Darcy nodded, willing to let him brave the weather even though she felt guilty for doing so. "Thank you."

Garret flashed her a gorgeous smile and left the vehicle, his shoulders hunched in deference to the cold. She shivered from the influx of cold air and cranked up the heat. It was good of him to let her stay here. A lot of men would worry that the stranger they'd helped would drive off in the expensive Cadi.

She huddled deeper into her seat and frowned at an ad for the radio station's upcoming Valentine's Day contest. There'd be no roses for her this year. No candy or jewelry or candlelight dinners. But that was okay. She'd learned the hard way that flowers and candy didn't make the man. And they most certainly did not make him father material.

Drowsy, she rubbed her belly. "I love you, Annabelle. I hope it's enough."

GARRET SCOWLED at the twentysomething kid in front of him. "You have *nothing* available?"

"Nope."

"I'll make it worth your while. She's pregnant and stranded and she was just released from the hospital. Don't you have a sitting room or something?"

"No, man. Sorry." The guy grinned, and a crackly laugh emerged. "Weird, huh? You know, no room at the inn?" He sobered when he realized Garret wasn't amused. "Um... look, there's nothing here. This storm caught a lot of people by surprise. We're full and then some." He glanced behind him, then leaned forward across the counter. "We're not supposed to recommend anyplace else, but have you tried the motel on Route 9?"

"Call them," Garret ordered. "Call them right now and find out if there's a room available. Tell them we'll take anything."

The guy gave him a leery, you're-going-to-get-me-in-trouble glare, but did his bidding. Garret paced in front of the counter and blatantly listened to the one-sided conversation. Finally the guy hung up. "Um…nothing, man—uh, sir. Sorry."

Jaw locked, Garret stalked out of the lobby. There wasn't a hotel closet left for Darcy to stay in. Scowling, he climbed into the Escalade only to hesitate when he realized Darcy was sleeping so soundly she hadn't heard him.

He quietly closed the door, free to study her without being observed. She was certainly attractive, but the symmetry of her features was off. Her nose was a little large for her face, her top lip as full as the bottom. Put together, there was nothing awe inspiring about her appearance. Nothing to make him feel so…curious?

He shook his head at himself. Who was it that said if you rescued someone you were responsible for them?

Garret drummed his fingers against the steering wheel. Snow blanketed the windshield despite the frequent swipe of the wipers. They had to get to wherever they were going or be stranded. But there was no way he could leave her sitting in the lobby of some hotel at two o'clock in the morning.

Frowning, he checked her seat belt once more and put the vehicle in Reverse. Someone had to take care of Darcy and her baby. And right now it looked as though that someone was him.

SHE WAS IN A BOAT, sun-warmed air blowing on her face, the chop of the waves slapping against the hull, the radio playing eighties hits by rockers with big hair.

A jolt startled her and Darcy blinked, drowsily surveying her surroundings and wondering why the GPS looked different than she remembered. With a start, it all came back. The wind was a heater cranked full blast, the waves dirt- and sand-encrusted sludge hitting the undercarriage of the SUV.

You expected something else?

Not really. She hadn't been on a boat since the last time Stephen had taken her out and they'd made love beneath the stars.

You made love, he had sex. Big difference.

The SUV slowed for Garret to make a turn. A garage door opened ahead of them and they pulled inside to park beside a Land Cruiser. She lifted her head.

"Hey. You were out the whole way."

"Obviously." The last thing she remembered was sitting outside the Station House. And now they were where? "This doesn't look like a hotel." She eyed the pricey-looking bicycle hanging on the wall in front of them.

"Because it's not." Garret released a heavy sigh and turned toward her. "Look, Darcy, the Station House didn't have any rooms. I had the night manager call the last motel near here and they were full, as well. So I brought you home with me."

Home? As in *his* home?

Garret tilted his head to the side and held both hands up, palms open. "I'm not a pervert or a rapist. And even though *you* could be an ax murderer, I'm going to take a chance and let you stay here for the night because I don't know what else to do."

He was exhausted. One glance into his weary gaze told her that. While she'd been dozing, he'd battled the elements to get them to safety and with no where else to take her—

"I'll sleep on the couch and you can have my bedroom. It has a lock on the door and I'll even give you a baseball bat if it makes you feel better, but honestly, you have nothing to worry about from me. Or Ethan."

That startled her. "Ethan?"

"My older brother lives here, too. I'll introduce you in the morning. He's completely safe. What do you say?"

What could she say? They were here and the thought of a bed compared to a booth in the hospital cafeteria was too tempting to resist. "Where's that bat?"

In response, Garret winked, then got out and grabbed their cases before leading the way into the house. Darcy followed him down a short hallway past a utility room, the kitchen and living room beyond.

"The bedroom is that way, first door on the right. Let me find some sheets and I'll change the bed for you."

"I'll do it." Her voice emerged scratchy so she cleared her throat and tried again. "I don't want you to go to any more trouble than you already have."

The melted snow left little diamond drops of water in his dark hair. They sparkled beneath the light.

"We'll change them together."

Garret left his briefcase near the couch and carried her suitcase into the bedroom. Within moments he located fresh sheets and they silently made up the bed together. The act was strangely intimate and brought a blush to her cheeks.

"Done. I'll get out of here so you can rest."

He grabbed some workout pants from a drawer and his toothbrush from the attached bath, then made one final trip into a walk-in closet where he retrieved a baseball bat. He held it out to her, and when she lifted a hand to accept it, he placed his free hand over hers.

"Sweet dreams, Darcy. To you and Butch both." He lowered his gaze to her stomach quickly before glancing back up and smiling at her, the look soft and sexy. Her heart raced and lost its rhythm. The feel of his touch, the expression on his face. The man was lethal. Letting go, Garret paused to lock the door on the way out.

She yawned as she donned her cold pajamas in the bathroom, brushed her teeth and climbed into bed, the bat propped within easy reach. The fresh scent of detergent and fabric softener smelled heavenly, but it was the other, more intriguing scent of Garret's cologne that had her pressing her nose into the pillow.

She slowly relaxed, amazed that the store-bought scent combined so well with the essential oils she'd rubbed on her neck earlier. Within moments she slipped into a cozy, dreamy state.

"So, Butch," she murmured, her hands on her belly, "what do you think? Is he for real?"

A firm, solid kick was her response—that and the sudden, urgent need to pee.

CHAPTER SEVEN

GARRET HAD JUST SET a skillet on the stove when he heard his bedroom door open. "In the kitchen!"

Darcy walked in bellyfirst, dressed in a brown velour track suit that matched her eyes and a blue T-shirt with a sparkly design on the front. Her curls were bouncy and shower fresh, her appearance alert although still more than a bit tired.

A rosy blush bloomed on her cheeks when she saw him. "Um…good morning." The color on her face deepened to a fiery pink. "I'm sorry I slept so late. You probably needed something from your room."

"I only just got moving myself. Did you sleep well?" He winced at the inane question. Anything was better than a hospital cafeteria.

"Yeah, I did. Thanks for lending me your room." Darcy stepped deeper into the kitchen. With a silent, sweeping glance she took in the black granite countertops, the sleek cabinets and stainless steel appliances. "This is nice."

"Thanks."

"I didn't see your brother. Is he still asleep?"

"Ethan's the surgeon on call this weekend. He left for work about five o'clock this morning because of an accident."

Darcy pursed her full lips at the news, the move making

him want to lean over and brush his mouth across hers to ease the tension. Shock clenched his gut into a knot. Turning until he had his back to her, he planted his feet and swore softly. What was wrong with him? What was he doing? Thinking?

That her mouth would make any man want to kiss it?

"Did you burn yourself?"

"No." He waved the spatula. "Just forgot how to cook." Had the stress of his job pushed him off the deep end? Darcy was *pregnant*. Beyond the baby she carried and the complications that came with it, what about Joss? Harry? One wrong move would screw up everything.

"I hate to trouble you again, but I've got my stuff packed up. If you wouldn't mind giving me a ride to the garage to arrange things with Nick, I'll get out of your hair. I can take a cab to one of the motels from there."

Without uttering a word that might reveal his stupefying interest, Garret pointed the spatula toward the window. "Have you looked outside today?"

Darcy gasped. "It's *still* snowing?"

"Hasn't stopped all night. And—" he had to stop and inhale "—it's not supposed to clear up until tomorrow afternoon." Meaning they were snowbound for the next thirty-six hours—maybe more depending on the road conditions.

"You've *got* to be kidding me." She released a low, throaty groan. "I had no idea. I got up and saw how late it was and didn't even look out the window. I was hoping to get my car towed and find a room at one of the motels…"

Garret cracked an egg and muttered when there were more shells in the bowl than yolk. He set that one aside and grabbed another from the cabinet. "The whole town is shut down because of the storm. No one's going anywhere right now."

"But, Garret, I can't stay. We're strangers and I can't impose on you."

Strangers? Maybe, but it didn't seem that way. "I don't qualify as a friend?"

"Of course you do." Darcy's expression softened, her coffee-colored eyes filled with regret and wry amusement as she glanced over her shoulder at him, the light from the window turning her hair into an angel's halo. "But I wouldn't blame you if you wished you'd never stopped to help me."

This was a test. It had to be. He'd dragged his feet where Joss and commitment were concerned and now he was being tested. He faced a snowy weekend alone with a pretty woman who tempted him to think about her mouth.

He forced the direction of his thoughts into a U-turn. He wouldn't treat Darcy the way the baby's father obviously had. Nor would he subject Joss to the hurt that stemmed from betrayal. How had one simple act of kindness become so complicated?

Things are only as complicated as you let them get.

He watched Darcy nibble her lower lip. She was a worrier. The baby, the wreck, the snow and getting to wherever it was in Indiana she was going. The best thing for him to do was make things here as *un*complicated as possible for them both.

Drawn even though he warned himself to keep his distance, he moved to stand behind her and stare out at the snow. "I couldn't have lived with myself if I'd left you sitting by the side of the road last night, Darcy. Just like I couldn't have left you sitting in the cafeteria. I'd do it again without question. Stop worrying." He managed a strained chuckle and backed away when the smell of her made him want to step closer. "Admit it, you slept a lot better in my bed."

The image of which was now firmly ensconced in his head. He scraped a hand over his face, picturing her warm and drowsy, the two of them spooning.

"You know I did."

He had to clear his throat to speak. "So, we'll make the best of the situation until the roads clear up." And he'd keep his distance, ignore the scent of her that drew him like a bee to a flower and—

See if I pass the test.

JOCELYN PIERSON SHIVERED as she pulled her keys from her pocket to let herself into the back door of her dream-come-true. Her art gallery was the bane of her father's existence. It was scheduled to open in a couple months—albeit later than she'd hoped, thanks to a series of delays—and she was extraordinarily proud of her achievement. Not bad for someone with "a soft little brain and poor judgment" according to her father.

The wind whipped up the moment she pulled her keys from the lock, and the force of it rocked her already-unsteady stance. She fell against the door with a muffled gasp, the keys tumbling through the metal-grate stairs into the snow below.

Muttering words guaranteed to get any good Southern girl's mouth washed out with soap, she turned to retrace her steps and found herself staring down at Garret's best friend.

"Go on inside, I'll get them." Tobias Richardson jerked his head toward the building to confirm his words, his nose and cheeks red from exposure.

She grabbed the handle to open the utility door and then had to fight the wind to close it behind her. Her hair stuck to her lipstick, her eyes watered after being out so long and her toes had gone numb twenty minutes ago while getting breakfast. She'd packed a bag but hadn't thought to bring snacks to eat. Luckily the diner was open. She tossed her bagged brunch aside, wishing she'd brought something warmer and more comfortable to wear.

Joss hurried to repair the damage and make herself presentable, but the hair clip caught in the tangles created by the wind. Just when she'd gathered the mass into some semblance of order, the door behind her opened. The wind blew snow through the back room, strewing papers, scattering the dirt she'd swept into a pile but hadn't disposed of. The blast of cold air ripped her hair from her hands, and all attempts at fixing her appearance vanished.

Tobias pushed the door shut and stomped his feet on the rug.

Desperate, Jocelyn smoothed her hair as best she could and tried to pretend it wasn't a disaster. "Thanks for getting my keys."

He moved toward her with a slight smile on his big, dopey face, her keys dangling from his hand. She'd always considered Tobias handsome in an awkward, gauche sort of way. He had a tall, lean body with the rolling gait of a western wrangler and sun-streaked, mud-brown hair that was forever in need of a trim. By far his eyes were his best, and worst, feature. They were a startling golden brown so light they looked yellow. Hawk's eyes, Garret had once said. The term fit.

"Here." He held out the keys and she looked down. His hands were chapped, the calluses on the sides of his fingers white with age.

"Thank you. How's Maria? I heard they were going to induce her on Wednesday if she didn't go into labor this weekend."

"She had the baby at one o'clock this morning. A girl, just like expected." Tobias released the keys. Their fingers brushed during the exchange and, as if the act had tainted him with some incurable disease, he rubbed his hand discreetly against his leg, then lifted it and pushed his hair back from his face.

She turned, absurdly hurt by his behavior. With a silent, appraising glance he criticized her clothes, her appearance, everything, making her well aware that he thought her less than worthy of Garret. Once more she tried to gather her hair without making too much fuss.

"Leave it down. It doesn't look as stiff."

Stiff? She hesitated for a split second, then continued with her task. "Daddy always says professional women do not have wild hair, nor do debutantes."

"And you are that."

She turned, her gaze narrowing on him. "Pardon me?"

"A professional woman." Tobias lifted one of his ugly hands to indicate their surroundings. "The place seems to be coming together."

It was a mess. She knew it. He knew it. Why pretend? Normally he wouldn't. She'd often wondered what she'd done to earn his hostility, but figured her relationship with Garret topped Tobias's list of her many negative attributes. Then there was his mother and her role as the Piersons' maid once upon a time. Tobias hadn't liked Jocelyn then, either, referring to her as "princess" in his mocking tone. "I'm running a little behind schedule, but I'll catch up. I stayed here last night and got quite—"

"What?"

The vehemence in his tone surprised her. "I beg your pardon?"

"You stayed here? By yourself? Did Garret stay with you?"

Joss couldn't believe his nerve. She shifted her weight onto one hip and crossed her arms over her less-than-stellar chest. "No, he didn't. But somehow I managed to survive all by myself."

He looked as though he'd swallowed a lemon. "I meant with the weather as bad as it is and with this place in such a state—"

"You just said it was coming together."

"I lied. It looks like hell, but I didn't want to hurt your feelings."

"Like you care about that. You just informed me my hair looks *stiff.*"

"What do you expect when it's always scraped back and stuck to your head?"

Jocelyn stared at him, her mouth open in shock. Of all the—

"You shouldn't have stayed here by yourself. That's all I'm saying. It's dangerous."

"And you think it's dangerous because…what? I'm such a ditz I can't lock a door or turn on the alarm system? Can't call the police if someone were to break in? Can't use one of the many metal rods lying about to whack someone over the head if I needed to?"

He shuffled his feet as though he was suddenly being attacked by ants—or metal rods. "I forgot you had an alarm."

"I know how to work it, too," she said in her sweetest, most saccharine Southern-belle voice. "But I guess that shows your opinion of me, doesn't it? Just say it, Tobias.

You think I'm dumb. I'm so dumb, in fact, that Garret shouldn't be with me. And that 'professional woman' comment? We both know what you meant—it was a shot because I *was* a debutante. But, for the record, some of the most enterprising, take-charge women in this part of the country were *debutantes*."

"I don't want to argue with you, dammit, I—"

"Then don't. Just tell me why you're here and get o—" She broke off, but it was too late. They both knew what she'd been about to say. "I—I'm sorry. That was very rude."

He pulled an envelope from his pocket and shoved it at her, his unusual eyes glittering with anger and what looked to be…hurt?

"Tobias—"

"Make sure you lock up and set the alarm."

He was out the door in seconds. As though taking his side, the wind tore at her hair yet again before Tobias yanked the panel shut with a loud bang.

She opened the envelope and choked at the embossed slip inside. Coughing, wheezing, she collapsed against a crate, digging the paper from within to confirm the truth she already knew. It wasn't…surely it *wasn't*.

But it was. Oh, shoot, what had she done?

She was now going to have to apologize to one of the most obnoxious men on the planet.

CHAPTER EIGHT

"TOBIAS, WAIT!" Jocelyn hurried out the door after him. "Wait!" she called again, catching him halfway down the stairs. He didn't stop. "Tobias, please."

Manners did the trick. He turned to stare up at her, his thick eyebrows low over his eyes. "What do you want?"

The temperature made her teeth chatter. "C-can you come back inside for a minute?" Remembering what had made him stop, she added, "Please?"

Tobias ran his hand over his hair and messed it even more. Didn't he ever get his hair cut? She bit her tongue to keep from saying something else she shouldn't and waited for him to make up his mind. Stubborn man.

It bothered her that he didn't like her. It didn't matter, of course. But he was Garret's best friend and she had enough good girl in her to want everyone to like her. Including him. But the fact that Tobias behaved as though he couldn't stand to be in her presence—that he didn't approve of Garret's love for her—irritated her to no end.

Was he going to make her stand out here all day in the cold? Finally he released a disgruntled sigh and retraced his steps, following her into the gallery's back room.

"Thank you for the permit." It came out badly, as though her gratitude wasn't sincere or she didn't appreciate the effort he'd made to get the permit. "It was very nice of you to do that."

"You're welcome."

That's it? No explanation as to *why* he'd done it?

Champagne and beer don't mix, Jocelyn Renee. But you won't ever forget it again, will you? Her father's overbearing voice rang in her head.

No, she wouldn't forget. But in that moment she felt as though she owed Tobias a warning about her father. Over the past couple of years, Daddy had gotten in more than his fair share of snide comments about the son of their former maid, making it clear he wanted no one in his family associating with Tobias. Even though Daddy hadn't yet set down the law with Garret—as he was wont to do with her—she knew he didn't approve of the friendship between Garret and Tobias. It was only a matter of time before her father started vocalizing his displeasure and pressuring Garret to cease all contact with Tobias. And her father would not be subtle or fair. He wouldn't hesitate to use her to control Garret.

Regardless of her feelings about the man, Tobias deserved to know what her father would try to do.

Tobias shifted his too-big feet. She needed to say something, tell him that Garret was stronger, that he was a good friend, a good man. That Daddy would never control Garret the way he did her. But the words wouldn't come. Truth was Garret and her father were very close. They had been for years, even longer than she and Garret had dated.

Looking extremely put out by her continued silence, Tobias sighed. "Was that all you wanted?"

"No." She cleared her throat and lifted her chin, determined to make peace if it killed her. "I wanted to know why you did it."

His shoulders lifted and lowered in a tense shrug. "Don't

get too ahead of yourself, princess. I was at the courthouse and saw your name on a pending file. It was no big deal."

Oh, how she despised that nickname. Her father had called her that, too. A pretty princess in a tower who should be seen and not heard. "I don't get it."

"What is there to get?" he asked impatiently.

She made herself meet his unusual eyes. "I don't get *why*. You don't like me. Don't pretend you do because we both know better. Why would you go out of your way to get this for me? Seems to me you'd like to see me fail."

Indecently thick lashes lowered over his gaze. "That's not true. But you need the permit to open, and I thought I'd save Garret the hassle of having to get it for you."

So he didn't approve of her gallery, either? "I would've handled the permit myself. I've managed to get all the others. I admit this one has been a problem but— I appreciate the help. I asked Garret to see if he could hurry the process but he's been so busy he hasn't had the chance. I was going to remind him again when things settled down."

"You would've run out of time waiting for that to happen. Your father's got Garret's nose to the grindstone."

She knew well what that felt like. She'd been raised beneath her father's overwhelming aggression and constant disapproval. Never measuring up. Never doing enough or else doing it *wrong*. Right now he blamed her for Garret not proposing yet, but what woman wanted to nag a man into marrying her?

"I'd better go."

Tobias looked bored by the stilted conversation. And there he went, tugging on his hair again like a big old dog scratching at his ear. But she had to do something. She couldn't imagine spending her married life to Garret, having his best friend glare at her all the time. The tension between them had to end. "Tobias—"

"Toby."

"You look more like a Tobias." Why had she said that? She swallowed audibly. "Anyway, please wait. I owe you another apology."

"For what?"

It wasn't easy to bring up a subject that happened so long ago. "I'm sorry I didn't speak up. Years ago. That day at the house. Those girls were awful."

"You mean your friends?"

She faltered again. "They weren't my friends. Not really. Not at all, if you want the truth." He didn't look surprised by the confession. "I should've said something to them when they began saying those things. It probably embarrassed you—"

"It was a long time ago." A ruddy hue crawled up his neck to his cheeks.

She stared, dumbstruck. Was that it? She'd felt badly about it, but he'd acted like a jerk and— He was *embarrassed?* Nervous around her because that happened years ago? Was that why he kept fidgeting? And the way he barked at her and glared and acted so brooding when the three of them were together? Was that him trying to cope with the rudeness of a teenage girl who'd become his best friend's date?

How could she not have realized? "I should've said something. I didn't speak up and that was…unkind. And then my father didn't pay you after all the hard work— I wish you had kept the check I sent you."

"It wasn't your bill to pay. I didn't want your money."

She realized now she'd only made the situation worse by doing that. How could she have been so blind? "But you earned it." And she wouldn't have missed the money. She knew he'd needed it, though, to help support his mother and little sister. "How is your mother?"

Tobias rubbed a knuckle against his mouth. "She's fine. She likes being a grandma again."

"Good. That's good." She saw a clipboard lying nearby and picked it up to have something to do with her hands. "I'm glad things are going so well for you. All of you. Anyway, thank you. Again. You've done Garret and me a huge favor."

His mouth pulled up in one of his smirking grins, one that lit his face and made his eyes crinkle at the corners, giving him a devilish quality. The expression emphasized the deep cleft in his chin. She hadn't found those sexy since her crush on Tom Selleck, but on Tobias... Well, he had a certain quality. She'd have to give him more thought. Think of a female friend he might appeal to. Someone nice and down-to-earth. Heaven knew she owed him that.

Tobias turned away but paused. "Did you have to clean the pool?"

The question caught her by surprise, although it shouldn't have. She laughed, remembering her father's rage and her secret delight that someone had gotten even with him and his tyranny. "No. He called a service to do that. But they charged him three times what he owed you."

A gruff chuckle erupted from his chest. "Served him right."

"I agree." He looked startled by her agreement and faced her with an expression she couldn't quite decipher. The metal clip dug into her hand.

Tobias glanced around at the assortment of crates she needed to unpack, canvases she'd prepared for hanging, none of which could be done until the walls were painted. "You're going to try to do all this yourself?"

"I, uh, hired someone who was supposed to have come today to help me. With the weather, we thought it best to cancel."

"Would you like me to help?"

Was he serious? Or just being polite and making a peace offering after their talk? Probably the second, but did it matter? They seemed to have crossed a bridge in their relationship. Maybe he'd stop all the glaring and come to terms with her marrying his best friend.

"That would be great. You don't have plans for the day?"

For the first time since she remembered meeting him, Tobias's eyes warmed when he looked at her and shrugged. "Where do we start?"

WHILE GARRET SECLUDED himself in his home office to work and to call Nick about her car, Darcy took care of the breakfast dishes and picked up around the surprisingly clean bachelor pad. The two guys were neater than she ever hoped to be.

Shaking her head, she looked up, her gaze caught by the weather outside. Everything was buried beneath a ruler's worth of snow and ice. All she'd needed was one more day of driving and she could've made it to her destination. At least close. *Close only counts in horseshoes and hand grenades.*

She rolled her eyes at the juvenile saying. The thick layer of snow made her wonder about her car. What if it was so covered that Nick couldn't find it? Or worse, that some other driver hadn't seen it and slid into it after hitting that same patch of ice she had? What shape was her poor car in? How much money would she need to repair it?

Growing up dependent upon an ever-changing stream of "uncles" for food and rent had made her the stand-on-her-own-two-feet type, but the repairs and hospital stay could easily wipe out the majority of her nest egg. Living in Miami wasn't cheap—yet another reason to go home to Indiana where a dollar stretched a little further.

Garret's footfalls sounded on the hardwood floor outside the kitchen and she turned to see him looking as disgruntled as she felt. "Uh-oh, something wrong?"

His gaze swept over the stove and lingered on the now-spotless sink. "Yeah, but we'll get to that in a minute. I got hold of Nick. He won't be able to tow your car until the state of emergency is lifted, but he did say he'd make you a priority."

Being made a priority was great, but the weight on her shoulders pressed heavier than ever. She hated feeling so helpless, so dependent.

Garret ran a hand over his short hair. "Look, Darcy, I didn't bother calling the motels about vacancies. Right now, even if someone did check out and attempt to leave town, I wouldn't want to take you out on the roads. It's too dangerous, and you can't risk another scare after what you went through last night."

She felt like such a pain, but since it was the smart thing to do, she forced herself to nod. Waiting out the storm here might be best, but it didn't make her conscience rest any easier.

"Are you okay with spending another night here?"

"If you don't mind, I suppose that's fine." She hated imposing on Garret this way, hated feeling as if her life was racing out of control and she couldn't stop the skid. At the same time, she was grateful for Garret's gentlemanly behavior and the fact that she wasn't stuck in some grimy hotel room she couldn't afford. "I can't tell you how much I appreciate your help, Garret. I keep saying it, but it's true. I don't know what I would have done without you. And I'm happy to pitch in while I'm here. It's the least I can do."

He gave her a smiling yet disapproving look and heat bloomed in her face. Scruffy had never looked so sexy on a guy.

"Yeah, about that. You're supposed to be resting, not cleaning up the dishes." Garret tilted his head to one side and crossed his arms over his chest. The move delineated the muscles beneath his long-sleeved T-shirt. "Didn't I tell you to leave those?"

"You cooked. It was only fair."

Garret had been gorgeous in his dark suit and overcoat last night, but this morning he looked even more so in worn running pants and a lightweight U of T shirt that had seen better days. Both molded his body, and his size gave her butterflies. *No, definitely not a hardship.*

"Quit worrying about imposing. You just follow the doctor's orders about getting some rest. Take it easy, and pretend you're in a messy hotel."

He said that with a handsome grin, one that emphasized the deep creases bracketing his mouth. He worked hard, but he laughed hard, too. She liked that. And the way his hair stuck up at odd angles. Too cute. Just because she was pregnant didn't mean she was blind.

"This place is a far cry from messy. It's hard to believe two bachelors live here."

"Yeah, well, you can thank Ethan for that. He has a neat streak a mile wide. Just make yourself at home. When the snow lets up, we'll get you where you want to be."

Such a gentleman. "Thank you."

"You're welcome. Now I'm going to go grab a shower.

While I do that, why don't you go call your mother?" Garret walked to the counter and jotted something down on a notepad beside the phone. "Maybe you'll feel better if you hear her voice. Here's the number to give her."

It was a sweet thing to say. And for a guy who obviously loved his family and was obviously loved by them, she supposed that would be the case, but her mom? They really weren't that close. Although, to be fair, she did say she'd help watch the baby. Darcy accepted the slip of paper and smiled. "Thanks."

As she watched him leave the kitchen Garret seemed like true hero material. The manners, the consideration. His unbelievable good looks—a regular Raoul Bova look-alike. What more could a girl ask? If all Garret's brothers resembled him... *Da*—

Shaking her head, she remembered her vow to clean up her language. She so did not want her baby sounding like a guest on *Jerry Springer.* Her life had had more than its share of swear-perfect moments, but it was time to change; otherwise, her baby's first word would be of the four-letter variety.

Darcy left the kitchen and made her way to Garret's bedroom to the phone, smiling at the sound of Garret whistling farther down the hall. Door shut, her footsteps dragged as she made her way over to the bed. *Come on, Mom, be home. Be there for me.*

Seconds later she waited and counted the rings. Two. Three. Four. *Pick up!* A click sounded, then her mother's recorded message played. Where *was* she? Surely her mother wasn't off with another new guy? Darcy supported the idea of her mom finding true love and living happily ever after. But that was unlikely to happen with the losers her mother seemed to gravitate to.

The beep sounded. "Hi, Mom, it's me. Are you there? Pick up, it's important." She twisted the phone cord around her finger. "I'm still in Tennessee. My car has to be towed and repaired, and— The hospital released me last night, but I'm stuck in the snowstorm."

Out of nowhere, hope soared. Was her mom on her way here to check on her? Had her mom finally put Darcy ahead of her latest guy? *Please, just once let me come first.* "Call me as soon as you get my messages, okay? *Call me.*" She left the number and murmured goodbye, hating the tears that thickened her voice toward the end.

She couldn't help it though. Everyone deserved at least one grand gesture in their life. Deserved to have someone, a loved one, do something big, something *meaningful,* that showed them how much they were loved. Something that declared loud and clear, "Screw the world, you're more important!"

Lying back on the bed, she squirmed until she was comfortable, and sighed, tired even though she woke up only a little while ago. "I'll do anything for you, Jordan. I'll give you so many grand gestures you won't ever doubt you're loved," she whispered, rubbing her stomach. "I just want someone to do the same for me."

CHAPTER NINE

TOBY WIPED the sweat from his forehead and stared at Jocelyn. He had no business being here. People would talk if they found out, speculate about what happened between him and his best friend's almost-fiancée during these hours alone.

"Something wrong?"

Pulled from his thoughts, he searched her upturned face for any sign of the teenage bitch she'd been. Surprisingly, he didn't see a trace of the girl who'd received a red BMW for her sweet sixteen. "Is it straight?"

Jocelyn took a few steps back and eyed the section of gallery wall they'd been working on. "Tilt it to the right just a smidge."

Who knew it took this much effort to decorate a *wall?* They'd finished painting the one wall, assembled some shelving units, then started the tedious process of unpacking, displaying and hanging—and rehanging—the art. Sighing, he did as ordered.

"Wait. Back the other way. Perfect!" She gave him a million-dollar smile, and he thought back to middle school when her mouth had been full of braces. He'd had them at the time, too, and more than once he'd dreamed of locking metal with her.

She tucked her hair behind her shell-shaped ear, drawing

his attention to the one-carat diamond studs in her lobes. Garret hadn't blinked at the price of those. Over the past couple of years his buddy had dragged Toby into many jewelry stores to help pick something out for Jocelyn. Fact was, Toby had been the one to choose these earrings for her. They'd reminded him of her when he'd spied them— elegant and tasteful. Classy.

The same was true with the engagement ring Garret had purchased but had yet to give her. Garret had bought the damn thing, but *Toby* had been the one who'd selected it after shaking his head at the ugly monstrosity Garret had favored. Didn't Garret know Jocelyn's tastes at all?

"Are you going to stay up there all day?"

He didn't move. "Depends. You got anything else you want done?"

Her cheeks blushed prettily when she looked at her watch and gasped. "Oh, it's late! Where did the time go?" She gaped up at him. "Tobias, I'm so sorry. I had no idea the day had flown by. I was just so happy to be getting things done."

He'd noticed. That was why he'd stayed. Because she'd given him so many smiles and glances from beneath her long lashes. Because doing these tasks had made her happy and he'd liked seeing her happy. Maybe a little too much. "I'm glad to have helped."

"Well, I'm sorry to have kept you so long. With this storm it's going to take you forever and a day to get home." She smoothed a hand over her hair, drawing attention to the clasp she'd stuck back in.

He'd wanted to remove the thing all day, make her look the way she had that morning. She'd been more approachable then, whereas now she looked almost uncomfortable in her own skin. A little girl playing dress-up; her hair fixed—if messier than normal—lipstick in place. A smudge on the pantsuit she'd worn to muck around the gallery. Who worked in pantsuits, and designer ones at that?

"Is something wrong? You're frowning."

Caught unaware, he shook his head. "Don't you own any sweats?"

"Why do you ask?"

It was none of his business what she wore—or who she dated. "Never mind." He moved down the ladder and shoved aside the thoughts of Garret and Jocelyn together. He had no right to think of her that way.

"Sweats would be more comfortable, but Daddy hates them. Says women should look like women, not sports jocks."

"You'd still look like a woman, trust me." He said the words deliberately, knew it would send her into a tizzy of ums and ohs and fussing hands. She smoothed her fingers over her hair to capture all the baby-fine strands that had escaped, tugged at her jacket and pulled it down over her small breasts and raised her eyebrows high, her smooth forehead wrinkling.

"He says it's one of the rules of business, to always be presentable. I never know who might walk through the door whether here or at home. He insists Mother and I look our best at all times. Guess old habits don't die."

"You're presentable." Toby stepped off the ladder and walked to where she stood. "Your father's rules aren't the be-all and end-all, Jocelyn." He lifted his hand and tortured himself by grasping a flyaway tendril between his thumb and forefinger and tucking it behind her ear. "Beauty is in the eye of the beholder. Some men don't mind a woman looking a little ruffled."

"Garret—"

She stopped whatever it was she'd been about to say.

But the spell was broken. At the mention of his best friend, he berated himself for playing with fire. The diamond studs winked at him beneath the gallery lights, the reminder that she was out of his league transmitted loud and clear.

"I'd better go." He meant to step away. But the allure of Jocelyn—all striking blue eyes and full lips that he'd bet his hard-earned money had no collagen assistance—held him in place. Sophistication rolled off her from her pointy, spiky-heeled boots to her sculpted nose—another present from Daddy because, heaven forbid, her nose hadn't been perfect the way it was.

He'd like to see her in sweats. And drunk, just once. She'd be a silly drunk.

"You're staring again. Are you sure nothing is wrong?"

Something was wrong, all right. Having these powerful feelings for Jocelyn—for his best friend's almost-fiancée—was more than wrong. He'd best get used to wanting but never getting because the situation wasn't going to change. Jocelyn would never leave Garret, and eventually Garret would marry her. "Positive." Toby glanced at his watch. "I need to get out of here. And you should think about doing the same."

"Of course. Thank you again."

Needing air, Toby headed for the door. If he were a gentleman he'd wait for her. He'd lock up and clean the snow from her car. He'd drive behind her to ensure she arrived home safely. But he wasn't a gentleman. He was a man grasping for a shred of decency so he didn't give in to the urge to do all kinds of wicked and sinful things with this woman.

"Tobias, wait."

Hand on the door, he gritted his teeth and paused.

"I meant what I said earlier. About everything that happened years ago," she said in a rush. "I'd like us to be friends. For Garret's sake if nothing else."

He couldn't stop the smirk forming on his lips. *For Garret's sake.* "Okay. Sure, why not."

"Really?"

Toby pulled the door open, resigned. "Yeah."

THAT EVENING Darcy lifted her finger to her nape and smoothed lavender oil on her pulse point, inhaling deeply and appreciating how the scent instantly soothed her.

"Are you feeling okay?"

Garret's voice startled her. After a day spent alternately working, helping her with the meals, he'd disappeared into his thoughts. He'd been sitting here looking at the movie playing on the plasma screen yet he didn't appear to be actually watching it. Something was obviously on his mind, but the remote expression on his face kept her from asking. "I'm fine. What about you?"

He flashed her a fake I'm-okay, you're-okay smile. "Sorry, I've been distracted."

"Headache?"

"Yeah. I get them sometimes."

"Want to talk about whatever's stressing you?" Darcy twisted the lid on the tiny bottle of expensive oil before returning it to the case and pulling out another. She repeated the process, tipping the bottle until a drop of oil sparkled on her finger, rubbing it on her neck and inhaling the fragrance.

"There's a lot on my plate right now."

She looked at him, taking in the little lines of strain

around his eyes and mouth. Poor guy really was hurting. He needed a good massage or a long vacation. Better yet, both. "Do you work every weekend? Ever take any time off?"

A shudder blanked his features, as if he'd heard the question countless times before. "Things are more hectic than usual. The hospital was recently purchased by a bigger one and there is a lot of red tape to get through." He nodded toward her hands. "What is that stuff? I thought you smelled different. Is that why?"

She pretended outrage. "Are you saying I *smell?*" Her ploy worked because his expression turned teasing.

"That last one smelled like Christmas so it's a good smell."

Darcy held the latest bottle out for his perusal. "It's an essential oil. I use them in my massage therapy sessions."

Garret leaned forward a little and sniffed. "Cypress?"

"Very good."

"I can't take credit. My mother and grandmother really get into decorating the house at Christmas. They always have fresh greenery and cinnamon, stuff like that."

"Sounds nice."

"It is. What about you? What was your house like?"

"Oh, nothing spectacular. My mom was so afraid of setting the house on fire that we had a fake tree. One of the small ones that could be scrunched up and put into storage."

"Not us. Real trees, all the way."

"Trees? More than one?"

Garret got up and moved to sit beside her. He plucked the case of oils from her lap, held it up to his nose and sniffed cautiously.

"Yeah. Sometimes one in every room, sometimes more.

They always had a theme, so needless to say my mother's ornament collection is massive. Now it fills the attic."

"I'll bet they're beautiful."

More than anything else, for some reason the number and type of Christmas trees articulated their vastly different upbringings. What would growing up in that house have been like?

"What's this?"

"Huh?" Her gaze was drawn to his lips when he smiled.

"Where did you go?"

Heat crept into her face. "Baby fog," she said by way of an excuse. "My mind slips into la-la land a lot. What did you say?"

"What's this one?"

The bottle looked fragile in his big hand. "That's a blend of several of the oils. It helps with anxiety and depression."

"Wasn't this the one you used?"

She couldn't hold his gaze. "I'm pregnant, the father is a no-good, lying bas— *louse. And* I'm stuck in a snowstorm because I wrecked the first new car I was ever able to buy. Depressed? Maybe just a little."

"Things will get better, Darcy. Nick will have your car fixed up good as new."

"Maybe."

"Not *maybe.* You'll be good to go in no time."

Yeah, but would she still have a place to go *to?*

"Come on, talk to me. What are you thinking about?"

She didn't want to unload her burdens on him, didn't want him to know all the nasty details of her life she was embarrassed about and couldn't change.

"If you tell me to butt out, I will. But I'm not going to stop asking until you do."

She liked persistence. And the timbre of his voice sent

a shiver down her spine. But how silly was that? Seven and a half months pregnant and she felt shivers?

Darcy inhaled, sighed. Maybe talking would help. It would distract her from her fascination with her host if nothing else. "My mom had me when she was seventeen. I never knew my dad. He and my mom broke up before I was born. Life was hard for her. And despite always, *always* saying I'd never wind up like my mother, here I am. I've followed in her footsteps by having a baby alone." She tried to smile, but couldn't. "I mean, sure, I'm older than she was and I have career skills. But sometimes I'm not sure I'm ready to be a mother. Would the baby be better off with someone else? You know…adopted. But then I feel it move and I know I wouldn't be able to live with myself if I gave it up."

Garret's hand touched her shoulder. "Do you have to do this alone? It takes two to make a baby."

"Stephen wants nothing to do with it. Us."

"That's his loss, Darcy. As to being a mom, I'd say every woman has doubts. Wonders if she's doing a good job."

"The books say it's normal but…"

"But?"

"But I've always wanted too much. Wanted way too much."

"How so?"

She stared at the big screen and saw her plans for her life disintegrating. "When I had a baby I wanted to be married to the man I'd spend the rest of my life with, someone who'd share the good and the bad. And now, with everything that's gone on, I just don't know how that can happen." She paused. "I see these elderly couples holding hands and talking, and I wonder what have they done—

what secrets do they know—to make it so many years together. I don't know anything about that kind of staying power, so how could I have it?"

Garret took the bottle from her hand and put it in the case, then snagged her fingers and squeezed them gently. The trace of oils warmed with the contact of their skin, releasing the scent. "You can have anything you set your mind to. And I don't doubt you'll give your baby the best life you possibly can."

"I will." *I promise.*

"You're better off without that guy. Instead of wondering why Dad doesn't love him or her, your baby will grow up knowing your love and protection. You're saving your baby from that kind of insecurity."

"I don't ever want the baby to feel like she's a burden or a mistake. Stephen was a mistake, but not this baby."

"You are going to be a great mom." Garret handed the case to her. "Now tell me about the rest of those. What do they do?"

She welcomed Garret's attempt to distract her. To get her mind off whatever the future might hold. But she could see what the effort was costing him by the pain in his eyes, by the way he turned his head, rubbed his temple.

"Listen, forget the oils." She hesitated, then jumped up from the couch as fast as her beached-whale body could travel. "It's obvious your head is killing you and you're sitting there trying to take care of me when I'm the one who should be helping you. Have you ever had a massage?"

CHAPTER TEN

GARRET STARED at her, concern changing to confusion and then pure leeriness. No doubt he was thinking she'd gone off a hormonal cliff. From sad and reflective to happy and talking massages in less than five minutes? She supposed it would freak a few people out, but the sight of him in pain bothered her.

"No, I haven't, but it's okay. You don't—"

"I *do*. You want me to be comfortable here, right?"

"Right, but—"

"I can help you. I'm feeling really bad about you getting stuck with me and then—" she waved a hand toward where she'd been sitting "—going all gushy like I did. No guy wants a woman dumping on them, especially not when you look like your head is about to explode."

He chuckled and rubbed his neck. "I asked you to dump on me. I could tell something was bothering you and you needed to talk. Better out than in where it upsets Penelope."

She made a face at his attempt at a name. *Penelope?* Unless Cruz was attached to the end of it or there was a lot of cash in the bank account, the kid wouldn't stand a chance on the playground. It was yet another example of how different their lives were. "I'm not doing anything here but eating your food and kicking you out of your bed."

"You haven't been a problem, Darcy. If I thought you

were I would've braved the roads today. Ever think of that? But I didn't because I've enjoyed our time together. Maybe too much."

Too much? She smiled. "Me, too."

"Good. So don't worry about me sleeping out here. I don't sleep that well, anyway."

"I know."

He looked at her, confusion apparent. "How do you know?"

"I can tell." She shrugged. "This is what I do, remember? No offense, but you're as tense as a crossbow. Your head hurts, you keep twisting and turning your head and neck, shrugging your shoulders, and you've been blinking a lot, like people do when they're running on fumes. But I can fix all that *and* I can practically guarantee that you'll sleep tonight. Come on, aren't you just the tiniest bit interested? I'm not offering to do anything kinky or weird."

"I wasn't thinking that."

Heat flooded into her face. She'd been joking, but once the words were said she would have sworn he was thinking something along those lines.

And for one rash, split second she was thinking it, too. Obviously, her hormones were on an upswing. Sex at this stage of her pregnancy? With a man she'd just met? *So* not going to happen. "Right, I—I wanted to be clear. I charge a hundred dollars or more for my services and I don't want you to get the wrong idea and think something else is happening. Not that you would."

"A hundred bucks?"

"Yeah." Oh, he was definitely curious now. "What do you say?"

"Darcy, this isn't necessary. You don't need to repay me."

"Look, I know a massage doesn't come close to making

up for all that you've done, but it would help you and that would make me feel better."

"Why is this so important to you?"

She could lie and say it wasn't, but something about the look on his face compelled her to be honest. "Because I've been on my own since I was seventeen and I haven't taken charity from anyone. I don't want to start now."

"Seventeen? Is that why you identified with Nick?"

Darcy shrugged. She was more than a little ashamed of her upbringing, which Stephen's parents had combed through, then used to make their points for why she shouldn't be with him. After hearing Garret talk about his family, she didn't want him doing the same. "You may not see my staying here as a handout, but I do." She placed her hands over her belly. "I don't want Spike to think it's okay to mooch off people. You'd help me save face with my baby if you agree."

Garret regarded her a long moment, a sexy half smile pulling at his lips. "Well, we can't have *Spike* thinking that about his mother. What would I have to do?"

Darcy nibbled her lip, suddenly not sure her hormone-heavy body could handle him stripping down to his skivvies like her other clients. This was her job. One she did well with the utmost professionalism. But Garret was *not* her ordinary client.

"Nothing drastic. We're not set up here for a full massage, but I think your back and shoulders are the biggest problem so, um, just take off your shirt." She wouldn't ask for more. It was too intimate, too personal a thing, given the setting. Had they been in a more clinical environment she would be able to view him objectively as a series of body systems in various stages of distress. But with Garret on the couch, in his home…

He stood before she had time to do more than take in a steadying breath. He unbuttoned the shirt and for some reason the sight left her a little dizzy and thigh-clenchingly aware of him. Yes, she'd noticed how handsome he was, but a lot of guys were handsome. Stephen had been gorgeous with his Latin heritage. She'd worked on models. Even an actor or two. But with every button Garret released, she saw more of his chest and—*whew!*

A light dusting of black hair covered Garret's upper chest and pecs before tapering into the waistband of his pants. He didn't have a blatant six-pack, but his stomach was tight and firm, defined. He was beautiful. All big boned and raw sensuality.

She never got nervous when she worked on a client, but Garret was different. After everything that had happened between her and Stephen, she honestly thought it would be a long, long time before she noticed a man again. In any way. Before her pregnancy had started to show, she'd had invitations from guys saying they'd make her forget all about Stephen. She hadn't been the slightest bit tempted, but right now…

Before she could entertain more thoughts about exploring all that exposed skin in a purely unprofessional way, she turned to arrange her oils on the coffee table. That done, she grabbed the sheet Garret had slept on the night before and spread it over the expensive leather, busying herself so she wouldn't have to look at him. "Lie down when you're ready."

She found some gentle-sounding music on the television and waited until she heard Garret lower himself onto the couch. She peeked at the broad expanse of his back, the strength and texture of his skin. So much temptation. But there was no changing her mind now.

The first step was getting him used to her touch. Darcy grabbed the odorless massage oil, warmed it in her hands, then placed her palms on his shoulders and spread the oil on his skin. Careful to keep the pressure light, she smoothed it down his back, then started at the base of his spine and with increasing force, ran her thumbs up both sides. Just as she'd suspected. Tighter than a drum.

Starting at the dimpled base of his spine—so cute!—again, she stroked harder and felt Garret stiffen, as if he struggled to suppress a groan. Smiling, she repeated the motion, feeling him tense up whenever she got to the worst spot between his shoulders. Finally he gave in. A rough growl of pleasure emerged, one that had her holding her breath and suppressing yet another shiver.

"Darcy, that feels…good."

"See?" Ordinarily, she kept her voice pitched low so as soothe and not startle her client. Doing so now didn't require much effort given the surprising huskiness of her tone.

Moving outward, she found the trigger points in his shoulders and worked out the knotted muscles there. The poor guy was a mess.

Garret sighed and angled his head away from her, his eyes drifting closed. She could still see his profile, however, and after a few minutes, the tiny lines on his face eased. Guitar music played in the background, the strumming slow and soft. Beautiful songs that blended together with barely a break in rhythm.

Now that he was relaxed, she could introduce the scented oils. She left one hand on his back to maintain contact and grabbed one of the bottles she'd arranged on the table. Roman chamomile filled the air.

Darcy brushed her fingertips up his back in light strokes

to spread the oil, then firmed her touch at the base and started up again. Reaching his neck, her palms slid over his shoulders and squeezed. Another sexy-rough sigh escaped him. The sound echoed through her and she tuned into the feel of his silky, black hair as it curled over her thumbs, the steely strength of the corded muscles beneath his skin. She shook her head slightly to snap her out of the sensual spell. This was a *massage,* not a seduction.

With renewed purpose, she moved her hands in long, rhythmic patterns, gently pulling and loosening the muscles, working out the knots with single-minded determination that she would help him sleep.

One by one she added more oils and the scents of spruce and blue tansy filled the air. The knots behind his shoulder blades slowly released, as did those in his neck, too. The longer she massaged, the more pliant Garret became, and she loved the husky sounds he made as he lost himself in the experience.

Certain clients had a hard time relinquishing control because of body image or some other insecurity, but Garret was doing wonderfully. Unfortunately the same couldn't be said of her. After a while her back began to spasm and pull from leaning over him the way she was. She hesitated, then shifted her hips to perch on the very edge of the couch.

"Are you tired? You can stop." Garret's voice emerged gruff and husky.

"Just getting comfortable," she assured him as she returned to her ministrations. His winter-dry skin absorbed the fluid, so she added more massage oil, then kept her pressure and touch steady as she applied the last of the specialized oils she liked to use. Rosewood and lavender, sandalwood. The scents blended well together, a tantalizing, heady fragrance she associated with sleep.

Once more, Darcy ran her hands up to his neck, and across his back to his shoulders, upper arms and biceps until the muscles were completely lax beneath his skin. Finishing what she could of his arms with one of them scrunched up against the couch near his head, she returned to his back, her hands creating a friction she'd felt many times before, but never like this. She felt every tingle, the play of muscles and bone. The heat.

Hormones again. Had to be. Women were sexually charged beings during pregnancy, their bodies on overload. But it hadn't been a problem before now which meant it was…because of Garret? She tried to focus, gave herself another lecture about professionalism and hoped he didn't notice the slight hitch in her breathing. Still, she found herself pressing her knees together and once again thinking things she shouldn't be thinking about her host. Luckily Garret's breathing had eased. Had he fallen asleep? She wasn't sure, but it was definitely time to end the session.

She smoothed her hands over his oil-silken skin one last time, moving slowly so as not to disturb him. A portion of the sheet lay between the couch and his side, and she placed the body-warmed material over him. Normally she'd use damp, warm towels to let the oils "bake," but she'd improvise. Sheet in place, she rubbed her hands along his back to help create warmth through friction. Then she covered him with the lightweight blanket, as well, lingering over the task and knowing without a doubt that when she closed her eyes to sleep tonight she'd dream of Garret.

CHAPTER ELEVEN

GARRET AWOKE to the sound of laughter, throaty and feminine. Darcy. A smile formed on his lips before he opened his eyes. Muffled noises came from the kitchen, then Ethan's laugh joined Darcy's.

Huh?

He turned his head and squinted toward the clock on the electronics across from the couch. Nine-thirty. *Nine-thirty?* He hadn't slept that late in— Not in years. And on a couch?

Remembering the night before, he put both palms over his face and rubbed. When she'd started the massage everything had been okay. His headache had started to ease, his neck had stopped hurting. But then she'd sat beside him and it was like having a jolt of electricity zap him.

He didn't know if it was his abstinence of late, Darcy's touch or the oils, but he'd been hard instantly. His mind had filled with all of the ways they could make use of those oils, and his body had turned into a furnace. Every stroke made him want to roll over and do some touching of his own.

After reciting the alphabet—backward—then forcing himself to plow through legal briefs in his head, he'd resorted to faking sleep to end the torture.

Shrugging off the knowledge that he was one sick puppy to lust after a pregnant woman, he gave himself time to get his body under control and rose, donning his shirt along the way.

"There's Sleeping Beauty."

Ethan's tone mocked him from the stool where he sat as Garret entered the kitchen. He yawned and chose not to respond to the teasing. "When did you get home?"

"An hour ago. Good thing I didn't call, huh? You were dead to the world when I came in."

Darcy turned from the stove to smile at Garret. "I told you I could get you to sleep through the night."

Ethan raised a suspicious eyebrow, then sniffed the air. "What's that smell?"

He ignored his brother's question and Darcy's amused gaze, and focused on what she was cooking. His stomach growled. "Pancakes?"

"They're almost ready. You like them, don't you?"

"Love 'em. Do I have time for a quick shower?"

"Sure. Ten minutes?"

"I'm going to go get out of these scrubs." Ethan stood and dogged Garret's steps all the way into the bedroom.

Once there, his older brother shut the door and leaned against it. "Are you *nuts?* I heard all about you rescuing some woman, but I didn't know you'd brought her home. Why did you?"

"The state of emergency?"

"Like that ever stopped anyone from getting on the roads. I made it home, didn't I?"

"You risking your neck is one thing. Taking a pregnant woman out there when she's already had false labor would be the ultimate in stupidity."

Ethan's gaze narrowed. "No, the ultimate in stupidity is having her here in the first place. Does Joss know you brought another woman home?"

Garret had meant to call her yesterday and tell her what was going on but each time he'd picked up the phone, he couldn't do it. He didn't want to upset her since there was nothing he could do about Darcy until the roads cleared, so he'd told himself the conversation could wait. Guilt stirred suggesting that had been a bad decision. "Darcy's not another woman."

"She sure as hell looks like one to me." Ethan's voice lowered even more. "When I heard she was pregnant, I pictured a house of a woman with a wedding ring on her finger and some guy named Bubba for a husband. Not a cute blonde who looks like she's simply hiding a basketball under her shirt and no ring in sight. So level with me. Are you in some kind of trouble?"

Garret struggled to grasp what his brother was asking. Sure, Joss was likely to freak a little when Garret told her about Darcy, but she'd get over it. "What do you mean?"

Ethan stared at him as if he'd lost his mind. "Darcy's baby? Are you the father?"

"*No*. Not even close." Garret grabbed jeans from a drawer, a fresh pullover from the closet. "How can you even think that? I only met Darcy Friday night."

"Harry's going to think the exact same thing and he's going to go ballistic."

"Darcy and I are two adults—strangers—in a snow crisis. Harry and Joss will understand." Garret frowned, well aware Harry wouldn't like Darcy's presence in his house. But Harry was his boss, not his father and—

And? Harry would be his father-in-law soon. Garret stalked back to the dresser and grabbed underwear. "Eth, she'd just been released from the hospital. What else could I do when all the motels were full?"

"Hey, I would've done the same, but my situation is different in a lot of ways." He smirked. "No one would've thought twice about me picking up a woman. You, on the other hand, are all wrapped up in commitment and obligation. This deal with Darcy looks bad so you'd better be prepared for the fallout. People like a good scandal and this has all the makings of one."

"You're right." Garret sighed, frustrated. He hated being the object of speculation and having people leap to the wrong conclusions. At the sharp nudge from his guilty conscience he had to admit that, under different circumstances, those conclusions wouldn't be far from the truth. He *was* attracted to Darcy. Damn, why hadn't he thought through the consequences of his actions more thoroughly? He usually was so careful. "Well, you're here now. That should smooth things over."

"You better hope it does."

"I'll take her to a motel as soon as a room opens up."

Ethan sniffed again, walking closer to where Garret stood. "What *is* that smell?" He stopped sniffing and jerked back in horror. "It's *you?*"

"It's…scented oils. Darcy's an aromatherapist." Heat crept into his face at Ethan's expression.

"Wait a minute. Are you telling me—"

"I had a monster headache. She wanted to repay me for helping her out."

"So she *massaged* you?" Ethan's gaze narrowed. "You were dead to the world when I got home. Are you sure you didn't get a roofie in your drink? You'd better hope photographs don't wind up on the Internet."

"She didn't drug me. Trust me when I say I didn't fall asleep for a long time afterward, all right? I pretended to be asleep so she'd stop."

Ethan squeezed his eyes shut with a groan. "This just keeps getting worse. She's *pregnant.*"

"I know. I've already called myself every name you can think of and then some."

Ethan remained silent for a long moment. "For what it's worth, you wouldn't be the only guy getting a stiffy around her—if you don't look below her chest she's pretty cute."

Garret wanted to take Ethan to task for the statement but couldn't, not when he'd thought the same himself. "Just take it easy and don't give her a hard time, okay? Everything is fine."

But everything wasn't fine. *Screwed* didn't begin to cover the state of affairs he'd be in if his parents and Harry, not to mention Joss, misconstrued Darcy's presence. "I'm going to shower. Do me a favor and help her out in the kitchen. Without the attitude, please."

Ethan headed toward the door, but paused with his hand on the knob. "I understand why you picked her up. Even why you brought her home. You did the right thing. Just be careful. There are a lot of women who'd take one look at you and decide Junior could use a daddy."

DARCY BREATHED a sigh of relief as both Garret and Ethan left the kitchen. Breakfast had been a chore to get through with everyone pretending Ethan hadn't said anything to Garret about her being there. Did he seriously think his voice hadn't carried through the house? She hadn't made out every word, but the tone was clear. And the tension between them? Neither man would ever win an award for acting.

She blinked back ridiculous tears and plopped another plate on the counter beside the sink. It was stupid to be upset, but she couldn't help it. Who'd feel comfortable in a place where they knew they weren't welcome?

Garret cleared his throat from the doorway. "Sorry about

that, I had to take the call. And there you go again. Leave those alone, I'll put them in the dishwasher."

Ready to escape, Darcy nodded. "Okay. I think I'm going to go try calling my mom again."

"Maybe this time you'll have some luck."

She made her way through the house, glaring at Ethan's closed door as she entered Garret's room. *Please, Mom, be home.* She grabbed the phone from the base and punched in her mother's number. This time after two rings, the recorded voice told her to leave a message.

"Mom, it's me again. Where are you? Call me as soon as you get my messages." She left the number once more and hung up. Almost immediately the phone rang. Her mother? She grabbed the receiver. "Hello?"

A slight pause sounded on the other end. "Hello. You must be a friend of Ethan's."

A friend of Ethan's? Interesting assumption. "Um, would you like to talk to him?"

"Oh, no, I'm calling for Garret. This is Jocelyn."

The way she said her name she might as well have attached *his girlfriend* onto the end. The pancakes threatened to revolt. Of course Garret had a girlfriend. He hadn't mentioned her, but apparently even white knights lied by omission. Not that she'd expected Garret to tell her everything about his life, but she'd told him about Stephen. He couldn't have *mentioned* a girlfriend? No wonder Ethan had followed Garret into the bedroom to *talk.* "Hold on a moment while I get Garret for you."

Darcy returned to the kitchen, holding the phone in front of her, the mouthpiece covered by her hand. And even though she was disappointed, she didn't want to cause him any trouble. Garret had been nice to her, gone above and beyond to help her. Just because he hadn't mentioned a girlfriend, well, typical guy. Why had she expected anything else?

"Garret, it's for you. Someone named Jocelyn." And there it was. Garret's expression turned guarded right before her eyes. He excused himself and, phone in hand, walked out.

Darcy palmed her stomach and made a face, staring down at her belly. "Come on, Marcus, the snow's letting up. Let's finish the dishes, then go pack."

GARRET ENTERED his office and shut the door behind him, feeling more guilt than the situation warranted. Nothing had happened between him and Darcy. "Joss, I've been meaning to call you."

"Oh? Sorry. I haven't been home."

Concern overrode guilt. "Where are you if not home?"

"The gallery. After you dropped me off Friday night, I heard about how bad the storm was going to be and packed a bag. I thought it better to be snowed in here where I can get some work done."

"You could've come home with me."

"And still not gotten any work done?" She laughed softly. "Besides, Tobias came by yesterday."

"He did?"

"Surprised me, too. He stayed for hours and helped me get things organized. And you'll never guess why he stopped by."

"Why?"

"He, um, brought the permit I needed to open."

Crap! Garret made a fist and punched his thigh. "Joss, I'm sorry. I can't believe I forgot the permit. It completely slipped my mind." How many ways could he let this woman down?

"It's okay. I understand how busy you've been."

"That's no excuse."

"Hey, I'm a big girl. I know how things work. And I would've handled it myself if not for Tobias. I was floored by the gesture."

"Everything taken care of now?"

"Yes. Before he left we painted the far wall and hung some things. And we unpacked the displays for the pottery and assembled two of them. At this rate, I'll be able to open on time."

"Well, I'm glad you had help." He owed Tobe a day of golf, dinner. Something. "But I'm not crazy about you being there by yourself."

"I'm fine. So should I ask who Ethan's friend is? She's not another nurse from the hospital, is she? Didn't he learn his lesson about that after Daddy talked to him?"

"Ahh, actually she's not Ethan's friend." Garret inhaled and sighed. He couldn't put this off any longer. "Her name is Darcy Rhodes. I found her stranded by the side of the road Friday night. She was in labor."

"What?"

He told her the rest of the story. "I'm going to take her to a motel as soon as the roads are clear to travel. Until then I'm sleeping on the couch." He needed to clarify that, just in case Joss had doubts. "You're not upset because she's here, are you?"

"Of course not. Why would you ask that?"

"Just curious."

"It's sweet of you to look after her. Then again I'd expect nothing less. You've always liked playing hero."

Playing hero? "What do you mean?"

"Garret, you know you like fixing everything. Your family. The hospital. This is no different. Your second-child characteristics are very strong. It's very heroic and very admirable. That's a good thing."

Then why did she make it sound like a flaw? Because he hadn't remembered the permit? "Ethan thought you'd be upset."

"Yes, well, Ethan's experiences with women fighting over his attentions at the hospital would make him think that. But no, I'm not upset. For pity's sake, you just said she's how far along? If you'd left her by the side of the road, I'd have been horrified. I understand completely, Garret."

Her words rang with truth. She wasn't jealous, wasn't upset. In fact, it seemed as though Joss didn't mind at all. While he knew it was juvenile of him, it bothered him that she wasn't more troubled. He'd care plenty if Joss took another man home with her.

"Make sure you call the hotels before you leave this afternoon. There were so many power outages I heard the companies brought in extra crews and they're staying in the area."

"I'll do that."

"Good. Now I'd better go. I've got to call Daddy and check in before he calls out the National Guard. Take care of your guest and let me know how things go. Bye."

Just like that the phone clicked in his ear. No "I love you," no nothing. Just "Bye." Shouldn't she be the slightest bit jealous? Have asked more questions? Even Ethan had issued a brotherly warning about Darcy. Shouldn't his girlfriend be a little more curious?

He pressed the button on the phone and set it aside. He and Joss hadn't spent more than a few hours in each other's company the entire month. And most of that time they had spent was surrounded by his family and hers on Christmas day.

She trusts you. Be glad she's not upset. Then you'd be kissing up trying to make amends.

Garret got back to work and was nose deep reading a deposition when the phone rang. Ahh, here it was. Joss had thought about things and was calling him back. "Hello?"

"Garret, what the hell is going on?"

He stilled. Had Joss called her father with her complaints instead of voicing them to him? What kind of behavior was that? "Sir?"

"I just got a call from a board member who said there are ten-foot snowdrifts in the parking lot."

He switched mental gears. *That's* why Harry was calling? "There's a lot of snow out there, Harry. They were told to pile it on the back lots farthest from the entrances."

"I don't want it there at all!"

He gritted his teeth, his hand gripping the phone tight. "It has to go somewhere. When they scrape off the parking lot because *we* want the spaces clear, where are they supposed to put it? They can't put it back in the air." Did Harry not have any sense?

Harry hem-hawed and grumbled for a moment. "Fine, but if I go down there to check things out and there's a snow pile on any of the front lots, that team is history. Fired! Do you understand me?"

"Yessir." Garret rubbed his eyes and pinched the bridge of his nose. So much for Darcy's massage.

"Jocelyn called, too."

He braced himself.

"I don't approve of her staying in that rat-trap building, son. Why she had to set up shop in the old part of town, I'll never know."

"I, uh, think rent had a lot to do with it."

"It's a waste of time and money. You need to take her in hand, Garret, and the only way you're going to do it is if you put a ring on her finger. What are you waiting for?"

He smiled wearily. Yet another jab. Joss could've been more interested in him, but at least she hadn't told her father about Darcy. Ethan was right. If Harry got wind of Darcy's presence, however innocent, his temper would blow sky-high and the pressure would really be on. "She's fine. The security system is top-notch."

"If she had a home and family to take care of she wouldn't be going so far to entertain herself."

"She likes art, Harry, and she's good at what she does. You should be proud of her accomplishments."

Harry grumbled a bit longer about the hospital and Joss "wasting money." Garret hated that Harry couldn't see how great his daughter was. But the only way he would have was if she had been born a son.

"Go take care of business, Garret. I'm counting on you to keep maintenance and my daughter on track."

"Have a good day, Harry." Garret hung up and leaned his head against the office chair, palming his face with both hands and rubbing hard.

Harry would make Garret's life a living hell if he didn't propose to Joss soon. He loved her, cared for her. Could see himself spending the rest of his life with her. They had a solid, good relationship.

So what *was* he waiting for? Why did the idea of forever with Joss seem so unsatisfying? Why wasn't he eager to make their relationship permanent?

And maybe the fact that he avoided probing into the answers to those questions told him all he needed to know.

CHAPTER TWELVE

THE NEXT MORNING Toby entered Garret's office in a piss-poor mood. What kind of friend lusted after his best friend's soon-to-be fiancée? Not a good one, that's for sure.

"What's wrong with you?"

Garret sat in his standard position—phone glued to his ear with a pile of paper in front of him and pen in hand. A workaholic at his best.

Ignoring the phone since Garret was doing the same, Toby got right to the point. "Jocelyn needs help at the gallery. I think she's overwhelmed trying to get ready for the opening. Did you go help her this weekend?"

Garret tugged at his tie and shook his head. "No, I couldn't get out. The roads didn't open up until late last night."

Like any cop in the area would ticket a Tulane. "I made it okay. I did some stuff for her."

"She told me." Jerking to attention, Garret spoke into the phone. "I'm on hold for Benjamin Thomas. Yes, I would like to leave a message, thank you."

Toby approached Garret's desk and perused the surface, reaching out to grab a picture of Jocelyn before hesitating and picking up the one next to it. Garret's family was gathered around one of his mother's Christmas trees,

Jocelyn included. And right there in full color he saw the way Jocelyn and Garret complimented each other—her sleek blond up-do and insanely expensive-looking red dress the perfect foil for Garret's jet-black hair and suit. A debutante and one of Beauty's founding families' sons. Go figure.

"Hey, sorry about that." Garret hung up and settled back in his chair. "The board meeting was postponed and one guy's already in transit, so we're trying to track him down before he gets here and has a fit. And thanks for helping Joss out. Especially with the permit."

"I thought you'd taken care of it for her."

A disgusted expression flickered over Garret's face. "I was going to but I forgot about it. The mess with the buyout has me forgetting my own name. I owe you one."

"You don't owe me for the permit." If anything he owed Garret, seeing as how Toby had enjoyed the time with Jocelyn way more than he should have. "But you do owe me for not making our racquetball slot this morning. Where were you?"

Garret fiddled with the pen and cleared his throat. "I tried to call."

"I got the message when I got back to the locker room. Don't tell me your twenty-two-inch wheels couldn't take a little slush."

Making a face, Garret motioned for Toby to shut the door behind him.

He did as requested. "What's wrong?"

"I picked up a woman who wrecked Friday night. After the hospital released her, I drove her to the motels but they were full so...I took her home with me. She spent the weekend."

Toby stared at Garret, the urge to deck him so strong his

knuckles cracked. Garret picked up strangers when he had a woman like Jocelyn waiting for him to make the next move? "Did you *cheat* on her?" Toby barely got the words out. Not because he actually thought Garret *had* cheated on Jocelyn but because he was shocked to his core that, in a sick and twisted way, he wanted it to be true. Why? So he'd have a chance with Jocelyn?

Garret glared at him. "Of course not! It was nothing like that. And I've already talked to Joss about it, so stop being an ass."

He'd been Garret's friend for over half his life. Toby knew Garret wasn't like that. But if Garret had cheated on her— What? Toby would tell her? Be happy about it? What kind of friend was *that?*

"Who is she?"

"No one you know. She's just traveling through town."

"She could be anyone. One of those women who go home with a guy, drugs him then opens the door for the boyfriend so they can rob him before murdering the guy."

"You've been watching too much *Dateline.*"

"Ethan wasn't at the house the whole weekend. I saw him in the cafeteria when I went down to get something for Maria. Which means you—" he pointed a finger at Garret "—were at the house alone with this woman. What did you do with her for hours on end?"

"I did exactly what you gave me such a hard time about the other night—I worked. Darcy rested and hung out. She'd just been in an accident—and she's pregnant. Why is this such a big deal to you?"

"It's not." Toby raked his fingers through his hair and moved to the door of Garret's office. "You didn't say she was pregnant." Like that made a difference? Toby had to get out of there. Liking Jocelyn was one thing, admiring her from afar, fine. But this feeling was more than *like*. And Garret was his best friend.

"Tobe, nothing happened."

Maybe not, but a lot had happened in the past five minutes. Garret had to propose to Jocelyn soon. With his ring on her finger, she really *would* be off-limits—that was a boundary Toby wouldn't cross. Ever. But until that happened, he had to stay away from her—them—altogether. It was only right.

"What's with you today? You look ready to self-combust."

He gripped the knob, wishing he could rip it off and throw it. "I thought maybe you'd…done something you shouldn't have."

"I didn't."

A look flashed over Garret's face, though. Guilt? Toby turned and leaned against the door. "You sure?"

Garret avoided his gaze and stood to pace to the window. "Nothing happened."

"But?"

"But how do I know Joss is the one?" Garret glanced over his shoulder at him. "Don't go mentioning this to your mother or sister but— You nailed me for not giving Joss the ring, and this is why. How do I know she's the one?"

"You're having second thoughts? You think it's a mistake to marry Jocelyn?"

"Not a mistake. Joss would never be a mistake. She's as perfect as a woman can come but…"

Toby struggled to find the right words, the things guys were supposed to say in situations like this. Somehow they all sounded false in his head while he silently cheered getting an opportunity to pursue Jocelyn. "You've just got cold feet. It's hard for a guy to think that he's giving up the field." He knew Garret was a stand-up guy who cared for and honored the woman he was with. If Toby thought for a second that Garret used women when they were convenient, that his feelings for Jocelyn weren't sincere, Toby would consider her free for the chase. But Garret wasn't like that and Toby had to respect their relationship.

"You're right. Cold feet. What else could it be, right? I love her, why shouldn't I marry her?"

Toby opened the door. "I can't think of a single reason."

Not one he could say out loud, that is.

GARRET STARED out the window a long time after Toby left. Once his engagement to Joss became official, his mother and Joss's would go off the deep end planning the wedding. It would be the first in the family and sure to create a fuss. He'd be asked to discuss parties and seating arrangements, colors and flowers. Stuff he didn't have the time or desire to mess with. This was exactly why people eloped.

A soft knock sounded on his door. "Come in."

"Hey, what's going on?" Joss asked as she stepped into his office wearing a sleek blue pantsuit that matched her eyes. "I saw Tobias getting in one of the elevators. He looked angry."

Maybe he needed a little reminder of the spark between them. Maybe it had been so long since they'd had sex that he was forgetting the way they connected. He crossed the room and pulled her into his arms, lowering his head for a kiss. Their lips brushed, but when he tried to deepen the caress, she pulled away.

"Where's Daddy?"

"Not due in for another hour." He stepped close once more and kissed her cheek, nuzzled his way toward her mouth, but sighed when he felt her straight-arming him.

"Garret, come on."

"I'm trying to."

She shook her head at him and wouldn't meet his gaze. "You know how Daddy feels about public affection and appearances."

"We're in my office." He reached behind her and shut the door. "Private. Kiss me."

Glancing over her shoulder toward the door one last time, she obediently raised herself on tiptoe and pressed her mouth to his, her lips parting, but after a quick, chaste taste, she broke contact.

"How's the woman you rescued?"

Garret fought his frustration with her lack of response and tried not to think about precisely how long it had been. "She's fine. She's here in the hospital, actually. She has a follow-up this morning."

"Good."

Joss started to move away but he snuggled her deeper into the embrace. "Why don't I take an early lunch? We can lock the door—"

"And have Daddy barge in and interrupt us?"

Good point. "I'll take a break and come by the gallery instead."

"I have deliveries scheduled this afternoon."

"The house?"

"Mother's home and neither one of us has time to drive to your place."

He stared down at her. "Are you sure that's it?"

"What do you mean?"

"You won't stay with me because you feel uncomfortable at the house with Ethan, don't want to risk the gallery or here. Joss—"

She stiffened. "Don't get that look. I came by to say

hello, not to argue or have a quickie. Does everything always come have down to sex?"

"We're not talking about sex, we're talking about us."

"But you're making it about sex." She backed away from him.

"Joss—"

"Forget it. I'm PMSing, all right? I didn't want to be blunt, but I'm moody and there it is. I've got to go."

"Don't leave angry."

A knock sounded on the other side of the door. What now? "I want to finish this," he told her. "Don't leave. Whoever it is can wait."

"I don't want to be late." She opened the door so abruptly she surprised his father on the other side. Alan Tulane took a step back, his gaze moving between the two of them. "Am I interrupting?"

"No, not at all. Goodbye, Garret."

"Joss—"

She gave his father a strained smile before she headed out the door, the sharp click of her heels loud on the tiled floor.

His father's eyebrows rose. "Bad time?"

"Depends on the perspective."

"Could it have something to do with this woman I'm hearing you rescued?"

Garret sighed. "Maybe. Probably. Joss said she wasn't mad about her staying, but—"

"I wondered about that. I heard on the news that the hotels were overflowing. She spent the weekend at the house with you?"

"And Ethan. Don't look at me like that, Dad. She's almost eight months pregnant. What else was I supposed to do? I couldn't leave her in the lobby."

"No, I suppose not." Alan made a face. "Unfortunately, I've learned women can get upset over innocent situations, and I have a feeling you're going to have to make up for this with Joss. Send her some flowers, take her to dinner. A little romance will go a long way."

Garret nodded his agreement. "I'll do that. We've both been working a lot lately and haven't seen much of each other."

"Then that's probably it. She's feeling neglected. Everything else all right?"

"Yeah." He indicated the brown paper sack his father carried. "Are those my cookies Mom promised?"

His dad tossed the sack to him with a smile. "Don't eat them all at once," he said, like he always had when they were kids.

"I know." He pulled out one and consumed half of it in a single bite.

Chuckling, his father headed out. "I've got patients to see, much to your mother's upset."

"Still wanting you to retire, huh?"

"I'm considering cutting my time down. I don't have the energy I used to."

"Are you feeling okay?"

"Fine, fine. Oh, and son?"

Garret tucked the cookie into the side of his mouth. "What?"

"If the girl is trustworthy and safe—"

"She is," he said, knowing exactly who his father referred to. "I'd stake my life on it."

"That's high praise coming from you."

"It's true. She pitched in all weekend, trying to make up for us taking her in. The dad's out of the picture, too. She didn't say much about her finances but she's worried about getting her car fixed and getting settled in Indiana before she gives birth. I took it to mean things are tight."

A medical doctor for nearly forty years, his father sighed. "Always sad when that's the case. Expectant mothers shouldn't be stressed, especially so close to delivery. You call Nick?"

"Yeah." He saw the question in his father's eyes and wished things were different. "He sounded good. He said Matt was excited about the snow and they were getting ready to go sledding."

"He's a good dad."

"So are you."

His father shoved a hand into his pocket. "I've made more than my share of mistakes. Still, I'm sure Nick appreciates the business."

"Dad—"

"You're a good judge of character, Garret. Always have been. If you think this woman is safe and she needs a place to stay while her car is fixed, why don't you try your grandmother? Gram could probably use the company. It might also get Joss off your back—and your mother off mine when she hears what's going on."

That was the best idea he'd heard all day. Darcy would be safe; he wouldn't worry about her or wonder why he'd reacted so strongly to her. And neither Joss, Harry or his mother could complain. "I can't believe I didn't think of that. Great idea."

His father tapped his temple with a finger. "Marriage smarts. Don't forget to call the florist," he said as a parting shot.

Rounding the desk, Garret dialed the local florist and requested a bouquet be delivered that afternoon. After that he punched in the garage's number.

"Make it quick," Nick said. "Business is good at the moment."

"Hello to you, too, little brother. Did you have a chance to tow the VW I called about Saturday?"

"Just got it in. The driver did a number on the passenger side. The fender collapsed into the wheel, but I don't know yet if it damaged the axle."

"How long and how much?" He could practically see Nick running the numbers through his head. The guy was a whiz at math. "Depends on parts. If that piece is damaged, it'll be expensive regardless. She a friend of yours?"

"You could say that. Pregnant, too. She's alone and in between jobs."

Nick whistled softly. "That's rough." A pause came over the line. "Let me see what I can do. Maybe I can find some junker parts. If I can, that'll cut the cost down considerably. I won't put anything substandard on there, but it might take longer to get it since I'm not ordering it straight from the factory."

"I'd appreciate whatever you can do to help." Garret hesitated. He and Nick talked as though they were strangers or business acquaintances. Not family. He hated the distance between them. How had things deteriorated to this point? "Give me a call when you hear something?"

"Why don't I just contact her?"

"I, uh, don't have a number for her offhand."

"You can call and leave it with Sara when you get it."

So Nick wouldn't have to talk to him? "Okay, sure. Nick, listen, thanks for the help. Maybe we can get together for dinner sometime at the Grille?"

"Maybe. See you around."

Garret hung up the phone, angry with his parents and Nick for being so stubborn. And angry with himself for

letting anything come between family members. His dis-
agreement with Joss and his resentment toward Harry with
his frequent absences that tripled Garret's already overwhelming workload piled in along with Toby's censure to
create a mountain of dissatisfaction with his life. He just
needed a break.

His thoughts strayed to Darcy's massage Saturday night
and how relaxing it had been. Well, relaxing until his body
had gone into hyperdrive at her proximity and touch.

Had Darcy had her appointment? Was the baby okay?
He glanced at his watch, then stood. His guilt pricked at
him but he shrugged it off. His own girlfriend wasn't concerned about Darcy, so why should he worry about wanting
to see her again? That's what friends did.

CHAPTER THIRTEEN

DARCY SMOOTHED her shirt over her stomach and waited impatiently for Garret's brother to pick up the phone.

"This is Nick. Can I help you?"

She twisted the wire phone cord around her finger. "Hi, Nick, my name is Darcy Rhodes. I believe your brother Garret talked to you about my car? A Volkswagen? I was wondering if you could give me an estimate on the repair cost and timetable?"

"I just got off the phone with Garret. We're looking at two weeks or more. I'll have to get back with you on the estimate. I'm going to call around to see if I can get a better price. Do you have rental coverage?"

"No." She groaned, then winced at her manners. "Sorry, I didn't mean to sound ungrateful. It's just— Don't worry that I won't pay you or anything. I will, I promise. But if I'm going to be here that long waiting on my car to be repaired, I'll have to find a part-time job."

"What do you do?"

She hesitated, then told him and waited for the snarky comment that sometimes began with "Oh, yeah?" and ended with "Well, maybe for a little extra you'll massage my—"

"Oh, yeah?"

Don't say it!

"You're certified?"

The question stumped her. "Uh, yes. Yes, I am."

"I've been looking for a massage therapist for my gym. Maybe we could work out something that way. You interested?"

Another white knight? "Seriously? That would be—" She fumbled for a word to express her gratitude. "That would be great. Thank you." After everything Garret had told her about Nick, she had no qualms working for him. And Nick had already proven himself by not degrading her profession.

"I'll get back with you later today and we'll see if we can't work out a deal. Sound good?"

She closed her eyes in relief. The women in this town were crazy for not scarfing the Tulane men up. "It sounds perfect but— My cell phone is in my car and I'm not sure where I'll be later. Perhaps I could call you when I'm settled?"

"Great. Talk to you soon."

Darcy murmured goodbye and hung up, relieved and worried at the same time. Her back ached, and she pressed her hands against the base, rubbing.

"You okay?" Garret asked, walking toward her where she stood at a pay phone.

She'd asked about his schedule this morning on the way to the hospital, so she knew he'd ducked out of a series of meetings to come see her. "I'm fine. What are you doing here?"

Garret stopped in front of her and, the way it had every time he stood so near, her heart picked up its pace. He was so handsome. Especially when he looked at her with that expression of tender concern and— No, he wasn't interested. Not any more than the average guy would be interested in a very rounded, pregnant woman. Sex appeal? Yeah, right. Somehow she'd managed to stumble upon a genuinely nice man.

"The meeting ended early and the other one was canceled. I came to find you and let you know you're not going to a motel."

"I'm not?"

"No, come on. You can tell me what the doc said on the way."

Minutes later Darcy was seated in the Escalade beside Garret getting grilled on the ob-gyn's every word.

They left the hospital parking lot and drove around the outer belt of road surrounding the area. Lined with bare trees and snowbanks, the houses had been made commercial. Now they were quaint-looking doctor's offices, a law firm, three florists and a health food store.

And there it was again. That flash of a smile, the look, and—a firm nod? "Why are you nodding?"

"Because it makes me feel even stronger about you not staying alone while you're here."

"Dr. Clyde said I'm fine. I just need to take it easy for a few days and then I can get back to work. My blood pressure is up, but she thinks it'll go down once things are settled."

He turned and traveled down a quiet street. On the right was a large sign. *The Village.* Garret slowed and turned again just in front of it, waving at the guard at the gate. They passed small, two-family homes with one-car garages on either side of the houses, then several buildings two and three stories tall.

"You brought me to stay at a *nursing* home?"

Still going, Garret chuckled and parked in front of one

of the three-story buildings. "That's only one section. You're staying in the condos."

"Weren't those condos back there?"

"Those are townhomes. They require more maintenance. The condos are maintenance free."

"Garret, I appreciate the gesture, honestly, but this looks out of my price range. Would you mind taking me to the motel?"

Garret stretched one hand across the interior of the SUV and gave her palm a reassuring squeeze. "Trust me. This is better than any motel room, and it'll ease my mind knowing you're safe."

She stared into his dark, moss-colored eyes and found herself wishing the impossible. It was scary how easily he reassured her. She was aware of him on so many levels.

Overactive hormones. They'd brought more than one woman low over the years.

"Don't move. I'll grab your suitcase and come get you. It's still icy." Her hand tingled long seconds after he'd released it.

Inside the building, Garret removed his warm palm from her elbow and knocked on a door. Someone else was in there? Absurdly nervous, she tugged at her maternity blouse, fluffed her hair where her coat had crushed it and tried to hide her misgivings.

The door opened. "Garret." An older woman greeted them. Seventysomething, she had jet-black hair streaked with silver and cut in a sleek style. She wore black pants and a black sweater with dangling earrings Darcy knew had to be diamonds. The only other splash of color came in the intricately woven silver wrap the woman had tied loosely around her shoulders.

Darcy watched as Garret bent to drop a kiss on the woman's wrinkled cheek. Whoever she was she'd aged well.

"You look beautiful as always."

"And you're overcompensating for the fact that you work so much you never come see me even though I'm practically right next door."

Garret looked embarrassed by the chiding statement. "I'm here now, aren't I? And I brought the company I promised you."

Darcy bit back a gulping moan when the woman turned her shrewd gaze on her.

"You must be Darcy. Garret's told me all about you, dear."

She wished she could say the same. "It's nice to meet you…" She looked toward Garret for help.

Garret appeared boyish as he wrapped his arm around the woman's shoulders and grinned. "Darcy, allow me to introduce you to Gram, otherwise known as Rosetta Tulane, my grandmother. Gram, Darcy Rhodes."

He'd brought her to stay with his *grandmother?* She pasted a smile on her lips. "It's very nice to meet you."

The woman's gaze seemed to take her measure, hesitating only briefly on her stomach. "Likewise, dear. Why are we standing here? Come in out of the drafty hall."

The temperature in the building was anything but drafty. Garret prodded her inside with a hand at her back, and Darcy followed his grandmother into the condo, waiting while Garret brought in her suitcase.

"I'll get us something to drink. Garret, take Darcy's coat and make her comfortable."

"Yes, ma'am."

As soon as Rosetta was out of sight, Darcy rounded on him. "How could you?"

"How could I what?"

"Not *warn* me." Darcy made sure to keep her voice low. "Your grandmother? You should've told me I was going to meet her. I would've—" What?

He tilted his head to one side, amusement lighting his features. "You look fine. What does it matter?"

Good question. It shouldn't matter. It wasn't as though she was a girlfriend Garret was bringing home to introduce. That position had already been filled. She just hated that Garret's grandmother's first impression was of her homeless, jobless and pregnant. "I can't stay here, that's why. And why on earth would she even agree to let me?"

"Because I asked her. She knows your situation with the car and the storm, and she wants to help."

"She doesn't even know me. *You* don't know me, not really."

Garret grabbed her hands from where they rubbed her stomach in fast strokes. "I know enough. Now calm down or the contractions will start again. What's the problem?"

He was right so she tried to calm her nerves. His grandmother was probably a lovely woman, but she couldn't imagine staying with a stranger. This wasn't a snowstorm emergency. "I don't want to be any more trouble and— Do you not remember what I said about not accepting charity? A motel is fine."

"Nonsense, dear." Rosetta appeared behind them, a tray in her hands. "A woman so late in her pregnancy shouldn't be alone, especially if she's having problems. And it wouldn't be appropriate for you to continue staying with my bachelor grandsons," she told her pointedly. "This is a perfect solution until your car is repaired. You must think of the future. You'll need to provide for the baby, not spend your money on overpriced lodging. You'll be much more comfortable here, too."

Darcy realized Garret had stood there the entire time holding her hands in his, and she yanked them away, praying his grandmother hadn't noticed.

"I'm quite excited about your staying here. I lived at home when I went to college and I imagine this will be like having a roommate in one of those— Oh, what are they called?"

"A dorm, Gram. They're called dormitories."

"Yes, that." She set the tray on the coffee table, smoothing the ends of her silver wrap back into place when she settled herself on the couch. "Please don't be angry with my grandson, Darcy. I really do want to help. Things get a bit lonely here this time of year when so many of the residents go south to warmer areas. I have a spare bedroom to offer and insist you think about your little one. Perhaps you would consider your room and board payment for being my companion? I'd love the company."

Darcy glanced at Garret again, and found him awaiting her response. "Well…"

"Come sit down, dear. Let's get to know one another. Garret, you go to work and stop by again this evening. Darcy will have made her decision by then, and if she still wants to go to a motel you can take her. How does that sound for a compromise?"

Darcy knew there was little choice to be made. Garret had disrupted his schedule enough for her, and Rosetta had a point. Her options were to stay here with someone who seemed like a very nice woman, or a hotel she couldn't afford. She took in the homey interior of the condo, then studied Garret's and Rosetta's expressions. "That sounds good. Thank you."

Garret squeezed her shoulder on the way out the door, standing close and smelling heavenly. "Have fun," he murmured, his breath sending a shiver over her. "Just remember to rest. Gram can be a party animal."

PAIN STABBED through Jocelyn as quickly as the box cutter had sliced into her hand. She gasped and swore, dropping the utility knife and then jumping back when it clattered onto the floor at her feet.

"Careful, you don't want Daddy to hear you."

Pressing on the cut to try to dull the pain, she turned and saw Tobias weaving his way through the boxes and crates that had arrived today. Pottery and glassware carefully packed, a sculpture from Spain. All she was missing were the pieces by a Montana artist she desperately wanted to showcase. Why wouldn't the silly man call her back?

Tobias's gaze dropped to her hand. "What the—" He hurried around the last of the obstacles and grabbed a towel she'd been using to dust the pieces after she removed them from their packing. "Give me your hand."

"That's dirty."

"It's better than letting that bleed." He took the decision away from her and wrapped the towel around it, pressing firmly.

"What are you doing here?"

His jaw locked. "I came to look at some office space that's available and thought I'd drop by and see if your help arrived. Looks like I'm just in time."

"Office space? Why are you—"

"It's a long story."

Joss lifted her hand and placed it over his. "What happened?"

His scowl deepened. "I turned in my notice."

"What? You've been with Wellington, Wellington and Deere for years. How could you quit when you're up for a...? Oh, Tobias."

His hair hung over his forehead as he stared down at their tangled hands. "They gave the partnership to someone else." He smirked, but she could tell it was for show. One glance revealed his hurt, the anger rolling off him. He had every right to be angry, too.

Mr. Wellington was one of her father's friends, but she knew him well enough to know he played favorites and often made promises he had no intention of ever keeping, all in the name of business. "Are you looking for office space to open your own practice?"

"Maybe. I don't know. I'm going to check into things and I thought I might contact a headhunter."

She stiffened. "You can't leave town."

"Why not?"

"Because...your family would be upset. Garret, too. You had a bad day, Tobias, but you don't want to leave."

"What about you?"

Jocelyn swallowed, the sound audible in the otherwise quiet building. "What do you mean?"

"Would you care if I left?"

CHAPTER FOURTEEN

"OF COURSE." She tried, oh, how she tried, but his lion eyes wouldn't let her look away. "I know you're angry but—"

"Why?" he insisted.

"Garret—"

"I'm not talking about Garret. Would *you* care if I left?"

What did he expect her to say? "You're a good friend, Tobias. If you hadn't helped me with the permit, I wouldn't be able to open."

"In other words, I'm the go-to boy when Garret is busy."

"Of course not! I meant— What do you want me to say?" The words came out sharper than she'd intended.

"Nothing. I don't expect you to say anything. I was just wondering if you'd actually have an opinion of your own."

The cut on her hand hurt like crazy but Tobias's comment caused more pain. She had plenty of opinions, plenty of brains and— "I'd care. What kind of space are you looking for? There's an empty office above the gallery here."

Joss turned away and stooped to pick up the box cutter. Her father would be furious. Garret wouldn't care, of course, but her father—

"You want to rent me the space upstairs?" He sounded surprised. No wonder. She wasn't sure why she'd offered.

"I merely mentioned it's available," she corrected, trying to backpedal and not doing a good job of it. "It's sitting there and the rent would help meet my payment. Never mind. You obviously aren't interested."

"I'm interested."

She closed her eyes. "I should probably mention it to Garret before—"

"Can I see it?"

"Now?"

"Why mention me renting it if I don't like it? Show it to me, and then I'll help you unpack all of this and put it wherever it needs to go. I don't have anything else to do at the moment. Wellington told me to get the hell out so I packed up my stuff and left."

"You said you gave notice."

"I lied." He shoved his big hands into his pockets. "It sounded better than saying I told him where he could stick his partnership and got fired."

"Good for you." She swallowed, her heart beating a little too fast. Why should she care that Tobias told Wellington off? Why should she feel proud of him? But she did. Because she wanted to do the same with her father. Wanted to stand up to him and people like Mr. Wellington, prove their meanness and hatefulness would come back to haunt them because the people they disregarded would rise above their sad behavior. "Let me get the keys and a Band-Aid."

"I'll come with you."

Too aware of Tobias following her, she entered the office and grabbed the first-aid kit. While she sprayed the cut with antiseptic, he opened a Band-Aid. Did his hands tremble, just a little? Or was that hers? Finally the protective strip was in place and they were on their way upstairs in the old-fashioned elevator.

"So...have you talked to Garret today?"

"Earlier, yes." Why hadn't she noticed how slow the elevator was before? "Briefly." Finally the elevator settled into place. "Here we are." The third floor spread out in front of them. "The area is only about two thousand square feet. I doubt it's what you're looking for but—"

"It's perfect."

"Oh." She watched Tobias look around the area, his big body moving with surprising masculine grace. Strong lines, the proud tilt of his head. He'd be a hard man to sketch but she'd love to tackle the challenge. A bronze nude would—

She blinked, her heart beating out of rhythm. She had no business, no business at all, looking at Tobias like that. Why had she? She loved Garret. But the last few times they'd been together she'd left the encounters feeling frustrated and uneasy. It was silly, nothing more than stress. She loved Garret, and how many couples didn't share one iota of love between them? They could be happy, *would* be happy if he ever proposed. It was silly to let absurd, inconsequential things irritate her the way they seemed to be doing of late.

But she couldn't help it. She hated the way Garret rubbed his chin anytime he was sitting still, and his awful taste in movies that lacked even the most basic plot. More guns and action did not a blockbuster make. And art? How could anyone *not* appreciate art on some level?

"Are you planning on doing anything with it soon?" Tobias's gaze narrowed on her. "What's wrong? What were you thinking about?"

Her mind scrambled for an appropriate topic. "Rosetta's birthday party. It's coming up."

"Not for a month." Tobias moved close. "Jocelyn..." He

ran a hand over his face, and she knew he didn't want to say whatever was on his mind. "You and Garret are bound to have some rough spots. You just have to stick it out and be strong."

Stick it out? Be strong? Why did she always have to be the one to give in? Conform? What about Garret? Realizing Tobias knew nothing of her thoughts, and the topic probably had more to do with Garret's actions over the weekend, she sighed. "If this is about the pregnant woman he rescued, I'm not worried."

A muscle ticked in his jaw. "Sure about that? You looked worried."

"Tobias, he's Garret. He's just doing what he does best, what he's always done. One of the ladies from The Village stopped by this morning to congratulate me on snagging such a hero, and then proceeded to grill me on what I knew about the woman staying with Rosetta. Think he'd take a mistress there? I'm *not* worried."

As she spoke she felt, saw, his attention shift lower. To her mouth? A low throb unfurled in her stomach. "Garret and I are fine. We're both busy. Besides, I couldn't plan a wedding now, anyway."

"Some people think that's what wedding planners are for. And your mother and his would handle everything if you'd let them."

"I'd want to plan my own wedding."

"Does that mean you're going to turn Garret down if he asks?"

"No! Of course not. How could I after all this time?"

"You just said you didn't have time to get married. Surely you wouldn't do it simply because your father wants it to happen?"

She released a hollow laugh. Where was he going with

this? "I'd make time. And I'm sure everyone in town has heard Daddy's views on when and where and how Garret and I should get married, but I wouldn't do it unless I wanted to."

"Do you?"

"Any woman would be nuts not to want to marry Garret." That wasn't an answer and they both knew it. He watched her too closely, made her afraid to blink, to move, because if she did, he'd see the truth. The doubts. "Really, Tobias, why all the questions? Do you doubt my sincerity?"

"I've known you long enough to know you generally do what your father says."

"Not always. He didn't want me opening this gallery and I'm still doing it. And that's the second time you've indicated you *think* you know me better than you do. How is that possible when you've always disliked me and kept your distance as if you're afraid to be near me?"

Her comment spurred him to action. Jaw rigid as though he ground his teeth into nubs, Tobias took slow, deliberate steps toward her. Joss backed up, the trembling inside her growing.

"I'm not afraid to be near you. Why would you think that?"

"You always seem…uncomfortable around me."

He took in her quivering stance with a sweep of his gaze. "The same is true of you."

"Only because you glare at me all the time."

"With good reason. Maybe *I'm* uncomfortable because I don't like thinking of you as a sacrificial lamb willing to sell herself for a ring and a bank account to make Daddy happy."

"How *dare* you!"

"Admit it. Harry wants a toehold in the Tulane family, and you're his ticket. Am I wrong?"

Her back hit the wall. She swallowed at the abrupt end of her retreat and hated the expression of superiority on his face. "Is that why you're friends with Garret? Because *you're* using him?"

She knew in an instant she'd said the wrong thing, but it was too late to take the words back. Tobias closed the remaining distance between them, not stopping until he stood so close she could see the gold flecks in the burnt sienna in his eyes, such a beautiful amber. Garret was more handsome by far, but Tobias—

He braced a hand on the wall beside her head, his body blocking her escape. "He's going to ask you to marry him soon, and it kills me to think that you might say yes just to make your father happy."

The words came out an angry growl, and a sizzle of excitement raced down her spine. This was the man she'd seen in the teenager she'd known. Angry, driven to right injustices, determined to protect those he loved and valued as friends. *Passionate.* What would it be like to be the object of that passion?

Scalding heat rushed into her cheeks.

"You want to know what I think? I think you've avoided Garret for months because it's starting to dawn on you that there's more to life than always doing what your daddy says and being Garret's eye candy. First it was charity work and finishing your art degree. You even used Garret's work schedule as an excuse. Now it's the gallery."

"You don't know what you're talking about. Garret and I are both busy and my life is none of your business. Why do you care?"

"Because he's my friend. Because he never treated me

like I was second best and I'd hate to see him wind up in a second-rate marriage."

Staring at Tobias, she lost the ability to breathe.

Was it true? Heaven knew her father would overlook a lot of things, but he'd never forgive her if she ruined her future with Garret and the running of his precious hospital.

"What's wrong with me?"

"What do you mean?"

"I don't know what's *wrong* with me," she said again. "Garret is… He's wonderful. He's smart and kind and giving. So handsome." She held eye contact with him, pleading with him to understand. "But sometimes he drives me *crazy*," she admitted, her voice shaking. "He sings these godawful ditties that don't make sense, and he always has a pen in his hand that he won't stop *clicking*. And when he kisses me, it's like he's afraid I'm going to break. I *won't* break. I'm not some kind of china doll too expensive to play with and I want— I want *more!*"

She stared up at him, horrified at what she'd said. And to Garret's best friend? But Tobias listened to her every word. As if he heard her, *really heard her.*

Breathing hard, she dropped her gaze to his mouth and she didn't stop to think of the consequences. Desire singed her veins, the same desire reflected in his eyes. In the flaring of his nostrils when he realized her intent. But he didn't move away. No, as she flung herself against him and pressed her mouth over his, he groaned, but he didn't back away.

A second, that's all he gave her before he took control. Not a soft gentle kiss but one that rocked her head back with the force of it. She moaned when his tongue swept inside to stroke. It was rough and fast and just what she needed. She was bombarded from every direction. The taste and feel of him as he flattened her to the wall with his body, the ache in her breasts as they pressed against his chest. Through his open coat and clothes, her suit, she felt him and she liked it. The steely strength and heat, the rock-hard arousal she wanted to rub against.

All from a kiss? One that used teeth and tongue and created too much need, whip-fast pleasure that made her want to forget everything else. Her father and Garret and the ring she knew would be beautiful.

Lost, wanting to be taken wherever this led, wanting to *feel* one last time before having to face the numbness of regular, everyday life, she kissed him back, seeking, finding a white-hot passion guaranteed to send her soaring. But at what cost?

The thought brought painful clarity, instantaneous regret. The raw wound inside her opened up as though split by a bolt of lightning. She jerked out of Tobias's arms and slid sideways along the wall, watching as comprehension dawned on his face.

What had she done? Not only to herself but to Tobias? He was Garret's best *friend*. And Garret— *Oh, Garret.*

Glaring at her, Tobias spat out a curse so full of disgust with her and the situation she'd created, the boundary they'd crossed, she flinched and closed her eyes, didn't open them again until she heard him slam into the stairwell.

Her hand over her mouth, she leaned against the wall, rubbing to remove the feel of him, but only managing to taste him more. *Stupid* was messing up a good thing, kissing her boyfriend's best friend.

What goes on in that soft little head of yours, Jocelyn? Sometimes I think you're either too smart for your own good or too stupid to live.

Stupid was proving her father right.

TOBY BURST out of the gallery via the back door. *Where all the bottom feeders come and go in Debutante World*.

He shook his head and kept going, sludging through the deep snow and not giving a damn about what it did to his best suit.

Garret was going to kill him. It wasn't anything less than Toby deserved after what had just happened, but he'd already lost his job. He didn't want to lose his best bud in the same day. *Then why did you kiss her back?*

He growled out a curse and climbed into his Jeep, but after starting it he sat there a long moment, too angry to drive, too dangerous behind the wheel until he calmed down.

Jocelyn's passionate speech about not being a china doll had nearly destroyed what was left of his restraint, but the hold he'd managed to maintain unraveled the moment she'd crushed her lips to his. It was the desperation in her that had gotten to him. The way she'd gripped him, clung to him, the little moans in her throat because it had felt so right.

He hit his palm against the steering wheel. Screwed. He. Was. *Screwed.* No job. No best friend once Jocelyn went running to Garret, desperate to save her own neck in case he told Garret that she'd made the first move. Did it matter who'd crossed the line when all he'd wanted to do was have her up against the wall?

Maybe it *was* a good time to contact that headhunter, he thought, shoving the vehicle into gear. A job in Siberia might come in handy right now.

CHAPTER FIFTEEN

"I JUST WANTED to let you know I received the flowers. They're beautiful, Garret. Thank you."

A slow smile spread across his face at the sound of Joss's voice on the other end of the line. "I'm glad you like them. Joss, about today—"

"I'm *sorry*. Garret, I had no right to go off on you like that and—I love you. You know that, right?"

"I love you, too." He frowned at her tone, the thready, anxious pitch so unlike her. "Is something wrong?" He thought he heard a sniffle. "Joss?"

"Garret, I—I need to tell you something."

"What?" He listened carefully, but didn't hear anything that sounded like she was crying. It was winter, a sniffle could mean anything.

"I—I…" She inhaled shakily. "I'm going to Montana."

"What? Why? When?"

"Tomorrow morning. Early. An artist I want to showcase isn't returning my messages, so I've decided to fly out and talk to him in person."

"What about the gallery? Won't this throw you even more behind schedule?"

"A little."

"It's only one guy. Can't you find someone else to display?"

"No. I want this artwork. And things will move more quickly than I'd thought. It's just a matter of hiring some help. I'm sure I can get an art student to come work for a good recommendation. I won't be gone long. A few days at most."

"I'd love to see Montana. If I could get away, I'd come with you. We could spend a little quality time together."

"That would be nice, but I know now isn't a good time with the buyout, and this is a business trip. I won't be sightseeing."

"You'll be careful?"

"Yes. But I'd better go. I have a lot to get done before my flight in the morning.... Garret? I'm sorry about today. Really."

"We just had a spat, Joss. It's okay. When you get back, we'll go out to dinner and you can tell me all about your trip. We'll make a special date of it. Maybe go to Biltmore and spend the weekend."

"That sounds lovely. Good night, Garret. Don't work too hard while I'm gone, and remember I love you."

"I love you, too." Hanging up, Garret frowned down at the phone and sighed. Joss had sounded tired and stressed and upset, so maybe taking off and getting out of town for a few days would do her some good. And in the meantime?

He glanced at his watch and groaned. It was late; he was dead tired; and he still had to drop by Gram's and check on Darcy. How much longer could he go on like this? He could feel the candle slowly burning out, but too many people depended on him and he couldn't let them down. Grabbing his briefcase, he headed out the door.

Exactly twelve minutes later he shoved his thoughts about his job aside and drank in the sight of Darcy's smiling face on the other side of the condo's threshold. The mountainous tension inside him eased. "I take it things are going well?"

Her smile widened, her brown eyes warm and sparkling with welcome. "She's fantastic as you well know. Garret, it seems all I ever do is thank you, but thank you. Again."

"You're very welcome." He waited for her to step back before entering the condo and closing the door, noting immediately that Darcy's suitcase was no longer in sight. "You've unpacked?"

"Are you kidding? The moment I agreed to stay, Rosetta wheeled my suitcase down the hall herself."

He chuckled, able to picture the scene. "I knew she'd convince you." He looked around but neither saw nor heard Gram. "Where is she?"

"Taking a bath. She should be out soon." Darcy led the way to the living room and dropped onto the couch. "Have you had dinner? We made stew."

"I ate at my desk around six. I should've called but it's been one of those days. Are you tired? I could go and let you get some rest."

Darcy hugged a pillow to her side as though trying to disguise her stomach. The move was automatic and reeked of her being self-conscious around him, but he thought her beautiful in her pregnancy, not awkward or ungainly. He had to fight hard not to stare at her full breasts.

"Actually, Rosetta insisted I lie down this afternoon. I did it to humor her and wound up falling asleep for three hours."

"You're still recovering from your adventure. Spike must've needed more rest." He'd referred to the baby as Spike several times now, but for some reason it seemed to fit. Darcy's child would be feisty and independent—just like its mother.

"Maybe, but now I'm not sleepy at all. I've been sitting here playing solitaire." She raised an eyebrow and gave him a cheeky grin. "You're not a card player are you? Black-jack? Gin?"

A quick game until Gram emerged might be just the thing to help him relax before heading home. He needed something to take the edge off. "Black Jack."

She shuffled the cards with the expertise of a cardshark.

"I think I've been had."

A soft, sexy laugh was his answer.

"YOU CAN'T DO THIS. Jocelyn, have you lost your mind? You leave now and that woman will have Garret to herself. You'll be history."

Jocelyn stalked into her bathroom carrying the bag she'd retrieved from the closet and began packing her toiletries. Of all times for her father to feel the need to talk to her about Garret, why did it have to be now when she already felt so bad? "Daddy, please. We're fine. For pity's sake, she's *pregnant*."

"People are talking."

"Then let them talk! You know as well as I do that if the baby were his, he'd have married her already."

"You should never have started that monstrosity. It's ruining your relationship with Garret. Your future!"

That *monstrosity* would be her saving grace one day, that much she knew. "Oh? What am I supposed to do while Garret works eighty hour weeks? Sit home and twiddle my thumbs?"

"Your mother gave up this nonsense when she married me."

Which is why her mother was downstairs on her third glass of wine instead of in a studio creating. "Thank God

Garret would never ask me to do that." Her cell phone rang, and she left the bag to hurry and dig it out of her purse.

"Let it ring."

"I'm waiting on a business call."

"At this hour?"

"Overseas," she muttered, uncaring who it was so long as it ended the conversation. "Hello?"

"Garret hasn't come after me and tried to kill me. You didn't tell him?"

Tobias. Oh, what next? "Yes, I have been waiting on your call. Please hold for a moment." She pressed the phone to her chest. "I have to take this."

Her father glared at her. "You'll do well to remember what I said, Jocelyn." He stalked out of her bedroom and slammed the door behind him.

Joss took a deep breath and reluctantly raised the phone back to her ear. "What do you want?"

Toby made a tsking sound. "Using me to get rid of Daddy? Whatever should I think?"

"Tobias—"

"You didn't tell Garret."

What could she have said? *Oh, Garret, of course we're getting married when or if you ever ask, but I kissed your best friend and that's okay, right?*

"No, I didn't say anything. And I'm sorry. I don't know what came over me. But it's done and it won't happen again. I was upset and— You must think I'm a horrible person, but I regret it and I *am* sorry."

"I'm not."

"You don't mean that. I'd appreciate it if you'd keep the matter between us, too. Garret doesn't need to know. It would only hurt him."

Silence. What was he thinking? Would he tell Garret anyway? Had he already? No, no, Garret would've been upset when she'd talked to him.

"Have you seen him? Has he kissed you since then?"

She'd thought about going to say goodbye to Garret in person but couldn't bring herself to do it. She needed space, time to process and deal with whatever had made her behave the way she had.

It won't happen again. No, it wouldn't. Passion couldn't be trusted, couldn't be controlled, and she valued control. Needed it. This afternoon was an example of that and why it was all wrong. She'd allowed her body to lead her astray once, how could she have succumbed again?

No, she wanted a normal life with a normal man, not one who made her do things she'd *never* otherwise consider.

"Answer me, Jocelyn. Have you seen him? Did he kiss you?"

"That's none of your business. Good—"

"Don't hang up, we need to talk about this."

"No, we don't. What is there to say? I'm sorry. It shouldn't have happened. It was a *horrible mistake.*"

"Then why didn't it feel like one?"

She couldn't answer that, not even privately to herself. If she did, she feared her entire life would unravel. "It never happened. Do you hear me? It never happened and it will never happen again. Please, Tobias, don't tell Garret. I want to marry him. I love him. Don't ruin our future together because of one moment of insanity."

"Was it—"

"I have to go. Goodbye, Tobias."

CHAPTER SIXTEEN

GARRET WHISTLED as he waited outside Gram's condo. The sun was setting outside, and for the first time in ages he'd exited the hospital when it was technically still daylight.

The door opened and even though he hadn't been to The Village to visit much in at least two years, Gram didn't seem surprised to see him for the fourth night in a row. He and Darcy had played cards, watched movies, talked about everything from UFC Fighting to deep-sea fishing and helped with Bingo night downstairs. It was the most fun he'd had in years.

"Well, don't just stand there, come in," Gram ordered.

A burst of laughter filled the air and he frowned. *Nick?* Garret crossed the threshold and sure enough there sat Nick and his son, Matt, with Darcy around a table full of food.

"Garret, you're just in time." Darcy's cheeks colored with a pretty blush. "Are you hungry?" She scooted back her chair to stand.

"No, dear, you sit. I'll get my grandson a plate and something to drink." Gram pulled out the chair opposite Nick on her way to the kitchen.

"Thanks, Gram." Garret nodded at Nick and turned his attention to his nephew. "Hey, Matt. Wow, look at you. You've grown two feet since I saw you last."

"You saw me at Christmas."

"Has it been that long?"

Matt grinned, his mouth missing a few teeth. "Dad says I'm the bottomless pit. Maybe that's why." A third-grader, Matt had taken a growing spell this past year and no longer looked like a little kid. He was tall for his age, lanky, growing into that awkward stage. Something all the boys in the family had suffered through.

He felt bad that Matt was growing up and none of them were getting to see it happen.

Garret seated himself and smiled at Darcy. "What's going on here?"

Darcy fussed with her napkin and unleashed one of her amazing smiles on Nick. "Your brother came by so we could celebrate our deal. He finished the estimate on the repairs and he's going to let me work off the cost at the gym. I'm his temporary massage therapist. Isn't that sweet of him?"

Nick shrugged like it wasn't a big deal. "I've been looking for someone and already had a massage table on order. This benefits us both."

Darcy turned her cocoa eyes back to Garret, excitement etched on her features, and his gut pinched in response. How could he ever have thought she wasn't beautiful?

"It's more than that. He's already talked to some of his members and lined up clients for me. I start Saturday."

Jerking into the present, he frowned. "Are you sure you're up for it?"

"I'm fine."

"I'll keep an eye on her," Nick promised. "She won't overdo it." He settled back in his chair and palmed his coffee cup, raising it to his lips to drink.

Garret knew he ought to be reassured by Nick's words,

but was Nick helping Darcy to be nice—or because he was interested in her? And what if he *was?*

Garret rubbed his chin. The fatigue was getting to him. He hadn't slept more than a few hours each night since Darcy left. Maybe he should get a massage? Help her out financially? Remembering what happened last time, he quickly decided against it.

"Something wrong?" Nick asked.

Gram returned from the kitchen. "Matt, be a dear and carry in the dessert for us?"

"Yes, ma'am." The kid took off like a shot, eager to please. "Gram, you made my favorite!" Matt returned with a broad smile on his face, the heaping plate of chocolate chip cookies balanced precariously in his hands. "Can I take some and go watch cartoons since I already ate?"

"Yes, sweetheart. Just take a napkin and try not to spill, all right?"

"Yes, ma'am."

"I didn't expect to see you tonight, Garret. Joss hasn't made it home yet?"

He glanced at Darcy, noticed her gaze focused on her plate. "She'll be back tomorrow afternoon. Her persistence paid off. She handpicked some pieces and is bringing them with her."

There was a lull in the conversation and he glanced at Nick, found his brother's gaze on Darcy. Not good. With her belly hidden and the light shining through the window behind her, it was all too easy to find Darcy attractive. Any man would.

A jab of anger slid through him that smacked of jealousy. Nick and Darcy might understand each other because of the similarities in their lives, but Nick needed to keep

his distance. She didn't need the complication of a temporary romance at the moment.

Of course, she was strong enough to take care of
herself—she'd proven it time and again. So why was he
worried about Nick? Why was he feeling so protective?

Over the next half hour he didn't come up with any
answers. The talk continued and eventually made its way
down memory lane, thanks to Darcy asking questions
about what it was like growing up in a large family. He and
Nick talked about the good times they'd had, keeping
Darcy and Gram laughing while they told on themselves
and relived the pranks they'd pulled. It took him a while
to realize Darcy worded her questions so that he and Nick
remembered the good times and not the arguments over
school and the split Nick had made from the family.

"I need more coffee. I'll be right back." Gram excused
herself, wiping tears of laughter from her eyes, but Garret
saw her linger at the door and smile in Darcy's direction.
The sight was a punch to his gut. Gram loved Joss, but he'd
never once seen her look at Joss that way.

"So, Darcy, you all settled in?" Nick asked.

"Yes, I am. The spare bedroom is beautiful, and
Rosetta's—"

"Somebody's cell phone is ringing!" Matt called from
the other room.

Darcy gasped. "That must be my mom. Excuse me."

And that's when he knew he was in deep.

He was protective because after knowing her only a
week, he hated the thought of her leaving.

IN THE BEDROOM Darcy grabbed the phone from the bedside
table where it charged. "Hello?"

"Darcy? Baby, are you all right?"

Relief poured through her. "I'm fine now. Mom, where have you been? I've left messages every day."

"Well—" her mother laughed "—I didn't check them because we took a little vacation to Vegas."

We? She knew that tone. "Mom, I told you I was on my way. Please tell me you didn't—"

"Things happen fast around here. You know that."

"What things? Mom, what did you do?"

"I got married! Now, I know what you're thinkin', but he's a good man, Darcy. It's sudden, but I think he's got sticking power."

For how long? Before she could ask, she heard the distinct sound of her mother lighting up a cigarette. "I thought you quit."

"I did, but Arnie smokes, too, and I got started back. You know how it is."

"Mom, you know how I was with my allergies as a kid. It won't be good for the baby to be around smoke." A long pause sounded on the other end and with every second that went by, Darcy's dread grew. "Mom? You are still planning on helping me with the baby, aren't you?"

"Darcy, I was, honest. But I've been thinking about that a lot and I've decided you can't expect me to pitch in and take care of your problems."

Take care of her *problems?* "Mom, please. Don't do this. I only asked you to help until I could get back on my feet. Until I can find a job and an apartment. Day care I can trust. I make good money, it won't take long."

"You don't know that. We're not the big city here and it could take a while before you find something. Which made me think— Darcy, you're plenty old enough to handle things on your own."

"But right after the baby is born—"

"You'll do fine. Why, women used to have babies and go out into the fields to work. Some still do. Having a baby is nothing these days. I'm sorry, honey, but I've changed my mind."

"Mom, you said you would help me. You promised. I packed up and *moved*."

"Don't take that tone with me. Beggars are beggars and I've got enough stacked against me without you being here with a squalling brat and— Look, don't take this personal and get all upset like you always do, but I never told Arnie I had a daughter, much less that I'm going to be a *grand*-mother, and I'm certainly not going to tell him now that we're married."

Hurt cut deep. She'd always known her mother lacked maternal warmth and depth, but to pretend she didn't even *exist?*

"Arnie's a bit younger than me, but we get along fine. If you come home and move in, well, I don't think a new marriage should have that much stress."

A bit younger? "How old is he?"

"Now, Darcy—"

"How old, Mom?"

"Twenty-eight."

Her mouth dropped. "He's only three years older than me?"

"Now do you understand? You'll do fine on your own, you always have. See if the daddy'll pay you to keep the baby away from him. Maybe then you could hire a nurse or something if you need one right after."

Keep the baby away. Like her mother wanted her to *stay away.* "I don't want Stephen's money. I never did."

Her mother snorted. "If you had his money now, you wouldn't be in this mess, would you? Darcy, I don't want to fight. As soon as you get your car fixed, you let me know where you wind up. Send me a picture of the baby at work. Not at home, okay? Don't forget and mess this up for me. I've got a good thing this time. Oh, I hear Arnie pulling in. Don't be mad, baby. Mama loves you."

The phone clicked in her ear. Darcy flipped the cell phone closed and tossed it aside. Then grabbed the doll she'd set on the bedside table and flung it to the floor. Glaring at its twisted appearance, she laid gentle hands on her stomach. "Mama loves you," she whispered, hugging her baby. A knot formed in her throat, too big to wish away.

Using her toe, she rolled the doll over so she could see its face, remembering when she thought her mother had given her the doll to show her how much she loved her. What a joke. Her mother didn't feel anything for her. "Don't worry. I'll protect you and take care of you, hold you when you're scared and always help you because that's what mommies are supposed to do. Don't be scared, because we're going to be all right. I'm not her. I'm not *her.*"

GARRET AVOIDED his brother's suspicious expression after Darcy left the room. He'd seen a lot of pregnant women come and go at the hospital, but Darcy was surprisingly graceful, and his gaze had lingered on her a lot longer than it should've. If not for the mound of her stomach, she wouldn't even look pregnant. And if she wasn't? Would that make anything easier?

"The baby yours?"

His attention snapped to Nick. "No."

"You sure?" Nick lowered his voice. "Because the way you're looking at her makes it seem like a possibility."

Garret clenched his jaw. It was one thing to have doubts

about Joss and their relationship, but tossing Darcy—and her unborn child—into the mix was just insane. "I feel bad for her. She's going through a hard time right now, and needs a friend."

"That may be, but you weren't looking at her like she's a friend."

Garret shifted in his chair. "You're seeing things. She's pregnant, or didn't you notice?"

"She's still a pretty woman. Not to mention smart and funny." Nick smirked. "And there are ways around a pregnant belly."

The comment sent images through his head and his body reacted in an instant. He realized then and there the baby wasn't a problem for him. What kind of man held an innocent baby at fault for his or her conception? Darcy would've stuck by the baby's dad if he'd been man enough to take on the responsibility.

"What are we talking about now?" Gram asked as she returned from the kitchen, coffeepot in hand. "Where's Darcy?"

"She got a call on her cell. She thought it might be her mother," Nick informed her.

"Oh, I hope so. The poor dear. She's tried all week to act like she wasn't worried, but I could tell she was. It's obvious she doesn't have the family support the two of you grew up with." She shook her head. "The ones who have it always seem to take it for granted."

Nick scowled at the gentle reprimand and stared at the table, a muscle ticking in his jaw.

Garret grabbed a cookie from the plate and stood, his body well under control thanks to Gram's appearance. "I'm going to go spend some time with Matt, then check on Darcy."

In the living room Matt had zoned out in front of the television watching *SpongeBob SquarePants.* Glancing over his shoulder to make sure Nick and Gram weren't behind him, he gave Matt the cookie, then continued on down the hall toward the bedrooms. The door across from Gram's was open, a three-inch crack allowing him to hear Darcy's choked sobs.

His heart thudded in his chest as he approached. "Darcy?"

She snapped to attention and wiped her face with trembling hands. He crossed the room, stepping over an expensive-looking doll dressed in Victorian-era garb and sporting a head full of curls similar to Darcy's. He shoved the cell phone aside to sit on the bed beside her, pulling her against his chest and ignoring her stiff posture.

"Shh." He pressed a kiss to her hair, rubbed his hands up and down her back. "Whatever it is, it'll be fine. Remember what Dr. Clyde said. You don't want to upset Spike, right?"

A muffled noise escaped her—a laugh?—before she buried her face deeper. The scent of her hair reminded him of orange groves and flowers, the feel of it soft in his hands. "What happened? Tell me, sweetheart." Her voice emerged muffled against his chest and he couldn't make out her words. "What?"

"She got married. To husband number *f-four.* She was in Vegas and that's why she d-didn't call me back." Her fingers gripped his shirt, the ragged sound of her voice tearing at his insides. "She *promised* me. She said she'd help with the baby and let me stay with her while I got on my feet. She promised."

He cursed the woman who'd treat her daughter this way.

Darcy was on her own? Completely? What kind of person did that? What kind of mother?

"He doesn't even know we exist. She didn't tell him because she doesn't want us. Doesn't want me. She never did."

Biting back a curse, he pressed a kiss to her temple and cradled her closer, Gram's comment about family support repeating in his head. "Darcy—"

"It was stupid of me."

"What was, sweetheart?"

"Believing in her. I knew better. I *know* better. All my life she's tossed me aside any time a man came around. Why did I think she'd put us first now? Why did I think I could depend on her?"

Because she saw the good in people, not the bad. That insight into Darcy's personality came easily. She'd had a rough childhood from the sound of it, but Darcy still believed in the good. He gently wiped away the tears. "You'll be okay. You're not alone, Darcy." Her gaze shifted to the doll lying on the floor and he wondered at the connection. He bent and picked it up. "Who's this?"

Darcy glared at the doll but made no move to take her from him. "Miss Potts. My mom gave her to me when I was little."

"Looks like you've taken good care of her." Whether she'd thrown the fragile, expensive-looking doll or it fell off the bed, it was no worse for wear. Darcy on the other hand…

"Now you know why I didn't say much when we talked about family. My family isn't like yours."

Darcy's lashes were spiky, her nose red, but she was beautiful, her eyes liquid pools of glazed brown. Her full mouth turned down at the corners, trembling. He wanted to press a kiss there to still them, wanted to make her smile. Do something to ease the pain she was feeling.

"She gave me the doll for my birthday." A rough laugh escaped her chest, thick and throaty. "We didn't have a lot of money and I'd begged for Miss Potts forever. Mom always said no."

He didn't like the tone she used. "What happened?"

"I came home from school and let myself into the house. But hours passed and she didn't come home. Not until my birthday the next day. Then there she was, all smiles and apologies. She admitted she'd forgotten to call someone to come watch me because she was…having too much fun partying with a guy. I wouldn't have wanted her to stop having a good time, would I?"

Dear God. How could someone be so reckless? So un-caring about their own flesh and blood? "How old were you?"

"Eight." A bitter smile flashed. "A self-sufficient eight. There was food in the house. Cereal and juice. I didn't starve and I was okay, but—I was alone. My mom…she had a lot of boyfriends. She made it easy for them. Anyway, I was afraid if they knew I was there alone, if I left the lights on… I kept a flashlight on under the blankets. Then there she was, carrying the stupid doll like it made up for what she'd done. She said it was to keep me company next time because ob-viously I was a big girl and didn't need to be watched."

He rested his chin on her head, holding her close be-cause he couldn't make himself let go. "She didn't know what a treasure she had."

Darcy inhaled raggedly. "*I'm* the gatekeeper in my family, Garret. The one who always took care of her when the guys dumped her and moved on. She said it was my fault because they didn't want another man's kid."

"Not all men are like that." He wasn't.

"I knew I had to get out of there. If I didn't get away from her I'd never be my own person. I couldn't deal with her life and have the one I wanted for myself. It was hard to break ties, but I did it. I went to school, moved wherever the job paid best. Then I found out I was pregnant and I didn't want my baby to be completely alone. I thought my mom had changed. She said she had. It just makes me so angry." Her hand fisted in his shirt. "I *believed* her."

"You wanted your baby to know its grandmother. You left the father because he didn't deserve you or Spike. Those are good traits, Darcy, not bad. You're fighting to do what's right, and no one can fault that."

She sniffled, a husky chuckle emerging from her throat. "Another pep talk. You need to charge for those. Oh, look at you." She plucked at his tear-soaked shirt. "I'm sorry for crying all over you. You poor guy, it's hard being my friend, isn't it?"

CHAPTER SEVENTEEN

"NOT AT ALL." Garret tucked a curl behind her ear. "I like being your friend."

"Thank you. Me, too." She blinked rapidly. "You're a good man, Garret."

"Sweetheart, I don't want to put more pressure on you, but what are you going to do now?"

She inhaled a shuddering breath. "I'm not sure, but I'll be fine. It's good that I have to do this on my own. I have to get used to being a single mom, and there's nothing like jumping in with both feet, right? As soon as my car is fixed I'll figure something out. We'll be fine, just the two of us."

He smoothed his hand over her hair. "I don't doubt you will, but it's okay to admit you need help sometimes, that you need someone to lean on. You've got that in me, okay?"

"Do you ever feel that way?"

Maybe it was the moment, maybe it was the way she looked at him. Whatever it was, he had to answer honestly. "Yeah, I do." He smoothed his thumb over her cheek, his gaze dropping to follow the movement. Her lips were parted, moist, and he found himself unable to look away, unable to stop the tide.

Garret lowered his head, hesitating a scant millimeter from her lips. Warnings clanged in his head, but he breathed her in, so close but not touching, not kissing. So close that with every breath, every tremble of her lips, he wanted more.

A small, muffled moan escaped her throat when he finally closed the distance and brushed her mouth with his, softly, barely a kiss at all. But his every muscle tensed at the touch, molten lava firing his veins until his whole body burned.

He sealed his lips over hers and suppressed a groan. Darcy tasted hot and sweet, like Gram's chocolate chip cookies and tears and woman. He filled his hands with her soft curly hair, tilted her head and deepened the caress, unable to stop, each nudge of their tongues a delicious slip and glide.

"I have to say goodbye to Darcy first!" Matt's running footsteps thundered down the hall.

Garret practically launched himself from the bed. Darcy gasped and covered her mouth with her fingertips and a scant second passed before Matt barreled into the bedroom.

"Darcy, we're leaving."

Darcy remained on the bed, her face blazing with color, but thankfully Matt didn't seem to notice—or comment on Garret standing in the corner with a death grip on the dresser's rounded edge.

"Will I see you at the gym Saturday?"

"Of course." She cleared her throat. "Absolutely. I'll be there, just like your dad and I discussed."

Watching the interaction from the sidelines, Garret attempted to harness the explosion of desire and was startled when the boy threw himself at Darcy and gave her a hug. Matt was usually reserved and shy, not one for making contact. Had he ever hugged Joss?

"Will you play Alien Racers with me?"

Darcy nodded, returning the embrace. "I sure will,

sweetie. You'd better practice, though, because I got really good playing it on my breaks at the hotel."

Matt released her with a grin. "You won't beat me."

"Matt?" Nick appeared in the doorway.

He hadn't heard his brother walk down the hall or else he'd have headed Nick off. One look at Darcy's face and his brother would know.

Garret watched, the knot in his gut growing, as Nick took in the scene. Darcy on the bed, a fiery blush remaining on her cheeks, and unable to make eye contact, Garret standing as far away from Darcy as possible, as if—

They were guilty of something.

He met Nick's gaze briefly and knew that while Nick was curious about whatever was going on—something Garret would like to know himself—his brother was the last one in the family who'd judge.

"Matt, come on, we've got to go. Darcy, I'll see you Saturday."

"Um, yes. Thanks for getting my portable table out of the car and bringing it to me. I have three appointments here over the weekend."

Nick nodded. "You're on a roll. You'll earn the money in no time. I'll pick you up about twenty to ten."

Darcy smiled at Nick in thanks, and Garret's gut tightened in response. He didn't want her smiling at Nick. And he didn't have the right to want anything where she was concerned.

"Thank you. I appreciate it."

Garret ran a hand over his head and squeezed the muscles in his neck. Protective was sounding damn possessive.

"Matt?"

"I'm coming." The boy shuffled off with one last wave to Darcy.

Garret stared at his feet. The ability to speak and say whatever needed to be said, the gift he'd relied on his whole life, didn't appear. He had nothing but a truckload of guilt and self-recriminations. Emotions he couldn't begin to name. Joss deserved better than him kissing another woman. Wanting another woman. He'd always despised men who strung women along, used them, uncaring of their feelings. He wasn't like that. People expected more of him. He expected more of himself.

"It's okay, Garret."

He looked up to see Darcy watching him, her gaze much too astute.

"Believe me, I understand how complicated this is."

"I didn't mean to take advantage of your upset. That wasn't my intent."

A sad smile pulled at her lips. "I know. We're both stressed and feeling… I don't know. It's no big deal, just a kiss."

"You're sure? You're okay?"

Her chin raised, but her lashes lowered. "I'm fine."

She didn't look fine. She looked unhappy and dazed. And he felt like the lowest of the low because he had no right to make things worse. "I should go, too. Darcy, I'm sorry. That shouldn't have happened."

JOSS EMITTED a surprised shriek before clamping her hands over her mouth, staring in horror-filled shock at the sight that greeted her on the other side of her bedroom window. She'd tossed the drapes back to investigate a noise and there he was. Tobias glared at her, a hundred-eighty pounds of furious man. She glared right back. "What are you *doing?*"

"Open up."

She shook her head firmly back and forth.

"Do it or I'll go knock on the front door."

She opened the window a scant inch. "Go away. I don't want to talk to you." She tried to slam the window closed, but Tobias's hand shot out and kept that from happening. He raised the window higher, inserting one leg into her bedroom, then the other. "No, no. Get out. I said go away, not come in. I don't want to talk to you."

"Fine. I'll leave." Tobias headed toward her bedroom door.

"Stop! Wait!" She ran after him and flung herself in front of the door, glowering at him.

"Make up your mind, princess."

"Go out through the window."

"Not until we talk."

"I have nothing to say to you."

"Why did you take off? I've been through hell this week wondering what was going down with you."

"I—" she started to automatically say *I'm sorry* but refused to apologize again "—had a business trip."

"Uh-huh. You left because of what happened."

"Your ego is huge, you know that? I went to buy art-work."

"And to escape the fallout if I told Garret about what you did?"

"You wouldn't do that."

"What makes you so sure?"

She stared into his lion eyes and knew they both felt the same in one aspect if nothing else. "You wouldn't hurt him that way. Just like I wouldn't."

"We kissed—"

"And I said I was sorry. Just *leave it be.*"

"I can't. I can't, and do you want to know why?"

No.

"Your tongue was in my mouth and you kept inching your leg higher, like you wanted to wrap it around my waist." He eyed the paneled wood behind her. "Ever done it standing up?"

"Stop it."

"The idea getting to you? Join the club. I've thought of nothing else since that day."

She didn't comment. She wouldn't. He could talk all he wanted and when he was through, he'd leave. And if he so much as put a finger on her she'd scream.

With pleasure?

"How can you marry him knowing you want me?"

Her face burned. "It was a very *brief* moment in time. A mistake. And I'll marry him because I care for him and it's the right thing to do. This conversation isn't right. Nothing about this is *right.*"

"You weren't thinking it was wrong when you kissed me."

"Would you stop saying that?" She slid sideways against the door and crossed the bedroom to get away from him but he followed her. "You're supposed to be his best friend. Where's your loyalty? Your honor toward Garret?"

"I guess I'm thinking that if you're kissing me, maybe this marriage isn't such a great idea. *There's* my loyalty. Maybe I'm doing my part to keep you both from making a mistake. He hasn't asked you, and you haven't been pressuring him to hurry up. That doesn't spell trouble to you? There's still time to fix this."

"Fix it? How could we possibly fix what we did?"

"By doing it again? If it was a fluke or—what did you call it? A mistake? Then we'll feel nothing and there's no reason for either one of us to be worried. Let's try it and see."

"That's ridiculous." She tried to put a wing chair between them, but Tobias snagged her arm and wouldn't let go. Still, he didn't attempt to follow through on his threat to kiss her again. "Let go." She yanked her arm free, knowing full well if he'd wanted to hold on to her, he could have.

"Is that what you want? Him? Take me out of the equation. If things were all right between the two of you, you wouldn't have kissed another guy. Admit it. Who's to say you're not going to go kissing someone else?"

"You know I'm not like that."

"How's that when you did it to me, his very best friend?" Tobias tilted his shaggy head to one side. "That mean desire got the best of you?" He looked extremely pleased by the thought.

"It shouldn't have happened. I regret it."

Tobias crossed his arms over his chest, his gaze narrowed on her thoughtfully. "Are you sure you regret it? That kind of passion doesn't happen every day."

She struggled to focus, her hands fisting even though she'd never struck another living soul in her life. "That kind of passion leads nowhere and I won't be a part of it again." The moment the words were out of her mouth she knew she'd said too much.

"This is getting interesting. Again, huh? Who was he?"

"Leave. Now."

Once more he stopped her and kept her close. "Does Garret know about the guy or are you keeping him a secret, too?"

"It was a long time ago."

"He doesn't know, then."

"He knows I was with someone."

"What happened?"

"I fell in lust and thought it was love. End of story. Surprised?"

"That you could experience lust? No, you're a very passionate woman."

Garret didn't think so. She saw it in his eyes whenever they were together. Sometimes she'd been able to get into things and enjoy the closeness, but lately…

Tobias stepped forward, lifted his hand and smoothed his knuckles along her cheek. "Jocelyn? What are you afraid of? Are you afraid of feeling too much? Is that it?"

"I'm *not* discussing this with you."

"Why not? Obviously you can't discuss it with Garret. Tell me."

"Fine. You want to know? I don't trust blazing, gotta-have-you-now desire. It's pure lust and it means next to nothing. I had that and I got burned."

"How?"

"He used me for money and when I couldn't give him any more to fund his art, he left. End of story. Are you happy now?"

A muscle ticked in his jaw. "So you're going to marry Garret because he *doesn't* make you burn?"

Why wouldn't he just shut up?

"I don't like the thought of you getting hurt because some ass used you and abused you. But I'm not him. I don't want your money, and I'm man enough to know something special when I see it. When I *feel* it. That kiss—"

"Was nothing. Just like I had before. What about the guilt and pain we'd feel? What about decency? What about Garret?"

"He's a man, not a little boy. The question is, are you a woman or a little girl playing at being an adult? You only get one life, Jocelyn. You either live it or you drag yourself through it. I love Garret like a brother, but the two of you are not married. You're not even engaged. You have time to fix the mistake by ending this before it gets worse."

"You don't care that it would hurt him? Humiliate him? We've been together three *years*."

"Garret is going to hurt a lot worse when you finally realize second best isn't good enough. You think he won't feel that? Living with you every day? Men aren't as stupid as women think."

"Garret and I are fine."

"Keep lyin' to yourself, honey. But we both know differently, don't we?" His yellow-gold eyes were hooded, darkened by thoughts she could easily read. Why? Why did she feel this way toward Garret's friend? Toward *anyone* else? Garret had supported her dreams, been faithful and kind. Loyal. He deserved more than to have her behaving like this or having this discussion at all.

She could be happy with Garret. Would be happier if Tobias— What? Stayed away? So now she was going to turn into her father? "Sex isn't everything. The grass isn't always greener on the other side. There are a million and one reasons why we'd never work. Even if Garret and I split up, I wouldn't be comfortable dating his best friend. What kind of woman does that?" Her father would never approve.

You're nearly thirty years old; why do you need Daddy's approval?

"Garret and I make a wonderful couple. We're friends. We complement each other very well, what with our backgrounds and—" She broke off abruptly, not wanting to hurt Tobias but managing to anyway. She saw it in his eyes, the sudden stillness in him.

"Your backgrounds and upbringing in Beauty's elite?" His face turned into a mask of disdain. "I'm just the maid's son, is that it? Someone to play around with and tease when you're bored but not to be taken seriously?"

"Tobias, please, I didn't mean it like that. I meant—"

"I know which damn fork to use, Jocelyn." He smirked. "One of the perks of being the housekeeper's son is that you pick up on things like that."

"I'm sorry. I didn't mean to insult you."

Tobias swung his leg over the sill, pausing long enough to say, "You didn't. You insult yourself by not seeing what you could have if you were brave enough to stand up to your old man and Garret instead of floating along afraid of your own shadow."

He was gone in a flash. One minute he sat on the edge of the sill and the next she saw him slip over the side of the roof out of sight.

Her shoulders sagged. Shaken, she closed the window and locked it. Pulled the drapes so that her room looked the same as it had before he'd arrived. He was crazy. Everything Tobias had said was just crazy. *Garret* was her future.

Not his best friend.

CHAPTER EIGHTEEN

DR. CLYDE FROWNED at Darcy after looking over the contents of the file folder in her hand. "Darcy, I'd hoped things would change since I saw you last, but I'm afraid I'm going to have to get strict here and put my foot down. You are not to travel alone, much less finish this move by yourself." The woman pulled off her reading glasses and gave Darcy a regretful stare. "Your blood pressure is still up and those cramps we talked about probably are some strong Braxton-Hicks contractions. But the fact they're not ending concerns me. I don't want you taking off and going anywhere without a traveling companion."

Darcy tried to unglue her tongue from the roof of her mouth. "But—my blood pressure is probably just up because of stress." *And Garret's kiss.* She'd had the hardest time forcing herself back into the kitchen to help Rosetta clean up and she'd caught the older woman looking at her suspiciously more than once. After the dishes were done, she'd claimed exhaustion and locked herself in her room, somehow managing to avoid the subject of her mother's call. Thank God the woman didn't pry. "I'm fine," she told the doctor. "I feel a lot better since I've rested."

"Stress is another thing you must get under control. Even with all that you're facing. If you don't, your problems are going to get worse. Stress manifests in health issues, and we can't have that with this baby. Surely you have someone who can fly down and drive you home to Indiana?"

"There's only me and my mom, but she can't come. Actually, I'm not sure I'm going to move to Indiana now." She had the week until her car was repaired to figure it out. Not much time in the scheme of things. Was she seriously thinking of driving off on her own after what Dr. Clyde said? What about being responsible?

"You aren't going to stay with her?"

Feeling the doctor's censure, she shook her head, unwilling to part with more humiliating details. She could only imagine what the doctor thought of her situation. For all intents and purposes, she was homeless. Dr. Clyde wouldn't report her or believe her unable to take care of her baby, would she?

"Darcy, look at me." The doctor waited for her to obey. "Your baby doesn't need a lot of expensive toys or gadgets. But it does need you to be as healthy as possible. You need to establish roots and *quickly*. Getting settled and having plans for the future should bring your blood pressure down. I'm going to be blunt and give you advice you probably don't want to hear. I think you need to rent a place in Beauty and stay until after the baby arrives. I don't think we need to put you on Brethine yet, but if the low-grade cramping turns into more, I want you here immediately." She patted her hand. "I don't want you to be alone and I hope you feel you can trust me to help you through this. I'll do as much as I can for you to make sure you and your baby are okay."

"Thank you." Darcy struggled to keep her emotions under control. The past twenty-four hours seemed surreal. Her mother, Garret and his horror over the kiss. This. Dr.

Clyde's advice was sound. She had to find her own place. No way could she stay with Rosetta until the baby was born. And Garret? Would he feel strange visiting her now? Probably so if his reaction last night was anything to go by. But her car wasn't ready yet, and she couldn't leave or move without it.

"We'll need to set up weekly appointments from here on out, but come before then if you experience any changes or problems. Go back to where you're staying until your car is repaired, prop your feet up. Check out the apartment rentals in the paper, and get some rest. Doctor's orders." She ripped off the diagnosis sheet and handed it to Darcy. "I'll see you in a week."

Outside the office, Darcy put one foot in front of the other. What now? Stuck on that highway that night, she'd prayed for a miracle and received a series of disasters instead. The knot in her stomach grew to monstrous proportions and she ducked into the ladies' room. The panic grew larger, more strangling. She had limited funds. Maybe Nick would let her stay in the massage room at the gym until she got some money together. Surely there was a locker room. An office? Sleeping on a couch would be fine. The gym had showers.

Darcy left the restroom and rode the elevator, ignoring the curious looks from the smocked nurses and orderlies because no matter how hard she tried she couldn't stop biting her lips and twisting her fingers into pretzels. What was she going to *do?* Why had she kissed Garret? If they hadn't shared that kiss everything would be normal between them now. She'd feel comfortable staying at Rosetta's until she found an apartment, her conscience clear. But not now.

Darcy left the elevator and turned the corner only to

hesitate beside the foliage of a ten-foot ficus tree, her gaze locking on Ethan and Garret standing about four feet away arguing, if the expressions on their faces were anything to go by. Stepping closer but remaining behind the tree, she listened.

"Darcy is nice, okay? She's *great,* but do you know how long I've waited for the chief of surgery to retire? I planned to toss my hat into the ring officially, but when I went in to talk to Harry, I couldn't get a word in because Harry was on a rampage about you and how you've betrayed Joss by having an *affair* this week while she was gone."

Garret ran a hand over his face. "Didn't you explain?"

"I didn't get the *chance.* Garret, you've gotta fix this and do it quickly. Propose to Joss as planned, put the ring on her finger and make it official so Harry will calm down."

Darcy caught her breath. *Propose? As planned?* They were *that* involved? But Garret had kissed *her* and— *It meant nothing.* He'd regretted kissing her, said he was sorry. She was the one who'd thought that maybe it wasn't such a mistake. That friends could become more.

"When I propose to Joss, it won't be because Darcy needed a place to stay and Harry's using it to his advantage to force my hand."

When, not *if.* The ache in her back increased and Darcy lifted her hand to rub it. The movement drew Garret's attention and she smothered a groan, but managed a shaky smile. "Good morning."

Ethan swung to face her. "How long were you standing there?" His expression softened into one of doctorlike compassion. "You weren't meant to hear that, Darcy. This isn't your fault."

"Don't. I'm glad I know what's going on. And I'm sorry for causing you both trouble."

"You're no trouble. Everything is fine," Garret insisted.

"Yeah, once Garret explains the situation to his boss, it will all blow over. It's the old-fashioned mind-set around here, that's all."

"It might be old-fashioned, but I guarantee your family isn't any happier about this than I am."

Darcy jumped at the sound of the deep, angry voice, and turned to face the man it belonged to. Garret's boss? He had three chins, a rounded stomach way bigger than hers and wore a brown suit, overcoat and brown hat with a two-inch band of black piping at the base of the brim. The man regarded her with an uncompromising stare, his gaze sweeping over her and lingering on her belly before shooting back to her face.

"Darcy, this is my boss, Mr. Pierson. Harry, Ms. Darcy Rhodes."

"I can't say that I'm happy to make your acquaintance."

"Harry—"

"I do not appreciate the situation you've forced upon Garret or this hospital."

"She didn't force anything." Garret glanced at her, his moss-green eyes soft with regret.

Harold released a loud *harrumph*. "You're a brilliant man, Garret. I'd never have guessed you'd fall for some money-hungry bed-hopper's tricks."

"That is enough. Harry, I know why you're upset, but you have no reason to be."

Ethan moved so that he stood beside her. "I agree. You're insulting Darcy and Garret both—not to mention Joss—by suggesting something more happened than us simply giving a stranded, *pregnant* woman a roof over her head in the midst of a natural disaster. What kind of image would it have set if two of the hospital's employees had turned their backs on her?"

"Lending a helping hand is one thing, but it did not have to involve her sleeping in the same house—or visiting her every night this past week."

She should've known people were gossiping about them. How could she have forgotten that about small towns? In Miami no one knew or cared what went on with the neighbors unless the police showed up. But Beauty was even smaller than her hometown in Indiana, and everyone had known *everything* happening with her mother there. Thank goodness the kiss hadn't taken place outside the condo door.

The argument continued. People—hospital employees and visitors alike—gawked as they walked by. The pain in her back caused the muscles on her sides to ache, and she rubbed her stomach in rhythmic motions when the latest cramp grew stronger.

No. No, she wasn't doing this again. It was stress. She had to calm down and the pains would go away. Everything would be fine as soon as she could get away from them all, even Rosetta. She needed to retrieve her things from the condo and find a cheap room somewhere and lick her wounds in private.

Desperate to sit down, she spotted a bench nearby and lowered herself to the seat, earning a frowning look of concern from Garret. "Just resting. I'm fine."

"You don't look fine," Ethan murmured. "You're having contractions again, aren't you?"

She moved her head calmly back and forth. She was not their problem, not anymore. "I'm fine." But maybe she should go back upstairs. Things were getting a little… intense.

"Of course she's fine," Harry added. "Don't think a little playacting on her part is going to change the subject, Garret. You owe me and my daughter an explanation and an apology. How dare you treat Jocelyn this way?"

His daughter? Mr. Pierson was Garret's boss *and* future father-in-law? A pain sharpened.

Oh, yeah, you definitely need to go upstairs. Darcy pushed herself to her feet, hating that she appeared so awkward and huge. Tears pricked her eyes, the norm these days. She wasn't the type to cry over problems. Why bother when it didn't make them go away? She was more of a plow-through-until-you-figure-it-out kind of person. That got results and kept her too busy for tears.

Darcy worked to keep the discomfort from showing on her face. *Okay.* As soon as she could walk, she'd go upstairs. Calmly. Without an audience.

"That's it. Don't move." Ethan jogged to the nearby information desk and grabbed the handles of a wheelchair.

She shook her head in denial, but Garret took hold of her hand and wrapped an impossibly strong arm around her shoulders, lending her support. Her face burned. "Garret, please. Let Ethan help me. I don't want you to get into any more trouble."

Ethan turned the wheelchair around and set the brakes.

"I can walk."

"You ride or I carry you," Garret murmured, the look in his eyes stating he'd do just that. And how would that appear to the gawkers watching this scene? Before she could take him to task on giving her orders and kissing her when he planned to *marry* someone else, she found herself in the chair.

Garret squatted down in front of her. He lowered the footrests and placed her feet on top, maintaining his hold longer than necessary. "I'm sorry, sweetheart. We'll talk later, okay?"

"What's there to talk about?" she asked pointedly. "I understand." But did she? Garret didn't seem like the type of guy to go around cheating on women.

"Garret, shut up and get out of the way." Ethan unlocked the brakes and got them moving.

"I'm not finished with either one of you." Harry followed them to the elevator. "I want answers and I want them *now*."

The elevator doors opened, but as the brothers wheeled her inside, Rosetta called Garret's name.

"Aww, great," Ethan murmured.

Darcy glanced up and saw Garret close his eyes as though summoning the depths of his patience—or in embarrassment. She'd bet the latter. The older woman stepped onto the elevator with them, Garret's boss following her.

"What on earth is going on here? You've got people talking about you throughout the hospital."

"How are you, Gram?" Ethan kissed the woman on the cheek. "You look beautiful."

"Good morning, Gram." Garret smiled, but it was a strained effort.

Ethan pushed a button and the elevator began its ascent.

Harry dipped his head in a respectful nod. "Just the person I need to talk to. Rosetta, I want to know how you could condone such behavior. Why would you allow Garret to bring his pregnant mistress into your home and—"

"Harold Pierson, you should be ashamed of yourself! Don't let me hear another word like that." Rosetta glared at Garret's boss, then dropped her gaze to look Darcy over, her eyes narrowing shrewdly. Swallowing, Darcy prayed for them all to go away. As though sensing her thoughts, Rosetta nodded and patted Darcy's shoulder. "Let me handle this and don't fret, dear. It's not good for the baby."

The elevator arrived on Dr. Clyde's floor and Ethan pushed her down the hall at a breakneck pace, the others hurrying behind them. To her horror, the entire group followed her inside. Everyone in the waiting room looked up from their magazines and books. On the other side of a plexiglass partition, Dr. Clyde spoke with one of her employees, but the moment she noticed the hospital president and the rest of them in her waiting room, she walked out of sight. A second later the door to the examination rooms opened.

"Bring her right back. Darcy, what happened?"

She shook her head mutely, unable to speak.

"Oh, I know that look. They're back, huh? Room three. Becky will get you hooked up to a monitor and we'll see what's happening here. The rest of you, please, wait in my office."

Rosetta rested her hand on Darcy's shoulder. "May I stay with you, dear?"

Darcy nodded even though she knew she should say no. Things were complicated enough and she needed to get used to being entirely on her own. Right now, however, Rosetta's friendship was too precious to pass up. Within moments a fetal monitor was in place, a blood pressure cuff on her arm.

"Even higher than before. Darcy, I know you were upset by what I told you earlier. I could tell, but—"

"Excuse me for interrupting, but what did you tell her?"

Rosetta looked at her expectantly, and somehow Darcy managed to repeat the doctor's warnings.

"Oh, Darcy. Child, don't you dare worry about a thing. Do you hear me? You can stay with me. I don't mind."

"Rosetta, we're not talking about a week or even *two*."

"She's right," Dr. Clyde interjected. "She'll need a place to stay until she's cleared to travel, which could be anywhere from two to six weeks after birth."

"And I'm fine with that," Rosetta stated firmly. "Darcy, you shouldn't be alone now. And since your mother isn't able to come get you, I'd be honored if you'd consider my home yours. I have plenty of room and you can't think of yourself as a bother when you'd be giving us old people a lot of excitement waiting on a baby to arrive. You're welcome to stay as long as you need."

Her nose tingled with yet more tears. Were these people for real? How could anyone—total strangers—be so generous?

"I'm afraid we have a more serious problem here. The contractions started too easily and could progress without medication and monitoring. It's feasible that you could go into labor if we let the contractions continue. Darcy, you've got a little less than five weeks until your due date, but we need every one of them."

"I have to take the medication, don't I?"

"It would be best," Dr. Clyde said with a nod.

"Will I be able to work? I have to pay for the repairs and rent." She turned toward Rosetta. "If I stay with you, I have to pay rent. I'm *not* a charity case."

Rosetta's features softened with a look similar to... pride? "I know that, dear."

Dr. Clyde set her file aside. "In an ideal world I'd insist you not work. But given the situation, I'm not opposed to it if doing so will make you feel better, and provided the medication is effective and you aren't contracting. But you need to rest between clients, and I insist on half your normal load. Understood?"

Darcy nodded, unable to take it all in. It should've been her mother standing here beside her, should've been her mother holding her hand in support. Offering to help, to take her home. Garret wouldn't like this. Not after what happened between them. And his boss.

My baby comes first. And it's not like I'll be kissing Garret again.

Darcy forced herself to lift her chin and stare directly into Rosetta's eyes. "Are you sure?"

"Without a doubt."

"Then I'll stay on the condition that I pay you rent and get to help around the house."

Rosetta beamed. "Done. You drive a hard bargain."

Darcy smiled weakly. They all knew she was getting the best of the deal.

CHAPTER NINETEEN

LATER THAT EVENING Garret sat back in his chair and tried to tell himself he wasn't responsible for how complicated his life had become. It didn't work.

Despite Gram's assurances that she had things under control and that nothing had happened between Garret and Darcy, Harry had made life hell. When the hospital president wasn't muttering about Darcy and public display, he'd wreaked havoc throughout the hospital, causing numerous problems. And why not? Harry knew Garret would be the one left to clean up the mess. Garret didn't doubt it was Harry's version of revenge and the man's way of keeping him so busy he wouldn't have time to see Darcy.

After months of negotiations with the union representative and coming within inches of signing a new contract with the nurses, Harry had blown everything by informing the union official that the nurses didn't *deserve* a raise. Harry and the rep had nearly come to blows, and Garret had spent the entire afternoon on the phone trying to repair the damage. He was sick of Harry's temper and holier-than-thou attitude. The man didn't have a clue how to relate to the hospital's many employees. Months of work down the drain and for what?

As they had throughout the day, his thoughts drifted to Darcy. That her latest scare came on the heels of their kiss had been on his mind all day, and he tossed the pen he held onto the desk in frustration. How was she? Did she think he'd kissed her because— Why *had* he kissed her? One minute he'd offered comfort, the next he couldn't think of anything but tasting her. Friends didn't do that.

The phone rang and he hesitated before picking it up. "Garret Tulane."

"Sounds like you and I had the same kind of day," Joss said. "I just wanted to let you know I'm home and that I talked to Daddy a few minutes ago. He was awfully fired up."

"Yeah." He sighed. "Joss—"

"Don't worry about me, Garret. Daddy's in a mood. You're such an honorable man. I trust you and I know you'd never deliberately hurt me. And I would never deliberately hurt you."

Tell her what happened. But it was only a kiss, and not deliberate, like she'd said. Why make the situation worse when it wouldn't happen again?

"Listen, I, um, called to cancel our date tonight. I know we talked about going out to dinner, but I'm really tired and—"

"No."

"What?"

"Joss…I don't care what we do. I don't care if you sleep all evening, but I'd like to see you."

"Oh… How sweet. Okay, I think maybe I feel a second wind coming. I'm at home. Want to swing by here?"

"I'll be there in half an hour."

"Good. Now stop brooding. Daddy will calm down soon."

He wasn't so sure. At least not without a major concession on his part. Maybe he should ask Joss tonight? Get it out of the way?

There you go again. That's nice and romantic.

"How is Darcy?" Joss asked, matter-of-fact. "Daddy said she went into labor again."

He'd bet that wasn't all Harry had said. "From the stress."

"Poor thing. Be honest, was Daddy involved?"

He blamed himself for upsetting Darcy, but Harry certainly hadn't helped. "Some. Anyway, she's stuck in town until the baby's born now. Ordered not to travel. If she can handle it, she'll be able to work. Nick's hired her on at the gym."

"That's great."

It was. If he didn't think too much about Darcy putting her hands on other men. *Why* the thought of that bothered him was a question he couldn't answer.

"Garret, if you want to check on Darcy, don't let Daddy's temper stop you. Go right ahead."

He cleared his throat. "That's very understanding of you."

"She's pregnant and alone in a strange town. I can't imagine being that way and having no one. It's...sad. I understand why you feel the need to watch out for her—you're the one who found her that night. Now, I've got to go make myself presentable before you get here. See you in a little bit." Murmuring goodbye, she hung up.

Garret set the receiver on the base, his thoughts focusing on what Joss had said about Darcy. He was concerned about her, worried. Responsible. Maybe *that* was the source of his interest in her?

He grabbed his briefcase from the floor behind his desk and started to fill it only to pause. Harry had come in that morning with nothing in his hands, gone home the same way. Right or wrong, Garret had been performing Harry's job in a lot of ways of late. Anger surfaced. Harry had no right to terrorize the hospital with his tantrums, and he needed to learn the consequences of his bullying.

Garret mentally quelled the rising tide of guilt and self-imposed responsibility, and determinedly returned the briefcase to the floor. Nodding to himself, he grabbed his keys and coat and headed toward the door, feeling very much like a kid playing hooky from school.

Maybe it was time to not be so ready to step in. Time to back off and let Harry appreciate him a little more. Time to make some changes.

FORTY-FIVE MINUTES LATER Garret sat across the table from Joss at his uncle's bar and grille and thought of all the reasons she was perfect for him. Joss could play the social-ite when expected, be charming and poised. She could also laugh at herself on occasion, and she was a smart, astute businesswoman. So why didn't he ask?

She looked up, her fork raised halfway to her lips. "Something wrong?"

"I'm proud of you. You've done an amazing job on the gallery." Her lashes lowered, but Garret thought he saw a flash of resentment.

"Thank you."

"What?"

Joss stared at him blankly. "Pardon?"

"Don't give me that. You're angry. Why?"

"It's nothing."

"Obviously it's something."

She lowered her fork to her plate and gave him a be-nevolent stare. "How do you know I've done an amazing job? You've barely set foot inside the gallery. I didn't say anything because I don't want to fight."

"I've been busy."

"I know."

"Your father's my boss and not an easy man to take."

"I know that, too. How about we talk about something else? Your mother said the cake recipe for Rosetta's birthday party is divine."

So that's what they were down to? Discussing cake recipes because they couldn't talk about *them?* "How about we go back to the gallery after we eat? It's after hours so the phones will be quiet, no deliverymen will show up. You can give me a private tour."

She hesitated for a long moment. "Now? Oh, well…I suppose I could. No, I will. That sounds like…fun."

"What sounds like fun?" Toby walked up to the table from behind Joss's left shoulder.

Garret sat back and grinned at him. "Where have you been? You haven't been to the gym all week."

Toby glanced at Joss and then back at him. "Jocelyn didn't tell you?"

"Tell me what?"

"Tobias, I thought—I wasn't sure if—"

"I'm job hunting."

"What?" Garret looked at Joss and saw her staring at Toby, her expression hard to read. What was up with that? He focused on Toby. "What happened?"

"Same old thing. I got strung along like a mule with a carrot, but didn't get the partnership."

"Ah, Tobe, tough break."

"Yeah, well, while I look around I've been taking some time to kick back and sleep in. I've been going to the gym later in the day."

"That's an excuse. You're just afraid you're off your game and I can take you down. Admit it, your record is history."

Toby smiled at the teasing. "Bring it on."

A pause followed the words and Garret shifted on the booth's seat. "I'm surprised I haven't talked to you if you're on the hunt. How many times have you mentioned partnering up? Change your mind?"

Toby shoved his hand through his hair. "You've, uh, got your hands full right now. I know it can't happen so why ask? Looks like my takeout is ready. See you around. Jocelyn…enjoy dinner with your guy, here."

"Later." Garret watched Toby walk away and then glanced back at Joss to see her gaze following him, too. "I can't believe Wellington did it to him again. Toby's a great attorney."

"He'll find something."

He frowned at her tone. "Joss, is something going on?"

She flashed him a cool, measured smile. "Nothing unusual. I have a headache. After I arrived home today I got another lecture from Daddy. He says we don't spend enough time together and that our relationship is suffering."

"Do you feel that way?" Garret watched her closely, looking for clues to what she was thinking.

"I'm not complaining if that's what you're asking. *I've* canceled our dates, too, remember? I haven't been able to spare more than a few minutes for you these past few months, and I understand that things are the same way with you. It just makes me wonder—" She broke off and jabbed her fork into her food.

"Wonder what?"

Another shrug. The silence between them lengthened, the weight of the ring box burning a hole through his pocket. If he asked, they'd be able to spend more time together and the tension between them would ease…right?

Garret finished off the last of his steak and downed the soda, noticing for the first time that other than the few bites she'd taken at the beginning of the meal Joss had barely eaten.

As though sensing his perusal, her light blue eyes rose to meet his. Out of nowhere he pictured a warm, rich toffee-colored gaze.

"Garret, can I be honest?"

"Absolutely."

"I'm not feeling very well tonight. Can we postpone the tour and make it an early night?"

He wasn't expecting that, but reminded himself that timing was everything. She had tried to call off the date and he hadn't let her. This was no less than what he deserved for forcing her to come. Still he wanted to talk to her about how she felt, what she saw for the future. Kids, house. What did she dream of?

He pushed his plate out of the way and leaned his elbows on the table. "Are you sure nothing's wrong?"

Her gaze darted away from his. "I'm really tired and not hungry at all. I have a nasty headache and there's this on-going list of things to do buzzing around in my mind. I feel like I need to go to sleep and start fresh tomorrow."

"I was kind of hoping we could talk. There's something important I'd like to ask you."

The fork slipped from her hand and clattered onto her plate before bouncing to the wood floor. "Sorry. I'm such a klutz. I'll go get a new one from one of the stations. Your uncle won't mind, will he?"

"You just said you weren't hungry. Use mine, I'm finished."

"I'm not hungry, but—"

He grabbed his fork from his plate and placed it on the edge of hers to use or not use as she liked. "Joss, listen, I'm sorry I haven't been around to help you with the gallery. I apologize for that. I hope you're not upset with me and just not saying anything. You can talk to me."

"Don't be silly. You're busy and you've got more important things to do than mess with my little gallery."

"Joss—"

"Daddy certainly wouldn't want you wasting your time there when you could be working at the hospital. Besides, you're not interested in art at all."

"It's just not my—"

"Not your thing. I know—" she pushed her plate away "—and it's fine. Garret, really, I'm not very good company tonight. I think it's best if we go. I think I'm coming down with a touch of the flu or something. You know what? You stay. Go have a drink at the bar. I'll call a cab."

"Joss, sit down. You look pale. Maybe you're jet-lagged. Give me a second to take care of the bill and I'll drive you home."

JOCELYN GAZED out the window as Garret drove her home. He'd asked if she needed more air, if she felt sick. If he'd done something to upset her. All of which she answered with a low no. All of which she should have answered with a yes. She needed more air because she couldn't breathe, felt sick because of what she'd done. Was furious at Garret for spending so much time at the hospital with her father instead of with her. Where were her guts? Her backbone? Why did she play the good little girl and pretend?

Turning her head, she watched as the streetlights played

over Garret's face. He was gorgeous. Strong and tall and handsome. A man's man. A man she'd be thrilled to call her husband. But was Tobias right?

Garret pulled up to the house and stopped, shoving the vehicle into Park before he reached for the door handle.

"No," she said quickly, unable to stomach the pretense a moment longer. "Don't bother walking me to the door. I'm going straight to bed. Thank you for dinner."

He snagged her arm before she could let herself out. Watching her closely, Garret slowly tugged and she moved toward him willingly, hoping, praying, that while she'd been gone something had changed.

Garret brushed his lips gently over hers. "Feel better."

She nodded, hesitated, then wrapped an arm around his neck and kissed him again, the kiss too hard. Desperate. Awkward and totally different from the way she'd felt with Tobias. She pulled away with a murmured goodbye and rushed out of the Escalade.

"Joss?"

"Yes?"

"I love you."

She turned to shut the door, blinded by tears. "I love you, too."

CHAPTER TWENTY

DARCY STARED up at Garret and laughed. "Shut up! Are you serious?"

He winked at her. "No one suspected a thing."

She lifted the hammer up to him and watched as he nailed the closet supports into place. Darcy was fairly sure Rosetta's maintenance contract covered such things, but the woman had insisted Garret was a better hand at completing the chores. Darcy was glad to see him again. After the kiss and that scene at the hospital, she wasn't sure how he'd treat her. If he would even come to see her.

"What's next on the list?"

"The shelf above the washer. It wobbles, apparently."

He tested the support, made sure it wouldn't budge and climbed down, seemingly as at ease on the ladder as he was at his job. The power player had a domestic side. Who knew?

Garret put the hammer back into the tool chest, hesitating. "Darcy, about the other day—"

"We're good. Right, Spike?"

He chuckled, his eyes warm on hers. "I'm glad. You and Spike have enough on your hands without me adding more to the mix."

"Or hurting your girlfriend," she murmured softly, nixing the easygoing mood with four words.

Garret hesitated, his expression darkening with a mixture of regret and sadness. "Or that."

GARRET FROWNED and hung up the phone when he got Toby's voice mail again. He knew his friend was upset about Wellington and the loss of the partnership, but Toby had bills to pay. He had to get something going soon, and a week had come and gone since that night at the Old Coyote.

A knock sounded outside his door. Garret swiveled in the chair, hoping Toby had come to see him, but his mother stood there instead. "Hey, Mom, what's up?" He stood and walked over to give her a kiss.

"You tell me." His mother hugged him back and sent him a look he recognized well. "Garret, is everything all right?"

Sighing, Garret leaned his hips on his desk and scowled. "If everyone would mind their own business, it would be."

"Have you been out with Joss lately?"

He inhaled and sighed. "She picked up a cold in Montana. I've talked to her on the phone several times, but she's been taking it easy and puttering around the gallery. Why?"

"Garret—"

"It's not my baby."

"Well, of course it's not. I know Darcy would be wearing a wedding band if that was the case." She smoothed her carefully styled hair. "Sweetheart, I hate to sound old-fashioned, but appearances do matter and—"

"Harry said something to you."

The first time or two he'd seen Darcy since the kiss, her responses had been reserved, but then she soon warmed up and seemed to have forgiven him. Once he started noticing the ripe fullness of Darcy's breasts pressing against her top, the curve of her lips and the shape of her behind, the way she jumped up to help Gram every time she thought the older woman needed it, he left. *But you still noticed.*

His mother drew herself up to her full height. "He's concerned. And frankly, so am I."

"It's fine, Mom."

"Then why are you doing this?"

"Doing what? Darcy is literally stuck here in town until after the baby's born, and Gram's great, but don't you think it's a little heartless to drop Darcy there and not see her again?"

"So it's friendship? She's your friend?"

"I'd like to think so, yes."

Exhaling what appeared to be a sigh of relief, his mother said, "We want you to be happy, Garret." She palmed his face in her hands. "Marriage is supposed to be forever. No one would hold it against you if you need more time before you propose to Joss."

"Harry would disagree with that statement."

"Harry can disagree all he likes. I don't want you or Joss hurting over something that could've been prevented if it wasn't rushed."

"Me, neither. Thanks, Mom." He forced a smile. "Now, tell me how the plans are going for Gram's big birthday bash."

DARCY ACCEPTED the gift with a smile. "Thank you, Mrs. Colby. I don't know what to say."

The older woman beamed. "You don't have to say a word, honey. I'm glad to help. My grandbabies have more than enough. I thought you might be able to use a little, too, with your baby on the way."

"I can. I appreciate it." It had been that way all day. All of her clients had come bearing gifts, and she was overwhelmed by their generosity. As she set the gift aside and selected music for Mrs. Colby's session, she reminded herself this was a temporary situation. She wouldn't be staying here, best not get too attached to the people.

But they're so nice. Why not stay?

Moving close to the door, Darcy spotted the flyers that had appeared that morning. Jocelyn Pierson's name was displayed in bold letters as the event contact for donations benefitting the children's ward at the hospital. Garret's hospital where he worked for Jocelyn's father in the position Garret's grandfather helped him get. Garret was too nice a guy to screw with his life.

She enjoyed the time she spent with him. Loved how he made her laugh and blush and feel like a woman instead of a beached whale. But she liked it too much. He was too handsome, too flirtatious, too kind. Too nice a guy for her to have to sit back and watch him marry another woman.

That's why you can't stay.

JOSS APPEARED in front of Garret during his workout, looking every inch Harry's daughter in her sleek suit and high heels. "Hey, feeling better?" he asked.

"Yes, I am. Thank you."

"What's wrong?"

"You tell me. I just got off the phone with Daddy." Her light blue eyes narrowed in concern. "I can't believe he had the gall to say what he did to your *mother.* I'm so embarrassed. He treats me like I'm a child, not a woman."

Maybe if Joss spoke up more, Harry wouldn't do that. Garret smiled, grim, almost wishing she *had* put Harry up to it. At least then it would mean she cared enough to fight for him. How juvenile was that? But her mood of late worried him, and he wouldn't mind a little better idea of where he stood. They were two adults, but the pressure to keep their families happy was intense. This was why guys didn't bring the girl home to meet the parents until he knew for sure what he wanted. "Mom was fine. We had a nice chat when she came to see me about it." He nodded toward her clothes. "You working out?"

"No. I had to take my car to Nick's. It's making a funny noise."

"You should've said something. I could've had a look at it."

"You're too busy, and Nick said it would take ten minutes. A fan belt or some such. I saw your car and thought I'd come to apologize. I don't know what's gotten into Daddy lately. He's so insistent that we make things permanent."

"I'm sorry, sweetheart. You don't need that pressure on top of getting ready for the opening."

"I'm okay. So why are you here now? I thought you always worked out in the morning?"

"I was hoping to run into Toby."

"Oh? Any particular reason why?"

"I think he's feeling pretty low about not getting the partnership. Thought I might try to cheer him up. Guess I'll track him down some other time. Want to grab some dinner? I'm almost done here."

She shook her head. "That sounds lovely. It really does, but I can't. I need to meet with the caterer about opening night."

"This late?"

"She works out of her home and we need to go over some things. Did I tell you I'm hosting a charity toy drive the night of the opening? I'm coordinating it with the hospital to help supply the toy bin in Pediatrics and send every child home with a new or gently used toy."

"That's great."

Just then the door to the designated massage room opened and a drowsy looking woman emerged. She paused in the doorway to say her goodbyes. He couldn't see Darcy.

"I've got to go. Nick promised to have my car ready. Give me a call later tonight if you get a chance."

"Uh, yeah, sure. Be careful." He shifted to make it easier for her to give him a kiss.

"Ick. You're all sweaty. Don't muss me for my meeting." She kissed more air than lips, flashed him her practiced smile and then walked away.

Garret glanced back toward the massage room only to find the door closed once more. Swearing beneath his breath at the strange situation he found himself in, he grabbed his gear from the locker room and headed out of the gym.

The February air cooled the sweat on his skin with numbing swiftness, but that was nothing compared to the surprise he felt when he saw Joss standing outside her car talking to Toby. Joss looked flustered, her normally ultra-cool persona nowhere to be found as she stared up into Toby's face and gave him what for about something. The scene caught his attention because she looked so fiery and passionate. So *unlike* the woman she was with him. The woman she'd appeared inside the gym. If he wasn't mistaken she almost looked—

Interested in Toby?

The thought came out of nowhere, a sucker punch that couldn't have shocked him more. No way. It was his imagination. One of the first lessons in law school was that in domestic cases the guilty are usually the first to accuse the innocent of their own crimes. The fact he liked Darcy, was curious about her and had been thinking about her as something other than a *friend,* that was why he saw what he thought he saw.

He took a step forward to join them but something held him back. Garret watched, unable to take his eyes off the scene playing out before him. Joss said something he couldn't hear, but Toby's reaction was instantaneous. His buddy bent forward, his head lowering, his posture that of a man about to kiss a woman senseless—or quiet. At the last second, Toby stopped and pulled away, but there was no denying the sexual tension flaring between the two of them.

Had he been played for a fool? Was that why Joss was so uncomfortable of late? Was that why Toby was avoiding his calls? *Guilt?*

Doubts bombarded Garret's head. All those hours he worked. Jocelyn's distance. Tobe stopping by the gallery, pressuring Garret to decide. This was *why?* He ground his teeth until his jawbone popped loud in his ear, angry, furious at Toby's trespassing and yet not sure what to do. The rational, don't-go-off-half-cocked mediator-attorney in him demanded proof before he considered confronting them, and seeing them talking in a parking lot did not qualify as such. But the tension. What about *that?*

Toby stalked off and got into his SUV, peeling out of the parking lot and heading west even though he'd been dressed in work-out clothes and *hadn't* stepped foot inside the gym. Joss did the same but headed east, both of them seemingly trying to stay as far away from each other as possible.

A gust of wind hit him but did nothing for the anger simmering inside him.

Was Joss cheating on him with his best friend?

"Eighteen."

"Twenty-one." Darcy swiped the cards from the couch cushion between them and looked up to find Garret in the same mood he'd been in all night. No amount of teasing or questions had drawn him out of it. If anything it had gotten darker, his expression more brooding.

The condo was quiet, Rosetta out on a date with one of the men who lived in the building. Garret had scowled when he'd heard the news. He'd hesitated outside the condo door, freshly showered and dressed casually in khaki slacks and a lightweight black sweater that emphasized his good looks, but then asked if he could come in anyway. She hadn't been able to turn him away.

"Ow. Wait a minute, I have to stretch." She made a face and shifted her sideways position on the couch.

"Where's it hurt?"

She smoothed her hand over her lower back and without warning, Garret moved closer until their knees met, putting them face-to-face. Just like that his arms were around her. Despite the surprise of it, she didn't move away. Garret placed his hands on her lower back and began a slow massage.

"Oh, wow." She tried to hold in a moan, but his touch felt too good. "Oh, that feels wonderful."

He chuckled huskily. "You like that, huh?"

Oh, yeah. And he seemed to like it, too. "Don't stop." She tried to hold herself upright and away from Garret's hard, broad chest but the slow push and pull of his hands on her back made that impossible. She dropped her head to his shoulder and closed her eyes with a sigh.

His lips brushed her temple. "How do you do that?"

"Do what?" she whispered, feeling the tension inside her rocketing up by degrees. How was that possible with her the way she was?

"Make me want you when all you're doing is sitting there."

She caught her breath. Seriously? The moist heat of his breath against her neck, her ear, sent shivers through her. "It's all a figment of your imagination. I'm pregnant, or have you forgotten?"

"I haven't forgotten."

Meaning…what? "Garret, stop."

"You said I couldn't." He kissed her temple again. "And I don't want to."

She squeezed her eyes shut at the pitch of his voice. "I don't want to make another mistake. We've spent a lot of time together these past few weeks and it's been fun, but…Garret, you wouldn't be a rebound for me." She lifted her head, looked into his eyes and bared her soul. "This is… It scares me how easy it would be to fall for you." Nothing like a little honesty to send a guy running.

"Would that be a bad thing?"

"Did you and Jocelyn break up?" He shook his head no. "Then, yeah, it would be a bad thing."

"We're close, Darcy. I'm not going to lie to you. Joss and I never made a verbal agreement to be exclusive, but we have been, almost from the beginning."

She plucked at a button on his shirt, needing something, anything, to do rather than face him. "If you tell me you're one of those guys who says he's in love with two women—"

"I'm not." He lifted her face to his. "Darcy, I'm going

to be honest here. I'm not sure what I feel for you. Am I interested? Attracted to you?" He rubbed his thumb over her chin, a slow drag of warmth. "Yes, I am. Does it freak me out that you're pregnant? Yeah. Big time." He smoothed a hand along her jaw until it rested on her nape. "I've thought about marrying Joss for a while now. I bought the ring before Christmas," he admitted softly.

"But something happened?"

He brushed his thumb over her cheek, her mouth, his eyes a turbulent sea. "Yeah…you. You have me thinking things I shouldn't be thinking about a soon-to-be mom."

Garret stared into her eyes, and she saw a reflection of what she felt: a conflict between duty and desire. How often had she wanted to go out and have fun, but was afraid she'd end up like her mother? Afraid she'd end up on the losing end of a string of guys who wanted to get off and nothing else? And when she'd taken the risk, jumped into a relationship with Stephen, look what had happened. How did people know what was right and what was wrong?

"Darcy, say something."

"I know what it's like to want something you don't have. I understand being confused. But I need to know this isn't a joke or a game for you. Whatever *this* is. I understand being confused, but I don't want my heart broken."

"I don't want to break your heart." He settled himself more comfortably against the back of the couch. "I don't want to mislead you, and the last thing I want to do is hurt you, Darcy. I don't know where I stand on a lot of things and you're one of them. All I know is that right now, right here, I'm where I want to be. Is that enough for you for now?"

CHAPTER TWENTY-ONE

HER FANCIFUL IMAGININGS wanted her to think there was a reason she'd had the accident that night. A reason Garret was the one to find her, the one with her now. But she had learned to be a realist. "Why would you want me?"

The question emerged raw, revealed her vulnerability. But her own family didn't want her, why would he? Especially in the condition she was in.

God has the best in store for us, but you have to believe to receive, Darcy. You remember that and you'll have a good life. Nana's voice filled her head, bringing forth a rush of memories and emotions. Rolling out pie crusts on summer afternoons, the radio on an oldies station, Nana in her flowered apron singing "You Are My Sunshine."

But how could she believe in anything—trust in anyone—after what had happened to her with Stephen? After what happened repeatedly to her mother at the hands of the men in her life?

Garret pulled her close, kissed her gently, his mouth lingering on hers. "Because you're you," he murmured against her lips. "Because you look me in the eyes and you're honest with me about what you feel. Honesty is…hot."

She laughed at him. At them. "I'm scared of screwing up."

"Me, too."

There it was again, that fairy-tale feeling. Why was she doing this to herself?

"You are the last thing I expected to enter my life at this point, but I'm glad you did," he said.

She nuzzled her nose against him. "This is crazy messed up. You know that, don't you? I'm *huge*. My back hurts, my ankles are puffy and I should *not* be thinking about you this way."

"But you are?" Garret's eyes warmed with blatant interest. In the space of a heartbeat an arrested expression crossed his face, one of hunger and excitement and curiosity that made her body tighten in response. "Come here." He snagged her with a hand behind her nape and kissed her. Not the sweet, chaste kisses of before, but hungry, urgent, drowning get-to-know-what-you-like-best strokes that turned her muscles to mush.

Darcy moaned, unprepared for the onslaught of desire Garret unleashed, and found herself gently pulled upward onto her knees and shifted about, until she was draped across his lap and well able to feel the steely strength of his arousal against her hip. Oh, yeah, he wasn't kidding her. That couldn't be faked.

Garret raised his head briefly as though to check to make sure she was okay, but when she didn't utter a complaint he kissed her again, using his teeth to nip, his tongue to soothe, delving inside to explore. He didn't rush her and she knew if she were to protest, Garret would immediately stop. But she didn't want him to. No, she wound her arms around his neck and kissed him back, shivering when his broad palm slipped from her thigh to her breast and squeezed.

"Beautiful. Do you have any idea how many times I thought about doing this?"

Yes. Because she'd dreamed of him doing it more than once. This morning she'd donned a baby-doll style dress, scoop-necked at the top and loose around her belly, the bottom of which reached midthigh, and lace-trimmed leggings beneath, and now she relished her choice when the material posed little barrier to Garret as he smoothed his hand back down her body to her knee, up again. When he reached her shoulder he dragged his knuckles along her collarbone, into her cleavage and then slipped beneath the material and her bra to cup her again, this time flesh to flesh.

"Oh." Her breasts had never been all that sensitive, but with her pregnancy they were. And the feel of him touching her— "Garret, please."

"You're killing me, sweetheart." He kissed her mouth, her cheek, her neck, following the course of his hand, all the while giving her gentle little scrapes of his thumb. Back and forth, so slow. The arm supporting her back tightened, lifting her toward him and she held her breath, waiting for the moment his lips touched her, laved and sucked with all the pent-up hunger she felt radiating from him. The shock of it shot straight to her core, and she stiffened before curling into him, desperate for more.

Garret groaned. "Beautiful." Still holding her so that he could play with her breasts, he slid his hand to her knee and raised it, settling her foot on the couch just so, before he went back to what he was doing. Touching, tasting, making her gasp and moan, his decadent mouth on her throat, her chest, his free hand meandering up and down her body and leaving a blazing trail behind. What was he doing to her?

Garret's heart thudded beneath her ear, his breathing unsteady, proof that he was enjoying himself and wasn't simply going through the motions or doing this for her. He wanted to, because he wanted her. Amazing. Dangerous to her heart, but amazing all the same.

A rough sound escaped him, a growl, a chest-deep rumble, and he shifted so that she laid more fully across his lap, more open to his touch. His hand slipped lower, inward on her thighs, between.

"Garret."

He cupped her, the thin barrier of her leggings not protecting her from the heat of his thumb, each movement sending a sizzle of excitement through her until she could scarcely keep from crying out. Over and over he touched her, kissed, rubbed, his mouth on hers long enough to capture her moans before moving on, lower, focusing on her breasts since they brought her pleasure—a devastating suck and stroke that made her writhe. If someone had said she could feel like this now...

Then Garret's hand found exactly the right spot. "There." He kissed her, hard and fast and sexy rough, his breath hitting her cheek when he broke contact to laugh softly. "Ah, yeah, sweetheart, right there. I love the look on your face."

He repeated the motion, varying the pressure and angle of his touch until she clutched his shoulders, kissing him, desperate, for more. Harder, faster, *more*. Whimpering, moaning, struggling to breathe as Garret built the tension inside her body to an unbearable degree. Finally, oh, *finally*, he cupped his hand around her and pressed, palming her and taking her mouth with his as he ground his hand against her until she shattered, her soft scream of pleasure captured by his mouth.

Darcy laid sprawled on his lap afterward, her nose buried in Garret's neck. Doubts, fears, total embarrassment bombarded her, but she shoved all the emotions aside to enjoy the moment, knowing she felt more for Garret than she ever had for Stephen. How scary was that? How sad? She'd known Garret a matter of weeks and yet he meant more to her than her baby's father? What did that say about her?

But it was true. She'd spent almost every evening talking with Garret, getting to know him, and what they'd just shared? It was nothing short of…magical.

Which made it all the more terrifying.

Garret shifted his hand between her thighs and aftershocks rolled through her. He made himself more comfortable on the couch, holding her on his lap, silent.

What was he thinking? Did he regret what they'd just done? Shoving those thoughts aside, she brushed her lips over his jaw, his throat, moving lower, shifting to have better access to his clothing.

"Darcy, no."

"But—"

"Gram will be home soon." He held her hands, bussed his lips against her forehead. "You were beautiful. This was wonderful. But I should go."

Tears pricked her eyelids and she blinked rapidly. "I know." But she didn't want it to end. Didn't want reality to intrude even though it was crashing back in drowning waves. She was too impulsive. She shouldn't have let things go so far, shouldn't have been so eager, but—

Garret hugged her close and raised her head with a hand under her chin, his mouth finding hers with unerring accuracy. And just like that her heart kicked up speed, the trembling started deep inside.

"I don't want to hurt you, Darcy. I'd never deliberately hurt you. Whatever happens, will you please remember that?"

And there it was. Reality. He wanted her to remember that—if he chose Jocelyn?

When, not *if.* "I'll try."

"YOU'RE AWFULLY QUIET. Something happen back at the gym?"

Nick's voice startled Darcy from her thoughts. She hadn't been able to concentrate all day. All she could think about was Garret and what had happened between them last night.

Was she more like her mother than she thought? A few pretty words and she gave in? She glanced over her shoulder and saw Matt in the backseat playing a handheld game, oblivious to the adults thanks to the earphones tucked in his ears. Would she have a boy like Matt? A little girl? What kind of shape would she be in when she gave birth if she let herself fall for Garret only to be cast aside? Getting closer to Garret had seemed like a wonderful idea last night, but in the harsh light of day— *Face it, you acted just like Mom.*

She settled herself against the seat and tried to stave off the upset and embarrassment. She'd never done that before, gotten so close to a guy so soon after meeting. Stephen had said he'd practically had to pry her thighs apart and that was after dating him nearly six months. She didn't do easy, didn't do one-night stands, didn't feel like she owed a guy anything just because he bought her dinner. So why did she want to do all those things and more with Garret?

"Darcy?"

"Do you ever wonder," she asked softly, "if you're making the right decisions?"

Nick smiled. "Only every day. Are you talking about parenting or something else?"

"Life in general. I want…I want whatever happens next to be right for both me and the baby. And I really need it to happen quickly given, well, this," she said, indicating her belly. "Rosetta says I'll go into labor soon because I've cleaned the apartment from top to bottom and washed everything that wasn't attached to something."

Nick chuckled as he drove her home to the condo. "I remember Matt's mom doing that."

She glanced at Matt again. The child was oblivious to their conversation but she lowered her voice to be sure. "What happened? If you don't mind my asking?"

Thirty seconds passed before he shrugged. "She had stars in her eyes at the thought of being a Tulane and moving to the top of the mountain. When she realized I wasn't going to go crawling back to my parents and marrying me meant she was just going to get me, she left. But she left the best thing between us behind." He cleared his throat, his jaw locking and unlocking at his thoughts. "It hasn't been easy, but kids are resilient, Darcy. They'll love you no matter how screwed up things get sometimes."

She let that pass without comment. She loved her mother because she was her mother, but a deep, caring love? If not for Nana's love until her passing and a deep-rooted sense of right and wrong she wouldn't know *how* to love her baby. Her mom hadn't taught her that. But was her version of love dark and twisted? Was it the *right way* to love or was it only a matter of time before she screwed that up, too? "Do you think your parents regret not being close to you?" The question slipped out before she could stop it. "I can't believe I asked that. How rude, Nick, I'm sorry. My mom and I are— We have a lot of problems, and I'm worried they'll carry over and come between me and my baby. That the pattern will repeat. I didn't mean to sound insensitive about you and your family."

"It's okay. And the answer is yes. I do, too. But I can't see them making any other decision at the time." He grimaced. "I did the right thing by leaving, they did the right thing by setting down an example for my brothers and sister. Who's right? Some people need distance to be themselves and I'm one of them. Maybe you are, too. Things are undeniably tense and awkward when I'm with my family, but short visits work well. Usually no one gets hurt that way."

She smiled sadly. Would short visits work with her mother? *Only if she'd want to see you.* Who wanted to live their life that way? Waiting for a phone call from her mother to say it was okay to come visit? A phone call that probably would only come when her mother was between men, canceled at the last minute if the guy came back or a new one entered? No, she wasn't going to do that, put her child through the drama. She had to build relationships and connections on her own, for them both.

With a man who wasn't sure where he wanted to be?

"No matter how hard you try, you can't live for other people. You have to be your own person first, a person you can live with so that whoever you're involved with can't make or break your happiness."

Wise advice. Until the baby came and she recovered, she was stuck in town with Garret. That was a given. But what about afterward? What did a person do when she was sure what the right decision was but wasn't ready to make it?

"GARRET, we need to talk." Harry bulldozed his way into the office and shut the door.

Garret set the supply report aside and frowned at his

boss. "I didn't think you were coming in today. Something wrong?"

"Yes, something is wrong. You listen to me and listen good. You know I'm not a patient man, and I've had enough of this Darcy person and the talk that's going around. Whatever it is that has you going over there nearly every night to see that woman won't last."

"Darcy is on her own and doesn't know anyone in town. You can't sympathize with that?"

"Don't give me that bull. That may have been true when she first arrived, but she knows plenty of people now. I know about her working for Nick, and isn't that supposedly *why* she's staying with Rosetta? As her companion?" he demanded pointedly. "She doesn't need you babysitting her. Joss is—"

"Joss and I have discussed this, Harry, and she's okay with it." He couldn't say that *they* were okay because they weren't, but the last thing he'd do was discuss his suspicions with Harry. He wasn't sure whom to confront first. Joss, Tobe. Or himself. Had too many hours working and his friendship with Darcy pushed Joss into Toby's arms?

People cheat because they want to, no one makes them.

And before he could throw stones he had to take a hard look at what he'd done with Darcy last night. That factored in, too. Complicated things more.

"I don't want you seeing that woman."

"I'll see whomever I damn well please."

"Then you're a fool. She's taking advantage of you and you're blind to it. Just like you've always been to Richardson hanging on to your family's coattails."

He left the subject of Toby alone. "Darcy hasn't asked for a thing from me. If anything I have to make her accept my help because she doesn't like charity."

Harry growled. "I'll prove to you what kind of person she is. All I have to do is offer her some money and you'll see how fast she runs with it."

He stood but didn't move from behind the desk, knowing it gave him the position of power in the room. Two could play Harry's hard ball. "Stay away from her. Darcy isn't like that, and if you upset her, you'll answer for it."

"To who? You?"

He smirked. "I won't have to say a word. Think my grandmother will let you get by with tormenting a pregnant woman in her care?"

"She needs to go."

"Go *where?* Darcy can't travel."

"There are ways. I'll *hire* someone to drive her out of here if I have to."

"Harry, I mean it. You keep your foul moods away from her. Upsetting Darcy could send her into labor."

"If it means she'd leave sooner, that would be a good thing. Garret, fix this. You end it now or else."

"What are you saying?"

"Do you really think your job will survive, treating my daughter this way? Think your brother will get that promotion if this continues?"

"Now you're resorting to *threats?*"

"Take it however you like," the man drawled. "The gallery opening is in three weeks. The place will be crawling with reporters and people ready for a party, and I expect you to help give them one. Propose to Jocelyn beforehand and let the damn opening night of that nightmare be for something meaningful. After dragging her along for years, she deserves a special evening. In the meantime, stay away from that pregnant tramp or I'll see to it you aren't left standing."

Garret watched Harry leave, all the anger and frustration inside him reaching critical mass. He was sick of this. Sick of the drama, the godlike haul-ass-and-get-it-done-now-or-else behavior Harry had displayed for the past couple years. Sick of it all.

He sat and stared out the window, not giving a flying leap about the supply lists or contracts on his desk, not even the one he'd worked so hard to get. He'd crashed and burned a long time ago, he just hadn't wanted to face it.

"Deep thoughts for such a beautiful day." Gram regarded him from the doorway, concern in her eyes. "I take it Harry is on another rampage?"

Normally he would've brushed her off with a smile, laugh and firm no comment, but he didn't. He shoved himself upright, deciding Harry could review the contract if he wanted nurses working the hospital in the near future. "Want to go get some coffee?"

A smile lit her features. "I'd love to."

Fifteen minutes later they were in a coffee shop off main street, the place mostly empty because of the time of day.

"Harry's applying pressure, is he?" Gram murmured.

"You could say that."

"Did something happen between you and Darcy?"

His head jerked up. "Why do you ask?"

Gram smiled in that knowing way she had. "Because she's looking much the same way you do. I know the two of you are getting close. I can tell. And I'm worried about you. Both of you."

He stared into the murky depths of his drink. "We were just friends, but now—" How could he describe how he felt?

"Now you're more? Is that wise considering the relationship you already have in your life?"

"No. I can't say that it is. I'm…confused, Gram."

"Darcy is a wonderful girl. She'd make any man a good wife."

"But so is Joss," he added.

"Very true."

"You're not helping me here, Gram." He took a sip of the coffee he didn't want. "Harry wants me to propose to Joss the night of the gallery opening. Make it a big to-do." He couldn't look at her.

"Is that what you want?"

"I want…peace. I want things to settle down with my job and with Harry on a rampage all the time and me doing his job and mine, I can't find it unless—"

"Unless what?"

He'd been about to say *unless I'm with Darcy* but would Gram understand? How could she when *he* didn't? "Joss is a good woman. We're good together and I love her. I do love her."

"I know."

"Three years is a long time to wait, but she has and she's been patient. She's been fantastic. She hasn't pressured me, has stood by me working long hours and weekends. But lately things have been…strained, and I'm wondering if it's time to fish or cut bait."

"Because you're interested in Darcy now, too?"

He didn't answer right away. Wasn't about to mention what he'd seen to Gram. If he did marry Joss, he didn't want Gram suspicious of Joss every time she saw her talking to Toby. *It was nothing. They were just talking— you are the one who's crossed the line.* "With Darcy I feel…different." He made himself meet her gaze. "I want what you and Grandpa had, Gram. But how do I know which one is *the* one when both of them would make me happy?"

Gram dabbed at her eyes with a napkin.

"I'm sorry. All I've done is upset you. I should've known you'd—"

"No, Garret. No, that's not it. Some people go their entire lives never finding someone to love. You've been blessed with two wonderful women."

"Joss is great and we're good together, but how do I know good couldn't be better?"

"Darcy?"

He managed a nod. "I don't want to hurt either one of them."

"Then I suggest you figure out where you stand and quickly," she told him, "because the longer you drag this out, the worse someone is going to be hurt."

CHAPTER TWENTY-TWO

THE WEEK of Rosetta's birthday party passed with surprising swiftness, but with it came more anxiety and stress. Darcy sighed. Trying to protect herself was impossible. It was too late for that. So she simply tried to take the days one at a time and distract herself from the fact that Garret had distanced himself from her.

Twice during the week she'd overdone things at the gym and needed to take the medicine to end the cramping. A little rest and she was back on her feet again, even though she could barely see them. Garret called three times to check on her, claiming work kept him away. She wasn't convinced, and came to the conclusion that he regretted what they'd shared on the couch, just like he'd regretted the kiss in her bedroom, which made her all the more embarrassed by her behavior. And angry. At him, at herself.

Garret didn't come to see her and Rosetta as he had before. Was he spending the time with Jocelyn? What were they doing? Did he touch Jocelyn the way he'd touched her?

Jealousy sucked. How did women *do* this? Here she was going to have a baby, for pity's sake. The timing couldn't have been worse for her to meet Garret, but she had and it was too late. She cared for him. Wanted him—and he wasn't hers to want.

"Something wrong, dear?"

Darcy started and realized she'd been staring into space. She finished drying the plate she held. "Just thinking about how giving my clients have been. The gifts and all. It won't be easy to pack up. I'll have to rent a U-Haul to move everything."

"You're thinking of moving? Not staying?"

"Why would I stay?"

"Well, there's plenty of time to decide. And plenty of places around town to live if you change your mind about making Beauty your home. Not that I'm in a hurry for you to leave. I like having you here."

"Yeah, well, if Nick continues at the current pace on my car, I'll never be able to move." Rosetta looked away and busied herself scrubbing an already-clean counter. "Did you tell him to do it at snail speed?"

She knew she was right in her thinking when Rosetta had the grace to blush. The two-week time frame had come and gone—three weeks ago.

"I'll only admit to suggesting to him that I was afraid if he got the work done right away, you might decide to ignore doctor's orders and drive on alone."

Darcy inhaled and sighed once more. She'd decided to do just that a million times over, but common sense prevailed when she remembered what it was like to be stuck at the side of the road in labor.

"We both agreed it was a good idea to…delay things a bit. Are you upset with me, dear?"

She put the plate away and grabbed another, careful not to drip on her dress. "No. It's sweet that you care so much. Rosetta, I'll never be able to repay you for all you've done for me."

"You've done as much or more for me, Darcy. You've

been a wonderful friend and I don't like the idea of you out there alone. I like watching over you. I've come to think of you as family."

That was the problem. It was becoming all too easy to pretend the Tulane family *was* hers. Rosetta's grandmotherly love and support was so precious, so reminiscent of Nana. Darcy liked the feeling of being watched over, too. Nick and Ethan, they were the brothers she'd never had. And Garret— Her feelings for him could only deepen at this point. A useless act since they could only develop so far. A week of his keeping his distance was proof of that.

"Darcy?" Rosetta's face softened. "Oh, honey. You're falling in love with him, aren't you?"

"No." Denial was automatic, a built-in life preserver. "No, I'm not." It was time to grow up. For her baby's sake, if not her own. Which meant not becoming any more involved with a man destined to marry another woman.

A sharp knock sounded on the condo door before it opened and closed, ending their conversation.

She turned away from Rosetta, putting the last plate away and trying to brace herself for the barrage of feelings overwhelming her. She wasn't falling. She'd *fallen*. Hard, fast. How could she have allowed it to happen? Staying in Beauty was temporary. *Garret* was temporary. How awkward was it going to be to meet the infamous Jocelyn Pierson, caretaker of the hospital's poor and underprivileged? How difficult would it be to look the other woman in the eye knowing Garret had kissed *her?*

He might've kissed you, but where has he been?

She heard heavy footfalls enter the kitchen and her heart picked up speed. If Garret gave her that look, she'd know everything would be all right but— She turned to see Ethan smiling at them both. "Wow. You two look hot."

Ethan had come to pick them up. Not Garret.

Because he would escort his girlfriend *to the party, not you.*

Darcy clutched the countertop, closed her eyes briefly. What *was* she thinking? *Doing?* She had a baby to care for, a life to build, and here she was thinking about a man? What about her baby? Garret had turned her into—

"Are you all right, Darcy?"

"I'm fine."

"You look a little pale." Ethan frowned at her, wearing his doctor face. "Are you sure you're up for this?"

She saw the gentle warning in his eyes, as if he was well aware of what was going through her mind. Rosetta, now Ethan. They'd known all along what she hadn't been able to see. The gossip was true. She'd become the other woman.

Somehow she managed to pin a weak smile to her lips, her stomach in knots. "Let's get this party started."

Because the sooner it was over, the sooner it was *all* over, the sooner she could leave.

JOSS SMOOTHED a hand over her dress and frowned at the Jeep they neared. "Isn't that Tobias's?"

Garret shot her a glance, then shrugged. "Yeah. Why do you ask?"

"No reason. You'd said the party was mostly going to be family and friends, that's all."

"Toby's a friend. You don't think so?"

"Of course. I spoke without thinking." Or had she? Was this the beginning of her filling her father's shoes?

They continued on, entered the large double doors leading into the Tulane family home.

"There he is. Let's go."

Her head snapped up, her gaze immediately locking on Tobias. He'd been watching them.

"I see a friend I need to speak to." Jocelyn dug her four-inch heels into the opulent carpet. "I'll join you in a minute."

Garret's gaze sharpened. "Something wrong?"

"No. Why would you think that?"

Before he could answer she saw Garret's attention leave her. She followed his gaze and found Ethan escorting Rosetta and her pregnant guest into the room. So this was Darcy Rhodes.

She wished the woman was prettier. Not that Darcy was ugly by any means. But she was *attractive*, not beautiful, which made Garret's talk-of-the-town friendship with her all the more disturbing. Was something going on between them? "We need to say hello to your grandmother and wish her a happy birthday." She didn't know why she said it. She didn't want to meet Darcy face-to-face and knew that to walk over there she forced them both into a slew of speculation. But she didn't care. No, there was a reckless-ness taking hold inside her, one that had grown every day since she'd broken all the rules and kissed Garret's best friend.

"If you like."

Joss fell into step beside Garret and forced her chin high, aware that Tobias's mocking gaze followed.

THREE HOURS after the string band played "Happy Birth-day" for Rosetta's arrival, Darcy accepted the cake handed to her by one of the catering staff and looked around for a quiet spot. Not finding any nearby, she escaped the crowded main rooms and made her way down a hallway. Spying an open, darkened room, she slipped inside and collapsed into the closest chair, her nerves raw, her emotions under a thin thread of control.

Garret's parents were warm and welcoming and had made her feel very much a part of things despite the questions she saw in their expressions. Garret's family was… awesome. They hugged and congratulated each other over the slightest accomplishments, complimented each other, missed each other. Only Nick stood off to the side, listening, watching it all, the quietest of the bunch, speaking when spoken to and obviously on edge.

Worse, her feet hurt, her back hurt and she felt totally inferior and out of place in her bargain-basement maternity dress compared to Garret's gorgeous girlfriend. She wore Vera Wang on her size-four body and wore it well.

Meeting Jocelyn had been just as painful and awkward as she'd feared. Another eye-opening smack to the face because she and Garret looked so perfect together. If not for Rosetta's presence at her side, she would've left then and there. Maybe it was a good thing Nick hadn't returned her car because had she had it, she would've jumped inside and driven to the next town at least. Anything to establish some distance.

Sighing, she propped the cake on her built-in belly tray and closed her eyes, concentrating on relaxing her tense muscles in the hopes that the cramping she'd felt off and on all night would fade. The last thing she wanted to do was ruin someone's enjoyment of Rosetta's party by having to ask for a ride back to the condo. Or the hospital.

Multiple footsteps approached the room where she sat. *Keep walking. Don't come in, keep walking. Please.* She needed a moment alone to regain her composure.

"For the last time, go away and leave me alone."

"You can't *talk* to me?"

Darcy recognized the voice of Garret's girlfriend and Toby Richardson. She shrank down in the high-backed chair, wanting to disappear.

"What are you doing, Tobias? Do you want people talking about us? I've had enough gossip these past few weeks."

Darcy winced, her guilt growing.

"Then what's a little more? Stop treating me like the plague."

"I'm marrying Garret."

"If he asks."

"He's going to. He told Daddy that he planned to ask the night of the gallery opening."

Her throat closed. So that was it. That explained Garret's absence. He'd felt guilty about their make-out session, he'd made his decision and that was that, wasn't it?

Darcy lifted a hand to her mouth. Jocelyn's announcement was proof positive that she had to get out of there. Out of Rosetta's condo. Out of Beauty. Far, far away.

"When are you going to see what a mistake this is?"

A mistake? Darcy waited for Jocelyn's answer, holding her breath when a cramp sharpened and became uncomfortable. She squirmed in the seat.

"It's *not* a mistake."

"He's interested in someone else. You're just going to overlook that? Do you really think that little stunt you pulled, having Garret introduce you to her, fooled anyone?"

"It's your motives that are suspect, Tobias. What if he'd seen you that night in the parking lot? Walked out and heard the things you were saying to me? He was right inside the gym."

What night?

"We were talking. What was he doing that night?"

"What do you mean?"

"He went to her. I drove around for a while to cool off, and since I was curious to see if he was with you, I drove by Rosetta's. Garret was there. The thing is, I kept driving and ran into Rosetta. She was out with friends. They'd been to a movie, had dinner. Which means Darcy and Garret were in the condo alone. If you love him so much, are you going to stand there and tell me that doesn't bother you?"

Darcy fisted her hands, trapped, angry and hurting. Garret had come to see her that night because—

It doesn't matter. You're leaving anyway. Soon as the baby is born, you're outta here. Why does it matter?

Because it hurt so much. She'd sensed Garret's upset that night. His distraction and unwillingness to talk about whatever had put him in his brooding mood. Now she knew why. Her face burned with anger and embarrassment. Garret had given her pleasure and not taken any for himself, but she still felt used. As if she were the toy he'd played with because the one he wanted wasn't available.

"No. No, it doesn't bother me. He's her friend, just her friend."

Just her friend. Of all the people to forget that fact, why did it have to be her?

"You're really going to do this? You're going to marry him because Daddy says so?"

"I'm going to marry Garret because I love him. Nothing you say can change that."

Darcy closed her eyes.

"Now be a true friend to Garret and me both, Tobias. Leave us alone."

The sound of Jocelyn's heels faded as she continued on

her way down the tiled hall. Darcy stayed where she was, unmoving. Another pain slid around her stomach, harder than the one before.

The gallery opening was two weeks from today. Which meant she had to leave town before then.

Toby cursed, then shoved open the door, startling her. The light above her head flicked on, and she winced at the blinding brightness, grimacing as she waited to see if she would be discovered.

He stalked over to the wet bar at the far side of the study, poured himself a drink and turned, spotting her immediately. He froze, the glass halfway to his lips. "Aw, hell."

Darcy set the forgotten cake aside, managing to get to her feet without too much trouble.

"Darcy, wait."

"Why? Does anything really need to be said?" She rubbed her back in slow, hard circles, thankful for once her body was cooperating. Two weeks was plenty of time to recover. At least enough to get out of town.

"I'm sorry."

Another contraction began, slow and insidious, spreading around her, through her, becoming sharp and piercing. She bit her lip, closed her eyes.

"Please don't tell me— No way. I just went through this with my sister," he complained.

The comment made her laugh despite the tears setting her throat on fire. "Traumatized you, did it?"

"You could say that." Toby set the drink on the bar and hurried toward her. "Need a ride? I know a back way out of here. If you're interested?"

"Definitely."

"Think you can make it around the porch to the front? If so, I'll meet you there with your coat."

She didn't move until the contraction passed. "Yes. I...I can do that. But don't tell anyone. I don't want to ruin the party."

"No problem. Let's go."

Toby showed her the French doors that opened out onto a wraparound porch. She headed toward the front of the house slowly, careful to watch her step on the moisture-slicked planks, thankful for the moon lighting the way around expensive outdoor furniture and planters. Darcy rounded the corner of the house only to pause. Garret sat sprawled on a bench staring up at the night sky.

He heard her and turned, immediately shoved himself to his feet. "What are you doing?"

"Leaving."

"Where's your coat? Are you feeling all right? What happened?"

"I'm fine. I just want to go ho— To the condo. Please give Rosetta my best and tell her I'm tired. I'll see her in the morning."

"Don't leave." He shrugged his suit jacket off and wrapped it around her. "I'll take you upstairs. You can lie down in one of the bedrooms. If you're not feeling well, you shouldn't be alone."

She shrugged the coat off and handed it back to him. "Thanks, but no. And I won't be alone. Your friend Toby is driving me."

"Toby?" He tossed the jacket aside. "Why are you going with *Toby?*"

"He's leaving. He's going to drop me off on his way home."

He took another step closer. "Are you sure that's it?

Where were you? I've been looking for you. I wanted to tell you something."

"I— In the bathroom. Pregnant women, you know?"

"Darcy, what's going on? Did someone say something to you?"

"No. No one said a thing to me. In fact, everyone has been amazingly nice, considering."

"Considering what?"

"Considering who I am. I see where you get your kindness and manners. Your parents are great. And Jocelyn is— She's beautiful. I heard about what she's doing for the children's ward at the hospital, using the gallery opening to get donations. That's sweet. You're going to be happy with her."

Garret stiffened. "What did you say?" He grasped her elbow and gently tugged her deeper into the shadows along the side of the porch.

Embarrassed to be seen with her?

"You're upset." He swore softly. "Darcy, I'm sorry about this week. Work has been a nightmare with Harry arguing every change, and I thought, given timing, it might be good for both of us to take a breather and make sure we're doing the right thing."

"It was perfect timing," she agreed. His expression softened into one that tugged at her heartstrings—until they broke.

"If this is about me not picking you up tonight—"

"Of course not. I mean, why would you bring me? I'm not your girlfriend. Or should I say fiancée?"

CHAPTER TWENTY-THREE

SEEING GARRET GRIMACE at her wording didn't make Darcy feel any better.

"This hasn't been fair to you or Jocelyn."

"You're right. Which is why I'm going to do what I should've done from the beginning—keep my distance and ask that you keep yours." She shook her head when he opened his mouth. "I mean it, Garret. This week, tonight, helped me realize I've turned into someone I *swore* I'd never be—the other woman." She laughed, the sound bitter to her own ears. "My mother may be on husband number four, but it's not for lack of trying to get other women's husbands to notice her. I know better than to think situations like this end happily. It's ironic to think of myself as a homewrecker, big as I am, but it's true. That's what they consider me, too. The people in there."

"You're—"

"You care for me. I know that, I can see it in your face. It's not enough. This isn't what I want."

"Stop. Before you say anything else, hear me out. I—"

"I can't *do* this! No matter what you say right now, no matter how you look at me or make me *feel,* I can't handle a baby and a relationship. Especially one like ours would be."

"How would it *be?* Are you saying you won't even give me a chance?"

"It would be awful." She waved a hand to indicate the house. "I've been in there wandering around all night, listening to everyone talk about you and her and how soon you'll be married. They're all excited about it. Then there were the whispers about me that would stop when I got near. They love you, Garret. They're concerned about you." She smiled up at him, the effort costing her more than he'd ever know. "I didn't want to like her but I did. Jocelyn could've been really mean and hateful toward me because of all the talk, because of what we've *done*."

"Darcy—"

"But she wasn't. She went out of her way to be nice, and that only made me feel worse." Now she knew why Melanie irritated Scarlett O'Hara so much. All that goodness and kindness was hard to take.

"You're both nice. You're both beautiful and friendly but that's what made this—"

"Garret, *stop*. She was *nice*. Three years is too long a time to date someone only to throw it away when someone like me crashes into town and gets your attention by foisting myself on you. That's all it was, too. You reached out to me, connected with me, because you thought I was safe. I'm pregnant, passing through. I was someone you could talk to. Mess around with."

"Dammit, Darcy, it wasn't like that." Garret stepped close, but she backed away. He stopped with a low growl of frustration. "You're more than that. Darcy, you have every right to doubt me, to be scared, but I need you to hear me. I've made this situation worse by being so indecisive, but I needed to bring Jocelyn tonight. I felt like I owed her that because—"

"Doesn't that tell you something? Because it tells me

what I need to hear, loud and clear. Garret, I have to put my baby first. And I'm doing it tonight."

"Don't do this. Not now. I just need a little more time."

"Whatever we had is over, Garret."

Darcy shook her head, tried to ignore the cramp growing stronger, taking her ability to breathe normally.

"Darcy?" His gaze narrowed. "Darcy, are you—"

The door opened behind them. "Darcy?" Toby's low murmur couldn't have come at a better time.

"I'm h-here." She needed help. Knew she couldn't walk away from Garret on her own.

"I'm taking you to the hospital."

"No."

"Dammit, Darcy—"

"Stop swearing at her," Toby ordered, moving to her side.

"Tobe, stay out of this."

The contraction finally ended and she released the breath she held in a gush. "Don't talk to him like that. At least Toby knows what he wants."

Toby helped her into her coat. "Come on."

"No. Darcy, wait."

She laughed, surprising both men if their expressions were any indication. "I said that to you," she told Garret. "The night you found me in the snow. Now I wish you had kept driving."

"You don't mean that."

"Yeah, I do. My baby deserves the best I can give it, and that means being with someone who can put us first. I refuse to be second anymore. I can't be my mother, Garret. Not even for you."

"You're not your mother, sweetheart. You're scared

because you've convinced yourself the only person you can rely on is yourself, but that's not true. Don't do this. I needed some time to think, but I know what I want now. I know I want *you*, Darcy."

Pain coursed through her, but whether it was from the contractions or her heart shattering, she wasn't sure. "No, you don't. You want what you can't have," she whispered, struggling to hold her head high. "Goodbye, Garret. Be happy."

"Darcy, don't do this. Not now. Let me come with you."

She shook her head, sad, terrified, afraid she was broken inside where it mattered most.

Toby wrapped an arm around her back and helped her to his Jeep. Darcy stared out the window at Garret's imposing form looking so masculine against the wide white columns of the house, the image bringing back more memories of the first night she'd met him. Tears blurred her eyes but she didn't let them fall. She'd cried enough. Now it was time to be strong.

As Toby drove her down the mountain to the hospital, her contractions began to hit closer together, harder, more intense. *Oh, Nana, I need help. Why aren't you here?*

"You okay?"

"You stared at her all night," she whispered. "I saw you watching her and wondered…before I ever heard what you said. Do you love her, too?"

Toby didn't pretend to not know what or who she was talking about. "Yeah. What about you and Garret?"

"Yeah."

"Fine mess we got ourselves into, isn't it?"

She wrapped her hands around her rock-hard stomach. *Mama loves you.* "Yeah."

GARRET PULLED JOSS out of the crowded house and onto the porch.

"Garret? Where have you been? I haven't seen you for over an hour."

"Darcy's in labor."

The words made her blanch. Already pale, she turned positively ghostlike. Before Darcy had found him he'd sat here and reviewed everything in his head. Three years of dates with Joss—laughs, sex, holidays and vacations spent together. Family gatherings like the one tonight. The feeling of dissatisfaction he'd felt for too long. The scene in the gym's parking lot. All of it jumbled up inside his head, combining with the time he'd spent with Darcy. The way she smelled, laughed. Her heart of gold and the kindness she'd shown toward others in little ways. Extra time working at the massage table because someone had had a bad day, the way she jumped up to help Gram when he knew Darcy had to be hurting and uncomfortable. The way she'd welcomed him into her arms, was honest about her feelings. Her fears. What had he done? Why had he waited so long?

Straightening, he turned around and took Joss into his arms. Her eyes widened when he palmed her face and brought her mouth to his, kissing her for all he was worth. Lips, teeth, tongue, seductive strokes and all the finesse he had in him. After a moment he lifted his head and watched her closely. But other than blinking her eyes open and giving him a weak smile, his kiss had garnered no more passion than a brotherly kiss on the cheek. More proof of what he already knew.

"Garret, what's wrong?"

"Do you love me?"

She hesitated a split second. "Of course I do."

"No." His hands fell to her shoulders. "Do you *love* me? Are you *in love* with me? Do you imagine the two of us together for the next *fifty* years? Day after day, night after night? Do you dream about me making love to you?"

"Garret, I—"

"Do. You. *Love*. Me?" He shook her gently. "Do *you* want to marry me, or are you simply doing what you think you're supposed to do? What we're supposed to do because it's been three years and everybody says it's the next step?"

She inhaled a sharp gasp. "*What?* You're asking me this now? *Here?*"

"I need to hear you say it. I wouldn't hurt you for the world, but I need to hear you tell me you love me, that you can't imagine living your life without me. Because if you can't say it, we both know something's wrong."

"You're making this about *me* when it's…it's really about you. Can *you* say it?"

He didn't want to hurt her. "No."

"Because of Darcy."

"Because I need more from my wife than you're willing to give. When I kiss you, touch you, what do you feel? I just kissed you and you looked bored by it. Are you going to stand there and say you want *years* together after that kind of response? That you haven't pulled away from me lately because you're not feeling me?"

She opened her mouth, but other than trembling lips and the sound of her breath panting, no sound came for a long, long time. "Garret, I…" A tear trickled down her cheek. "I care for you. *So much.* I'd do anything for you. You are such a good man and a wonderful friend. My best friend. I never wanted to hurt you or endanger your position with my father because I *know* how he can be, but I don't—"

"Love me? Not like that? Not like a *husband?*"

Trembling from head to toe, she shook her head.

"Thank God. I don't love you, either. I do—" he dropped a kiss to her forehead "—love you, but not like a wife."

She looked as shell-shocked as he felt. "Oh, Garret. How did we let this happen? How did we let it come this far?"

"I guess at the time, no one else made us stop to take notice. Now they have."

She smoothed a trembling hand over her hair. "We've been together so long. Like everyone else, I thought we were it. I couldn't stand to hurt you, and Daddy never let up about us getting married. I didn't want to ruin things at the hospital or your relationship with him after all this time. It sounds so fatalistic now, but—"

He hugged her close. "I know. Joss, I was going to do the same thing."

Her arms surrounded him, held tight. "What are we going to do? What happens next?"

"I'll go along with whatever you tell people. Whatever you want to tell Harry."

She exhaled roughly. "Daddy is going to be furious with us both. Oh, this is a nightmare. And right before the *opening*. Oh, no."

Garret moved back far enough to lift her chin with his hand. "Blame me. Tell him I'm a jerk who strung you along, tell him anything you want. Just know Darcy and I haven't slept together. This isn't about her. It's about us not living the lives we want."

Her lashes fell over her eyes. "I kissed someone else. Once."

He grinned, knowing without a doubt who that person was and unable to believe the mess they'd both have been in if he'd done as ordered and proposed. He bussed the top of her head and squeezed her tight once more. "You're the best, Joss, but I have to go. I have to get Gram and go to the hospital. Darcy can't have the baby alone."

"No. No, of course not."

Garret released her, then hesitated. "I don't know if Darcy will forgive me for making such a mess of things, but this is a lesson for both of us, you know. Maybe you could make this the night you stand up to your father and go after Toby."

Her eyes widened, her mouth parting in a sharp gasp. "You knew?"

He shook his head. "A good guess, now confirmed."

"I'm sorry, Garret. We both felt horrible that it happened. We didn't want to hurt you."

He accepted that with a nod. "Don't hurt each other trying to figure things out. And don't wait like we did, Joss. Three years is way too long to keep your true feelings to yourself. If you care for him, tell him."

Amazingly, Joss smiled. "Maybe. We'll see. Go to Darcy and tell her…tell her good luck. Give her my best. Maybe we could be friends later. When the weirdness goes away."

Garret grinned, winked at her, then raced for the door. "Gram!"

DARCY COULDN'T BELIEVE her eyes when Rosetta and Marilyn Tulane entered her delivery room. Hot on their heels was a nurse.

"Ladies, I'm sorry, but you're going to have to wait in the waiting room."

Rosetta zeroed in on Darcy's bed and headed toward her without pause, leaving Marilyn to speak with the nurse. She took Darcy's hand and bent over the rail, giving her a motherly kiss and a glare. "Don't you ever think a party is more important than you."

"I didn't want to ruin your fun," she whispered, touched by the woman's words.

"Well, now the party is over and we're here."

She glanced at Garret's mother. "Um…"

Marilyn Tulane smiled at her. "Do you mind? Between Rosetta and me, we've both been through this many times. We'd like to help you if we can."

But Garret's *mother*?

"Darcy, what do you say?" one of the nurses asked. "Do they stay or go?"

Marilyn came to join Rosetta by the bed. Her expression softened when she got a good look at Darcy's tear-streaked face. "Or would you like someone else? Garret wants to come in—"

"No. Absolutely not."

"He said you didn't want to see him anymore." Rosetta looked as if she couldn't quite believe the news.

"I don't. I don't want to see him because it's not right. For either of us. He's—"

"Ladies, let's not upset her, please," Dr. Clyde said, coming into the room. "Darcy has quite a bit on her plate as it is."

Marilyn nodded, her expression sad. "I understand. And all that can wait until later, but Garret can't stand the thought of you being here alone. If you send us out, he'll likely break the door down and make a scene. We'd love to keep you company and lend you our support, Darcy. Please?"

Darcy gripped Rosetta's hand, afraid to believe in the kindness she saw in their eyes. Afraid to think too much about why she'd been born to a mother who didn't want her around instead of someone like Rosetta or Marilyn who took on responsibilities not their own.

Ask and ye shall receive.

"Oh, Nana."

"Pardon, dear?"

"You can stay. I'd love for you to—" Tears filled her eyes, a lump the size of Texas in her throat. "Thank you." *Thank you.*

"Oh, honey."

Both women patted and fussed and assured her that no thanks were needed, and Darcy cried even harder because it was just too sweet. Too much. Their presence, their caring, their love for a stranger who'd crashed into their lives and caused so many problems.

Marilyn brushed her bangs out of her eyes. "We'll get you through this, and when you hold your baby, it'll all be okay, Darcy. You'll see."

She doubted that. Nothing would ever be okay again after knowing these people, but she didn't argue. Couldn't when a pain started low in her back and spread, deep and hard, leaving her curled up on her left side on the bed. She closed her eyes and tried to breathe, felt someone surround her hand in a reassuring, comforting grip. Seconds later her other hand was taken—and she held tight to the mothers she'd always wanted.

TOBY HEARD HIM first. Head low, Garret sat on the floor of the L&D waiting room, staring at the secured doors and muttering to himself between curses. Unlike the night Toby had brought Maria in, the room was empty.

He hesitated briefly, then continued walking and lowered himself onto the floor beside Garret with a sigh.

"Haven't seen you in a while. Now twice in one night. You been lying low?"

"Just busy." He made the statement before he noticed Garret's expression, the knowledge in his friend's eyes. He suppressed a groan and braced himself for a blow, determined he wouldn't block it.

"You'd better treat her right, Tobe."

He decided it was a good thing he was sitting down. "What?"

"You heard me. You'd better treat Joss right. She's a good woman and if you don't get your butt in gear and—" Garret pulled a box from his pocket "—give her the ring you picked out for her, some other jerk will come along and claim her." He tossed the box up in the air.

Toby caught it instinctively.

"Harry hates you, you need to know that up-front. All hell is going to break loose when he finds out about you and Joss, but I think with the gallery and all this, she's finally ready to be her own woman and stand up to him. Take advantage of it."

Toby sat there. *Stunned* didn't begin to describe how he felt right now. "You, uh… What about you? You know… us?"

Garret rolled his head along the wall and shot him a glare. "I don't like it that you didn't speak up, but who am I to talk after falling for Darcy under the circumstances?"

Toby stared at the box in his hand. Opened it up and there it was. The ring he'd chosen for the woman he loved.

"You can pay me in installments, but everything about the partnership has to be fifty-fifty."

Flipping the lid closed again, he tucked it into the inside of his coat pocket. "Deal."

And then they waited.

CHAPTER TWENTY-FOUR

SIX HOURS LATER nurses swarmed into the room to break down the bed, and Dr. Clyde told Darcy to push. She thought it would be over then. Who knew it took so long to have a baby? After another forty-five minutes, she bore down one more time and the baby made its way into the world.

Dr. Clyde looked up, her eyes crinkling behind her glasses and mask. "Congratulations, Darcy. You have a beautiful baby girl."

Rosetta and Marilyn smiled and laughed and wiped away tears as they oohed and ahhed over the squirming bundle in the doctor's hands. Darcy watched them all, unable to believe the baby was finally here and feeling out of sorts and dizzy now that it was over.

"Would you want one of these ladies to cut the cord?"

The question stumped her. She glanced up at Rosetta. "If Nana was here, she'd be the one I'd ask, but— Would you want to? You don't have to. I understand if—"

"I would love to, Darcy."

The nurse draped a blanket over Darcy's knees to give her some modesty and then the older woman moved into position.

Marilyn dabbed at her eyes and alternately patted Darcy or else gushed over the baby still in the doctor's care. Her daughter continued to cry as she was briskly wiped of fluid and wrapped in warmed blankets, then Dr. Clyde gave Darcy her daughter. "Support her head, yes, like that."

She was so light. So tiny. Her baby girl had blond hair like hers, long enough to curl at the ends, and her eyes were a dark, dark blue.

Tears trickled down Darcy's cheeks, but she smiled and laughed all the same. Ten tiny fingers and a button nose. Rosebud mouth. Definitely worth the pain.

Marilyn pulled her camera from her purse and snapped a shot of them gazing into each other's eyes. Another of Rosetta sitting beside her on the bed. One of each of them holding the baby, lots of her and her daughter together.

One of the nurses took the baby for its bath at the far end of the room, and Rosetta and Marilyn followed to watch, camera in hand, while Darcy stayed in the bed and tried to recover her composure while the linens were changed. She was a mom.

Dr. Clyde entered the room looking frazzled. "Darcy, Mr. Tulane is outside and quite insistent. He'd like to come in."

Ignoring the questioning, concerned stares of the women across the room, she shook her head firmly back and forth. Sad and tired and happy all at once. "Would you tell him we're fine and that— Tell him Spike is a girl."

"Darcy, are you sure?" Rosetta asked. "He's been out there for hours, dear. Waiting to talk to you."

Darcy shook her head, not about to be dissuaded. Her daughter's birth was a new start. A new life. *I won't be her.* "I'm sure."

DARCY FROWNED at Rosetta. Using winter colds and the baby's near-term birth and risk of respiratory problems as an excuse, Darcy had managed to avoid visitors after being released from the hospital. Most especially Garret, much to his grandmother's upset. "I don't want to see him."

"He's been by every day since you came home."

Yes, he had. With gifts, no less. A pumpkin seat to put the baby in, a car-seat-stroller combo, a bassinet. Then there was the gigantic pink giraffe, enough baby toys for four families, including a rocking horse with a curly mane. There were gifts for her, too. A set of silk pajamas in brown—to match her eyes, the note read. A new CD she'd mentioned in passing. Flowers, lots of flowers. Sunflowers and daisies—in *March*. And the last and boldest gift of all—business cards with her name on them, listing Nick's gym as her place of employment.

Once upon a time her entire life had fit in the storage compartments of her VW Beetle, allowing her to pick up and leave when and how she needed. Did stuff equal roots? "I haven't changed my mind."

The older woman frowned and went back to what she was doing, piling a third box full of donations from the residents of The Village.

"Rosetta, can't you understand why I find Garret's sudden turnaround questionable?"

"Of course I do. But you haven't seen him, Darcy. You don't know how haggard he looks. He's not sleeping, not eating much if at all. A man doesn't behave that way over a woman he *doesn't* love. He and Joss are no longer together."

"That has nothing to do with me."

"Oh, Darcy. How long are you going to punish him for being a caring man?"

She snuggled the baby closer, unable to respond.

"Garret loved Jocelyn in his own way, but I knew they

weren't right together. They were too comfortable, like friends, which is what they've turned out to be. When you came along and I saw the way he looked at you, I knew. The way he loves you—"

"He doesn't love me."

"No? I disagree. How many men would've given up on you already? Do you know how many people go through their lives searching for that kind of love and never find it?" She left the toy-filled boxes and garbage bags by the door and moved to sit on the couch beside her. "Think of your mother. She's searching for it man by man and here you are throwing the real thing away. I think you're afraid to love him."

"Rosetta, please."

"I think," Garret's grandmother continued determinedly, "that after watching your mother make so many mistakes and having made one yourself with the baby's father, you're afraid to love. You think it won't last."

"It usually doesn't."

"Is that why you haven't named the baby yet?"

"Deciding on a name isn't easy."

"It isn't. But Garret mentioned your penchant for trying out names, and after all this time, I can't help but wonder if you're afraid to name the baby because it'll eliminate the distance you're keeping between you and your daughter."

"That's a horrible thing to say!"

"Am I wrong? You claim to want roots and a family, but when the perfect opportunity comes along in Garret and the baby, you back away. If you name your daughter, you'll feel a mother's emotions, a mother's love, and you're afraid it'll make you face all the things you still haven't faced about your mother."

"I know exactly who my mother is."

"Yes, you do know. But have you accepted it?"

How could anyone fully accept their mother's not wanting them? Wouldn't everyone want that attitude to change? Want a miracle to happen? *Reality bites, Darcy. When are you ever going to break those stupid rose-colored glasses?*

"You've been taught what *not* to do, Darcy. Motherhood makes you vulnerable in ways you've never imagined, but it also makes you strong. It binds your hearts and there's nothing like it, but you have to be open and want to experience it, to feel it. Are you going to let your mother rob you of loving your daughter? Rob you of a man worthy of your love and who loves you?"

Little by little Rosetta's words sank in. Was she letting that happen? She didn't intend to, but was she? She could lie to Rosetta until she was blue in the face, but she couldn't lie to herself. She was letting her fear of messing up overshadow her love, her feelings. Naming the baby…and loving Garret.

"What if I screw it all up?"

Rosetta smiled. "You'll make mistakes. You'll *all* make mistakes. If you let yourself love and forgive, it'll work out exactly as it's supposed to."

She stared down at her baby's sweet little face, the knot in her stomach growing.

"If you stop running from your past and the fear your mother instilled in you, if you face it, Darcy, you'll see the love you feel for Garret and your daughter is returned. But to receive it, you must first believe in it yourself."

Darcy buried her nose into her daughter's blankets, breathed in her baby smell. "Nana used to say something similar to that."

Rosetta nodded. "Because it's true, dear."

"Why did Garret move out of the house?"

"Why do you think? He wanted a place for you and the baby to come home to when you're ready."

"His job?"

"He's been frustrated working for Harry and was more than ready to quit. And when taking such a fresh step in life, why not go all the way? I've heard the office space above the gallery is coming along nicely. He and Toby will make a wonderful team."

"How do I know it's real? Two weeks ago Garret couldn't decide if he wanted me or not—"

"He knew, Darcy. But he had other responsibilities that needed to be taken care of before he could commit to you. He didn't know how to end things with Joss. He isn't a mean person, he didn't want to hurt her. Oh, Darcy, *think*. You knew where his heart was leading him. It's quite obvious he isn't the type of man to be with you if he didn't care for you, but now that he's free, you won't give him the time of day. Do you really think that's a coincidence?"

She could blame her hormones, her fears of becoming a mother, for her behavior. But the truth was she *ached* from missing Garret, wanted him in her life. Loved him. The way he smiled, the silly songs he sang. What was she *doing*?

A knock sounded at the door. "Rosetta?"

"That's Toby's mother. She's come to pick up the donations for Jocelyn while the boys work on the office."

Rosetta's words weighed on her mind. While Rosetta answered the door, Darcy carried the baby back down the hall to her bedroom. She laid the baby in the bassinet, then moved toward her dresser where the doll sat propped against the mirror. She stared down into Miss Potts's face a long time, memories sliding over her. She'd treasured Miss Potts for so long, but why? Why keep her when she represented everything that was bad in her life? A bad childhood, lack of emotional commitment from her mother.

Ready for a fresh start like Rosetta said, Darcy hurried down the hall to the only box left by the door and put the doll inside. Out with the past, in with the future. She wouldn't let her fear override the gifts she'd been given. The life she had to lead if only she were brave enough.

Back in the bedroom she sat on the edge of the bed and stared into her daughter's beautiful face. "Gram's right," she whispered, using the name Rosetta insisted the baby would use. "It's time to stop running. Time to start believing and being the person I want to be. The mommy you need me to be, not my mother's daughter. I won't get it right all the time, but…I'll do my best." She smoothed her fingertips over her daughter's downy head. "So, before I go and tell Garret how much I love him and want him, what do you think about Elizabeth? You could go by Elizabeth or Beth, Eliza or Lizzie. Liz. You'd have a lot of options and," she added, "it's Gram's middle name and she's the best great-grandma you could ever possibly have. Do you like it?"

"I love it."

Darcy gasped and turned to see Garret in the doorway, looking just as haggard as Rosetta said he did, the doll in his hand. She got to her feet, her trembling legs barely able to hold her. He wore jeans and a pullover, both loose and hanging on him.

He lifted the doll. "Why are you getting rid of this?"

"Because she's part of the past and I want to concentrate on the future…with you," she whispered. "If you still want me."

Raw hope crossed his face. "Sweetheart, I've always wanted you. That hasn't been the problem. You love me?"

She nodded shakily.

"No, you've got to say it. I need to hear it. Do you love me?"

"Yes."

Some of the tension in his face eased. "Dream about waking up beside me for the next fifty years?"

"Yes."

He took a step closer, his eyes fierce. "Making love to you?"

"Yes."

"Do you believe I want you—only you—because I love you and...Spike?"

He said that with a grin, a heart-stopping, love-filled smile that stole the breath right out of her lungs. Garret had given up every constant in his life—his girlfriend, his job— for her. All for her and her baby girl. He'd put them first. He'd put them *first*. It was romantic in the movies, but it was more romantic when it really happened. More special. More...amazing.

"Darcy?" Garret opened his arms and she flew across the room, slammed into him but knew he'd catch her, hold her. Love her. Because she finally understood what she hadn't been able to before meeting Garret.

"I love you, Darcy." He buried his nose in her neck and inhaled. "Ahh, I've missed the way you smell. The way you feel. Not being able to see you has been killing me."

She swallowed, unable to believe she'd come so close to losing everything she'd ever wanted. "I know. I've missed you, too," she whispered, drawing back to trail her fingertips over his mouth. "I see it now."

"See what?"

Smiling through her tears, she leaned forward and kissed him, slow and deep, not breaking contact until they both breathed heavily. "I see that Nana's always right."

EPILOGUE

DARCY HAD NEVER GIVEN much thought to being a June bride, but she and Garret were married the second Saturday in June, five months to the day from when Garret rescued her. Rosetta was her matron of honor, Toby Garret's best man. She and Elizabeth wore white—just to give the gossips more to talk about—at her husband's insistence.

"Penny for your thoughts," Garret murmured later that evening, his arms sliding around her waist and turning her so that she snuggled against him. "Darcy, you okay, sweetheart?"

"I'm better than okay. I'm happy. Blessed. It's amazing." And even though her mother hadn't come to the ceremony, she was *still* okay, happy and blessed. Her love for Garret and Lizzie, for Garret's family, made it okay. Because she felt like her family *had* all been there. Garret's brothers and sister had flown in for the ceremony, his many aunts and uncles, cousins. So many cousins! It would take years to learn all their names.

Garret's fingers speared into her loose hair and he lifted her head so his mouth could close over hers.

"Mmm." He tasted of champagne and buttercream icing, desire and hard, hot man. His tongue coaxed her, eased her into a deeper, more possessive caress.

She fingered the buttons on his tuxedo shirt and then

began unbuttoning them, hungry, needy, wanting her husband the way she'd never wanted anyone. His hands slipped out of her hair, pulled down the zipper in the back of her dress, but she didn't notice him tugging on the thin, spaghetti straps until the cool air made her shiver. She lowered her hands, one at a time, and let the white silk drop to the floor, aided by his hands. Garret shook. She could feel him trembling, and it touched a place deep, deep inside, burrowed into her heart, her soul. Love could hurt, took an extraordinary amount of trust, but when it was right, it was so, so right.

Garret dropped his head to her neck, scoring her skin with his teeth just hard enough to send goose bumps over her entire body, make her nipples pucker. He chuckled huskily when he felt her response. "Still sensitive there, huh? Let's see where else."

It was a game they'd played a lot since declaring their feelings. Every time he bared more of her, his head lowered, his lips, teeth and tongue alternatively kissing, nipping or sucking at her until it was all she could do to remain on her feet. His hands roamed over her full breasts and around to the clasp of her strapless bra. Down to push her panties away until the only things she wore were her spiky, sparkly heels and lace-topped, thigh-high stockings.

"I think we'll leave those on." Her husband's green eyes were heated, filled with love and desire, all for her. Pulling at his shirt, he held her gaze as he removed it. "I know what to expect, Darcy." A small smile formed on his mouth. He nodded toward the bed and she followed his stare, searching until she spotted the bottle of gel Garret had purchased to ensure her comfort. They'd waited to make love, pleasuring each other in different ways while they grew even closer and made things official, giving her body plenty of time to heal from giving birth.

Smiling ruefully, she reached for his belt and unfastened the catch, the snap of his pants. Garret took care of the zipper, and she slid her palms around his waist beneath the band, smiling when she heard him release a husky groan the moment her body touched his full length. She kissed his chest, sidled closer still, and relished the hiss he released when his arousal pressed against her stomach.

"You make me crazy." Garret's palms slid over her back, cupped her rump and squeezed. He kissed her, hard and fast and with dizzying thoroughness. By the time Garret raised his head, she stood dazed, knees weak and wobbly, while he shucked his pants and underwear and gently pushed her backward until she sat on the edge of the king-size bed.

Kneeling on the floor in front of her with an appreciative leer, Garret arranged her just so, her legs on either side of him. Holding her gaze, his hands roamed. Her shoulders, the valley between her breasts. Her thighs. Back up again. Changing course, his fingers plucked at her nipples and rolled, drawing a sharp gasp from her because of the corresponding spear of desire that shot from her chest to her womb.

Garret leaned forward and fastened his lips over hers, leaving her awash with need. His stomach pressed against her warmth, and he slid an arm around her hips to pull her into closer contact, rubbing, teasing. Darcy squeezed her knees tight against his ribs to hold on to the sensation.

He trailed his lips lower, across the curve of her belly, lower, watching her with his passion-darkened gaze. Her heart pounded out of control, each breath harder to catch than the last because of the way he looked at her, unwavering as he pressed kiss after kiss lower over her stomach.

Her belly button. Her thighs. She waited, never realizing how sensual it was to—

She gasped when he kissed her there, moaned because he stroked and laved, and pleasure overtook her until she couldn't think at all. Her hips lifted into the strokes, her lips parted to take in more air, and slowly, so slowly, her body began to tighten. Garret's excitement was tangible as he watched her responding to him, and she embraced the moment. Another stroke, two. Slow, decadent drags of his tongue in just the right spot that sent her skyward with a broken cry.

Time passed, she wasn't sure if it was seconds or minutes, but she slowly became aware of Garret's words of praise as he kissed his way back up her body.

"Beautiful. So beautiful."

She was vaguely aware of Garret moving onto the bed, using the bottle of lubricant generously to better ease his way. She caught her breath at the feel of him, the ridge of him inside her, a bit more, then tightness.

His breath rushed out of his chest. "Are you okay?"

She nodded, eyes closed due to the sensations bombarding her. He felt so good. So right. Like two halves of a whole. Tears stung, and she blinked rapidly.

"Darcy— Sweetheart."

"Don't stop."

"I don't want to hur—"

"You're not. I'm just…happy." She managed a watery smile. "I'm *happy*," she repeated with a laugh. "I never thought I'd have this. You. *I love you.*"

She caught her breath when she saw the sheen of tears in his eyes before he closed them, felt the trembling inside him that revealed so much. He took her mouth in a powerful kiss, his hips moving in rocking motions, back and forth, until she slowly eased him all the way inside. They both groaned at the pressure, the sensation of him buried deep for the first time.

Garret kissed her, then set about pleasuring her all over again. She was amazed by the depth and breadth of this experience versus those of her past, relished the awareness because she knew she'd never treat Garret's love lightly having craved this for so long.

"Sweetheart, please. Ahh, you're killing me."

She smiled, lifted her knees around his hips and drove him deeper, tightened around him and pushed him over the edge. She savored his groans and the heat of his breath, the way he clutched her to him and held her like she was the most beautiful woman on earth—and she climaxed again.

Amazing.

She smiled up at the ceiling, her fingers in his hair, her mouth against his skin. *Amazing.* But then with Garret she'd come to expect nothing less. Garret and Elizabeth, her new family; they just proved that fairy tales could come true.

* * * * *

An Unexpected Delivery
LAURIE PAIGE

In honour of the two Graces –
Emma and Katharine.

Welcome to the world!

Chapter One

"Yes. Yes, I'll take care of it," Stacy Gardenas said into the telephone. She finished writing her boss's directions to his country house on a notepad.

"Repeat that," he ordered.

"Take 66 west to 81," she read from her notes. "North on 81 to the first exit. Go west. Take the second right turn onto Pine Valley Road. Look for a paved lane on the left side of the road two and half miles from the turnoff."

"Okay, you got it. Tell the courier to watch for the left turn. It's tricky. Travel time will be an hour and a half. Call me back if you run into trouble."

"I'll make arrangements as soon as we hang up."

"I suppose my partner has long departed?"

Stacy grinned, but when she spoke, her tone was neutral.

"Yes. He called Shirl and said he wouldn't be back today. The case was settled out of court."

"Out of court," Gareth Clelland repeated. "I'll be damned. For how much?"

She gave him the details.

"I suppose he's going to take tomorrow off, too." His voice, a baritone-bass, vibrated through the wire like the low murmur of the cello in one of Mozart's melodies. It was a voice that reflected its owner—quiet, confident and self-contained.

"Tomorrow is Friday," she answered. "And Monday is a holiday, Presidents' Day."

"Damn, I'd forgotten." There was a brief silence. "You may as well close the office after the courier picks up the package. You can take tomorrow off, too. Shirl can cover the phones."

"Right. And thank you for the time off." She waited for further instructions, pencil poised, her mind focused. Gareth didn't like to repeat himself.

"That's all, I think. It's 1:35. I'll expect the package by 3:30."

She checked her watch and adjusted it forward five minutes to match his. "I'll get right on it."

"Okay. I'll see you Tuesday then."

"Have a nice weekend," she said before he hung up.

Maybe it was mule-headedness on her part, but she persisted in inserting a few basic pleasantries into their conversations. Her taciturn employer wasted few words on amenities. She got a hello in the morning and a goodbye at night and very little in between. She added the extras.

He hesitated before replying, "Yeah. You, too."

The line echoed the faint click when he hung up. She grinned. Her niceties always seemed to surprise him and disrupt his thought processes. Well, he needed them jarred loose once in a while. All work and no play, blah, blah, blah...

She called the courier service. Then another. And another. They were booked solid. "All the gov'ment officials in D.C. are trying to clear their desks and head out of town for the long weekend," one of the dispatchers explained.

A common saying in the nation's capital—when government officials got a day off, they took another one to rest up for it.

She replaced the phone in its cradle and stretched her aching back. It had been hurting from the time she woke up that morning. She must have slept wrong. Or maybe it was the fact that she was eight months pregnant and counting.

Rising, she went into Gareth's office and unlocked the file cabinet. The brief was still in the folder, right where she'd placed it the other day. She wondered about that. Her boss rarely forgot anything.

After finding the other papers he wanted, she placed them inside a courier briefcase, clicked the locks on and spun the combination cylinders. Returning to her office, she tried three other delivery services before giving up.

She pondered the situation. She could deliver the documents herself since she didn't have anything pressing to do. Besides, she loved long drives in the country, and she was restless.

Grabbing her coat, purse and the briefcase, she went into the outer office to tell the secretary her plans.

"Gareth won't like your coming up there," Shirl warned.

A pebble of misgiving plunked into her stomach, adding to her discomfort. Gareth had never invited anyone to his pied-à-terre at the northern end of the Shenandoah Valley that she knew of. "Well, he can always fire me." She gave a fatalistic shrug.

She knew he wouldn't. Gareth might not like the fact that she was pregnant, but he wouldn't do anything to jeopardize her livelihood. He knew her circumstances. She turned to leave.

"Hey, wait!" the secretary called after her, "I just remembered—there's a storm moving in. The forecaster said it was going to be the biggest one this winter."

"I listened to the noon report. The snow isn't supposed to get this far south. We're only expecting freezing temperatures tonight or early tomorrow. I'll be okay. I'm going straight out there, then straight back. Besides, I'm in the ute." She waved and left the office.

The ute was a four-wheel drive, bright red sports utility. It had been her husband's pride and joy.

While she waited for the elevator to take her to the parking garage of the quiet, marble-corridored office building located on the banks of the Potomac in Arlington, Virginia, Stacy thought of Bill.

It had been a year since they'd bought the ute. Eight months since his promotion to detective on the narcotics squad. Eight months since they'd celebrated the event with candlelight, champagne and passionate delight. Eight months minus three days since he'd been killed during a stakeout at a drug house.

Six years of marriage gone. *Snap*. Just like that.

Sometimes she wondered if it would have lasted much longer. Bill had been all flicker and flash, a bright sparkle in her life after her father's death, drawing her to his radiance.

But a person needed more on a daily basis. A marriage needed a steady flame to warm it during the ups and downs of life. She'd tried to provide the balance in the relationship, but it had been difficult.

Her husband had resented her caution and had scoffed at

her worries. He'd craved excitement, lived on the edge. He'd taken one risk too many.

Stacy laid a hand on her abdomen. Neither had he wanted children. She'd been stunned when she'd realized a new life had taken hold inside her—stunned and thrilled and, yes, scared, too. She was alone in the world, with no relatives to help out. A baby was a big responsibility....

The elevator stopped. The cold of the unheated garage hit her when she stepped off. She pulled her coat close around her neck and hurried to the ute.

She cranked up the engine, then eased out of the garage and into the flow of traffic heading to and from the Pentagon, which was farther down the road. In a few more minutes, she was on the highway, breezing along at sixty-five miles per hour. She loved leisurely drives in this part of the country.

The Allegheny Mountains. The Shenandoah Valley. The Rappahannock River. The Appalachian Trail.

Having been born in Wyoming, which was relatively new as a state, she was constantly amazed at being in the very heart of American colonial history. She'd toured all the battle sites, the winter quarters of Washington's ragtag army and the homes of the first Americans when she'd moved to the area to live with her handsome new husband. They'd been twenty-two. So full of hopes and dreams...

A sigh worked its way past her lips. At twenty-eight, she had few dreams left to nourish an empty heart. The ones that remained were centered on the coming child.

A gust of wind shook the truck. It snarled at the trees along the side of the road, whipping them back and forth without mercy. Dark clouds hunkered over the terrain.

She wondered if the weatherman had called it right when he said the storm was going to miss them.

Thirty minutes later, she found out.

The first snowflakes hit her windshield as if they'd been dumped from a bucket. They were big and fluffy, shattering against the glass in silent explosions. She flipped the wipers on for intermittent swipes across the windshield.

A few minutes after that, she turned them on faster. The flakes were smaller now, but falling at a furious rate. However, it had barely coated the shoulders of the road. The steady flow of traffic prevented it from collecting on the pavement.

She relaxed and turned on the radio to listen to music and maybe catch a weather update. A little snow was nothing to worry about. The ute had tires with heavy-duty treads.

An hour and twenty minutes later, she swept around the curve onto the next highway and headed north. Taking the first exit, she was pleased at the good pace she was maintaining.

Humming along with a popular tune on the radio, she thought of what she would do with the extra time that weekend. Clean house in the morning, then finish painting the secondhand crib she'd bought and sanded down to the bare wood. She wanted to be sure there wasn't any lead paint around her baby.

She squirmed in the seat and tried to find a comfortable position. It wasn't possible.

A road led off to the right. Good. That was the first turn. She was supposed to take the second. Peering down the little-used road through the snow, she wondered how far it was.

Ten minutes later, she turned right at the intersection.

She slowed to a safe speed. The road was not only winding,

it was rough. The county needed to repave it before the potholes and the creeping grass and vines completely overran the blacktop.

In fact, she might write them a letter suggesting it, she decided, after dodging one hole and hitting another, less visible one. She groaned as pain jolted up her back.

Her pace was now ten miles per hour. The road wound its way up into the hills, narrowing until it was only one lane wide. She hadn't spotted any roads going off it.

She risked a quick glance at her notes. Two and a half miles, then there should have been a paved lane to the left. He'd said the left turn was tricky. She wondered what, exactly, that had meant.

Surely she'd driven more than two and a half miles. She hadn't seen one road, either to the left or right. This had to be the wrong one. She'd better look for a place to turn around.

That was easier said than done. With the road clinging to the side of a steep hill, she didn't come across one place she considered wide enough to turn the ute. She drove on.

The snow was still coming fast and thick. An inch or more had built up on the road. Along the side, the wind piled it into drifts. Didn't anyone live on this godforsaken mountain?

Growing desperate at finding a turning point, she finally chose a wide spot at a ninety-degree curve and stopped.

She pulled close to the edge, put the truck in four-wheel drive and backed up against the slope of the bank. Then she eased forward, turning the wheels as far as they would go. After three such maneuvers, she faced downhill.

She struggled out of her coat and wiped the sweat from her face. Taking a calming breath, she eased off the brakes and headed down. The snow obliterated the tire tracks within a few feet. No one on the highway would notice where she'd turned off and taken the wrong road.

It occurred to her that she should have called Gareth and told him she would be bringing the documents he wanted.

The tires skidded sideways through the snow as she rounded a turn. She cut the wheel the other way, which was toward the tree-lined cliff that edged the road. The ute came out of the skid. She steered into the curve again and prayed the tires would hold.

They did.

Sweat popped out and dried on her skin, making her feel both clammy and cold. The temperature was certainly dropping. She could vouch for that. And the storm was growing worse.

Finally, she came to the intersection. She glanced at her watch and groaned aloud. She'd spent over two hours on this trip and hadn't reached her destination yet. Perhaps she should go home while the road was still navigable....

A strange pain gripped her. It started as a clenching sensation in her lower back, then swept around to embrace her. She gasped and clutched one arm across her abdomen.

It was almost a minute before it let up.

She sat there, dazed by the attack. That's what it had felt like—as if something had grabbed her body and put a Vise-Grip on it, pulling tighter and tighter.

Her hands trembled as she resumed her trip. A mile down the road, she realized she needed to stop again.

Pressing the brakes hard, she slithered on the fresh snow. She let up on the pedal and pumped it. She came to a stop in the middle of the road and briefly worried about traffic.

Since there wasn't another set of tracks of any kind to be

seen, she didn't think getting run over was going to be a big problem. Laying her head against the back of the seat, she clasped both hands across her body and held on while another contraction squeezed her like a ripe orange.

A moan broke through her control. The pain was worse this time. She felt heavy and strung out when it was over.

One thing she knew, she had to find the cabin. If this wasn't Braxton Hicks contractions, as Dr. Kate called false labor, then she needed help. She drove on.

Just when she was ready to give up to despair, she spied a road sign. Pine Valley Road. Thank heavens.

Gareth's house was on a paved lane two and a half miles from there. She turned, then set the trip mileage indicator to zero and drove down the county road, relieved to be nearing the end of this treacherous journey.

A few minutes later, she came upon a curve in the road that curled downhill. Glancing at the trip indicator, she saw she'd gone the required distance. She looked for the left turn.

Gareth had been right. It was a tricky turn. The lane wasn't visible until she was almost past the entrance. She swerved sharply in surprise when she realized this was it and automatically hit the brake pedal.

For a second, she thought she was going to make it. She should have known better. Fate was working against her.

The back tires broke loose first. Then the front. The truck slid gracefully off the road into a shallow ditch like an ice skater performing a trick. With a jarring *thump,* the truck hit a telephone pole and came to rest.

Stacy couldn't move. She gripped the steering wheel as another pain shot through her. She tried to remember how she was supposed to breathe, but the instructions went completely out of her mind. Instead, she held on and waited for it to be over.

One minute and twenty seconds. Was that too long for false labor? It couldn't be. She couldn't be having a baby a month early out here on some road in the middle of nowhere during a raging blizzard. She couldn't!

She took her foot off the brake pedal and eased down on the gas very gently. The truck jumped a bit but it didn't move forward. She bit her lip and tried again. The tires spun uselessly, unable to get a grip in the snow.

Getting out, she pulled on her coat and gloves, then bent to inspect the problem. Her heart sank. The truck was buried in mud and snow right up to the axle.

Well, one good thing—she knew she was at the right place. The truck had clipped another post as it cavorted across the road and into the ditch. A mailbox lay on its side, half buried in the snow. G. Clelland was painted on it in block letters.

Stacy stood the post up and propped the mailbox on it. Using a rock, she pounded the nail down into the wood to hold it on. To her delight, the post stayed upright when she finished.

She glanced down at her clothes. At least she had on warm wool flannel slacks. She kept snow boots in the truck that she could pull on over her flats. She would walk to Gareth's place.

From there, she could call a tow truck to get her out. She tugged her boots on, pulled a toboggan hat down over her ears, buttoned her coat to her chin and slung her purse over one shoulder. With the briefcase in one hand, she locked the truck and started down the road. With her luck, his house was probably located ten miles from the beginning of the lane.

Fifteen minutes later, she was afraid she'd been more right than she wanted to be. Not a house in sight.

What she wouldn't give to see a friendly chimney sending up a plume of smoke like a welcoming signal.

She stopped and placed her hands on her knees. From a half crouch, she rocked through another contraction. If she was in labor, walking was supposed to move things along faster.

Poor baby. He might be born in a snow bank if his mama's luck continued the way it had started. She remembered a saying—if it weren't for bad luck, I'd have no luck at all.

She laughed. The sound was high and thin. She worried that she was succumbing to hysteria. She had to keep her head. Her child depended on her.

Who could she depend on? No one. But she'd be okay. She just had to keep walking…keep walking….

The words echoed through her brain with each step. She put one foot in front of the other and kept it up. She remembered to watch for a house. To walk right past the place would be really stupid…even more than making the journey in the first place.

The scent of wood smoke caught her attention. She paused and sniffed the wind like a deer trying to find its way.

The snow fell all around her and the pine trees with little rustling noises. Taffeta rubbing against taffeta. Her breath was the only other sound.

She imagined being alone, the last person in the entire world. The silence of the woods made it too real. She shivered and hurried on, following the scent of wood smoke.

Finally she came into a clearing. And there was the house. She stopped, her mouth agape.

It wasn't a simple cabin by any means. Glass panels soared upward to form a spire at the highest peak of the roof. A huge wooden door, surely belonging to some medieval castle, stood below the second-story wall of glass. The lower floor of the building was made of stone, the upper of wooden beams.

Smoke wafted from a stone chimney in lazy curls of gray-white, barely visible against the falling snow.

She walked up the steps and thumped the brass knocker in the middle of the massive door. Five seconds later, the door opened. Her boss stared at her, his face closed and remote.

"Hi," she said spritely. "Sorry to be late."

She handed the briefcase over, then bent forward and clutched her thighs as another pain tightened around her.

"What is it?" he demanded, definitely in a foul mood.

With her teeth clenched, it was hard to speak. "Baby," she said. "I think it's coming."

"God in heaven," he muttered and set the briefcase down.

"Yeah. He's wise to stay in. It's a terrible night."

Under the circumstances, she didn't think it was that bad a joke. However, the Great Stone Face didn't crack a smile. The pain eased. She straightened slowly, her legs shaky from strain.

Gareth swept her into his arms and carried her inside like a hero in a melodrama. Too shocked to protest this odd behavior, she rested her cheek against his shoulder. His warmth made her realize how cold she was, his eyes how unwelcome.

"I'll just rest a minute, then I'll be going," she said.

He kicked the door closed, his face grim as death.

Chapter Two

Gareth muttered a curse, then set his teeth together and held back the rest of the words.

Why him?

There was no answer. There never was. Fate waved its evil hand and catastrophe struck. Humans had no say in the matter, nor any way to guard themselves against it. He cursed again.

Then wished he hadn't.

His assistant gazed up at him. Her eyes, usually the color of milk chocolate, were wells of darkness, reflecting pain and... Could that be fear he saw in the depths?

He frowned, finding it difficult to associate her with fear. She had such a dauntless spirit.

Surprised, he wondered where that thought had come from. If asked, he'd have said his assistant was competent, neat and quiet around the office. Other than those bare facts, he knew next to nothing about her.

That wasn't true. He'd stood beside her at her husband's funeral, ready to catch her if she fainted or to restrain her if she tried to throw herself into the grave. Neither of those heroic deeds had been necessary.

She'd been quiet then, too, and stoic in the face of the tragedy. She'd taken the standard three days off, then quietly returned to work and got on with it.

Only one time had he witnessed uncontrolled emotion in her. That was when her doctor had called to confirm the pregnancy. He'd hung up the phone on a client and had run into her office, thinking something terrible had happened when he'd heard her initial shriek. Then he'd realized she was laughing, sort of hysterically, but it was laughter.

"I'm pregnant," she'd cried, her eyes shining. She'd whooped with excitement. "Pregnant! Oh, God, pregnant!"

He'd been in no doubt about her joy then. He studied her face. She didn't look so happy at the moment.

The bit of lipstick that remained on her mouth contrasted starkly with the pallor of her usually tawny complexion. He couldn't figure it out. What the hell was she doing here?

She moved her head against his shoulder. A strand of hair, damp with snow, caught on the beard he hadn't bothered to shave in a couple of days. A spicy scent drifted up to him, one of vanilla and cinnamon with a hint of lemon and the sweetness of honey. He inhaled, drawing the fragrance deep into his lungs.

A sound, not quite a groan, not quite a sigh, escaped her parted lips. A funny sensation ran through his chest, a sort of tightening or clenching feeling.

Striding up the stairs, he became aware of how delicately

her body curved against his, how weightless she seemed compared to his much larger mass, although he knew she was an average-size woman, five feet five inches, nicely rounded.

And pregnant, he reminded himself as his body stirred, shocking him with the tingling demands of passion.

In his room, he laid her on the king-size bed and bent to take her boots off. She put out a hand and stopped him.

"Wait," she said, then gave a little gasp.

Her fingers curled around his hand, squeezing harder and harder as she rode out the spasm. Her teeth sank into her bottom lip as she held back any sounds of distress.

Sweat poured out all over his body. His own muscles clenched involuntarily, straining with her effort to expel the child from her body.

"We need an ambulance," he muttered.

"There isn't time." She released the breath she'd held and let go of his hand.

Standing, she removed her hat and coat and handed them to him. He tossed them over the desk chair in the corner.

She wore brown slacks with a long-sleeved maternity top in a pastel pink. A multicolored scarf encircled her neck and was held in place with a dragon pin on the shoulder of her blouse.

"Do you have a rubber mat?" she asked.

A strange question. "There might be a plastic sheet left from some painting I did last summer."

"Better get it and put it on the bed. And an extra sheet. And towels."

"Right."

Relieved at having something to do, he hurried out of the room and down the stairs. He found the large piece of plastic he'd used as a drop cloth to catch paint splatters.

Pausing at the counter, he glanced at the stairs, then picked up the phone. They needed help. He didn't know how to deliver a baby.

There was no dial tone. He clicked the button several times and got nothing besides the static *hiss* of an empty line.

He glared at the instrument.

A noise from upstairs forced him to give up on the phone for the moment. He bounded up the steps three at a time.

At the door to his bedroom, he stopped. His executive assistant was down to her skivvies and about to take those off.

Need, heavy and urgent, jolted through his nether regions. He glanced down at his jeans as if discovering a new part of himself. Clearing his throat, he entered the room.

Her shoes and snow boots were lined up like toy soldiers at attention against the wall. Her slacks were folded and placed on the chair where he'd thrown her coat and hat. These, too, were neatly arranged.

"Uhnn."

The groan brought his eyes back to her. Her blouse ballooned around her as she bent and clutched her thighs.

He stared, half in fascination, half in horror, as her body tightened around her abdomen. The involuntary hardening of the muscles reminded him of a charley horse he'd once had in the calf of his leg. It had hurt like hell. He remembered that, too.

Another part of him—a part he couldn't seem to control—noticed how smooth and shapely her legs were.

The blood throbbed deep in his body. He couldn't understand it—getting all hot and bothered because a woman was in his bedroom. A woman about to have a child, at that. Weird.

He called himself a name, but couldn't stop the sensations that assailed him. Having a baby reminded him of the process of making one. A very pleasant process, if he remembered correctly, he cynically remarked to his alert libido.

"Help me," she said on a gasp.

He forced his mind back to the problem at hand, a much more serious one than his. "How? What should I do?"

"Need to…sit down."

He lifted her as gently as he could and placed her on the bed. She began breathing in quick pants.

"Easy," he said. He hunkered down in front of her and took her hands. "Slow and easy. Take a deep breath. Let it out, nice and easy. That's the way."

Gradually she eased her hold on him, then released him. "We need to fix the bed." Twin lines grooved the space between her eyebrows. She sighed as if weary beyond bearing.

"Right." He made her sit in a chair while he pushed the top sheet to the foot of the bed, then spread the plastic over the bottom sheet. He covered it with the clean one.

"Do you have an iron?" she asked.

"A what?"

"An iron. To iron the sheet. It kills germs."

"Oh." He thought there might be one in the kitchen. "Be right back." Like a marathon racer, he sped to the kitchen and returned. "Got it."

He felt as if he'd achieved some great feat and should be rewarded with a crown of laurel leaves.

She was all business. "Plug it in and run it over the sheet. Turn it on high."

He followed the orders as if his life depended on it.

Hers might.

He shied from that thought. Women had babies all the time, all over the world, without medical help.

They also died. Sometimes with the best medical treatment in the world. He shook his head, negating that worry. There was no time for anything but the crisis at hand.

"How are you feeling?" he asked.

"Not too good." She removed the pin and scarf, fastened the pin back on the material and laid it on his dresser. "I'm sorry about this. I never dreamed… It was just… I was so restless and I thought… Anyway, I'm terribly sorry."

He waved her apology aside. "What are you doing here?"

"There was no courier available. I decided a drive would be nice. It's lovely here in the mountains. In the city, you forget they're so close."

"Yeah. Not like Wyoming where you can go for seconds and not see a mountain." He was pleased when she smiled at his joke.

"Do you have a T-shirt I could wear? Extra large, if you have one."

"Sure." He retrieved one from a drawer.

After handing it to her, he stood a couple of feet away, waiting for her next instruction. It occurred to him that in this situation she would have to call all the shots.

"Uh, would you mind?" she asked.

It took him a second, but he finally caught on. She didn't want him to watch her remove her blouse. Heat ran under his skin, and he felt like a kid caught spying on a pretty neighbor. He spun around so his back was to her.

But in his mental vision, he could see her, looking fragile and incredibly beautiful. He wondered why he'd never noticed the curve of her lip, the shape of her nose, the indentation of her chin that wasn't quite a dimple, during all the months they'd worked together. A year, and he'd never looked at her?

"Okay," she said.

When he turned, he found her in bed with his T-shirt on. She'd pushed the pillows into a pile against the headboard and spread the top sheet over her. Her knees were drawn up, making a tent so he couldn't see her pumpkin shape. Her hair was in a tangle of curls on his pillow.

The strangest thing happened. For an instant, no more than the time between one heartbeat and the next, it seemed perfectly right that he should crawl into bed and make love to her. He clenched his fists, fighting the insane urge that was so strong, he feared he'd do it before he could stop himself.

"I really am sorry to trouble you," she apologized again. Her gaze slid away from his. He realized she was embarrassed.

He could hardly rail at her for coming out here in her condition, not at the moment. Adopting a light tone, he gave a snort of sardonic laughter. "I'm a little put out about it myself."

"I think you'd better call that ambulance," she advised, closing her eyes and pressing against the pillows. A fierce frown turned her lightly spoken request into a serious one. He realized she was having another pain.

How long since the last one? Wasn't someone supposed to time them or something? Yeah, *he* was that someone.

She looked at him. Her eyes had the depth, the texture of velvet. He could lie down in them and… Fear flickered through those dark chocolate depths.

He swallowed and concentrated. "The phone's out. I tried, but there's no dial tone." He strode to the desk and picked up the extension. "Still no luck." He managed to keep the worry out of his voice. He'd have to be the clam one here.

"Probably my fault. The truck hit the telephone pole when it went into the ditch, also the mailbox. But I fixed it. Where's your cellular phone?"

"At my apartment. I forgot it." He couldn't believe he'd understood her right. "You went off the road?"

But she couldn't answer. Her hand reached out. He caught it in his. Sitting beside her, he held both her hands as the gripping thrust of her body racked through them both.

The sweat was standing on his brow as much as hers when it was over. "That was a long one," she informed him.

"Yeah, I know." He glanced at the alarm clock. Over a minute and a half. *God help them.*

"You'll need scissors and thread," she told him, wiping at her face with a towel. She handed him one of the extras he'd brought in at her request. "Clean them with alcohol. Or boiling water will do, just like in the movies." She smiled.

Any minute now, he'd wake with this strange, restless night behind him. He glanced at the window. Night had fallen, but it was hours before dawn. This was no dream.

Grim reality took over. This was really going to happen. Stacy, the quiet, the competent, was going to have a baby. In his home. In his bed.

"Anything else?" he asked.

She flashed that smile again, a brave smile. He knew it was a facade, and that she did it for him. That gave him another odd jolt inside.

"Iron a towel to wrap the baby in. Billy," she added. "To wrap Billy in."

"Billy," he repeated. The baby's father had been Bill, a nickname for William. He nodded and set about doing the tasks.

When everything was clean and laid out to her satisfaction, he sat on the bed beside her. "Take my hands," he offered when he saw the frown start on her forehead.

She grabbed hold of him as if she'd never let go. She

breathed deeply, then started panting. She released him and pulled her knees toward her chest.

"Ohh," she moaned softly. She drew a deep breath and held it. And held it. And held it.

He knelt beside the bed and checked the progress. "I see it," he told her. He swallowed hard as a knot formed in his throat. Then there was no time for thoughts or feelings.

"Can you…see his head?" she asked, panting again.

"Uh, yes." He thought it was the head. Then, "Yes, yes, it is. It's coming. Here it comes."

She moaned and strained as hard as she could.

"That's it," he said. Excitement crept into his voice. "You're doing good. The head is out. It's facing backward."

She breathed deeply, relaxing. "I think that's how it should be. Make sure the cord isn't around his neck."

"No, it isn't. I don't see it."

"Okay."

Relief swept over him. He didn't know what was supposed to happen next. She seemed to be resting.

Minutes ticked past. He noticed how loud silence could be. The sighing of the wind, the whisper of snow at the windows, the creaks of the house reminded him of the isolation of the place.

Stacy made a slight sound. He saw the tightening of her abdomen and knew she was going into another contraction. He looked up and met her eyes.

Something invisible reached out and grabbed him, dipping right into his soul. Threads of light wove around them, drawing them tighter and tighter together. He waited, spellbound by this phenomenon that was beyond his previous experience.

Stacy shifted restlessly. She clutched at the sheets and breathed deeply, then began panting.

He wanted to kiss her. "It's okay," he murmured.

She made another giant push and the child was born, sliding into his hands like a wet watermelon seed. The baby gave an indignant yell, then settled into a mewling cry.

"A boy!" he said. "It's a boy! By damn, we did it!"

"Let me see him."

He held the baby up. "Everything's there. Fingers, toes. Eyes, ears. All the right parts in all the right places." He was grinning like an idiot.

She smiled, too. "Now finish," she told him.

"Right." He managed to sever the cord without fainting, although he'd never be fooled into thinking men were the stronger sex again. Stacy told him everything to do.

"Give him to me," she requested when it was over. She lay against the pillows looking pale and beautiful.

Gareth laid the baby in her waiting arms. He removed the used towels and the sheet, replacing them with fresh ones. Then he leaned over her and the baby. He brushed the hair from her temples with fingers that still trembled ever so little.

"You are one of the bravest people I've ever met," he said in reverent tones. His heart felt too big for his chest.

Her eyes widened.

He left before she could reply. After cleaning up and starting the washing machine, he tried the phone again. Still no luck. He went up the stairs.

Stacy had her eyes closed. The baby nestled beside her, wrapped in the towel he'd ironed. He needed to fashion a diaper for him, but for right now, he'd let them rest.

Fatigue washed over him. He went to the glass panels that

formed one wall of the room. It was separated from the outer wall of windows by a sunroom, designed to collect solar heat during the day and radiate it into the house at night.

Opening the door silently, he crossed the heat-absorbing tiles and stood by the outside windows. The snow still fell. It was eight inches deep, more in the drifts. The snowplow wouldn't get through until Monday or Tuesday.

He forced his mind to practical matters. He had plenty of food, even with unexpected guests....

God, he couldn't believe he'd delivered a baby, one that seemed to be okay. So many things could have gone wrong.

Blackness pushed out of his soul, engulfing him.

Gripping the window frame, he quit fighting and let the memories wash over him, unable to hold them back any longer.

Three years ago, he'd rushed to a hospital on an emergency. His fiancée had been in an accident—a drunken driver had swerved into her lane going almost one hundred miles an hour.

"Where is she?" he'd asked, spotting the doctor, also a friend, who'd called him with the news.

The doctor had gestured toward the Intensive Care Unit. "She's waiting for you."

It wasn't until later that he'd understood what his friend had meant—that Ginny had waited until he could hold her one last time. One last kiss. A few desperate murmured words.

And then she was gone.

One week before their wedding. She'd been two months pregnant with their child.

Guilt and despair pummeled him. Her death had been his fault. He'd called her while in flight and asked her to meet his plane. They'd been apart a whole week. His desire to see her had overcome common sense.

He beat the anger and other useless emotions back by force of will. What was gone, was gone. He'd survived. He hadn't wanted to, but he had.

He shook his head, wondering why he was remembering the past at this moment when he'd been able to avoid it for three years.

Remembering was no good. It served no purpose. He had other things to do. Like check on Stacy's truck to see what kind of mess she'd gotten herself into.

Returning to the bedroom, he stood there watching the new mother and her child sleep. A chasm opened in him, like a sealed vault whose lock had been breached. Stacy and her son somehow exposed the emptiness that dwelled inside him. He didn't like it. Laid bare, the void hurt like a raw nerve.

He pushed the thought aside. Stacy was his assistant, well educated and trained to his way of doing things. He'd been planning on talking to her about studying to be a paralegal. She had the brains for it and the self-discipline. The pregnancy had halted his ideas on that.

The birth of the child changed things, too. He just didn't know how yet. He didn't want to think about it. After this incident was over, he wouldn't have to see the baby again. Stacy had a nursery school lined up.

He'd give her some time off, all she needed. When she returned, everything would be normal again.

If it wasn't, he'd help her find another job.

Stacy woke with a start. The baby gave a tiny, forlorn cry that wrenched her heart. "There, now. You're fine. We're both okay. Thanks to Gareth," she added.

Her boss might never recover from the shock of delivering a baby—he'd looked pretty green there at the end—but he'd been wonderful during the ordeal.

She sighed and moved cautiously. To her surprise, she didn't feel sore. That was one fast delivery. From the time she'd felt the first real contraction until the birth had been less than two hours.

"Well, I'm not sure what comes next, but perhaps we'd better try feeding you," she said to the baby. She pushed upright against the pillows and fumbled with the lamp until she found the switch. Soft light illuminated the large bedroom.

Outside the windows—a double set, she saw, with a room between them—night had settled in. Snowflakes bounced off the glass panels and piled up on the outer ledge.

Glancing at the bedside clock, she discovered it was only a few minutes after eight. She thought she'd arrived around five, but she wasn't sure. Time had ceased to have meaning during that last hour or so.

She laid the baby down and tucked the T-shirt under the strap of her maternity bra. She unhooked the flap and the cup peeled down, exposing her breast. She lifted the baby and rubbed his rosebud mouth against the nipple.

That seemed to excite him. He opened his eyes and bobbed his head around frantically. She guided him in the right direction. He latched on like a pit bull.

"Ouch!" she exclaimed, jerking against the pillows.

He lost his hold and let out a wail. She helped him find the nipple again. This time she was prepared and didn't move when he tugged.

Odd sensations shot off into her chest, sort of painful, but not entirely. The baby lost his hold. Again they went through the finding and latching on procedure. This happened several times until he dozed off.

She wondered if he'd gotten anything. She tried squeezing to see if anything came out. Nothing did.

When she heard footsteps in the hall, she yanked the sheet over her, baby and all, while she fumbled beneath it to close the bra clasp and pull down the T-shirt.

Gareth entered the room as the baby let out a wail. He checked on the threshold, then entered the room. "Is he all right?" he asked.

"Yes." She laid the baby on her tummy, which felt so odd in its newly flattened state, and struggled with the bra under the cover. The baby wailed louder.

"What are you doing?" Gareth frowned at her warily.

Heat flowed up her neck into her face. It was rather ridiculous to be embarrassed at this late date after what she'd put him through that afternoon, but she couldn't help it.

"Well, uh," she said, stalling while waiting for a brilliant reply to pop into her mind.

"What's wrong with the boy?" He leaned over her, menacing in his bigness.

He was a powerfully built man, over six feet tall, with shoulders like a football player in full uniform. His hands and feet were proportionately large. He hadn't shaved that morning and a dark stubble swept around his strong jawline, giving him the ominous appearance of a tramp.

His jeans, scuffed boots and blue corduroy shirt, worn out at the elbows, added to this impression. His dark hair was tousled. It was a contrast to his usual urbane appearance.

There was one thing that wasn't different from what he was

like at the office. His gray eyes still looked directly at a person as if he could see right to the back of the skull.

Her gaze went to his hands, now tensed at his sides. They were big, too. And, unlike the hard gaze he turned on her, they were gentle.

Those hands had trembled when he'd tied and cut the cord, then positioned a plastic bowl for the afterbirth as she'd directed. When he'd held the baby up so she could see that her child was all right, they had been gentle—large, capable and so very, very gentle. She loved his hands.

"Stacy," he snapped.

She blinked up at him. She dropped the sheet and brought the child up to her shoulder. "He's fine. I was trying to feed him, but he keeps going to sleep. I'm not sure if he got anything to eat or not."

All at once, she felt helpless and stupid. What did she know about raising a child? Nothing.

She'd had no brothers or sisters. Her mother had died a long time ago, her father during her junior year in college. She was the only child of two only children. No aunts, uncles or cousins. She'd never been around babies in any capacity, had never earned money baby-sitting....

A wet warmth spread over her stomach. "Oh," she said.

Gareth followed her gaze. "I'll find something for a diaper." He left the room practically at a run.

Poor man, he was probably scared to death something terrible was going to happen. As if helping birth a baby wasn't terrible enough for a hardened bachelor like him.

She giggled. She couldn't help it. It was too funny. Gareth Clelland, hotshot legal eagle, one of the foremost attorneys in the country who argued cases in front of the Supreme

Court, was stuck in a cabin with a nervous new mother and a crying infant, acting as midwife and nanny.

When he returned, looking grim and remote, she burst into fresh giggles. This was something to write about, if she'd had anyone to write to, which she didn't.

"Stop it," he ordered.

She wiped the smile off. "Yes, sir," she returned smartly. Then she giggled again.

"Are you hysterical?" he asked in a milder tone.

Taking a firm hold on her runaway emotions, she shook her head. "Sorry. It struck me as funny—you a high-powered attorney having to play nursemaid."

He gave her a quizzical glance. One dark eyebrow rose in sardonic humor. When he grinned, lines appeared at the corners of his eyes. "Yeah, it's a barrel of laughs."

She loved his smile. Even if it was laced with cynicism, it appeared genuine, not like the social ones she'd seen at the office. "I'm also embarrassed."

"You needn't be." He laid several dish towels on the bed, plus a piece of plastic cut from a garbage bag. "I thought you could use these." He reached into his pocket and laid two safety pins beside the dish towel.

"Good." She unwrapped the baby, dried him, then folded the makeshift diaper and plastic around him and pinned them in place.

Gareth ironed a dry towel and brought it to her. She wrapped the baby in the terry cloth bunting. "I don't think you need to iron the towels anymore."

He unplugged the iron. For a second he didn't say anything, then he nodded. "Are you hungry?"

She considered. "I don't know. I'm still sort of numb...." She felt the blush start again. "I mean, after all that's happened and everything. I really haven't thought about it," she finished lamely.

His lips thinned. "I made some soup earlier today."

"Well," she said. "Multitalented—and all of them amazing." She clamped down on her runaway tongue. He was going to fire her for sure if she didn't control herself.

"I'll bring you some supper," he decided, not waiting for her to make a decision. He left the room.

Lying against the pillows, she wondered about him. He was almost forty. Why hadn't he married?

She knew he dated, mostly high society women from the capital or Virginia, where his office was located, although not regularly and no one in particular. She'd sometimes heard him make reservations or order tickets to concerts and events at Lincoln Center and places like that.

It must be pleasant to go someplace with a man like him. He could be charming when he wished. She'd heard him laughing once during a phone conversation with one of his dates. His tone had been low, deep and intimate. It had given her goose bumps.

That had been when she first started to work for him. For the past few months, he'd been so busy he hadn't gone out.

Or maybe he didn't make the arrangements so she could hear. Her mouth dropped open. That was it. She hadn't heard him on the phone with one of the many women interested in him since…since the funeral. Was he being considerate of her?

When a woman occasionally called him at work, he closed the door between their offices before taking the call. He must have realized seeing or hearing other couples had been painful for her for the first few months after her own loss.

Until she'd found out about the baby. Then the world had seemed bright again.

She'd point out this considerate aspect of Gareth to Shirl when she went back to work. He wasn't a heartless beast at all.

When he returned with a tray in one hand and a clean T-shirt in the other, she was composed. He placed the tray on the bed and tossed the shirt to her.

"Oh, thanks." She hadn't wanted to ask him for a dry one. She didn't know how many clothes he brought with him or kept at the mountain retreat.

Sniffing the comforting aroma of homemade chicken noodle soup, she realized she was indeed hungry. It had been a long time since lunch. She looked around for a place to lay the baby and decided the other side of the bed would have to do.

Gareth placed the tray, which was on short legs, on the floor. He went to a closet and returned with an armful of pillows. These he placed around the child on the other side of the king-size mattress, making a safe nest.

"Perfect," she said as he leaned down to set the tray across her lap.

He was very close, his face no more than six inches from hers. Smoky blue-gray color outlined his irises in a most attractive fashion, emphasizing the light gray in the middle.

For a minute he paused, holding her gaze with his while currents of some ephemeral substance wound around them. She tried to think of something to say…anything….

He straightened, breaking the strange connection, his face its usual mask of polite indifference.

She wasn't sure what had happened. If anything.

He muttered something and walked out, leaving her staring after him like a dolt.

Feeling the damp T-shirt against her, she quickly slipped it over her head and pulled on the fresh one, her mind elsewhere.

She'd read about the hormone changes and mood swings motherhood could bring during the first few days or weeks while the body got back to normal and life settled down. That must account for the knot in her throat and the clamoring of her pulse. That and the fact she'd forced her boss into a most embarrassing position by coming to his hideaway.

Pulling the tray closer, she picked up the spoon and wished she could wiggle her nose and be back at home in her own bed with this day just starting. She'd certainly change a few things about it.

The baby stirred and tried to suck his fingers. A funny feeling attacked her insides, a mixture of love and tenderness for this tiny creature given into her care.

She continued to watch him while she ate. He was the one thing she wouldn't change about the comedy of errors that had happened that day.

Realizing she was tired, she finished the chicken noodle soup. Homemade, no less. By her boss.

Wow, as Shirl would say.

She'd almost gone to sleep again when Gareth stalked into the room. "Finished?"

"Yes. That was delicious." She offered him a smile.

He didn't notice. With admirable efficiency, he removed the tray and damp T-shirt, taking them with him as he left the room.

"Wait," she called.

He turned at the door.

"Do you happen to have a cardboard box or something I can use for a cradle? I'm afraid I'll roll over on the baby if I go to sleep."

He hesitated, then nodded and left.

She wondered about that pause. A muscle had jumped in

his jaw before he'd nodded. And in his eyes... She must have imagined that odd bleakness, the pain and despair.

Yes, her hormones were acting up. She was the one with the emotional upheavals, not him. She waited anxiously until she heard his footsteps on the stairs.

He strode in and set a wooden cradle on the foot of the bed. "Will this do?"

She stared at it. "Why, yes." She reached out to stroke the satin-smooth wood. "It's beautiful. Was it handmade?"

"Yes."

"It must be an antique."

"A replica," he said and walked out as if he had an important meeting to attend and she was detaining him.

Giving a wry glance at his retreating back, she picked up the sleeping baby and held him with shy tenderness.

Gareth stalked back into the room, filling it with his masculine bigness. He placed a folded bath towel in the cradle and set it on the side of the king-size bed within arm's reach.

She laid little Billy down, then examined the cradle in detail. The sides were made from spindles, the head and foot of solid wood. An intricately carved scene of trees and grass, a flowing brook, rocks and wildflowers decorated each end piece. An owl sat on the branches of a tree, looking wise as owls were supposed to.

Why, she wondered, would a bachelor have a handmade cradle at his hideaway in the mountains?

Looking at his closed expression, she was afraid to ask.

Chapter Three

Stacy slept fitfully during the night. So did the child. She kept the bedside lamp on so she could check on her son often during the slow hours until dawn. She tried not to think of all the things that could go wrong. Besides, it did no good to worry. A person had to face things as they happened.

Billy seemed to like the cradle. When she woke to the faint light of the cloudy morning, she found him with his eyes open, looking around as if checking out the world instead of whimpering as he'd done each time he'd stirred during the night.

"Good morning. Like what you see?" she asked, lifting him to her lap and trying another feeding.

Her nipples were sore from the latching on, losing it, then latching on again. Babies, although driven by instinct, had to learn to suckle. She hoped he caught on soon.

"Ouch, ouch, ouch," she murmured as he settled in for some serious feeding. Her breasts were engorged and rather tender. "Could you be a little easier?"

"He'll learn by the time he's twenty-one," a masculine voice predicted with a sardonic edge.

Gareth stood in the doorway, his hands thrust into his pockets. He was freshly shaved, otherwise he looked much the same as the previous day—boots, jeans, T-shirt under the same out-at-the-elbows blue corduroy shirt.

"But that'll be too late to do me any good," she groused, then realized the innuendo behind the words. Heat climbed from her breasts, up her neck and into her face.

"Yeah. Tough," he said in mock sympathy. He laid a clean supply of dish towels on the bedside table.

As an ice breaker, it wasn't much, but the good-natured heckling helped her over the initial embarrassment of facing her boss after yesterday's events.

"Did we keep you awake last night?" She thought it was time for a change in subject.

She was acutely conscious of her son making little noises at her breast as he nursed, not to mention the fact that her breast, which to her eyes resembled a huge pale melon of some strange species, was visible and that she had to hold it away from Billy's nose so he could breathe. She flattened her hand over the bulging mound to hide as much of it as possible.

"No, I slept fine."

"Where...that is, I can move to another bedroom. This one is yours."

He shrugged. "There are three bedrooms downstairs. I'm in one of them. It's quieter up here for you and...Billy."

She wondered at the pause before he said the baby's name.

His eyes flicked to the child in her arms, then away. It came to her that he might not like children. Or their mothers.

"What would you like for breakfast?" he asked.

"Cereal or toast, if you have it," she said, keeping a bright note in her voice with an effort. She glanced at his hands and remembered how gentle he'd been while tending her and her son during the delivery. "Yesterday," she said impulsively, "you were magnificent, simply magnificent."

To her amazement, he flushed brick red. Her stone-faced boss was blushing?

"Yeah, well, I don't think I'll take it up as a hobby," he informed her and abruptly left.

The hard edge had returned. She looked down, disappointed. She'd imagined that moment of emotion between them.

She finished feeding Billy. He seemed to get enough for he settled into sleep immediately afterward. She placed the baby between two pillows, then eased out of bed.

Going into the bathroom, she wet a washcloth in warm water. She washed her son and changed his diaper, then laid him in the cradle. He was sound asleep.

After considering for all of two seconds, she decided to take a quick shower. Using Gareth's soap and shampoo, then his deodorant and powder and comb, she was in and out of the bathroom faster than she'd ever been in her entire life.

Little Billy slept peacefully, his puckered mouth moving as if sucking. His lips had a blistered look, but that was normal, the baby books reported.

She found a blue velour robe on the back of the bathroom door and put it on, wondering which of Gareth's female friends had given it to him. It didn't strike her as something he'd buy for himself. She slipped into her flats and went downstairs. Gareth was in the kitchen. He was scrambling eggs.

He took in her appearance in one glance, then removed two plates from the oven. He spooned out the eggs beside the sausage and toast on each plate and carried them to the table.

"Breakfast," he announced.

She sat down. He joined her after pouring coffee in thick mugs and bringing them over. She picked up her fork and started in when he did. "This is delicious," she told him. "I didn't realize how hungry I was."

"You didn't eat much last night." He stopped, then rose as if he'd thought of something. He fetched a glass and filled it with milk. He brought it to the table and placed it beside her plate. "Nursing mothers need milk," he said at her questioning glance.

"How did you know that?"

"I have a sister. She and her husband have two children."

She gaped at him in surprise. In the year she'd worked for him, he hadn't mentioned his family once. Sometimes she thought of him as an orphan like herself.

However, his parents lived in a small town about a hundred miles south of Arlington. She'd spoken with his mother a few times, taking messages regarding family celebrations and dinners, but no one else from his family had ever called.

She started to question him about them, but thought better of it. When he didn't volunteer any further information, she kept her curiosity to herself. He wasn't given to small talk, at least not with her.

Shirl knew less about him than Stacy, in spite of the other woman having been with the law firm longer. Neither of them knew what the middle initial of his name stood for.

He'd been named for one of his grandfathers, she decided. Butler. Or Buchanan. Beech. Barnett. Those were old Virginia names she'd found in the cemeteries she'd visited.

Gareth Butler Clelland. Gareth Buchanan Clelland. If he'd been named Adam, his initials would be A.B.C.

"What's so funny?"

Her unconscious smile widened into a grin. She explained about the initials.

"It's Beauregard."

"You're joking," she said before she thought.

He looked at her solemnly. Then she noticed his eyes. They were laughing at her. His mouth curled into a half smile. His expression was cynical, yes, but amused, too.

"You *are* joking."

"Don't look so surprised."

"Well, it is rather as if the Sphinx smiled," she blurted, then pressed her fingertips over her mouth. She was going to get herself fired if she didn't watch it.

Gareth could be pleasant. He had a low, sexy laugh when he chatted with his women friends. His laughter was usually sardonic, mocking whatever emotions the moment demanded. It was sometimes dark and sultry. And it was always enticing.

He gave the mocking version now. "It's Bainbridge, after my father's youngest brother who died in Vietnam."

Gareth Bainbridge Clelland. She thought of the sleeping baby. William Bainbridge Gardenas. It sounded important, like somebody who was somebody. She nodded decisively. Yes.

"I need your keys," he told her. "I'll see if I can get the ute unstuck and down to the house this morning."

"We could call a tow service," she began, then remembered they had no telephone. She sighed in helpless anger with herself for getting into this predicament and involving her boss in it, too. He probably *would* fire her when they got out of this mess. "In my purse. I'll get them for you."

"Finish eating. There's no hurry." He glanced out the window nearest the table. "In this snow, nothing is going to happen very fast, I'm afraid."

Was he telling her they were trapped there until someone came to dig them out and restore the phone line? She'd already deduced that for herself.

She ate the meal, then excused herself. She rinsed and stored her dishes in the dishwasher, then headed for the bedroom again. Billy was still sleeping.

Moving quietly, she dug the keys out of her purse, carried them downstairs and laid them on the table. Gareth's dishes were gone and he was nowhere in sight. The doors to the rooms off the hallway were closed, so she couldn't tell which one he was using.

She hurried back upstairs, feeling as if she were intruding on his private domain, although no place could be more private than the master bedroom where she and Billy were staying.

Going through the French door, she crossed the sunroom to stand before the panels of glass. Although triple glazed, she could still feel the cold seeping in from the outside. The temperature was below zero.

Too cold to snow. That's what her grandad on the ranch in Wyoming used to say when she was little. However, he was wrong. It was snowing now, big, lazy flakes that tumbled from the sky as if carelessly tossed out the window of some celestial mansion.

The world was white, a wonderland of powdered sugar icing on mint chocolate trees. She wished they could stay here forever.

It was a startling thought. She went into the master suite and closed the French door behind her, putting aside fantasies for the warm comfort of her boss's bed.

She smiled. Shirl would faint when she told her about this unbelievable weekend.

Gareth exchanged his old corduroy shirt for a heavy wool one in red-and-green plaid, his jeans for old bib overalls that had been supplanted by new ones for skiing. He pulled on a pair of insulated boots and a wool hat. With a waterproof jacket, he figured he'd be warm enough to face the elements.

Grabbing the keys off the table, he went out the kitchen door into the garage. There, he fired up the old pickup he used in the mountains. It had a snowplow blade on the front. Usually he would have left the task until he was ready to leave, but he needed to check on Stacy's ute and the telephone pole.

He began a methodical pattern of pushing the snow off the drive. It was slow work and, at the rate the snow was falling, would have to be done again within twenty-four hours.

The morning passed before he reached the end of the drive and saw the ute in the shallow ditch.

Some invisible force grabbed his heart and squeezed it without mercy. He winced at the sudden pain, then cursed until it disappeared. Stacy and the kid seemed okay, so there was no use getting maudlin about what could have happened.

After scraping the snow away from the ute's path, he attached a chain to it, then hooked it to his rear bumper. It took thirty minutes of digging and packing sand under the wheels to get it free.

His breath formed dense clouds of steam in front of his face as he leaned against the side of the ute and wiped his face with a dry handkerchief. The thought entered his head that maybe he wasn't getting any younger. He gave a cynical snort. He was thirty-nine, but it had been years since he'd felt young.

He climbed in and cranked the engine of the ute. It started immediately. Easing it into gear, he pulled around the pickup and drove it down the lane to the house. He parked it in the garage. Inspecting the side, he noted the damage was minimal.

After hanging the keys on a hook beside the kitchen door, he lingered on the threshold. Something was different. He tilted his head to one side and listened intently.

The house was quiet, but it was always silent when he was in residence unless he turned the television on. No, the lack of noise wasn't what made it feel different to him.

It was something else, something more elusive, but alluring, like a melody carried on the breeze, making a mortal wonder if the sound had been the wind through the trees or the fluted notes of a fairy dance—

The rush of water in the upstairs bathroom made him realize what the difference was. The house wasn't empty anymore.

He pulled off his snow boots and padded across the kitchen in his socks. Upstairs, he paused at the open door and peered inside. Stacy was still in the bathroom.

Drawn by forces he couldn't define, he went to the bed and looked at the sleeping infant. Billy had had a bath and looked fresh and contented. Gareth noted the baby's hair was thick and black. He wondered if the father's hair had been the same.

Stacy's hair was dark, too, of a shade that was neither black nor brown. It had no blond or red highlights, only a glossy shine that spoke of health and cleanliness.

While he watched, the baby puckered its lips and made a sucking motion. Billy searched around with his hands and tried to find his mouth. When he couldn't, his tiny face screwed up, ready to cry.

Without thinking, Gareth reached down to help. The baby grabbed his finger and brought it to his mouth. Billy sucked noisily.

Gareth didn't move. Unnamed emotions churned, filling his chest and choking off his breath. For a stunned moment, he couldn't think.

Then the pain descended, the terrible pain of love and loss that was like no other he'd ever experienced, a pain he hadn't felt since Ginny's death.

He reeled from it, jerking his finger from the infant's grasp as if from a firebrand and taking a stumbling step back from the bed. He whirled and rushed from the room, not stopping until he was in the kitchen. He pulled his boots on and headed down the drive, walking fast…almost running…but for the moment there was no escape from the pain of remembering…the pain of loving….

Stacy opened the bathroom door cautiously. She thought she'd heard footsteps. She glanced around. The room was empty.

Probably Gareth doing something downstairs. Maybe he was preparing lunch. It was after one and she was starved.

After checking the baby, she went down to the kitchen. No one there. She wondered what to do. Going to one of the closed doors off the hall, she knocked gently. No answer.

"Gareth?"

When she got no response, she went to the next door, then the last one. Still no answer to her taps.

Unable to contain her curiosity, she furtively opened the bedroom door and peered inside. She started in surprise and opened the door wider. There was nothing inside.

The room was devoid of furniture.

She couldn't say why that startled her so. She retraced her steps and paused outside the door to one of the other bedrooms. Bolder now, she opened it. And felt the hair lift on her neck.

It, too, was empty.

The room was attractively proportioned. It was painted a very pale peach with white woodwork. A fireplace outlined with ceramic tiles, hand-painted with wildflowers, took up most of one wall. Bookcases and cupboards formed an interesting and useful corner grouping to the right of it.

She imagined it as a sitting room, warm and cozy during cold winter nights. A family could read, watch television or simply gaze into the fire while the snow fell outside, which it was still doing at that moment.

Where was Gareth?

Going to the window, she saw a lone figure through the trees, facing into the wind, his head down, his arms pumping as he walked fast along the lane. He must be going to see about her ute. She'd heard the sound of an engine earlier and seen him from the upstairs windows as he plowed the driveway.

She closed the door and went to the one room she hadn't peered into. Opening the door without knocking, she again was startled by what she found. This room, too, had no furniture.

On the floor next to the inside wall, he'd unrolled a sleeping bag and added a pillow and blanket for his bed.

She pressed her fingertips to her mouth, distressed at the sight. The makeshift bed, the empty rooms…they cried out to her, speaking of emptiness…loneliness.

Tears welled in her eyes, blurring the outlines of the sleeping bag and silent room. She closed the door and leaned her head against it. The black despair she'd felt after Bill's death washed over her, only this time it was for her stern-faced, rarely smiling boss.

Taking a deep breath, she forced aside the despair, feeling utterly foolish for being so emotionally unstable.

She walked down the hall and stood in the middle of the living room. She let her gaze drift from feature to feature.

The room was comfortably, but expensively furnished. The sofa and love seat were of leather in a deep teal-green. An antique desk was littered with his legal papers. Shining brass lamps and candlesticks gleamed in the snow-filtered light of early afternoon.

She returned to the kitchen with its eat-in table, the two sinks and multiple work areas, the double ovens, the separate microwave oven area. This was a house made for a family.

But Gareth had no family—no wife or children to fill the house with laughter and the clutter of hobbies and homework.

The tears erupted, and she covered her face with her hands and cried for him, for things she couldn't put a name to, for the pain of living, of loving, for dreams that couldn't be.

When she heard a vehicle in the drive, she fled up the stairs, grateful for its isolation from the rest of the house. She washed her face and blew her nose while she regained her composure. Feeling better, she returned to the kitchen.

A woman's hormone changes after birth could lead to unpredictable emotional upheavals. That's what had caused the inexplicable tears. Gareth Clelland needed her sympathy like a leopard needed another spot.

She checked the contents of the refrigerator with an eye to

lunch. Finding sliced roast beef and cheese, she prepared grilled sandwiches. While they were browning in the skillet, she rooted through the cabinets and came up with baked chips and salsa to add to the fare.

When she heard the motor of the garage-door opener, she figured her boss was on the way inside. She placed the food on plates and carried them to the table. The door opened. She looked up and smiled. "Lunch," she announced. "Would you like beer or soda with your sandwich?"

His gaze ran over her, from the top of her head, over his robe that she wore, down to her shoes. "Beer."

She hurried to get it while he took off his snow boots and outer clothing. She brought it and a glass of milk to the table and took her place there.

"If you're bashful, you'd better keep your head turned," he told her.

She immediately looked his way to see what he was talking about. He had his bib overalls unsnapped and was in the process of sliding them down over his lean hips. He wore long underwear.

"My grandfather wore long johns in the winter. I've seen them before."

He shrugged and kicked off the denim garment. She got a glimpse of lean, muscled thighs and buttocks covered by pale blue waffle-knit cotton before he pulled on jeans and snapped them at the waist. He zipped them before he went to the sink and washed his hands, then splashed water over his face. He used a paper towel to dry with before coming to the table.

"I didn't expect a meal," he said, joining her.

"I was hungry when I woke up." She took a bite of sandwich when he did.

It felt odd to be eating across the table from a man again. She'd missed the companionship.

"Your ute is in the garage," he told her after taking a long swallow of beer.

"You got it out of the ditch?"

"Yeah. I thought I'd go back this afternoon and see if I could do anything about the telephone lines. The pole is okay. You didn't knock it over when the ute hit it, so maybe the line was jarred loose. I can probably fix it."

"Oh, good. I've felt terribly guilty for that. It was stupid of me to deliver the papers—"

"It was my fault," he broke in, his voice dropping to a deep growl. "I should have remembered the holiday and known everyone would be getting ready to leave town."

She nodded. "I wanted to get out, too. A drive seemed the very thing. If it hadn't been for the snow…" She trailed off, remembering it was more than snow that had detained her. "Well, anyway, I'm really sorry."

He waved her apology away with a sweep of his hand as if shooing a fly out of the way.

"I…uh…" She stared at the chip in her hand and wondered how to broach the subject. "I saw the sleeping bag," she blurted. "I thought you were sleeping in a bed." She couldn't keep the accusatory tone out of her voice.

He chewed and swallowed before speaking, his eyes on her all the while, making her feel uneasy, like the snoop that she was. She'd had no right looking into his empty rooms.

"I'm comfortable." He glanced outside. "The snow has let up. I'll be going out as soon as I finish lunch." He took a drink, cutting off further conversation while he finished.

Stacy ate more slowly. When he got up, she didn't say

anything. He took the overalls and went into the bedroom he was using. He changed in there. When he came out, he put on his snow boots again. "I'll be gone a couple of hours. If the plow has been through the main road, I'll go down to the store and bring back some milk. Anything else you need?"

She could have named a bagful of items. "Diapers. A toothbrush. A bottle of hydrogen peroxide. Uh, how are your T-shirts holding out?"

"I've got plenty here, and there's a washing machine, so feel free to use all you need. They're in the third drawer down in the bureau."

She nodded her thanks.

"Anything else?"

"There is one item," she said, then wished she hadn't. She could make do until she got home.

He waited.

"It's personal."

"Okay." He was beginning to look a bit impatient.

"For women only." If she could only vanish on the spot.

He frowned, then relaxed as a comprehending gleam leapt into his eyes. "Okay, I get the idea." He left the room, obviously having no problem with female personal items.

A feeling like jealousy darted through her. She shook her head, perplexed by her own emotions of late. Naturally, the female body was no mystery to a man of Gareth's cosmopolitan experience and life-style.

In a minute, she heard his truck start up. The sound faded when he drove off. She finished lunch and put the dishes away.

Going to the master bedroom, she looked out the window for a while. She read, talked to Billy when he was awake, then took a long nap. When the baby woke her up, it was late afternoon. She sat in the rocker-recliner and put him to her breast.

At the first touch of his mouth, a strange sensation washed over her. Her breasts swelled, hard and painful, then, like a dam bursting, something gave way. A warm, pale liquid spurted from them, soaking her bra on one side, showering her son's face on the other.

He waved his arms excitedly and latched on, not having to suck at all as the milk flowed into his mouth. When the rush slowed, he seemed to have the knack of it. He suckled greedily, feeding until his tummy was taut and her breast was soft.

Laying him against her shoulder, she patted his back until he gave a loud burp, surprising her and making her laugh.

She lifted him to the other breast. After raising the footrest, she drew her knees up and laid the baby against them, then simply looked at him, amazed that this tiny creature was hers and proud that she'd had a part in his creation.

Her heart was awash with love for him, so full she felt she couldn't contain all of it inside her.

When Billy was finished and had burped again, she continued to hold him, marveling at this miracle of life.

"I love you," she told him, feeling fierce and tender at the same time. She smiled and wondered if all new mothers felt this way. "You're the handsomest, smartest baby in the whole world. Yes, you are, and I love you, love you, love you," she murmured in a singsong voice.

When she bent to plant kisses on his forehead, he grabbed her hair with both hands as it swung forward and held on.

"Ouch. What a grip," she exclaimed fussing to free the locks.

Straightening, she saw Gareth standing in the doorway, watching them. The expression on his face kept her silent.

He was staring at her and the baby, but his thoughts roamed far away, fastened on some image that only he could see. She didn't know what memories he recalled, but she knew a tortured soul when she saw one.

She realized Gareth Clelland was capable of deep feeling, not only capable, but that he had once loved someone to the depths of his being…and that he had lost that love…and never gotten over the loss.

He spun around and left without a word.

Chapter Four

Saturday dawned, so clear and bright, Stacy needed her sunglasses to look out the window. Light glittered everywhere, bouncing off the snow-encrusted rocks and trees and meadows, making her squint. The world literally sparkled.

She showered and dressed in her wool slacks and blouse, then tucked washcloths in her bra to catch the overflow of milk that came at odd moments. Every time Billy gave a cry, her breasts seemed to think this was a signal to produce.

"I should go into the dairy business," she told him when he ate later that morning. She sat in the rocker-recliner and observed a redbird checking a pinecone for nuts.

An outside door opened. She didn't hear it, but from upstairs, she felt the swirl of air through the snug house.

Gareth must be back.

For no reason, her heart bumped around her chest like a frightened thing. Which was ridiculous. She wasn't afraid of her boss, and she'd gotten over her embarrassment regarding his help during the crisis soon enough. There were only so many times a person blushed over the same event.

In a few minutes, she heard his muted footsteps on the stairs. He was probably in his socks. She'd noticed he usually left his boots in the kitchen. Whoever had housebroken this tough hombre had been brave.

She couldn't see herself suggesting he remove his muddy shoes before tracking through the rest of the house. Her husband hadn't liked being reminded of little things like that….

It came to her that she was comparing Bill to Gareth and that Bill was coming out the loser. She tried to recall the things she'd loved about her young husband when they'd first met, such as his quick smiles and laughter, but that seemed long ago.

Gareth appeared at the door. He studied her and her son for a long minute before he spoke. "The roads will be clear in another hour. The snowplows are out now. The telephone is working. You can check in with your doctor."

"Oh, that's a good idea." She lifted Billy to her shoulder and patted his back. He fussed at being removed from his lunch.

"If it's safe for you to travel, I'll drive you home this afternoon. There's a break between storms, but more snow is expected Monday."

"I'm sure it's okay. We're both fine, and I really need to get home." Having one set of clothing and no personal items was darned inconvenient. Gareth hadn't been able to get to the store yesterday and making do was getting difficult.

He nodded and left.

When Billy finished and fell asleep, she laid him in the cradle and went to the phone. She called Dr. Kate, reached the answering service and left her name, the telephone number and a brief explanation of her circumstances.

The doctor called back in ten minutes. "Are you trying to beat me out of my fee?" she demanded. "What's the idea of going off to the woods and having the baby behind my back?"

"I didn't plan it, I assure you." Stacy told her doctor what had happened, detailing Gareth's part with generous praise.

"Tell him I'm going to complain to the AMA. Practicing medicine without a license is a serious offense." She clearly thought the whole episode was hilarious. "Sounds like you had an easy time. How large is the baby?"

After Dr. Kate decided Stacy and the baby were in good shape, she told her she could go home at any time and to come in and see her on Tuesday morning. "Eight o'clock Tuesday. I'll come in early so you won't have to wait."

After they hung up, Stacy hesitated then called Shirl. She got the answering machine and left a message. "Come have supper with me tomorrow night and admire my big boy," she invited. That would blow Shirl's mind.

She went downstairs to find Gareth and tell him she was ready to leave. He was sitting at the kitchen table, his hands cupped around a steaming mug of coffee, gazing out the window.

"I can go home anytime." She offered him a sympathetic smile for putting up with her. "I wondered if I could borrow the cradle to take Billy home in. I'll bring it to the office next week—"

"You can keep it," he said, his voice dropping into that deep growl that sounded dangerous but alluring at the same time. "For good," he added.

"Oh, but it's so lovely. You might need it when you marry and have children," she protested.

He smiled, surprising her with the bitter irony in it. "Do you think that likely?"

Marriage or having children? She didn't know which one he meant. One thing she knew—if he didn't marry, it would be by choice, not because of no willing partners.

She glanced at his boots next to the kitchen door. Some woman would be lucky. He was too sensuous a man to live life alone. The thought shocked her.

But really, her no-nonsense, rarely smiling boss was a man of unexpected talents and depths. She'd admired him from the first. She'd learned to like and respect him during the course of her job. Now she found herself evaluating him as something more than those character traits. She saw him as a man, one with a great deal of passion and tenderness to share…

Pulling her gaze from the boots, she met his eyes. He watched her with a serious, rather intense expression. Again she was held in a spell by that penetrating, lucid perusal.

He was the one who broke it. "Coffee?" he asked, rising and going to the coffeemaker next to the stove.

"Yes, please."

"I thought I would drive you home in your ute and spend the night at my place in town. I'll have a friend run me back out here in the morning."

Poor man. He couldn't wait to get rid of her. "I can drive. Dr. Kate said it was okay as long as I didn't feel weak or faint. Truthfully, I've never felt better."

"You look—" He stopped as if suddenly realizing what he was saying.

She wanted him to finish that statement. "Terrible," she

supplied and laughed shakily. "I don't have any makeup except lipstick with me."

"You don't need it." He brought a cup of coffee to the table for her. "I'll fix lunch before we go."

He was determined to see her home. She didn't argue. Although she felt fine, she was nervous at being alone with a new baby. She was tired, and it was a long drive.

She thought of the night ahead. What if she went to sleep and didn't hear him crying? What if he choked?

She sat opposite Gareth and sipped the hot brew while worry darted through her.

"What's wrong?" he asked, frowning at her.

"I..." It seemed silly to voice her fears. "New mother syndrome, I think."

He nodded. "You're worried about taking care of him, that you won't be adequate."

She stared at him in amazement. "How did you know?"

"I once knew someone who had the same worries." For a second, his eyes flickered with some emotion she couldn't name, but it seemed soul deep.

Who had he known that intimately? But she didn't ask.

He moved toward the refrigerator. "My sister was like that, but by the time the baby was a couple of weeks old, she didn't think anyone but her, or maybe her husband, knew enough to take care of her daughter."

He was lying. She knew he was deliberately directing her thoughts elsewhere. There had been a woman one time, one that he'd loved. Maybe the woman had been married to someone else. His best friend perhaps. Gareth had fallen hopelessly in love with her. But of course he'd never reveal it by so much as a smile or a look of longing....

Fantasy. Pure fantasy.

She knew nothing about him. Besides, she had enough troubles of her own without taking on her boss's tragic past, if he'd even had one. Which she doubted.

"Well, I'll be glad when I feel like an expert. Maybe by the time he's twenty-one…" She let the thought trail away.

Gareth chuckled. "Yeah. If you can get them past drugs, alcohol and teenage pregnancy, you can feel proud."

"Amen," she agreed.

They ate soup, from a can this time, and sandwiches. She cleaned up the kitchen while he brought the baby, cradle and all, downstairs. His face was curiously impassive as he glanced at the sleeping infant.

He drove the ute while she watched the scenery go by and kept a protective hand on the cradle strapped onto the seat between them. She couldn't believe it had only been two days since she'd driven out so blithely, thinking to enjoy a ride before going home to an empty apartment.

That seemed ages ago. She was a different person now.

She glanced at the baby, then at the man who competently handled the ute, his mind miles away from there. He drove with both hands on the wheel, relaxed but alert. She would willingly place her life in those hands.

Sighing with the strange emotions that ran through her, she looked away and planned the rest of the weekend. She had to get groceries, baby items, a thousand things.

At the apartment, Gareth parked in her space in the underground garage at her direction, then carried the cradle while they rode the elevator to her apartment.

When they stepped off, her neighbors, a new couple in the building, stared at them in surprise. She spoke but didn't linger in the hall to talk. She was tired and drained all at once. Tears threatened. Her emotions were in a turmoil.

Hormones, she diagnosed and held on to her poise grimly. There was so much to do. And only her to do it.

Now she was feeling sorry for herself.

After unlocking and opening the door, she stood aside so he could enter and set the cradle down.

He looked a question at her.

"By the sofa. Set the cradle there." She forced a smile. "Thanks so much for your help. I can't tell you…" She trailed off, not sure what to say. Words weren't enough to convey her gratitude for his patience and kindness to her.

He placed the cradle carefully on the floor by the sofa. When Billy gave a whimper, Gareth started the cradle to rocking. The baby quieted at once. He straightened and came to the door, where she still stood.

Impulsively, she rose to her tiptoes and kissed his cheek, actually the lower edge of his jaw. That was as high as she could reach. She stepped back. "Thank you," she whispered.

He put a hand to the spot and rubbed it slowly. His eyes seemed to darken with mysterious thoughts while he stared at her as if she were a stranger.

"Do you want to call a cab?" she asked.

"No. I'll walk. It isn't far."

The door clicked shut behind him. Stacy sighed shakily. She couldn't figure out why, but she felt very much alone.

"He's beautiful," Shirl crooned, sitting on the floor beside the cradle and setting it gently into motion. "I want to take him home with me."

"Yeah? Wait until two o'clock in the morning when he's

woken you up for the third time in two hours and tell me that." Stacy stretched and yawned wearily.

The previous night had been tiring. Billy didn't seem to know this was his real home and that being at Gareth's place had been an accident on their part. He'd been fretful most of the night, not sleeping for a long period until this afternoon. Stacy couldn't seem to regain her energy, but continued to feel tired.

"Being a godmother is like being a grandmother. We get to give them back when things go wrong." Shirl looked at her watch. "I've got to go. My latest heartthrob is supposed to call when he gets in tonight."

"I thought you'd sworn off traveling men after the last one," Stacy reminded her friend with a grin. "An airline pilot isn't exactly home every night."

"As soon as I saw him, I was smitten." Shirl stood and gathered her purse and jacket. She shook her head. Her gold hoop earrings swung wildly to and fro. "I can't believe the Great Stone Face actually delivered a baby."

"What else could he do? Throw me out in the snow?" Stacy smoothed her top down over her now flat tummy. "Why do you think a bachelor would have a handmade cradle at his hideaway?"

"It was probably there when he bought the place." Shirl studied her. "Hey," she said softly, "you aren't going off the deep end over him because of this, are you?"

"Of course not." Stacy was indignant at the idea. "But he was wonderful with me and the baby. So very gentle." She felt the heat rise to her cheeks at her friend's incredulous stare.

"'Cause if you are, let me tell you, I know a hard-shell case when I see one. No woman is going to reach his heart." Shirl paid no attention to Stacy's denial as she warmed to her subject. "I've watched him in action for three years. He never dates one woman exclusively. Never. And if one of them shows signs of wanting more, he cuts her out of his life ruthlessly." Shirl shuddered. "Hard-hearted is his middle name."

Stacy smiled. "Maybe it's Beauregard," she suggested, then stopped. That was their private joke, hers and his. She didn't want to share it, not even with her best friend. "Actually, it's Bainbridge. I'm going to name Billy for him. William Bainbridge Gardenas. What do you think?"

Shirl stuck her hands on her hips and studied Stacy. A knowing look came into her eyes. "Girl, you got it bad."

Stacy shook her head, denying her friend's conclusion. "He isn't like you think. Just because Gareth is..." She searched for the word. "...Serious and rather stern-faced at the office, doesn't mean he can't have a sense of humor as well, or that he can't be kind."

"Bad, girl, bad." Shirl pulled her sheepskin jacket closed and zipped it. She'd been to a dude ranch for vacation last year and was now into boots and Western clothes.

Stacy grinned and gave up. Once Shirl got a notion, it stayed until rooted out by the next great idea.

"I gotta go. See you...when? Are you coming to work next week?" Shirl stopped by the door.

"I don't know. I'll have to check with the day-care center."

"Okay. Call if you don't show up."

After her friend left, Stacy went to her desk and looked over the list she'd made earlier. She'd planned on another month's salary before she took a brief maternity leave.

She wanted to stay home with the baby, especially now that she was nursing. Since that was impossible, she'd have to make other plans. First thing Tuesday, she'd call the nursery and see how soon they would take Billy.

"It's really terrible," Shirl confided in a low voice over the telephone. She was at her desk. "Absolute chaos. Janine quit in tears when Gareth snarled at her about a mistake in a contract. 'Course she'd already gotten it wrong three times before he told her, in that deadly calm, deadly cold voice he uses with us lesser mortals, that his year-old niece could do better. Janine threw the papers down and walked out."

Stacy groaned, picturing the scene. As executive assistant, she supervised the four clerk-typists in the law firm, acting as a shield between the boss and them. Gareth did tend to be rather abrupt. In adjusting to her son and motherhood during the past month, she'd almost forgotten the office existed.

"Pete and Gareth had a shouting match last night after everyone had gone but me. They were close to blows," Shirl continued, whispering.

Stacy assumed Gareth was in his office.

"I was looking for something to hit Gareth with when he stalked out. Slammed the door after him, too. I'd never seen him do that before. I rushed in to check on Pete. He told me he was worried. He said Gareth had been acting strange for days. He'd never seen the man explode like that, and he's known him since their college days."

"What were they arguing about?" Stacy thought this was strange behavior, too. Gareth, while serious, was always a gentleman. She'd never heard him raise his voice.

"Who knows?" There was a tense pause. "When are you coming back? It had better be soon. Before someone gets killed."

Stacy ignored the hyperbole. "I don't know. The day-care

center won't take a baby until he weighs at least ten pounds. With Billy coming early, he's only a little over six."

Shirl sighed. "Gareth is going to be in court all next week. With him out of the office, maybe things will calm down."

"Yeah, maybe." Stacy knew how he got when a case was in court. If he needed documents, he expected her to find them and get them to him immediately. With that frosted-steel voice, he could instill fear in the stoutest heart.

She and her friend talked a while longer, then made plans for Shirl to have dinner with her on Friday night. The new love would be out of town, flying a charter plane to Mexico.

After hanging up, Stacy finished folding the tiny clothes she'd washed that morning. The washing machine, which she and her husband had bought secondhand six years ago had conked out. The charge for repairs had been too much.

She'd reluctantly ordered a new one after several trips to the coin laundry. Those had been hell, juggling a baby and all the paraphernalia he required in addition to the clothes.

Not to mention the cost. Those machines gulped down money like there was no tomorrow. She figured she could pay for a new washer in less than a year at the rates they charged.

However, the new machine had taken a bite out of her emergency fund. That made her nervous.

She couldn't afford to take another month off, which was how long Dr. Kate said it would probably take Billy to gain the ten pounds he needed. The law firm gave a generous maternity leave, but it was without pay once a person used up her sick days, and Stacy, having been there only a year, had used hers the first week. Now what?

What if she took the baby with her to work?

Tingles danced along her nerves at the idea. Some offices

let women bring their babies in while they were small. Until the children were big enough to crawl around, they shouldn't be a nuisance. Unless they cried a lot.

Billy was a good baby, sweet-tempered and usually content.

What was she thinking of? Gareth would have her head on a platter if she dared broach the subject. But it would solve a lot of problems.

If things at the office were as tense as Shirl indicated, she was definitely needed. And with Gareth in court all day…

The case would be a long one—patent infringement by a rival company against Gareth's client. It could take weeks. Or months. Certainly long enough for Billy to gain four pounds.

It was a crazy idea. But it would let her continue to nurse the baby for a few more weeks….

She tried to take a nap, but her brain kept buzzing with possibilities. Really, the baby wouldn't be a bother at all. She wondered who she was trying to convince—her boss or herself.

"Good morning. Clelland and Davidson," Stacy said into the receiver. She slit an envelope open with an efficient motion, checked its contents and laid it in the To Be Filed tray.

"Stacy?" a surprised baritone inquired.

She clutched the telephone as her heart zoomed up to mach speed. "Yes. Hello, Gareth."

"What are you doing at the office?" The surprise had disappeared and been replaced with a heavy dose of wariness, maybe even hostility.

She decided to tell the truth. "Shirl called me Friday and said Janine had quit and things were hectic. I thought I'd better come in and see what was going on."

A longish pause followed her explanation before he spoke. "Did your doctor okay it?"

"Of course. I had such an easy delivery, I could have come back to work the next week. Unfortunately the nursery school doesn't take babies that weigh less than ten pounds."

She shut up before she gave away the fact that Billy still didn't weigh ten pounds, and at the moment he was snoozing in the cradle under her desk. She pressed a hand against her midriff. As usual when she was nervous, her stomach felt as if she'd swallowed a boulder.

"Yes, well, I need a report," he said, ignoring her chatter about babies.

She wrote down the information and promised to send it by courier or cab at once.

"Or you can always bring it yourself," he suggested dryly.

It took a second for her to realize he was joking. "I only deliver during blizzards," she quipped, then realized that statement could be taken more than one way.

Heat crept into her cheeks as she recalled Gareth's aid in delivering the baby. It had been such a strange weekend, full of nuances and flickers of intense emotion and thoughts that remained unspoken between them.

"Same here." He chuckled, a rich, warm sound that dipped right down inside of her and dissolved the hardness in her tummy.

In sharing the birth of her child, they had shared something primal and instinctive, a thing usually reserved to the parents of the child. And she'd learned her stern-faced boss had a sense of humor. And a gentleness so sweet, she grew misty-eyed each time she thought of it.

"Will you be in the office this afternoon?" she asked.

"Not until late. I'm having dinner with the client, then I'll come by and check the mail. Leave me a memo of anything you think I need to do."

She was relieved. She'd be long gone with the baby before he showed up. "Right. I'm opening the mail now." She eyed the stack of letters. It was still three inches high.

"We got a little behind with it."

"I noticed." She didn't dare mention the problem wouldn't exist if he hadn't been so hard on the staff.

"You may as well say it—it's my fault Janine quit."

"Well, if the shoe fits…"

"A size twelve mistake," he admitted. "See if you can talk her around, will you?"

"Yes."

When they finished, she hung up the phone and pondered their conversation. Other than a couple of awkward platitudes and insurance questions they'd hardly spoken since he'd dropped her at her place a month ago. She couldn't believe she'd been brave or foolish enough to tease him, and he'd let her get away with it.

At a whimper from the kneehole of the desk, she bent and pulled the cradle out. She locked the door to her office, opened her blouse, then picked up her hungry son.

If her boss could see her now…

One week down. Stacy sighed in relief as she straightened her desk Friday evening. Gareth and she had corresponded by note and telephone during the day. He came in early and left for court before she arrived. He didn't get back until late.

So far, so good.

However, good luck only lasted so long. She'd checked with the nursery school earlier that day. They'd agreed to take

Billy when he was six weeks old, no matter what his weight. If she could keep him hidden one more week, all would be well.

"Hi, fellow, how's it going?" Talking nonsense to him, she settled into her chair to let him nurse before she joined the throng of Friday shoppers at the grocery.

The feel of her milk coming down no longer caused her breasts to ache, although it still felt a bit odd. Each time she stepped into the shower, milk shot out in little streamlets for the first few seconds.

Dr. Kate had been delighted that she was nursing. "It's good for the baby and it's good for the mom," she'd informed Stacy while she checked her and Billy over. "It helps the body get back in shape faster."

Stacy had eased into her regular exercise routine two weeks ago without mishap. She'd never felt better. After a midnight feeding, Billy slept until six, so she was getting enough rest, too. Motherhood agreed with her.

Each time she thought of leaving the baby at the nursery, she experienced a pang of worry. As Gareth had predicted, she felt she was the only person qualified to take care of her son.

After burping Billy, she changed him to the other side, then rocked gently and hummed while she waited for him to finish.

A noise from the outer office caused the skin to prickle on her arms. Probably the janitorial service. She knew Shirl had locked the doors when she left.

The light clicked on in Gareth's office. She stared aghast as it spilled through the narrow crack of the partially open door into her office. She hadn't realized she hadn't closed it all the way when she was last in there.

She looked down at her son. His rosebud mouth worked busily, then stopped as he dozed off. If she removed him before he was finished, he'd let her know of his displeasure. Gareth would hear his squall easily.

Her mind spun haphazardly from one solution to another. She could say she'd picked him up from the nursery, then remembered something at the office she needed to do. Or that Billy had a runny nose and the nursery wouldn't let her leave him.

Footsteps crossed the adjoining room, sounding closer. Oh, no, he was coming into her office!

Her arms tightened around the baby. His head lolled to one side as he relaxed and fell deeper into sleep. She considered hiding under the desk until the office was clear.

But what if Gareth stayed until midnight or later going over his mail and catching up on office work? Maybe she should—

That was the way he found her, sitting on the edge of her chair in panic and indecision.

"What the hell?" His eyes, gray and stormy, narrowed as he took in the sight of her with the baby.

Their eyes met. For a split second, emotion flared in those cool, gray depths. She saw hunger and knew it was more than desire, but didn't know how she knew. She saw pain, then it was gone. His eyes moved downward over her. The hunger became pure, raw desire as he stared at her body.

She followed his gaze. Her breast was visible, a drop of milk clinging to the dark pink nipple.

Embarrassment swept over her in a torrid wave of heat. She adjusted her bra and pulled her blouse into place as fast as her trembling hand would allow.

"I can explain," she offered, dismayed to hear her voice quaver like a school kid caught in some mischief.

"Please do," he invited, emotion and desire swept cleanly from his face as if they'd never been.

She prayed for a softening of his icy expression, for any sign of understanding from him as she gave a concise explanation of her problem.

"Why didn't you stay home until the nursery would take him?" he questioned her as if they were in a courtroom and she a hostile witness. "I told you to take off as long as you needed. Surely you knew the job would be waiting."

"Things were chaotic here," she defended her actions.

"I should fire Shirl for calling you." He looked big and mean and menacing.

She worried he might do it. "It was my decision. I needed the money," she added, hating to admit anything that sounded like a human weakness to someone who obviously had none.

Her words seemed to jolt him. An emotion, too brief to be read, crossed his strong, angry features. "Why didn't you say so? I'll have the accountant cut a check for the time off—"

"No!" She returned his glare. "I'll earn my pay or do without."

"You'll stay at home another month and accept a salary," he ordered. "This isn't a damned nursery school. You can come back when your son is big enough to stay there."

"I can't accept a salary for nothing." Her pride was at stake. She wouldn't accept charity from him if she had to starve. "Besides, I don't see why I can't continue. This week has been fine. Billy isn't any problem in the office at all. He sleeps most of the time. I—"

He took two long strides forward. He loomed over her and the sleeping child. "Go home. I don't want to see you or your child here again. Is that clear?"

The blood drained from her face. "Perfectly clear."

He'd fired her. She couldn't believe it. She'd never been fired from any job. Not ever.

He stared at her another moment, then walked out. His office door closed with a jar behind him.

She sat there, stunned. Fired. A wave of fear washed over her. Her hands trembled as she slipped the shawl-like carrier around her shoulders and placed her son in it, snug against her body. He moved his lips, then settled deeper into sleep.

After gathering her purse and personal belongings, she glanced around the office to see if she'd missed anything. The plants she'd brought in could stay. She'd ask Shirl to water them until Gareth hired someone.

Fired. The word itself was a disgrace, yet she didn't think she'd done so very wrong. When she took a step, her toe hit the cradle. She stared at it for a long minute.

The cradle provided a key to his mixed reactions during the delivery, but she didn't know what secrets it hid. The cradle, his anger upon seeing her with the baby—all clues that pointed to something traumatic from his past. Had he and someone he loved had a child? If so, what had happened to them?

It was a mystery, one he'd never explain.

She removed the pad and baby blanket from the cradle and placed it on the floor in front of his office door on her way to the elevator. He'd find it there and take it to his place.

In a daze, she drove home, parked the ute in her space, then, still gripping the steering wheel, laid her head on her hands and let her mind drift.

She'd felt this way before. When her father had died, she'd felt the loneliness as a vast plain stretching before her. It had been the same when her husband had been killed.

As if sensing her distress, the baby awoke and cried. She

pushed aside her worries. "This isn't the end of the world," she told him. "We'll be fine."

That felt like a terrible lie.

Chapter Five

Gareth paced the wall of windows in the penthouse that was his town residence. He stopped and glared at the cradle, then paced some more.

Get a grip, he advised himself. He'd hurt Stacy's feelings for no reason. No *good reason*. He had to apologize.

He closed his eyes and pressed a finger and thumb to the bridge of his nose. A steam engine chugged inside his skull, sending a shaft of pain through his head with each stroke.

Going into the kitchen, he found some aspirin and downed two tablets with a glass of juice. He refilled his coffee cup and leaned against the counter, wondering if Stacy was up yet.

Probably. Babies woke early as a rule.

A fresh pain lanced through his head. He couldn't figure it out. He'd seen other women with babies. They hadn't bothered him. But seeing Stacy with her child caused something to happen inside him, something painful that he didn't want, hadn't asked for and wasn't about to acknowledge.

That emotion-driven weekend at the cabin had started this internal battle. Before that, his life had been perfect. Well, not perfect, but certainly okay.

He paced into the living room. The sun was full up, spilling its warm radiance over the world. The cherry trees shimmered with new growth and ripening buds. Soon they would burst open. He realized it was the first day of spring.

There was no getting around his conscience. He had to apologize to Stacy for his hateful words yesterday. He grabbed up the car keys and the cradle that had silently accused him of unspeakable brutality all weekend and headed out the door.

There was little traffic this early on Saturday morning. He made it to Stacy's apartment complex in twenty minutes. In the elevator, he rehearsed what he wanted to say.

When the doors slid open, he stepped off, nodding to the couple who stared at him and the cradle in his hands. They got on the elevator. The man pushed the button. They stood there frowning at him until the door closed and hid them from view.

Going down the hall, Gareth realized they were the same people who'd seen him arrive with Stacy and her son the previous month. He'd been carrying the cradle then, too.

They probably thought the child was his. Did they also think he had refused to marry the mother?

A picture of Stacy leapt into his mind, her dark hair spread over his pillow, her courage greater than her fear as she told him what to do during the birth. Another facet of that odd weekend— he'd wanted her.

He'd looked at her in his bed and desire had poured over him like a flow of hot lava. Even in those moments of strain, when a contraction had her in its grasp, she'd looked beautiful to him, beautiful and desirable, the epitome of womanhood.

The trouble was, he'd still felt that way after the crisis had passed. When he'd walked into the office Friday and found her nursing the child, all the burning need he'd suppressed had gushed forth. He'd wanted to lie with her, not necessarily to make love, although that was part of it, but to hold her and the baby and…and what? Claim them? Keep them?

Some basic instinct had been awakened in him. He didn't know how to put it back to sleep.

Unidentified emotions churned in him when he stopped outside her door. He picked one out of the whirlpool—guilt. Stacy and her child were alone in the world, and he'd been an ogre to her about the baby. He'd make it up to her.

He rang the bell and heard it echoing in the entranceway on the other side of the door. He'd about decided she wasn't going to answer when he heard the click of the lock.

When she opened the door, he realized she'd been standing on the other side, observing him through the peephole and making up her mind whether to let him in.

"You forgot this," he said, his apology going right out of his head. He took in her appearance from the crown of shining hair gathered behind her head with a bow, down the loose top, past her slacks to the pink toenails visible beneath them. She was barefooted and looked like a girl.

Except he knew in the most elemental way that she was a woman and a very desirable one.

That fact frustrated the hell out of him. He didn't need to get involved with a transplanted wildflower from Wyoming.

He wasn't going to get involved with anyone, period. He had nothing to offer a woman, not since…

"It belongs to you." She didn't open the door and invite him in.

"Got any coffee?" he asked, forcing the issue. "I'm not going to eat crow out here in the hall."

A startled expression flicked across her face. She stepped back and let him in.

After the door closed behind him, Gareth motioned for her to lead the way. She went into the kitchen. He placed the cradle on the living room floor where she'd had him set it the last time and followed her into the other room.

"I like your place," he commented, taking a seat at the table. Double windows faced south. A macrame frame with glass shelves had been suspended from the ceiling in front of them. Pots of herbs and flowers covered the shelves, adding a splash of color to the white walls and whitewashed pine cabinets.

The floor was beige linoleum with irregular dots of green and yellow, blue and red sprinkled in it. Stacy's home was clean and well kept, yet comfortable.

"Why are you here?" she asked. She brought him a cup of coffee and took her place across the table.

"To apologize for my behavior yesterday."

He watched to see how she would take his statement. She didn't blink an eye. Hmm, still angry with him.

"I hope you'll be speaking to me by Monday, or else it's going to be darned awkward carrying on a conversation through Pete or Shirl." He smiled at her.

She didn't smile back. "I won't be at work Monday."

A pang, sort of like alarm, went through him. "Why not?"

"You fired me." She gestured to the paper on the table. "I'm looking for another position."

"The hell you are." He forced himself to set the cup down without slamming it against the wood. "I didn't fire you. Why would I fire the best assistant I've ever had?"

"For having Billy at the office." She returned his glare with stoic courage. Her hand trembled as she lifted her cup and took a sip. "You said you didn't want to see either of us again. I took you at your word."

"I said that?" He racked his brain. He couldn't remember what he'd said, but he did recall his reaction at seeing her breast, full of milk, with a drop lingering on its tip. He'd wanted to catch the drop on his finger and taste it. He'd wanted to taste her.

"Yes," she said coolly, "you did."

He forced his gaze away from the front of her shirt and looked her in the eye. She was not going to let it go easily. "I'm sorry. I didn't mean it. I was…surprised at seeing you and the boy there, that was all."

She gave him such a skeptical look, he felt the heat rise in his ears.

"Surprised must be the understatement of the year," she murmured. She broke eye contact and gazed out the window.

"I'll expect you at the office Monday," he said firmly.

"I won't be in. The nursery won't take Billy yet."

"Bring him with you." He couldn't believe he'd said that. Her eyes widened to their fullest.

He managed a grin. "Yeah, it shocks me, too, but I think it'll work. You can keep the baby at the office as long as you want. Until he gets to moving around."

"You mean it?"

"Yeah."

"But you hate children."

He glared at her. "Of course I don't. It's just that you caught me at a bad moment."

How could he explain what he didn't understand himself? Seeing her hold her child in love and tenderness opened a void inside him that he didn't want exposed. "You and the baby, you make me remember things I'd rather forget."

"Oh, Gareth, I'm so sorry."

Her voice, her impulsive kindness made him wonder just how far she would go to comfort him. And how far he'd let her.

When she made another murmur of sympathy, he felt it flow inside, warm and soft and healing. He'd liked her voice from the moment he'd heard it. While she had no discernible accent, there was a lilt to it, as if she'd been humming to herself before she spoke and the notes carried over into her words.

"It was years ago."

"But it still hurts." A pensive shadow crossed her face. "Sometimes it never goes completely away, does it? There's still the regret for all the things that could have been and guilt for those that did happen and shouldn't have."

It was startling to hear her voice the inner doubts that tore at him at odd, undefended moments. "Yeah, guilt," he echoed in the soft silence that followed.

"We have to learn to let it go, too. That's part of the process of grieving—letting all the useless stuff go."

"Have you?" He couldn't keep the cynical disbelief from the question.

"I think so. Having Billy helped a lot. There's an empty space inside, but it's a quiet place now."

"It doesn't hurt anymore?"

"Not unbearably."

He sipped the coffee and let the conversation settle in the back of his mind. The emptiness that haunted him receded until it, too, was bearable. He breathed deeply, slowly.

The peaceful tick of the clock filled the room with a busy cheer. Peace. Yeah, that's part of what he felt around Stacy.

"You have a soothing presence," he told her. "I noticed it at the first interview."

She looked pleased. "Is that why you hired me?"

"No. You had the brains for the job. Your references were glowing. Your old employer threatened me if I didn't treat you right. He said his son was a hired killer."

She laughed. "His son is a policeman. He worked with my husband for a time on the street. I was thrilled to get to work for you after Mr. Anders retired. He said you were one of the best trial lawyers he'd ever seen."

"So you'll stay on?"

"If you wish."

The tension melted out of him. "I do." His stomach rumbled. He hadn't eaten breakfast.

"How about some pancakes?" she asked.

He hesitated, knowing he should leave. But he wanted to stay. "Yeah, that sounds good."

They talked about world news while she prepared the meal.

The women he knew didn't cook. They hired a catering service. That was one thing he liked about his cabin in the woods. He prepared his own food. Simple meals for a simple soul, he'd once told his mother when she'd been horrified to discover there was no delivery service in a hundred miles.

Stacy glanced at him. "What are you smiling about?"

"Life."

"Care to explain that?" She brought a plate to the table and placed it in front of him. After setting out a pitcher of warm syrup, she returned to the stove. He noticed the smooth line of her hips in the snug slacks.

"When I was a kid, Sunday mornings were a big treat. My folks usually had some of their arty friends over for a brunch. Everyone would gather in the kitchen and talk and help with the meal. I'd forgotten how much I enjoyed those mornings."

"So there are good things to remember?" She gave him one of her encouraging smiles.

"Yes. Good things." He thought of the past, of being at the farm with Ginny, who'd found his mother's bossy ways and nosy questions somewhat intrusive. An understatement. "My mother thinks babies are the greatest. She'd probably bombard you with advice on raising yours."

"Does she know that you delivered Billy?"

He realized Stacy was still embarrassed by that. He wasn't, but he was irritated by the restless nights he'd experienced since the event and the recurring dream of coming home and finding Stacy in his bed again. Except in the dream her arms were open, inviting him in....

Stacy gave him a curious glance. He hadn't answered her question. "No, but I mentioned that you'd had a boy."

He waited for the pain of the past to strike with its memory of loss and emptiness, but there were other memories now...of Stacy holding on to him as she labored through a contraction...of her son, grabbing his finger, wanting nourishment from him....

Stacy left him alone and let him think about the past. That's what the police counselor had told her, remember the good things, let the rest go. She had, but having the baby had helped a lot. Gareth hadn't had that comfort.

She resumed reading the morning paper while they ate the meal. What a relief to know she didn't have to look for another job. She really liked what she was doing.

After a while, she looked up. Gareth was watching her. In his eyes was the hunger she'd thought she'd seen before. Now she didn't have to wonder if it was really there or not. It was.

"Gareth," she said, a protest. Or an entreaty? She'd sounded breathless.

He blinked, and it was gone. "Yes?"

She gazed at him in confusion. Didn't he know? "Nothing. It's nothing."

Restless, she turned on the radio, needing to fill the silence between them. Beautiful, haunting music filled the room. It fitted her mood, the restlessness inside her, the longing for things she couldn't name.

She stood by the window, letting her gaze roam the street and the tiny park across the way. Since the blizzard, the weather had turned warm, each day filled with sunshine as if apologizing for the earlier harshness. She closed her eyes and forced the moodiness at bay.

When she finally faced Gareth, she was surprised to see a look of intense sadness on his face. "Gareth?"

He gave a half smile. "Beethoven, isn't it?"

She nodded. "The *Moonlight Sonata*. It's one of my favorites." She didn't mention that its gentleness, then its passion called to her soul, making her want more than this meager existence. She longed for something...

Laying the paper aside, he stood abruptly as if suddenly deciding to leave. Instead he came over and stood beside her at the window. "I once knew someone else who loved it, too."

Her heart knocked against her ribs. He was sharing a tiny

bit of his past with her. She instinctively knew he'd loved the woman who'd loved this music. Had she loved him? What had happened to her?

Stacy didn't dare ask.

The next thing that happened utterly surprised her. He lifted a lock of her hair and rubbed it between his thumb and finger. "She was a lot like you—warm and loving and—"

She was disappointed when he stopped, cutting the words off as if realizing he was saying too much. She stared at him. He was no more than a foot away. One step and they'd touch.

The heat from his body caressed her. She drew a shaky breath, let it out. It blended into the music.

He dropped the strand of hair and touched the corner of her mouth. She held very still. He explored her bottom lip with his fingertip. The sensation, as light as the flicker of an eyelash, sent currents of electricity into her chest.

Unable to get enough air, she had to breathe through her mouth. He outlined her upper lip, then removed his hand.

Slowly, so slowly she thought she would die before he reached her, he lowered his head. His lips touched hers, a glancing touch like a hummingbird skimming the flowers to find the very best nectar.

A thousand sensations ran through her, both sweet and painful, all demanding more.

"You'd better send me away," he murmured.

"No."

She slipped a hand behind his head and raised on tiptoe until she could reach his hard, unsmiling mouth. She gave him the same type of kiss he'd given her—an experimental touching that awakened the need for more.

Longing, visceral and urgent, spread through her. She moved closer, instinctively seeking the warmth of his large, hard body. Ah, he was like the sun, radiating heat that penetrated all the way through her.

"You make me feel warm," she whispered, kissing along his jaw, feeling the tension in the set of the muscles there and in his shoulders. She sensed the struggle inside him.

"You make me hot," he told her in a harsh tone. He clasped her by the shoulders, not letting her come closer.

His admission flew like a thunderbolt to some hidden part of her, shattering wisdom and common sense, filling her with unnamed yearning while music filled her soul.

"Do you know what you're doing?" he demanded, his voice going deeper, becoming husky with desire. It raged in his eyes, turning their coolness into heat.

"No."

The simple honesty of the word seemed to throw him for a loop. He stared down at her for a long moment. "If this happens, it's sex, nothing else. Is that clear?"

She tried to think, to will her body into submission, but it was impossible. Some part of her, strong and insistent, wanted to absorb the wonderful warmth his body gave off like a hearth on a cold morning. Another part wanted to give to him, to share a part of herself so the emptiness that caused him such pain could be filled and put to rest.

But these were shadows and flickers of emotions that darted through her mind, too swiftly gone to be captured and put into words. Somehow she knew this was the way, that right now he needed her touch as much as she needed his warmth.

"Is it clear to you?" she asked, wondering if he understood

his own needs at all, or if he'd denied them so long, he could no longer recognize them. She leaned her head back so she could see his expression.

"Very."

He looked deeply into her eyes, probing to her very soul. Her heart beat rapidly, shaking her body while she waited, leaving the next move up to him. In that instant, she knew whatever was between them was much more than the desire of the moment, and that she'd waited for this all her life.

He moved his hands down her arms to her wrists, then to her waist and up her torso. He molded his hands over her breasts, measuring their size and fullness.

Stacy gave a little cry and pressed her face into his shirt. It had been so long since she'd experienced the spontaneous joy of passion, of letting herself feel the delight without fretting over the responsibility and worry that had gone with it.

"We're insane," he said. But he bent and kissed the side of her neck instead of letting her go.

And then his arms were around her. She locked hers around his shoulders and held on, shaking like a leaf in a gale. He held her closer. She felt every line and ridge of his body.

His lips found hers. This time the kiss wasn't a shy graze, but the full interplay of demand and answer. His tongue explored her mouth intimately. The kiss went on and on. An eternity of longing was exchanged. She knew the moment the kiss deepened and became more than a meeting of flesh.

Gareth felt her response as an explosion of fire and passion. With a soft moan, she twisted against him, merging planes and angles until they were melded into one. For a moment, he gave himself to it, to her, then with a wrench, he pulled his mouth from hers.

They stood locked together, their breaths loud in the silence and ragged with needs unmet.

"Gareth," she said.

Her voice stroked him as her tongue had, wringing floods of desire out of him like water out of a sponge. He couldn't bring himself to step away. He needed her like he needed air.

"No," he said. His voice made a mockery of the denial. It was filled with the husky cadences of pure, hot lust.

She smiled just a little. Her breasts, large and taut with nourishment for her child, rose and fell against him as she took a deep breath and let it out in a rush.

He took the necessary step to separate them. She let her hands trail down his chest, then drop to her sides. Her eyes, the barometer of her moods, showed disappointment.

That and the need to kiss her again had him clenching his hands in useless agony. He stuck them in the back pockets of his jeans and took another step back.

"I'm sorry," he said. The headache returned, a steam shovel digging through his brain looking for sense. It wouldn't find it. There was no sense in that ill-advised clench. And no future. "That shouldn't…I shouldn't have done that."

"It's because of what happened at the cabin," she said, her cheeks flushed, her hair disheveled from his caresses.

"Is it?"

He injected a note of sardonic amusement in his voice as a defense against feelings he didn't want to acknowledge. If they were going to be able to work together after this, he was going to have to find a method of communication that didn't include seeing or being near her.

"People who go through a crisis together often feel close

afterward," she advised. Her seriousness—so damned sweet and earnest—mocked his cynicism.

He picked up his cup and took a drink, aware that she watched him, that she'd kissed him in the hollow of his throat and along his neck. Heat gathered deep inside.

"I've got to go." He set the cup down and stalked away.

She followed him to the door.

He faced her before he left, angry for reasons too complicated to explain, even to himself. "I should have known. It was there before. Your voice, your laughter, your joy at being pregnant…it was all there. You're real, and I want you."

"I feel the same."

"You're not supposed to agree with me." He felt fierce and close to exploding. He had to get out of there.

"Sorry."

"The funny thing is I didn't know, not until this morning. During the birth, when you were in my bed, I was aware of desire, but it wasn't…real. Seeing you here…" He shook his head, not understanding any of it, then turned and walked out.

All the way home, he was haunted by her eyes, soft eyes that seemed to see inside his soul. He didn't like the feeling. It made him angry. He felt cornered, with nowhere to run to.

Worse, he hadn't wanted to run while he held her and she let him take all the kisses he could get. He'd been lost in the music and the frenzied beating of their hearts.

Desire—hot and sweet and urgent—rushed over him.

Gareth yawned tiredly as he settled deeper into a lounge chair on the patio. He hadn't slept worth a damn last night. Today was his mother's birthday, so he'd come out for lunch and to bring her a gold bracelet. She wore it now along with the diamond earrings his father had given her.

"There, what do you think?" she asked, adding a final dab of white to her painting. She sat back, then glanced at the two men in her life expectantly.

"Very interesting," her husband declared.

Gareth studied the picture. "I like the way the barn sort of teeters to one side. Looks as if it's on its last legs."

"Oh, does it?" She leaned close to examine her work.

His dad chuckled. "Perhaps if you'd use your glasses..." he offered as a suggestion.

"No." She straightened. "I tried those for a whole week. The world looked simply surreal, all stark lines and delineated colors. I like it better sort of misty."

"And no straight angles," Gareth added. He smiled when his mother wrinkled her nose at him.

She put her brush in turpentine and wiped the palette down. "How's Stacy and the baby?" she asked.

"Fine." As the pause lengthened, he added, "I don't see much of them. We're busy at the office."

"I spoke to Shirl Friday."

Gareth tensed.

"She mentioned the most extraordinary thing—that Stacy had the baby at your cabin during the blizzard."

Caught like a kid in mischief, he couldn't evade telling the story. He did so in as brief a manner as possible and made a mental note to tell Shirl to mind her own business.

"And you were snowed in for three days?"

He knew she wouldn't rest until she had the whole story. "From Thursday evening until Saturday morning. The snowplows were out by then." He provided a few more details.

"Well," she said and gave her husband a significant look.

"It was nothing," he insisted with proper modesty.

"I remember taking your mother to the hospital when you were born," his father said with a nostalgic smile. "It was during a concert to raise money for the symphony scholarship fund. She wouldn't leave until the intermission."

"You were very irritated over that, darling, but one can't walk out during a performance. It would be rude."

The two men looked at each other and burst into laughter.

She looked from one to the other. Her frown softened into an affectionate gaze. "I'm thinking of taking up archery," she announced suddenly. At their skeptical expressions, she explained, "Like one of those Greek deities...what was the name?"

"Diana was the huntress," Gareth reminded her. "A virgin goddess," he added, tongue-in-cheek.

"No, no, not that one."

"Cupid was the other archer. He carried a bow and quiver of arrows," her husband put in.

She clapped her hands together in delight. "Well, there you have it," she said as if a puzzle had been solved.

A tingle of misgiving went through Gareth. He witnessed his parents' exchange of smiles that indicated a lifetime of sharing each other's thoughts. He flinched involuntarily as if an arrow had pierced his heart.

Or at least pinged off it, he added cynically.

His parents shared a wonderful relationship, and he was glad for them. He just didn't want any part of it.

A face appeared in his inner vision—Stacy, her smile encouraging as she told him to remember the good times and let the rest go. It wasn't that easy....

Then he remembered how easy it had been to slide his arms

around her, to kiss her and take all the sweetness she offered in her kisses. He'd forgotten everything during those wild moments in her arms.

He sprang up from the chair, restless as emotion churned within him. He didn't like it. Passion…love…those were all part of the past. He didn't want to remember any of it.

"Are you leaving so soon?" his mother asked.

He realized he was standing in the middle of the patio, his fists clenched and ready for battle. He forced himself to relax.

"Yes. I have some papers to study before court tomorrow. Thanks for lunch." He kissed his mother's cheek and shook hands with his father before leaving.

On the drive back to the city, he realized his actions of late could be taken as *running*. From a woman and a kid? Ha.

Chapter Six

"I can't believe the Great Stone Face lets you bring Billy to the office." Shirl rolled her eyes.

Stacy rocked the cradle with her foot. Her son was sound asleep under her desk. He was such a good baby. "Billy weighs ten pounds now. I should put him in the day-care center."

"It's better for him to be with you. My mamma worked all my life, then she died. I never really knew her." Shirl collected the filing. "Take what you can while you can, is my advice."

"I could say the same to you. When are you going to meet the man of your dreams and marry and have children? By the way, how's your pilot?"

Shirl ran her fingers into her hair, which was in a frizz of bright tawny gold that was striking with her milk chocolate complexion. "I'm not seeing him." She pulled a long face. "I think there's something wrong with me. As soon as a man indicates he's really interested, I back off. He asked me to go visit his folks. Scared me to death."

"When the right one comes along, you'll not give it a second thought," Stacy predicted, laughing at her friend's frown.

"Yeah, right."

Stacy wasn't fooled by the flippant reply. Shirl was troubled. She knew the feeling.

Gareth was one of the most puzzling creatures she'd ever met. He'd finished the court case, winning it for his client after a tense, arduous trial. He'd been in the office during regular hours most of the week. They hardly spoke.

He dealt with her by phone, using the intercom rather than speaking directly with her as he used to. He kept the door between their offices closed.

Probably a wise course. It would give them both time to get over this madness. Of course there was the possibility they wouldn't. Then what?

"I've got to go." Shirl straightened and gave a yawn.

Stacy was tempted to tell her friend of Gareth's visit to the apartment, but she couldn't do it. It seemed much too private and intimate to share. Besides, she didn't want to hear Shirl's laughter when she confessed what had happened.

After her friend's departure, Stacy contemplated those passionate moments for the hundredth time. She touched her lips and remembered how his had felt against hers.

She couldn't fall in love with her boss. It wasn't done. It certainly wasn't wise. However, she had a sinking feeling that all the pep talks she'd tried for days weren't going to do a bit of good.

The ringing of the telephone halted the recriminations. "Good morning. Clelland and Davidson." She tipped the cradle with her foot, rocking it in case the noise woke the baby.

"Hello. Stacy?" It was Gareth's mother.

"Yes. Good morning and how are you, Mrs. Clelland?"

"Frightful. Would you believe I've sprained my ankle? Can you believe this would happen when I'm expecting a hundred people here for an auction Sunday?"

"Oh, that's really too bad," Stacy murmured in sympathy.

"It's a disaster." Actually she sounded quite cheerful about it. "That's why I'm calling. I wanted to know if you could help out this weekend. I wouldn't ask, but I'm really quite desperate, and I don't know where to turn."

"This weekend?" Stacy repeated as she scrambled for something to say.

"The proceeds of the auction go to the local children's literacy program. We have some really nice items. Gareth talked one of his friends into donating an antique automobile. Isn't that exciting?"

"Uh, yes."

"So do say you'll spend the weekend and be my legs. I know it's crass of me to ask, but Gareth has mentioned how terribly efficient you are. Please say you can come."

"Well, I…" Stacy didn't know what to say.

"Is Gareth there?" his mother continued. "Let me speak to him. It would be best if you came out tomorrow."

Tomorrow was Friday. Stacy had been looking forward to the weekend as a relief from the tension in the office. She certainly didn't want to spend it at his mother's home.

"I'm really sorry, Mrs. Clelland, but I have a baby—"

"Yes, I know. Of course I expect you to bring him, too.

Now, is my son there? Let me speak to him," she said without waiting for an answer.

"I'll get him." Stacy, feeling as if she'd been swirled around in a whirlwind and spit out, buzzed Gareth on the intercom. Five minutes later, he strolled into her office.

"How do you feel about spending a long weekend in the country?" he asked. "We'll go down tomorrow and return Monday."

Trying to read his expression was like studying a blank wall for a hidden message. "I don't know."

She realized she wanted to go. She'd like to meet his parents and see where he grew up. However, during the past two weeks, they'd regained much of their former equilibrium in working together. Perhaps it was best not to rock the boat.

"Don't be scared," he said on an ironic note. "I'll control my beastly impulses."

"I'm not scared." She spoke too fast. "I mean, of course I'm not scared. It's just that…the baby and all."

"He does okay here at the office. He'll be fine at the farm. There's a nursery. Mom will put you in the adjoining room so you'll be close." He hesitated. "She does need help."

He didn't like the idea of her being there, either. She considered the pros and cons of the situation and decided nothing could happen with his parents and a baby in attendance. "All right. If you think I would be useful."

"I can guarantee it. Mom will run you ragged. I'd advise comfortable clothes and shoes. Also, our guests will feel more at ease if the hostess is dressed casually."

She mulled over this last cryptic remark after he returned to his office. She wasn't a hostess. She was an employee.

Sometimes it was hard to remember that, especially when the

memory of that passionate embrace invaded her mind and refused to be rooted out as it had so many times the past few days.

Gareth gave her a critical once-over while he stored her bags in the trunk of his sedan. He affixed the baby's seat in the rear of the car, facing backward. Stacy strapped her son in and tried not to look as apprehensive as she felt.

Soon they joined the other residents leaving the Washington, D.C., area for the weekend. The interstate highway traffic was already bumper to bumper.

"It might take a couple of hours to get to the farm," Gareth told her. "Usually I can make it in half that time."

"The traffic is heavier than I'd expected." She couldn't think of any idle chitchat and so sat in silence, watching the urban crowding thin out into rolling countryside. When it did, they were able to pick up speed.

Mansions were sometimes visible behind fences and hedgerows. She wondered what kind of house was on his parents' farm. Was it a real farm, or some rich person's idea of a farm—twenty acres with a swimming pool and a couple of horses to add color?

The air in the luxury vehicle hummed with undertones of tension, or maybe it was just her. She was going as an employee, not a guest, and certainly not as a friend or…or anything. There was no need to be excited about the trip.

When they turned into the drive that swept in a circle along the front of a massive two-story brick house, she stared at it in dismay. It was grander than anything she'd imagined.

"It looks…old," she said inanely.

"About 150 years. My grandparents bought it and spent most of their retirement years restoring it. My grandmother still sends interesting bits and pieces back from her travels.

This drives my mom wild trying to find someplace to put all the junk, as she calls it. I think that's why she has the auction each year. So she can get rid of it."

Stacy didn't say a word. She held Billy while Gareth retrieved their luggage from the car. A tall, thin man in a black suit rushed down the steps.

"Mr. Gareth, welcome home. Here, let me take those." He took over the luggage.

"Stacy, meet Jacob. He can answer any question or provide any reasonable service." He spoke to the older man. "Ms. Gardenas is here to help Mom with the auction this weekend. Would your niece be available to keep an eye on Billy for us?"

"She'll be delighted. Your mother has already arranged it."

They'd arranged a baby-sitter without consulting her. Stacy didn't want one. Billy would stay with her.

"Ms. Gardenas will want to interview Kim to be sure she's qualified to take care of a very young child. I believe she's had experience with babies, hasn't she?"

"Indeed she has. Her older sister has three children. Kim has helped raise them. Also, she's majoring in child psychology at the university."

"How's she doing?" Gareth asked. "She was having trouble with one professor last year, if I remember correctly."

"Straight A's this time. She made the president's list."

"Great." Gareth glanced at Stacy. "Ready?"

She nodded and followed him up the steps and into the house. Her heart thumped very loud as she entered.

The inside of the mansion was as she'd expected—marble and brass and crystal chandeliers, scroll-footed sofas and lyre-back chairs and piecrust tables. A maid in a black uniform.

"Your mother thought Ms. Gardenas would be comfortable

in the nursery quarters." Jacob inclined his head toward a broad hallway, indicating she was to go first.

"I'll go find Mother and say hello," Gareth told her. "I'll be back for you in, say, a half hour?"

"Yes, that'll be fine." She hurried along the hall.

"Last door on the right," Jacob directed.

She opened the door and went in. Her breath caught. Done in pale green walls and white woodwork, with white furniture upholstered in a floral print with lots of green, the room looked like a garden.

Living plants lined a tiled area next to a window that started a foot from the floor and went almost to the ceiling. Yellow and white daisies in earth-toned ceramic pots decorated the three tables in the room. The four-poster bed was draped with gauzy white netting and swags to match the upholstery.

A door stood open at one side. Through it, she could see the nursery. A whitewashed pine crib and dressing table were aligned along one wall. A bureau sat in a corner. A rocking chair and table were next to a window that looked out on a sweeping lawn and swimming pool.

A barn was visible in the distance. A tractor, big and important-looking, was parked beside it. A horse grazed in the pasture next to the barn, and corn grew in the field beyond that.

A working farm. That made her feel more at ease.

"I'll send Maudie to hang your things," Jacob told her. With a smile, he left her.

She laid her purse on a table, then took Billy into the nursery and changed his diaper. He'd slept all the way there in the car, so he wouldn't need a nap before bedtime. She sat in the rocker and played patty-cake with him, then put him in the crib while she freshened up.

The maid she'd seen earlier knocked and entered at her call. "I'm Maudie. I'll hang your things. What do you want to wear for dinner? I'll unpack it first in case it needs pressing. The family usually gathers in the library between six and seven."

Since it was a working weekend, she'd brought office suits. "The black suit," she decided.

Maudie efficiently unpacked and hung her clothes. She surveyed the black suit, then selected a white silk blouse. "You won't need the jacket," she advised. "Did you bring a gold necklace and earrings? They would go well with the skirt and blouse. Ms. Clelland said you were to borrow whatever you needed from her."

Stacy lifted her chin. "I have my own things."

She wasn't about to borrow finery from Gareth's mother like a poor relative visiting from the sticks.

After changing into the other clothing, she cleaned her face and put on fresh makeup, using a bit more than she usually did. She hoped no one noticed her hands were trembly. If they had before-dinner drinks, she'd probably spill something all over herself. She grinned at her reflection.

She wasn't here to impress possible future in-laws. She was here to work. She'd keep that firmly in mind.

When Gareth knocked on her door at exactly six o'clock, her stomach went to her throat and remained there. She picked up her son and held him like a shield. "Come in," she called huskily.

Gareth opened the door. He, too, had changed and now wore dark slacks and a blue silk shirt that made his eyes resemble polished pieces from a summer sky.

"Won't you join us?" he asked formally.

She nodded. Billy grinned at Gareth and reached out a hand to him, surprising them both. She watched with suspended breath as Gareth put his finger in the child's hand and let Billy bring it to his mouth for a taste.

After an experimental nibble, Billy let go and waved his arms the way he did when he became excited. He wanted Gareth to hold him. Fortunately, her boss didn't get the message.

"Mother is dying to see the baby," he said. His gaze lifted from Billy to her. It lingered on her mouth. "She thinks I'm deliberately depriving her of one of her natural rights, that of being a grandmother."

Stacy's lips tingled with the memory of his mouth on hers. Sometimes that seemed more like a dream than reality. "Lots of mothers feel that way."

"Do you?" His smile was sardonic as usual when conversation turned to anything remotely personal.

"I might. When Billy grows up."

"Mother will also try a bit of matchmaking between us. Don't let it get to you." With that, he motioned for her to follow and led the way down the hall.

Staring at his broad back, too stunned for words, she felt a contraction in her chest. For a moment, the tiniest moment, she wished Gareth was Billy's father. And if he was Billy's father, then he would also be her husband....

His parents waited for them in the library or study or whatever they called it. Gareth made the introductions. "Stacy, the invalid, looking suitably wan and dramatic in black, is my mother. The gentleman in the smoking jacket is my father. He's the only person outside the movies I've ever seen wear one of those and get away with it."

Stacy quickly looked at his folks to see how they took his teasing. They were smiling easily.

"We're delighted you could come," Mrs. Clelland said.

Mr. Clelland stood and shook Stacy's hand. He escorted her to a chair next to his wife, who sat on a velvet chaise longue like a languid movie queen. Stacy kept expecting someone to shout, "Lights. Camera. Action."

"Oh, look at the little darling." Mrs. Clelland touched Billy's cheek. He grabbed her finger and sucked on it. She laughed as if this were a great feat. "He looks just like you at that age," she exclaimed, giving her son an oblique glance.

Gareth looked momentarily startled, then he laughed. "I suspect most babies look alike for the first few months."

"Not at all," his mother insisted. "Molly always wore that quiet, stubborn look from the day she was born. Our daughter out West," she explained to Stacy. "She married a rancher— he was a widower—and now has two children. He had a little girl by his first wife, and he and Molly have a daughter, too."

"How nice," Stacy said sincerely, again feeling caught in a whirlwind as Mrs. Clelland breezed through the family history.

"Our hopes are on Gareth for a grandson. Molly's husband says they aren't having any more children."

"What does Molly say?" Gareth slipped in with a wry twist.

Mrs. Clelland laughed and clapped her hands together. "She says they are."

The noise scared the baby. He held his breath, then let it out in a cry.

"Oh, I've frightened the little one. Here, Billy, would you come to me and let me comfort you? Come, let me hold you. It's been so long since I've held a baby." Mrs. Clelland took the baby from Stacy and held him to her silk-clad bosom.

Stacy worried that he would drool on the woman's elegant dress. "Here, you'll need this." She slipped a cloth diaper under Billy's chin on Mrs. Clelland's shoulder.

The conversation became general after that—a discussion of the weather and its effect on the farm. She discovered there was a farm manager who lived a quarter mile away and brought them fresh eggs and milk every morning.

"And we'll have lettuce from the garden with our dinner," Mrs. Clelland promised as if this were a rare treat.

Stacy ventured to ask about her duties while there.

"Mostly I need you to put number stickers on the rest of the items, then record the sales price beside the number on the master list," Mrs. Clelland explained.

Dinner was announced. Stacy retrieved Billy, who was trying to suck on Mrs. Clelland's pearl necklace.

"I took the liberty of having the bassinet brought down from the attic," her hostess explained while her husband tucked her into a wheelchair for the trip to the dining room.

"Did you now?" Gareth asked, grinning at his father.

"Yes, I did. Before I hurt my ankle. I'm not usually so helpless, you know." His mother waved him and his remarks aside and spoke to Stacy. "I thought I could help with Billy while you and Gareth finish the list of auction items."

"Of course." Stacy found the bassinet in the dining room, newly decked out in embroidered cotton frills, with a fitted sheet and blanket in blue with horses cavorting over them. "How lovely," she said softly, pleased at the thoughtfulness.

"I used it for both my children. It was so handy. See? It's on wheels so you can move it wherever you wish with no trouble. That's why the nursery is on the first level."

"How nice." That was all Stacy could think to say.

"Now about the auction," his mother continued when they were seated around an oval table of shining walnut. "You will be in charge. Gareth and the servants will do what you tell them."

Stacy darted a glance at her boss to see how he took this. A lazy smile appeared at the corners of his mouth. His voice, when he spoke, was vibrant with genuine amusement. "Mother thinks men were put on earth to do her bidding."

"Of course they were. Now, where was I?"

"Putting the sales price on the master list," Stacy reminded her. "Who takes the money?"

"Jacob or Maudie will do that. You'll collect and count it when the cash register gets full. You'll have mostly checks. Gareth will put everything in the safe for you."

"And what will Father be doing?" Gareth asked.

His mother gave him a lofty perusal. "Taking care of me. He'll push my wheelchair so I can mingle with our guests." She turned to Stacy. "There'll be a buffet at noon. The caterer will handle that. Check it once in a while to see that there's plenty." She paused and considered. "I think that's everything. If a question comes up, do whatever you think is best. I'm sure you won't have any problems."

Stacy wished she felt as confident. Mrs. Clelland seemed to think Stacy directed charity auctions as a matter of course in her spare time. She pointed out this was her first.

"I will be available to advise you," Mrs. Clelland stated.

While Mrs. Clelland beamed at her, Mr. Clelland gave her a sympathetic smile. She smiled back, instinctively liking the older man. He took his wife's bossiness with a becoming deference to her wishes, which in no way seemed to diminish him as a man. He shared his son's intelligence and dry wit, but without using them as barriers around his heart.

The evening passed pleasantly, but by ten Stacy was getting tired to the point of wanting to be alone. They had returned to the library after the meal. Maudie had taken Billy to the nursery and tucked him into bed at Mrs. Clelland's request. Stacy yearned to go check on him.

At a break in the conversation, Gareth spoke up, "I think Stacy needs to retire now, Mother. She's answered enough questions for one night. So have I."

"It's so delightful to have a baby in the house again," his mother told her warmly when she stood. "Tomorrow you must let me keep him. Would you mind?"

"Of course not."

"It was wonderful having our grandchildren here for Christmas. If Gareth would put his mind to it and do as well, his father and I would be so very happy."

Stacy couldn't suppress the flush that rose in her face at his mother's pointed look at her son. Gareth's soft laughter rang in her ears, mockingly amused.

He had warned her, but surely the woman wasn't really thinking of her as a mate for her son. Stacy sought his gaze, but he'd returned to looking out the window at the night sky.

She jumped into the conversation to break the escalating tension. "Christmas was made for children, wasn't it? I'm looking forward to Billy's first tree. If you will excuse me, I am rather tired."

She said good-night and started from the room. Gareth did the same and fell into step beside her. They walked down the broad oak-floored hall to the room adjoining the nursery.

"Don't let Mother run over you. Tell her to butt out when she oversteps your boundaries," he advised.

Stacy doubted Mrs. Clelland would listen to anything she said. The woman was a law unto herself, but very likable. "She's a lovely person. Bossy, yes, but kind, I think."

"Umm, yes. She likes people, but she tends to sweep them

into her projects, then it's like fighting a whirlpool to get out. Sometimes it can't be done. My sister moved out West and I moved to the city to get away."

Stacy felt her neck grow warm as he described her feelings concerning his parent.

He chuckled, catching her discomfort. He slipped a hand behind her neck and rubbed the tension away at the base of her skull. "Don't worry. I'll stay close in case you get sucked in over your head."

She smiled as if grateful and slipped inside her room. With the door closed between them, she wondered who was going to save her from *him*.

In the bedroom, she quickly slipped out of her clothes and into a thick cotton nightgown that buttoned down the front. She sat in the rocker and nursed her son, her mind on the man she'd left in the hall.

A thousand questions about him haunted her. If she ever got a moment alone with his mother, would she dare ask about his past, assuming his mother would tell her anything?

He was such an internal person, she doubted he'd ever told anyone if he'd been in love. But surely he had. That house in the woods cried out for a family. And she hadn't imagined the emptiness. Yes, she'd ask if the opportunity came up.

After feeding Billy, she changed his diaper and tucked him into the crib. He grabbed the blanket with one hand and stuck his thumb in his mouth. He offered her a sweet smile, then closed his eyes and went to sleep. She thought he was the most beautiful baby in the world.

Going into her room, she looked through a magazine and read an article on raising a generous child rather than a selfish one. Finally she went to bed. Just before she fell asleep, her mind went off on a tangent of its own.

Thoughts of how good life might be if she was married to Gareth danced through her brain. For a while she let the fantasy play itself out, but reality intruded before she got to the part where he was holding her and kissing her breathless.

Frowning at the wayward musing, she put it firmly out of her mind and drifted into sleep.

Saturday was an impossibly beautiful day. Stacy dressed in slacks and a pink blouse. Wearing comfortable sandals, she went to find her hostess. Maudie directed her to the patio on the shady side of the house.

Mrs. Clelland was in the wheelchair, her leg propped up to ease the discomfort of her injured ankle. "Ah, there you are. I trust you slept well?"

"Yes, thank you." Actually she'd been restless, waking several times during the night for no reason. Each time she'd been aware of dreams centered around Gareth disturbing her sleep.

"The men are playing tennis. They'll join us for breakfast when they're through."

Stacy had already noticed Gareth's tall, powerful form on the court. His father played opposite him. What the older man lacked in brute strength, he made up for in strategy, running his son from side to side, trying to force an error.

"They're both very good," Stacy commented, tearing her gaze from Gareth with an effort.

"Yes." Mrs. Clelland studied her while Stacy poured a glass of orange juice and a cup of coffee from a tray on a sideboard.

Stacy felt rather flushed and wondered if Gareth's mother

could see her reaction to the woman's handsome son. She took the glass and the cup to the table and sat opposite Mrs. Clelland.

"I think you would be good for my son."

Stacy wasn't sure she'd heard correctly. "I beg your pardon?"

"I've shocked you." Mrs. Clelland laughed merrily. "All mothers are matchmakers. Just wait until your little one grows up and starts noticing girls. You'll have definite opinions on the one he should choose."

Stacy tried to set the woman straight. "Gareth is my boss. There's certainly nothing…that is, we haven't…we don't…"

"Oh, I'm sure nothing has happened." Mrs. Clelland's tone was droll, her expression exasperated as she watched her son lob a tennis ball over his father's head. "Gareth is so circumspect, I sometimes wish he *would* do something illogical or illegal."

"He drove ten miles over the limit on the way down here," Stacy felt compelled to mention in his defense.

"Did he now?" Mrs. Clelland's eyes twinkled. "Would you pour me another cup of coffee?"

"Of course." Stacy refilled the cup, then returned to the table. The breeze lifted her hair away from her face, cooling the heat brought on by Mrs. Clelland's astute glance. It also carried the sounds of the men's conversation as they heckled each other or complimented a particularly good shot.

"It was three years ago last Christmas that Gareth's fiancée was killed," his mother said aloud as if musing on it to herself.

Stacy stared at her aghast.

"He was devastated. It was only a week before the wedding. They were expecting a child, a surprise because Ginny didn't think she could have children. Naturally, I was overjoyed. Neither of my children had married or given me grandchildren at the time."

"How did she die?"

"A car accident. The other driver had been drinking."

"How terrible." Stacy pressed a hand to her middle where pain lodged like a boulder ready to shatter.

That was the emptiness then—a fiancée, pregnant with their child. He'd never gotten over it. Her heart ached for him.

"Yes. Gareth retreated into himself. I was beginning to think no one could reach him. And then you came along." His mother smiled happily.

"Mrs. Clelland, I think you're seeing things that aren't there," she said as gently as she could.

"No. I saw the way he looked at you last night. He's aware of you as a woman."

"It's…you don't understand. He helped me when Billy was born. It made things seem different for a while, but not for long. It was a temporary madness."

"The first he's had since Ginny died."

"But he's dated other women. I've heard him on the phone with them."

"Dated, yes. He's a healthy male animal. With you, there's more. There's caring." She laughed softly. "I couldn't have planned anything better than your having the baby on his doorstep. It opened his eyes."

The conversation was getting out of hand. "Really," Stacy protested, "you're wrong…" Her voice trailed off. Gareth had told her he wanted her, and there had been those kisses….

"Marry my son," his mother admonished gently, watching the two men finish their game. "He needs you and your child. He needs to feel again, to trust life again. He needs to take a risk with his heart, but he's afraid."

Gareth afraid? Stacy didn't believe that.

Mrs. Clelland sighed. "You think I'm an interfering old witch. I probably am. But promise me you'll take anything he offers. My son is an honorable man. He'll take care of you. If you let him. I'm asking you to do so. His need is so great."

"I…I don't know what to say."

"Say yes." Mrs. Clelland gazed at her intently. "You're the one who can save him from the blackness that eats at him day after day. Make him laugh again, Stacy. Please."

"I…I'll try," Stacy heard herself promise. That wasn't much of a risk, to make him laugh. She hadn't agreed to seduce him or anything like that. She could imagine his anger if he'd overheard this strange conversation.

The moment might never have been. Mrs. Clelland was all charm and laughter when the men joined them at the table. It was so unreal, Stacy wasn't sure the conversation had taken place. Maybe it had been part of the fantasies her subconscious had been busily weaving around them for weeks now.

"How about a game before the slave driver puts us to work?" Gareth suggested after they ate.

"I'm too rusty. You would be bored."

"Do go," his mother encouraged. "Maudie will bring Billy out the minute he wakes up, so you mustn't worry about him."

That took care of her next line of argument. Feeling like a weed among the roses, Stacy changed to shorts and tennis shoes. She went to the tennis court and revived her college game.

"You're good," Gareth complimented when she placed a shot straight down the line, thus winning the point and the game.

Her gaze met his. For a minute, she was filled with pride because she could at least keep up with him. "You're going easy on me."

"A little," he admitted.

He won, but not by a terribly wide margin. Walking to the house, she realized she felt alive in every cell. When she peeked at him, he was watching her, a sexy, mysterious expression in the depths of his eyes. She looked away, flustered by the male interest.

"Were you always shy?" he asked. "Or is it just with me?"

"With you."

Maudie appeared with Billy. Stacy rushed to her son, glad for the distraction while she got her feet firmly on the ground once more. The conversation with his mother had sent her mind in directions it shouldn't go. When he looked at her as if she were beautiful, her imagination winged off on its own.

"Stay here," Mrs. Clelland invited when Stacy would have gone to her room. "Nursing is natural and done in the best circles today. Could I burp him for you?"

"You may as well give in," Gareth told her, "or else she'll hound you to death."

"Well, if you don't…if you think it's all right…"

He nodded. The two men spared her blushes by turning away from the table and talking about the corn crop in the field. She listened to their conversation while her son ate hungrily. She remembered her dad and grandfather talking about crops and ranch details in the same fashion.

A farm was a good place to grow up. Gareth had been happy here, she decided. He'd had a horse and lots of friends. His parents were somewhat eccentric, but they loved him.

He had loved a woman once, and she'd died.

Stacy observed his profile while he talked to his father. She recalled the bleakness in his eyes when his guard was down. Life was bleak when grief was your only companion. She knew. She'd lived through it.

It was foolish to think she could ever open that dark, empty place inside him and fill it with light. She wanted to, but only he could unlock the door and let another in.

However, she'd promised she would try to make him laugh. Perhaps that was the key. Lowering her gaze, she watched her son with grave tenderness. There were more ways than one to skin a cat, her grandfather used to say. Maybe there was more than one way into a stubborn man's heart.

Chapter Seven

Stacy began to understand the extent of Mrs. Clelland's maneuvering when it took her, Gareth, Jacob and the son of the
farm manager all of three hours to finish the master list and
tagging of the auction items. His mother could have directed
the entire operation from her wheelchair.

By midafternoon, the task was done.

Stacy stood in the middle of the carriage house. Like the
main house, it had been restored to pristine condition.

The scent of wax and lemon oil permeated the air. Every
piece of furniture had been shined to a high gloss. She'd had
Gareth and the men arrange the donated items like rooms in
a home. Smaller items were displayed on tables and dresser
tops as part of the domestic scene.

Outside, a buffet would be set up in a tent by the catering

company first thing in the morning. Tables and chairs would go under the maple trees. Champagne, fruit punch, coffee and tea along with various snacks would be served all day.

"That's it," Gareth declared.

His grin was one of satisfaction. He looked incredibly handsome in a pair of cutoffs, tennis shoes and a blue cotton work shirt he hadn't bothered to button.

Sweat gleamed on his chest. A couple of drops glistened from the thick swirls of dark curly hair. The waistband of his shorts was damp with it.

She longed to run her hands over him, to taste the salty flavor of his skin, to kiss the grin from his face. She thought of a quiet corner in a barn loft, hidden by the bales of hay usually stored there.

"We'll ask your mother what she thinks," she said.

"She'll love it," he predicted.

She did. "Yes, this is perfect, Stacy. Perfect. You did a wonderful job." Mrs. Clelland beamed all around at her workers and thanked each one warmly. After Jacob and the young farmer left, she turned to Stacy and Gareth. "It's time for our guests to arrive. You'll want to shower and change."

"Uh, guests?" Stacy questioned on the way up the flagstone path to the house. She glanced at her beige slacks and pink blouse. Definitely grungy.

"A few in for dinner, a few for cocktails. Six couples will be spending the night." Mrs. Clelland waved her hand airily as if it were nothing to have twelve people overnight. For her, it apparently wasn't.

Stacy pressed a hand to her stomach. "I can eat in my room," she ventured. "Or the kitchen."

"Nonsense. I'll need you to help with the hostess duties. I can't get around very well, you know."

Gareth gave a snort of laughter. His eyes met Stacy's as he held the door open while his father pushed the wheelchair.

"Mother is about as helpless as a boa constrictor," he muttered for her ears only after the older couple was inside. "You've probably noticed."

Stacy tried to hold in a smile, but it was impossible with his eyes gazing into hers in silent laughter.

"Ah, yes, I see you have," he continued as if complimenting her on being astute.

She fled into the house before she laughed aloud. "I'll go change now. What time are we supposed to...uh..." She couldn't think of a polite word.

"Report in?" Gareth finished for her.

His mother checked the time. "It's almost three. Let's have drinks on the patio at five and watch the sunset before we have dinner. By the way, we'll dress tonight, but tomorrow will be casual." She beamed a smile at Stacy.

Stacy felt her heart sink. How formal did they dress for dinner? She smiled uneasily and headed for her room. She'd hardly gotten inside before there was a knock on the door. She opened it, expecting to find Maudie.

It was Gareth.

He came in and closed the door.

"Yes?" Impatience coated the word. She wanted to check on her son. Maudie had brought him to her for his afternoon feeding. Now he should be asleep.

"Go check on him," he said, reading her mind.

She hurried to the nursery and opened the door. Billy was

asleep in the crib, a brown-and-white teddy bear, obviously new, tucked in with him.

Maudie was in a chair, reading a magazine. She looked up. "Hello. He was an angel, slept all afternoon," she assured Stacy, hopping up. "I'll go to the kitchen and help with dinner, if you don't need me anymore?"

"No, that's fine. Thank you, Maudie."

The woman smiled and left. Stacy peered over the railing at her son. He looked very contented. As usual, her heart melted.

"He's a fine boy," Gareth said quietly, coming to stand beside her. It was the first remark he'd made about the baby.

"Thank you," she whispered, her heart full. She turned her head and looked at him.

He motioned her from the nursery and followed when she left, closing the door silently behind them. They stood in the middle of her room, each watching the other. He took the two steps needed to bring them within an inch of touching.

He waited, his eyes on hers.

Unable to resist, she laid her hand on his chest, then raked her fingers through the matted curls. His skin was sweat-slicked and smooth under her caress. She detected the hardness of bone and muscle in his large frame. She sensed his strength.

He took her left hand and laid it beside the right one. To her surprise, he closed his eyes while she hesitantly explored his torso. She licked her lips, then bent her head forward until she could touch him with her tongue.

His breath caught, then released, but other than that, he didn't move. She moved her lips over him while her hands gripped his waist above the cutoffs. Finding his nipple, she tasted it with her tongue, then nibbled at it. It beaded into a tiny ball.

A tremor ran over his skin like a sudden chill, causing a similar one to run over her.

She lifted her head and stared into his eyes.

They were dark, the pupils wide in the dim room, burning with needs he didn't, or couldn't, hide.

"Gareth?"

"Yes," he said. "To whatever you're asking."

He enclosed her in his arms, bending his more massive body over hers, fitting them together carefully, as if their lives depended on an exact blending of curve and angle.

"Put your legs around me."

She did. An electric shock ran through her at the intimate contact. She felt him through the cutoffs, hard and rigid and ready for her.

He moved two steps back and settled in a chair, her legs to either side of his. He rubbed her back, soothing and exciting her at the same time. His gaze never wavered from hers.

"You need to rest."

"No, I'm fine." She spoke quickly, breathlessly.

A hint of a smile touched the corners of his mouth. "I never thought I'd feel this way again. It's been murder all afternoon, watching you, listening to your voice...."

Currents raced up her back as his voice trailed off. He slipped his hands around her and cupped her breasts.

"Does this hurt?" he asked, kneading her gently.

"No. It... I like it."

"So do I." He hesitated. "May I taste?"

Her breasts swelled against her bra. "Yes."

He opened the pink blouse and pulled the material from the slacks. He studied the maternity bra, then opened the nursing placket. "Beautiful," he said in a deeper, softer tone.

A drop of pale liquid formed at the tip. He caught it on his finger and brought it to his mouth. Then he dipped his head and rubbed the hard tip with his tongue.

Sensation pelted down her chest, into her abdomen and lodged in a secret, welcoming place inside her. She held the back of his head with one hand and rubbed his shoulder with the other.

"I didn't come here for this," he muttered, drawing back and looking at his handiwork. "Do you have anything formal to wear tonight?" He palmed her breast and caressed it tenderly.

"I brought a crushed velvet skirt," she managed to whisper. "And a lace vest."

"Good. I want to taste you some more." He waited for her nod before opening the other side and laving her breast with his tongue. She arched her back instinctively.

His hands cupped her hips and guided her forward. Through the layers of material, she was aware of his desire as much as her own. She moved against him, eliciting a groan or a growl from him. She wasn't sure which. She wondered if they were going to make love.

Gareth is an honorable man.

His mother's words echoed through her skull. An honorable man. If he made love to her, would he feel compelled to marry her? What of her own honor? Would she want to force him into marriage against his will?

She knew the answer to that.

But for this moment, she could pretend. He'd go no further than she indicated she wanted to go. Somehow she knew he would know where that boundary was.

Cupping his head in her hands, tenderness warring with fierce desire, she urged his mouth to hers.

The kiss shattered her world into a kaleidoscope of

whirling rainbows. They fought a lover's duel, the battleground roaming from her mouth to his and back again.

He caressed her a thousand different ways, with a thousand different nuances of pressure, on her back, her shoulders, her breasts. She did the same.

When she pushed his shirt off his shoulders, he helped her, letting it fall to the floor. Then they were wrapped in each other, flesh to flesh, hands moving, exploring, restlessly seeking the other.

It was the most wonderful experience of her life. His hands cupped her bottom. He pressed her hard against him with a sudden, desperate motion. "Don't move," he whispered hoarsely, burying his face in her neck.

She sat utterly still, except for her hands in his hair. She stroked through the damp, silky strands as if to soothe him.

When he at last raised his head, it was to gaze into her eyes for a long time. She returned the look as steadily as she could. He brushed the wisps of hair off her forehead with hands that weren't quite steady.

"Sorry," he said in an odd tone.

"That's okay."

His smile mocked himself. "No, it isn't." He grimaced as if irritated with the uncontrollable passion. "Worse than a teenager. Thinking with my body instead of my brain."

"So was I," she admitted. The intimacy of their position was somewhat awkward. She tried subtly to disengage her body from his.

He slipped his hands to her waist and held her. "I think we need to talk." His glance went to his watch. "But there isn't time, not with a houseful of people due any minute. I came to tell you not to worry about clothes. My parents' friends will be in anything from jeans to vintage clothing to formals."

"Thank you for telling me. I wasn't sure…"

It struck her as an odd conversation to be having with her still sitting astride his lap, her breasts against his chest, her arms around his shoulders, his big, warm hands moving over her.

He must have had the same thought. "This is insane," he murmured, then he kissed her again, a soft, sweet kiss that made no demands on her.

For another minute, they indulged the embrace, then with a sigh on her part, they parted. He let her slide off him, then stood with one fluid motion. He crooked a finger and lifted her chin until he could see into her eyes.

"That was the most exciting experience I've had in years. Next time, I'll make sure it's the same for you."

She forced herself to hold his gaze. "I'll hold you to that." She tried to look sophisticated and cool about it.

His eyes darkened. For a minute, she thought he would carry her to bed and keep his promise right then. But he heaved a deep breath, grabbed his shirt and, after one last caress, left her.

She sank into the chair, unable to stand on her own for a few minutes. Doubts rushed over her. Did he love her? Or were his kisses the impulse of the moment?

Hearing a clock strike the hour, she realized time was running out. She went to shower and get ready for the evening.

"Stacy, how lovely you look," Mrs. Clelland complimented her when she arrived on the patio a few minutes after five. "Good, you brought the baby. Is he awake?"

"Yes." Stacy wheeled the bassinet to her hostess.

Gareth sat on the low brick wall surrounding the patio, a

brandy snifter in his hand. He gave her a solemn perusal as if to see if she were all right after their tempestuous embrace. Mr. Clelland brought her a glass of fruit punch.

"Thank you."

"Isn't he precious?" Mrs. Clelland crooned. She looked from Stacy to her son, her eyes full of mischief. "You two would have lovely children."

Stacy nearly choked on the punch.

"Mother, you're embarrassing our guest," Gareth chided lightly. He turned to her. "You look lovely, by the way."

She glanced down at her skirt. The crushed velvet was deep amethyst. With it she wore a cream satin top with a lacy vest of the same color that reached almost to her knees. The vest was embroidered with jewel-toned flowers. She murmured her thanks and selected a chair close to the baby.

Something was wrong. She didn't know what it was, but she could feel it. Gareth had withdrawn into his office persona—polite but remote. The bleakness had returned to his eyes.

She wanted to protest, but what could she say? Don't remember the woman you loved? Don't remember she carried your child? It was impossible to say anything. He'd retreated to a place she couldn't reach.

"Our guests have started to arrive," Mrs. Clelland said. "They'll join us in a few minutes. I thought it would be nice to have some private time just for family."

Stacy glanced at Gareth to see how he took this blatant prod from his mother, but he was watching the clouds backlit by the sunset on the far horizon. Arriving at a decision, she rose and went to him.

He didn't look at her when she stopped beside him. She felt the barriers surrounding him like a barbed wire fence around a prison. She and the baby had brought his emotions to the surface. He was trying to force them into the void again. That wasn't the way to deal with the past.

She leaned against his shoulder, moving into his space and forcing him to acknowledge her.

When he looked up, she smiled at him. Although he returned it, sadness lay deep in his eyes along with other emotions too deep to read. Guilt, he'd told her when they'd listened to the music at her apartment. Guilt and regret and sadness.

A tough load to carry alone.

It was all a part of grief, and grief needed to be shared. She'd had him and Shirl when she'd needed help. Later the thought of the baby had brought her comfort. Gareth hadn't let himself need anyone.

The sound of other voices broke into her introspection. Two couples came in and were introduced. The other four arrived fast on their heels. Jacob lit the patio braziers when the air turned cool. Maudie served hot hors d'oeuvres while Mr. Clelland poured drinks for everyone.

Three of the couples were older friends of Gareth's parents. The other three were closer to Gareth's age, invited with him in mind. Stacy was acutely aware of the speculation in every pair of eyes as she was introduced.

"Stacy is helping me with the hostess duties," Mrs. Clelland explained in her breezy fashion. "She's been a life-saver, taking over the auction for me on short notice. This is her son, Billy. He's a darling baby, isn't he?"

Eyes darted from the child to her, then to her left hand. She no longer wore a wedding ring.

"I'm the executive assistant from Gareth's office," she quickly explained before anyone got the wrong idea.

"Stacy keeps things humming on an even keel," Gareth put in. He laid a hand on her shoulder. "Even me."

There was general laughter from the group. Mrs. Clelland beamed in open pleasure. The other couples seemed to take it as a given that she and Gareth were a couple, too.

When Stacy turned a questioning gaze on him, he returned it with a steady look that spoke volumes…if she could only read his cryptic thoughts. He pressed her shoulder, then let go.

The talk became general after that. They went into dinner at last. She didn't know if it was because of nursing the baby, but she was hungry more often of late. Later they returned to the library for coffee.

The baby woke with a whimper.

Stacy went to the bassinet and lifted him. "I think I should take Billy to his room now. It's getting cool out here."

"I'll help," Gareth offered. He held the door open and pulled the bassinet inside after them.

He led the way to the nursery at the back of the house. They were silent on the trip down the long hallway. She tried to thank him at her door, but he entered with her.

The nursery quarters were lit only by a night-light. The atmosphere shimmered with dark intimacy. Gareth pushed the bassinet into the baby's room and left it by the wall where it would be out of the way.

"They think we're a couple," he said while she changed Billy's diaper. "Do you mind?"

She hesitated, then shrugged. "I'm not responsible for what they think."

His wry laughter, quickly gone, surprised her. "Mother is. She's forcing us together. I'm sure she thinks she's helping some great cosmic plan." Now it was he who hesitated. "It would be easier to play along, if you think you can take it."

"Play along?" She looked up, then went back to putting Billy in his pajamas.

"Yes. For us to be seen together will please her. It'll also keep the other women off my back."

She couldn't help but smile.

He grinned, too. "That sounded incredibly egotistical, but it's a fact. Women...come on to me."

Stacy laid the baby in the crib. "It's a thing to be expected if you're handsome, wealthy and intelligent."

In the silence that followed, she glanced around. Gareth wore an odd expression, almost as if he were stunned.

"Surely that doesn't surprise you," she said. She removed her lace vest and laid it over the end of the crib.

"Is that the way you see me?" His voice had a rich, quiet timbre that soaked right down to her toes.

"Yes." She paused with her hands at her blouse. "I've got to feed the baby. I'll have to take my blouse off to keep from wrinkling it."

"Do you want me to leave?"

She didn't know quite what to say. To be embarrassed after he'd touched her so intimately that afternoon seemed foolish. "I don't want you to think I'm coming on to you." She gave him a bold glance, then spoiled it by laughing at his chagrin.

"I won't think that. We need to talk anyway."

She laid her blouse aside, then lifted the baby and sat in the rocking chair. Billy suckled hungrily, his tiny hand holding her finger where she pressed her breast away from his nose.

"About this afternoon?" she asked. Oddly, she found she

wasn't embarrassed by the passion they had shared. For those few moments, the bleakness had disappeared from his eyes.

"Yes."

Instead of talking, he turned the straight-backed chair they had sat in earlier and straddled it, his arms crossed over the back, and studied her while she fed her son.

"Your mother told me of your fiancée," she said at last. "Is that why seeing me with Billy makes you sad?"

"It makes me remember," was all he would admit.

"What was she like?"

His fists knotted and turned white at the knuckles. "Why do you want to know?"

"Grief is something that should be spent. If you store it inside like miser's gold, it will turn on you, becoming bitter and rancid. Talking about the good times can help. What did you and she like to do together?"

"Besides make love?" he asked harshly, his expression closed and angry.

She gazed at him steadily. He was hurting, and he wanted to hurt back. "All couples like to make love. What did you do afterward? What was her favorite date?"

He dropped his head and rested his chin on his hands. Ever so slowly his grip relaxed. He took a deep breath and started. "She liked music. I took her to concerts. After-ward…it was the best…"

"Yes, I know what you mean. Bill and I liked long drives and picnics in the country. Making love after a Sunday drive was the sweetest time of all. Once he got stung when we sat in a field of clover." She laughed softly at the memory.

"That must have put a crimp in his style." His laughter joined hers.

"Well, one does have to improvise at times." She put the sleepy baby on her shoulder and closed her bra. She patted his back until he burped, then turned him to the other side.

"That's incredibly beautiful," Gareth murmured. His eyes darkened to a moody intensity.

"Nursing the baby?"

"Yes. It's sexy, but something more…something tender and endearing…I can't describe it."

"I think I know what you mean. Nursing is connected to life and being human and caring about someone else."

He frowned. "It can hurt…this caring. Or cause others to get hurt."

"Sometimes it can happen that way." She gave him a sympathetic glance. His face had closed, his expression turning inward. The anger had returned.

He stood and pushed the chair aside, then paced the room. "Save your pity. I don't want it. My life is fine the way it is. If you'll carry out our little pretense until this weekend is over, that will keep my mother off our backs."

"All right." She kept the disappointment out of her voice. For a minute, she'd thought they might break through the anger. Gareth had to get past that and accept what had happened before he could come to terms with it. "Why do you blame yourself for your fiancée's death?"

He stopped dead still. "It was my fault," he said without looking at her. "I called and asked her to pick me up at the airport. Because of me, she died."

"Because of a drunk driver," she corrected. "You weren't responsible for him."

"But I was for her. If I hadn't called, if I hadn't been so impatient, she wouldn't have been on the road at nearly midnight on Christmas Eve. I was selfish, thinking of *my* needs, *my* wants, not her safety."

"No one can control events—"

"You don't know. You don't know anything about it." He strode across the carpet. The door closed with a soft click behind him.

She thought of the steps of grief the counselor had told her about. First, disbelief, then resentment, guilt, anger and last of all, acceptance. Gareth was still locked in guilt and anger. Until he let those go, there was no room in his heart for another.

The nightmares were back.

Gareth watched the activities around him as if he were a being from another planet, invisible to the Earth creatures. He felt curiously cut off from them, untouched by their humanness.

Except for one person.

Hearing Stacy's laughter, he searched the crowd until he found her. She was talking to one of the men his mother had invited to the cocktail party last night. A TV producer of nature documentaries. Stacy found that fascinating.

Yeah, she liked handsome, wealthy, intelligent men. The producer scored high on all three.

He turned away, his mood as black as the night he'd shared with the crickets and owls. Unable to sleep, he'd walked for hours, until fatigue had forced him to bed.

Then the tangled, twisted dreams born of desperation and guilt had taken over.

They'd been all mixed up, one minute featuring Ginny, the next Stacy. And the baby. In slow motion, the cars had collided in his dreams all night. Like a photograph, the scene had become imprinted in his mind—one of wrecked metal and torn bodies, of blood and death and horror. Stacy and the baby had died…

The need to see the child forced him outside. Walking past the guests who milled in and out of the carriage house, he stopped on the lawn and shaded his eyes with his hand. Stacy had been nervous about leaving the child with a stranger until he'd suggested Kim bring Billy outside.

There, in the shade of an old maple tree, Jacob's niece read a book, the bassinet with the baby within arm's length. Nearby, the caterers were laying out the buffet in the huge white tent. Pennants flew from the corners and center post.

The tent reminded him of a picture he'd seen in a book about King Arthur and his knights. The scene struck him as unreal, with nothing in common with the world as he knew it.

A world of law and logic, that's where he was most at home, not the one of rioting emotions and tantalizing passions.

"Gareth, hello. Did you see what that snuff box went for? I was amazed." Stacy lowered her voice. "Your mother's friends must have tons of money."

She laughed, and his heart went into a spasm. He frowned, not liking the feeling.

"Well," she said, her smile fading. "I have to feed Billy now. Kim said he'd been an angel all morning. I want her to keep a good opinion of him."

She walked away. Everything in him wanted to call her back, to say something to make her laugh again. He clenched his fists. He didn't need this. He didn't want to feel anything for anyone.

A flood of memories washed over him. Recent memories. Yesterday, holding Stacy, touching her, tasting the sweetness of her breasts, those moments hounded him. They, too, had been mixed up in his dreams.

There was one confession he hadn't made when she'd insisted upon talking about the past. For three years he hadn't been able to make love to another woman. Not once. His body simply hadn't responded to another female. Yet with Stacy, he'd responded fully, like an adolescent in the first throes of unbridled lust.

When Stacy spoke to Kim, then took the baby and headed for the house, he followed at a safe distance. In the privacy of the back patio, she settled in a chair and took the child to her.

Unable to look away, he watched, like some perverted Peeping Tom, while she nourished her son. Strange sensations raced along his nerves, making every muscle ache with tension.

He wanted...he wanted...he didn't know what. Something more than the life he had now, something more than he deserved. He closed his eyes, but the image of Stacy and little Billy stayed as if burned into his eyelids. Beyond that was the image of fire and wreckage...of death.

The anger rose in him. Useless, stupid anger. Anger hadn't been able to put Ginny back together and make her whole and well. He'd wanted to kill the driver who'd run over her, but that wouldn't have brought her back, either.

He opened his eyes, forcing himself to face the harsh light of day as he had three years ago. It had been his call that had brought her out on the road that night. It had been his selfish need to see her that had killed her. That was the truth he had to live with night after night. That was what haunted his dreams and turned them into nightmares.

There was no use in thinking about it. He forced the memories into the void where nothing touched him. Glancing at the patio, he saw Stacy watching him with a troubled expression. He walked forward and sat on the wall near her.

"Things seem to be going well," she said with a tentative smile. "Your mother was pleased with the number of people who showed up for the auction."

"She's always pleased when there's a crowd."

The smile fled at his harsh tone.

"I'm sorry. I didn't mean to sound cynical. Actually, I like people, too—the more, the merrier."

"Because you don't have to confront yourself when you're in a crowd?" she asked, giving him an assessing once-over, her gaze as cool as a breeze off a glacier.

He felt her words like a blow. "Who appointed you my counselor?" he demanded, dredging up the anger, letting it take over before he confessed his soul to her and crawled into her arms like a child needing comfort.

"Do you need one?"

Too restless to sit, he paced the patio. "No." He met her gaze and turned away, unable to face the sadness and pity in those warm, velvety depths.

"Then you'll have to work through this on your own," she advised. "You'll have to forgive yourself and realize that you have very little influence over other people's actions—"

He whirled on her. "Dammit—"

The baby let out a wail, cutting off the angry words that gathered like a knot in his chest.

Stacy held Billy to her shoulder and patted his back. "There, now, there, darling. It's all right," she soothed him.

The need to lash out increased. Gareth sucked in the balmy April air and held it along with the angry words. He wanted to tell her she didn't know anything about how he felt or what he was thinking. She could take her two-bit psychobabble advice and stick it—

With an enraged shake of his head, he stemmed the hot tide that trembled on his tongue. Anger was no good, he reminded himself. He'd learned that three years ago. The emptiness was better. No need to feel or react to anything. No emotions, no mind-blowing passion. Yes, go for the black void.

He tried a smile. It was probably more of a grimace, but he managed it. His effort wasn't noticed. Stacy was busy with her son, laying him across her arm while she brought him to her left breast to nurse.

Gareth couldn't tear his gaze from the very feminine sight or the tenderness on her face that went with nurturing her child. It tore into him, opening the chasm, ripping at its edges until the pain became too much.

With a curse, he headed for the auction and the safety of the crowd. Funny, he'd never before thought of himself as a coward, but here he was, running from a woman and a child again.

Chapter Eight

"The servants are off today. We'll do our own breakfast," Mrs. Clelland explained to Stacy. "How did the little one sleep last night? Did you get enough rest?" She poured batter into a waffle iron and closed the lid, then checked the bacon and sausage browning in the oven, limping a bit as she moved about.

"Billy and I slept fine," Stacy said. Hers had been the sleep of exhaustion. Running the auction and seeing to the buffet had taken a lot of energy.

After she'd retired to her room, she'd sat by the window for a time, her emotions churning with needs she'd given up on fulfilling years ago. While sitting in the dark, she'd spotted Gareth outside on the broad sweep of driveway.

The loneliness of his solitary figure, out walking in the night, still haunted her. She wondered if she and the baby were part of his troubled thoughts as he roamed the darkness in search of peace. She thought they were.

They had breached a gap in him that he didn't want breached. Their presence opened an old wound that had never healed. Before helping her with the delivery, he'd lived in a world devoid of emotion. He wanted to hang on to that void.

He was strong-willed enough to do it.

While no one could go back to yesterday, a person could remain stuck in the past, guilt forever eating at the soul and destroying the possibility of another love.

That would be a shame. Gareth was that rare man with the depth and steadfastness a marriage needed, who was also able to inspire the lusty flame of passion and romance every woman dreamed of finding.

She settled in a comfortable chair and pulled the bassinet close. "Have your other guests left?"

"All but one couple. They're at the tennis courts playing doubles with our men."

Gareth's mother's reference was so casual, Stacy almost missed the impact of it. When she realized what Mrs. Clelland had said, she protested. "Gareth isn't mine."

"He is if you want him." Mrs. Clelland whirred frozen orange juice and water in a blender. She brought a glass to Stacy. "Coffee?" She was walking on her injured ankle.

"Yes, please."

"You do want him, don't you?" Mrs. Clelland paused and shot her a piercing glance before going on with the meal.

With anyone else, Stacy would have found the conversation intrusive, but she knew Mrs. Clelland spoke from love of her son. "Yes, I want him," she admitted.

"Good. Be sure and tell him. Men are much more dense in affairs of the heart. Ah, here they are now." She beamed smiles on the noisy foursome who came into the kitchen, tennis rackets still in hand. "Who won?"

"Gareth and I beat the socks off them," the other woman said. She held up her racket in a victory sign, then set it in the corner and helped herself to a glass of orange juice.

The others did likewise, moving around the large kitchen perfectly at ease. Stacy subdued an unexpected burst of jealousy for the other woman, who was about Gareth's age and who didn't wear a ring or have the same last name as the man she was with.

The tennis players discussed the game with lots of laughter and teasing about each other's skill. The noise level in the kitchen went up several decibels, waking Billy. They stopped talking at his first wail of alarm.

"I'll take him to the nursery," Stacy said, wishing she'd been wise enough to leave him there in the first place.

She quickly wheeled the bassinet into the hall and down to the nursery. She placed the baby in the crib and tucked him in. When she sang a lullaby, he drifted into sleep once more.

Lingering beside the sleeping child, she decided she would call the child-care center the next day and arrange his keep. To leave him there each morning would tear her heart out…the way it would when she left Gareth and the law firm.

She didn't know where the thought came from, but once it settled into her mind, she knew that was what she would do. The passion between them was too strong to be denied if they stayed near each other. She wouldn't accept him on those terms. Her love was worth more than that.

With a troubled sigh, she left the quiet room and returned

to the kitchen. The table was set and part of the group had taken their seats. She resumed her former place.

Gareth brought a Mexican platter of bacon and sausage links and placed it in the center of the table. His father brought the first round of waffles while Mrs. Clelland started a new batch.

The scene exuded an innocent charm similar to a Norman Rockwell painting. *Breakfast in the Country,* it could be titled. Tears filmed her eyes. She blinked them away.

The chair beside her moved, then Gareth sat down and pulled closer to the table. His arm brushed hers, the sun-bleached hairs tickling her skin. She laid her arm in her lap.

"Bacon or sausage?" he asked and held the platter for her.

She took two pieces of bacon. He helped himself and passed the food to his right.

His body radiated a steady warmth. She leaned toward him, wanting to absorb as much as possible. Her heartbeat quickened, sending the thin, hot blood pounding through her.

Gareth forked a waffle on her plate, then his. "One enough?" he asked.

His voice flowed over her, warm and deep, as smooth as melted butter. She nodded and reached for the juice, needing something to cool her off. Her eyes met those of the woman who sat opposite her. Ruthie, Stacy recalled the name.

Ruthie looked from her to Gareth and back. In an instant, Stacy knew the other woman had wanted him, but had given it up as hopeless long ago. Now she was wondering what he saw in Stacy.

Stacy wondered, too, when she risked a glance in his direction. He was watching her with the same stark intensity she had noticed before. It made her tremble. Again he didn't appear to be aware of the flames that glowed in his eyes,

making her ache with longing for the promises contained in
those depths.

"You slept late," he said in a low tone while his mother
discussed the success of the auction with the others. "I
missed our game."

"You had plenty of competition and an able partner."

He glanced at the other female guest, then back to her. "But
she wasn't as much fun to watch."

Stacy's breath jumbled into a knot.

"And I shouldn't be saying this," he concluded, a brief
frown appearing on his face, his laughter mocking his own
actions. He shook his head as if disgusted with his lack of
control. "You need milk," he announced. He rose and proceeded to pour her a glass and bring it to her.

There was a lull in the general conversation. Four pairs of
eyes noted the thoughtful gesture with varying expressions reflected in them. His parents beamed approval, his mother
joyful, his father thoughtful. Ruthie's eyes gleamed with
dislike. The male guest eyed her in an interested fashion. The
attention made Stacy nervous.

She mumbled a thank-you and kept her eyes on her plate.
When the meal was over, she jumped to her feet and cleared
the table. Gareth rinsed and stored the dishes in the dishwasher.

Mrs. Clelland played the invalid to perfection. She had her
husband bring a pillow and prop her bound ankle on a chair.
"We have time for a lecture at the museum," she said. "Do you
want to attend with us, or do you have to rush off?" she asked
the visiting couple.

Gareth's mouth turned up ever so little at the corners. He
wanted them gone. Stacy kept a carefully straight face even
as she fervently hoped they'd leave.

"We have to be going," Ruthie answered without waiting for her escort's reply.

"Yes," the man echoed.

Stacy realized she hadn't caught his name. Not that it mattered. She wasn't going to be part of their circle of friends anyway. She didn't want to be.

By the time she and Gareth had the kitchen finished, his parents had retired to their room to dress. The other two had packed and said their farewells in a surprisingly short time.

Gareth poured fresh coffee into their cups and took his place at the table. He picked up a section of the paper and began reading. She did the same.

After his parents left, he laid the paper aside and studied her. His perusal made her nervous. She finally gave up on trying to concentrate and, holding her cup in front of her like a shield, returned his look.

"What is it?" she asked.

"Are you as glad to be alone as I am?"

"Yes."

His eyes roamed over her face, stopping at her eyes, the curly wisps of hair at her temples that had escaped the combs, then landing on her lips. "What bothered you about them?"

Startled, she jerked the cup, sloshing the coffee over the rim. She mopped up the splatter with a napkin. "I don't know what you mean."

"I think you do," he countered softly.

She stared into the steam rising off the surface before facing him again. "I wouldn't like to be part of a couple like them. They…there was no commitment between them. The weekend was a casual thing of no consequence."

"Adults today don't need a lot of false promises to be able to enjoy themselves and each other."

"I wouldn't want false promises, either, but I would expect to love the man I slept with."

"Would you expect the same from him?" The sardonic twist in the question conveyed his thoughts loud and clear.

She answered truthfully. "Yes."

His dark eyebrows drew toward each other until a nick appeared over the bridge of his nose while he considered the situation. He rubbed a finger around the rim of his cup.

She loved his hands—broad, long-fingered hands. Big hands. Steady hands. The hands of a good man.

Turning her head, she watched the morning sun sparkle off the grassy sweep of lawn until she could trust herself not to leap into his arms and demand he love her.

Gareth knew the moment Stacy turned her attention from him. He fought an impulse to reach over and tilt her head back in his direction. More than anything, he wanted to punish her mouth with his, to chastise her for making him want her with every fiber of his being. Yeah, some punishment.

He didn't want to want a woman. Like a limb that's been asleep, his heart throbbed painfully whenever he thought of Stacy. He didn't like yearning for her, listening for her voice and her laughter to the exclusion of all others. Most of all, he didn't like the fact that he felt alive only when she was near. He'd been through that turmoil, the death that wasn't death although he'd wished it had been....

He didn't want to think about it.

A smooth hand slid over his, rubbing until he relaxed his grip on the cup. He watched as she moved her hand along his arm until she arrived at his shoulder. Standing, she stepped behind him and massaged the muscles of his neck and shoulders.

Don't touch me, he wanted to say. "Don't stop," he said.

"Your muscles are so tight." She bent forward as she murmured to him, her voice as caressing as her hands.

Ah, God, it was pain. It was torment. It was wonderful.

"Why?" he groaned even as he melted under her care.

"Why what?" she asked, almost on a whisper.

He grappled with his control, but the words came out anyway. "Why did you let me hold you and kiss you?"

She was silent so long, he'd decided she wasn't going to answer the stupid question. "I think you know," she finally said, so low he had to strain to hear.

He turned and pulled her across his lap, his arms locking around her of their own volition. He was past thinking, past caring about pain or memories or nightmares. He had to touch her. It was as necessary as air.

Stacy was stunned at the impact of his kiss. His mouth closed on hers as if punishing her for the desire that bloomed like a sturdy weed between them no matter how hard either of them tried to keep it from sprouting.

Thoughts fled as the kiss became deeper, more demanding. His hand in her hair, the arm around her shoulders, locked her against him until there was no space left to think. There was only this terrible need that burned in her, hot and desperate.

The tears seeped out from under her closed eyelids. They ran down her cheeks into the corners of her mouth. She knew the exact moment he felt them.

He eased the pressure of his mouth, then kissed his way to the corner of her mouth. There, he sipped the salty tears from her lips, then licked them from her cheeks, first one side, then the other. He was so exquisitely gentle.

She fought the turbulent emotions until her control was once more assured. The tears stopped.

He licked her lashes clear of the last drops, then raised his head and studied her. "Why are you crying?"

"I don't know."

The silence stretched between them. She laid her head on his shoulder and remembered another time when she'd done the same. When she'd arrived at his cabin, his eyes hadn't been welcoming. They weren't now.

His hands were gentle, but his soul wasn't. He hated it that he wanted her. He hated the passion between them. Did it follow that someday he would grow to hate her?

He sighed and stood, making sure she was steady on her feet before releasing her.

"I'd like to go home," she requested. Weariness folded around her like a mist.

"Emotion is exhausting, isn't it?"

She started at his insight. "Very."

"My mother will have lunch and the afternoon planned. Can you make it until this evening?"

She summoned the last of her reserves. "Of course."

"Of course," he repeated. He touched her cheek, then dropped his hand to his side. "You would inspire a saint."

"Hardly. My response to you—" She stopped, realizing what she was about to say.

"Isn't saintly?" he suggested.

She met his eyes. "No."

"Neither is mine to you." He thrust his hands into the

pockets of his tennis shorts and strode to the door. He went outside, his stride long as he walked away.

Her eyes were drawn to the solid length of his legs. She'd felt those rock hard muscles against her thighs. She knew the strength in his arms. She loved the warmth of his body. He was an ideal man, capable of great kindness as well as great passion, but only he could choose to share those traits with another.

"Clelland and Davidson," Stacy said into the phone. She eyed the stack of mail still to be opened.

"Stacy, this is Shirl. Guess where I am?"

"Well, you're not at your desk, nor were you yesterday. Pete is fuming, Gareth is irritated, and I'm swamped with work."

"I'm married."

"You're what?" Stacy couldn't keep her voice from rising in a stunned shriek.

"Married. I...we eloped."

"Who...you're not seeing anyone...Shirl, are you all right?"

Laughter rolled over the telephone line. "My pilot. We're in Mexico. Tell the boss men I'm taking the week off."

"Heaven help us," Stacy muttered. "Gareth will kill you. Right after Pete does."

Shirl wasn't worried. "Wish me luck?"

Stacy heard the wistful note in her friend's tone. "You know I do, the very best of luck and everything else. You deserve it."

"Now I'm getting all teary-eyed. Oh-oh, here comes the groom. I'll call you as soon as I get home. Oh, you'll need to find a new secretary. I'm giving notice. I'll be moving to Houston in a couple of weeks."

The door between the offices opened. Gareth stepped into the doorway and watched Stacy as she finished the conversation. They'd hardly spoken in the eight days since he'd brought her home from the weekend at his parents' farm.

"Shirl is married," she told him, replacing the phone. "She's in Mexico, married to a pilot. She's moving to Houston."

"You look stunned. I take it this was a complete surprise?"

"Yes. She told me she wasn't seeing him anymore."

He shrugged. "She changed her mind. A woman's prerogative."

Stacy pressed a hand to her stomach, which felt as if she'd swallowed a fist-size rock.

"What's different today?" he suddenly asked. He glanced around the office, a frown deepening on his face.

"There's no baby stuff," she said quickly. "Billy went to the day-care center this morning."

Gareth strolled around her office, looking at the plants and her personal touches as if seeing them for the first time. "How did he take to it? Aren't babies supposed to have some time to adjust before you leave them all day at a new place?"

His eyes narrowed on her. She licked her lips, feeling like a witness on the stand. "I stopped by after work each day last week so he would become used to the surroundings and the woman who will take care of him. I spent half a day there on Saturday and let him wake up with me out of sight. He did fine."

Gareth frowned as if displeased.

She resumed slitting envelopes and checking the mail, which normally was Shirl's job. She'd already delegated several chores among the four typists and collected the reports of the four law students who were working for the firm this semester on a work-study program with the University of Virginia. The office was running almost smoothly.

"My mother asked about you and the boy," he said, pausing

at the side of her desk. "She said it livened up the house to have a young one about."

"Please thank her for me." Stacy looked over a letter, laid it in the correct pile and picked up another one. She cleared her throat. "You remember Mr. Anders, my old boss who retired?"

"Yes."

"His son, the one that's a policeman…was a police-man…has started his own investigation agency."

"A private eye? We might use him sometime."

"He investigates insurance fraud and apparently has all the business he can handle. He wants me to come to work for him."

There, she'd gotten the words out without fainting. It was a move she'd been contemplating for five days.

"No," Gareth stated.

She frowned up at him. He stepped closer, looming over her, large and mean-eyed and short-tempered.

"You don't want to get mixed up in anything like that. It's too dangerous," he informed her.

"Actually, I'll be running the office while he and his partner do the investigating. It sounds like…fun." And that sounded like the lamest excuse for leaving she'd ever heard. "It would be closer to the nursery school. I could have lunch there and nurse Billy, too."

"You can do that now. Take a longer lunch. I told you he could stay here until he gets too big. Why did you put him in the day-care center?"

"I thought it was best for him to get used to it before he got old enough to really notice his surroundings."

"Well, I don't."

Her hackles rose at his imperious manner. "Well, I do."

He glared until he realized she wasn't going to back down.

Turning abruptly, he ran a hand through his hair and muttered under his breath.

"I beg your pardon?" she said icily.

"You ought to," he snapped, spinning around. "I'm not surprised at Shirl's actions, but I expected more loyalty from you. Here we are in a crisis and you're going to walk out."

"Well, not right away. I mean...I will give notice. A month..." At his fierce glare, she added, "Maybe six weeks."

"Thanks." Sarcasm dripped from the word.

She lifted her chin. "I'll find someone and train her—"

"The hell you will! You're staying and that's that!" He stomped toward the door.

"I meant, to take Shirl's place. I'll call the employment agency today."

"For Shirl's replacement?"

"Yes."

"Good. I'm not accepting a resignation from you," he told her in a voice that rumbled like distant thunder, foretelling a storm just beyond the horizon. He stepped into his office and slammed the door. The glass rattled dangerously.

Stacy propped her chin on her hand and went over every word of the conversation. She couldn't figure him out. He obviously hated to have anything to do with her, yet he wouldn't let her leave. Did that make sense?

Stacy hung up the phone and sighed in relief. It had been a frantic week, but she had a replacement for Shirl lined up. The woman had worked for a judge who'd had a heart attack and decided to retire. She could start Monday. Shirl, due in from her honeymoon, could give the new secretary a week's training and then leave to join her husband.

And so it goes, as some news commentator used to say.

After stretching and yawning, Stacy turned off the computer and printer and locked her desk. Maybe she'd stop for a pizza on the way to the nursery and have that for dinner. A plain cheese one shouldn't flavor her milk so that Billy wouldn't eat.

Her son was growing and seemed happy in his new environment. Once more she concentrated her love on him and refused to think about Gareth and what might have been.

No regrets, she told herself firmly. Her love wasn't wanted. It would die a natural death soon.

She fetched the copper watering can from the top of the file cabinet and went to the ladies' room to fill it. When she returned to her office, Gareth was there.

"Hello," she said brightly. "You got back early. Did the case close or is this a recess?"

"We finished. Got a nice settlement, too." He mentioned the figure, shrugged, then spoiled the nonchalant act by grinning. Stacy knew how much he liked to win.

"Wow," she exclaimed. The firm would receive a six-figure fee. Of course they'd spent a lot on research and expert witnesses. Still, the net would be a goodly amount.

"I feel like celebrating. How about dinner?"

Her heart bounced off her rib cage before settling down to a regular beat again. "I have to pick up Billy," she said, injecting just the right amount of friendly regret in the refusal. "I think I'll stop for pizza on the way."

"I'll get it."

She finished her chore and replaced the copper can on the cabinet before answering. "I don't think that's a good idea."

"Why?"

"Because." She glared at him. He knew the answer to that as well as she did. They had to maintain a distance until they got over the insane passion they had for each other.

"I'd like to talk to you," he said after the silence grew to unbearable lengths.

"What about?"

"Life," he suggested philosophically.

She didn't trust him in this strangely mellow mood. "Yeah, right. It stinks, end of discussion."

Picking up her purse from the credenza by the window, she dropped her office keys into the side pocket. She watched the traffic eight stories down, her mind lingering on the dinner offer.

Behind her, she heard him pacing about the office, restless and probably irritated with her for refusing his invitation. He liked to get his own way and did so far too often.

Her mood turned to anger with herself for wanting things she wasn't going to get. She grabbed the strap of her purse and swung it over her shoulder.

Her fist connected with warm, living flesh.

"Damn!" her boss said and pressed a hand over his eye.

"Don't move," she ordered. "I'll get some cold water. Give me your handkerchief."

He handed it over. She rushed to the fountain in the hall and soaked it with the icy cold water. After wringing enough water out so it wouldn't drip, she ran to the office.

Gareth was seated in her chair, his hand still over his eye.

"Here," she said. She pushed his hand away and placed the cold cotton over his eye. She watched him anxiously.

"That's better," he murmured.

"I don't understand," she mused aloud. "How did I hit you? I mean, why were you bending over my shoulder?"

"Smelling your perfume."

"I don't wear perfume to work."

"I know." He sighed heavily. "I like your hair up like that. It makes you look sweet and young. I wanted to kiss the back of your neck."

Stacy's hand flew to the twist on the back of her head. She'd twigged the hair up to keep it out of the way. Billy was forever pulling on it when she left it in his reach.

"You were going to kiss the back of my neck?" she demanded incredulously.

"Yes." He cast her a resentful glance from his good eye.

"Well, you can't. Not in the office. It isn't…it isn't dignified," she spluttered.

"Spare me the lecture."

"You can't go around kissing someone's neck just because you want to. You're not allowed to do that. It's against the regulations of the…the Equal Opportunity Office."

His snort of laughter was cruel. "You can kiss my neck. What could be fairer?" Now he was acting his usual cynical self.

"This isn't funny!" She realized her purse was still hanging on her shoulder. "I can't stand here arguing about it. I have things to do."

She stomped out of the office. He could think again if he thought he could kiss her whenever he wanted. She wasn't that kind of woman. She wouldn't fall into his arms just because he wanted her to. Even if she had each time he'd touched her in the past. But no more.

She arrived home and changed clothes, then fed Billy before she remembered she'd forgotten her pizza. That made her angry all over again. Damn Gareth Clelland and his kisses!

Billy patted her breast while he nursed. Her mood softened.

Such a sweet baby. "How I love you," she whispered. "You make everything worthwhile."

Gareth had no one to make life worthwhile for him. He would grow old and callous, maybe become the type of man who thought he could take what he wanted without consequences. He would use his charm and money and influence to replace the ravages of time and dissipation on his handsome face and strong body.

Such a waste.

She shook her head in pity for what she imagined he would become. He had so much potential—as a lover and a husband.

A sigh escaped her. To find in a man the steady flame that could warm a marriage through all the years, to discover that same flame could erupt into a passion so intense it lifted her to the stars, and not to be able to claim it…

Life could be so unfair.

Chapter Nine

Stacy turned off the computer and picked up the employee review forms from the printer rack. She read them over word for word, determined to spot any typos or errors before Gareth pointed them out to her. Everything was in order.

Putting the papers on her desk, she glanced at the clock. Her boss was due back in the office anytime. She'd penciled in an appointment for herself to go over the employee raises with him, then she planned on leaving early, if possible.

It was Tuesday, May 11. Her son had been born three months ago today. Only three months, yet she could barely remember a time when he hadn't been part of her life. The biggest part.

Her breasts tightened a little as usual when she thought of the baby. She adjusted her bra to a more comfortable position.

The outer door opened. Gareth entered the office, filling it with his masculine presence. He looked extraordinarily handsome in a blue summer suit with a hint of gray stripe. His shirt was dark red, and his tie combined the three colors.

Her nipples contracted into hard points. Thank heavens for nursing pads which disguised the fact. "Hi," she said brightly. "You're right on time. I have the employee evaluations ready."

She rose, ready to follow him into his office. He stopped and looked her over as if she were an intrusive stranger. "I have a couple of calls to make."

"Yell when you're finished," she requested. "I'm planning on leaving early tonight, if possible." She'd been late getting out three nights that week.

He made a sound in his throat that might have been agreement. Or then again, it might not. He went into his office and closed the door.

She set her lips primly together and placed the papers back on the pristine surface of her desk. A minute later, she heard him on the phone. An hour dragged by.

When he hung up, she grabbed her forms and headed for his door. It opened wide just as she grasped the knob. She was yanked forward and off balance. Gareth's arms shot out, catching her against him as she fell.

Shaking the hair back from her face, she gazed at him in stunned surprise. Then sensation poured over her like a summer rain shower. She felt the rise and fall of his chest against her breasts. His thigh was wedged between hers. His arms enclosed her with rock solid strength.

Against her abdomen, she felt the rapid hardening of his body. Her eyes widened in shock while desire surrounded her in tentacles of warmth.

In the taut silence that followed, their joint breaths were

the only sound. Like track stars who'd crossed the finish line and were hanging on to each other, she thought inanely.

She saw his eyes go to her mouth. Her lips were parted as she drew quick drafts of air into her lungs. Longing burst through her. She wanted him to kiss her and make the hurt of the past month go away.

He licked his lips, his gaze narrowing as if reading her mind. Slowly his head lowered. Their lips had almost touched when a knock on the outer door froze them in place.

"Yo," Pete called. He opened the door and walked in. And stopped dead still.

Stacy's mind went completely blank.

Gareth muttered a curse and stepped back, his arms falling away from her. He whirled on his law partner. "What is it?"

Pete held up both hands as if to ward off danger. "I thought we were supposed to meet in the conference room an hour ago to go over the employee evaluations with Stacy. Did I get the wrong date?" He looked from one to the other.

Stacy began functioning again. "No. You're right. We...I was just going to remind Gareth of the meeting."

"Well, then, are we ready to begin?" Pete asked, his expression neutral while his gorgeous blue eyes gleamed with laughter. "I have a hot date tonight."

She stared at the papers in her hand. "Uh, yes. Yes, I have the forms. I just finished them a while ago."

"You two go ahead," Gareth ordered. "I'll bring some coffee and join you in a minute."

She nodded. Feeling as stiff as a new robot, she crossed Gareth's office and entered the private conference room. She took a seat at the gleaming walnut table and laid copies of the evaluation forms at two other places.

Pete came in and took a seat. He gave her a careful once-over, then picked up the papers and began studying them.

Heat suffused her face. Gareth had nearly kissed her. Another inch and their mouths would have joined. And she hadn't made one protest. Not one.

What had they been thinking—to almost kiss right there in the office?

Obviously, neither of them had thought at all. They had reacted mindlessly to each other. Both of them. Gareth as well as her. What had happened to common sense?

Gareth entered the conference room from his office. He carried three cups of coffee, which he set on the table, then pushed one to her and one to Pete.

"Thank you," she murmured. Her voice was so husky, she had to clear it twice. She felt her face grow hotter.

"Yeah, thanks." Pete took a sip from the plastic cup. "I've looked over the recommendations you made," he said to her. "I don't have any problems with them."

Gareth slouched into a chair. He'd taken off his jacket and tie. His collar was open and his shirtsleeves were rolled up on his forearms. The room was silent while he perused the forms.

"How's the new secretary working out?" he asked when he finished. He looked at her.

"She's very competent and is already finding her way around. She's familiar with law terms. I plan on recommending a raise for her at the end of her first three months."

"All right. These others look fine to me." He glanced at Pete. "You want to handle the next one?"

"Nah, you can do the honors. It's after five, and I need to leave." He stood, pushed the chair in with his foot and headed for the door. With a smile at her, he left.

Stacy realized the outer offices were silent. The typists, law clerks and new secretary had left. The blood slowed to a sluggish crawl through her veins. She felt dull-witted, her body heavy with needs she constantly had to deny.

"Pete and I are pleased with your management skills. The office functions well under your leadership. A tight ship and a happy one. We decided a ten percent raise was in order."

She blinked in surprise. "You've already given me two raises," she reminded him. "One at three months and one at the end of my first year."

He shrugged. All trace of the earlier desire was wiped from his eyes. He was the cool, impersonal boss, always polite, but rarely smiling. "I suppose if you don't want it, we can't make you take the extra money. We figured you could use it since you have two to feed."

"Of course I can use it." She fidgeted with the papers. "I don't want charity from you."

Anger settled like a cloud on his handsome features. "Charity isn't on our list of employee benefits," he told her in a voice straight off an Arctic ice floe. "You earned it."

"Thank you." She stood. "If that's all…"

He rose, his greater height making her feel small and stupid and helpless for some reason she couldn't name. Then the most ridiculous thing happened. Tears filmed her eyes.

Horrified by this emotional stumble, she said good-night and rushed out of the room. Back in her own office, she locked up, grabbed her purse and headed out the door before she disgraced herself completely.

She nearly ran over Pete when she lunged into the elevator before the door closed. "Easy," he said, catching her arm to steady her. She smiled weakly and regained her composure. "I didn't want to wait for the next elevator."

"I noticed." His eyes studied her face.

She pushed a smile on her lips. "Thank you for the raise. It was a nice surprise, I must say."

"You're worth it. You handle twice the load of our last assistant. The office has never run better."

"Thank you." She couldn't think of another word. The elevator swooped downward with a soft swish of cables and gears.

"How's the boy doing?"

"Fine. Growing like a weed."

"Good." The door slid open, and they exited into the parking garage. "I'll walk you to your truck." He fell into step beside her. "Are you happy here with us?"

"Of course."

"Now that you've got the polite answer out of the way, tell the truth—are you happy working with us?"

She stopped by the ute and unlocked the door. "I don't know what you want me to say."

"Gareth has been a bear lately, especially to you. A few minutes ago, I'm pretty sure he was about to kiss you. When are you going to put the poor guy out of his misery?"

"H-how?" She hated the telltale catch.

"Well, let's see." Pete's eyes sparkled as he pretended to figure it out. "If he's asked you to marry him, then I think you should...for all our sakes."

She gasped, then snapped her mouth shut.

"If he's suggested something more casual, then tell him it's marriage or nothing. Turn in your resignation. That'll wake him up." The law partner chuckled with delight. "I'll hire you as a paralegal assistant if he doesn't come through. You know as much about the law as most of us legal eagles."

"My father was an attorney. I stayed at the office with him after school and in the summer after my mother died."

"What are you going to do about Gareth?"

"I don't know."

"Well, you two are going to have to work it out," he said seriously. "I'm afraid there's going to be an explosion soon. I hope it doesn't happen at the office. If it does, I think you'll have to pack up and leave. No hard feelings, but he's my partner. I have to work with him. You're the expendable one." He gave her a sympathetic smile.

"I understand." She climbed in the ute. He closed the door, the smile hovering on his lips. She managed to return it.

She worried over the situation on the way to the day-care center and all the way home. At bedtime, she still hadn't hit upon a course that would allow her to remain at the law firm. Pete was right. The situation was too volatile.

After changing clothes, she sat in the rocker and fed the baby while she faced the truth. She would have to leave. The new secretary was an older woman with over twenty years business experience under her belt. She could take over the running of the office with no problem.

The detective, her old boss's son, had called and begged her to think about his offer. The secretary they had wasn't working out. He couldn't offer her as much money as she was presently making, but he'd promised her a bonus at the end of the year if the company continued to do as well as it was now.

Choices. Life was full of them.

Her son made a gurgling sound. She smiled at him. He let

go the nipple and gave her a milky smile in return. Three months old. It seemed like a lifetime ago—her going to the cabin, getting lost, having the baby, Gareth taking care of them.

Her smile became wobbly. She beat back tears by dint of will. "We'll be okay," she promised her son. "We can make it just fine. We don't need anyone else."

But Gareth would make a wonderful father, insisted some stubborn part of her that wouldn't give up the dream.

The resignation was typed and ready. All Stacy had to do was lay it on Gareth's desk. Or she could give it to Pete.

Coward.

Gareth had hired her as his assistant. More and more duties had been added to her list until she'd ended up managing the whole office, but Gareth was her boss.

Remembering his fury when she'd mentioned quitting when Shirl had left and his uncertain temper of late, he might strangle her on the spot when he saw the resignation. The other job was waiting for her. She had to give two weeks notice, but after that, she'd be out of there and out of his life.

She heard him enter his office. She stuck the letter in a file folder like a thief hiding her loot. Later. She'd give it to him later. As soon as she found out what kind of a mood he was in. She'd been waiting all week for his temper to improve. It hadn't. Today was Friday. She had to do it today.

She checked the letters one of the typists had finished and placed it in the folder. The will was finished. She handled most of the estate work like this, getting it put together with all the clauses and whereases and such. All Gareth needed to do was to look it over, then she would call the client to come in and sign it—

The door between their offices jerked open. Gareth scowled at her. "Where's the Lambridge file?"

"Right here."

"I need it." He strode across the short distance like a hungry bear smelling fresh meat, grabbed the folder and returned to his den.

"You're quite welcome," she muttered at the closed door. She repositioned the combs in her hair while sneaking a glance at her watch. Fifteen minutes to go. Thank God.

She'd slip her letter of resignation under his door and run like mad for the elevator. She frowned in disgust at her lily-livered ways.

Restless, she went out and told Pat and the typists good-night and wished them a pleasant weekend. The law interns had already left. And Pete, of course.

When the room was empty, she rushed back to her office. Now was the time to make her getaway. She grabbed her purse, wrote Gareth's name on an envelope and picked up the letter.

Except it wasn't her letter. It was instructions on the will from their client.

She stared at her desk. It was the only piece of paper on its smooth surface. She pressed a hand to her stomach while suspicion bloomed like poison ivy in her mind.

Oh, no. She hadn't. Please, no—

"Stacy, get in here." The roar shook the glass pane in the door between his office and hers.

She'd put her letter in the folder, the one he'd snatched off her desk. He was going to kill her. With fatalistic calm, she crossed the carpet and entered the bear's den.

"Yes?" She folded her arms over her rock-filled tummy and held herself very still.

He gave her the absolutely meanest look she'd ever received from him...or anyone. "What is the meaning of this?" He waved a sheet of white bond paper at her.

"What is it?" she asked. Maybe he'd found a mistake in the will. Maybe he hadn't seen her letter.

"You know what the hell it is."

Oh. He had found it. "My...uh...resignation?"

"Yes." He gave her a lethal stare. "I thought we'd had this conversation two or three weeks ago. I thought we'd resolved this particular matter at that time."

"Yes, we did, and no, we didn't." She thrust out her chin. She wasn't going to cower like a thief caught in the act.

His scowl could have downed a moose at twenty paces.

"We didn't resolve it...not exactly," she added.

"What exactly did we do?"

Witnesses must hate it when he used that soft growl to question them. It contained hidden mines that they knew were going to explode in their faces. Stacy felt the same.

"Well, we sort of left it open. The policeman, the one who started the detective agency, called again. He really needs someone in his office."

"How much is he paying you?"

"Uh..."

His eyes narrowed to silver stilettos. "He isn't paying you as much as we are." He watched her without blinking. *"Is he?"* he suddenly barked.

Every nerve in her body jumped. "No!"

"I thought not. So what's your excuse for this?" He waved the incriminating paper at her.

She blurted the truth. "I thought it would be better if I left since things were sort of…tense…between us." Tense was the least offensive word she could think of. Dangerous or explosive or deadly might be more descriptive.

"No," he said. He tore the paper in half. Then half again. And again. And threw the pieces in the trash can.

She was so angry, her voice shook. "You can't do that."

"I just did."

"I'll print out another one."

"We're going to waste a lot of paper."

She stared at him for one long, furious, confused minute. "Blast you," she said and whirled and left the office.

All the way down the elevator, she expected him to be waiting when she stepped out. He wasn't. She peered around cautiously, then dashed to the truck like the coward she was.

Once locked inside, she cranked the engine and left with a squeal of rubber on the concrete. On the street, she slowed as she merged with the heavy traffic.

Breathing easier, she considered the situation. She'd turned in her resignation. No matter what he said or did with it, it was valid. She knew her rights. Gareth Clelland wasn't going to intimidate her. She might not work out the two weeks.

So there.

After picking up Billy, she stopped at the grocery, then hurried home, anxious to be inside the safety and solitude of her apartment. Again she kept a sharp eye out for her boss as she rode the elevator up to her floor. No one there.

Sighing in relief, she let herself in, then flicked the dead bolt when she closed the door.

Safe at last.

* * *

Gareth paced the hallway, unable to make up his mind whether to knock on Stacy's door or go home and let the situation ride until Monday morning at the office.

Of course, she might not come in at all.

He stopped at the wall ten feet from her door and looked down into the street. Friday night traffic crawled along like a loosely connected caterpillar with lights on each section.

"Damn," he said, slapping the wall with the flat of his hand. He spun around and headed for the door.

Without giving himself time to think about why he was there and what possible ulterior motives he might have in coming over here at night instead of waiting for the formality of Monday and the office, he rang the doorbell.

No answer.

He tried once more.

No answer.

"Dammit," he said aloud. He banged the door with his knuckles and heard the faint wail of the baby. Ah, she was in.

But she didn't come to the door.

Fury overcame his better sense. He pounded the door with three hard raps. "Stacy, I know you're in there. Now open the damned door before I break it in," he bellowed.

The elevator doors opened. A couple stood there looking shocked to the gills.

"Got a crowbar?" he asked with a nasty smile.

The man shook his head. The woman pressed a hand to her bosom, her eyes about to pop out of her head. Gareth reached up to knock once more.

The door opened. Velvety brown eyes glared at him. His heart lurched like a drunk baboon. Stacy wore shorts, a loose

T-shirt, and no shoes. The baby was cupped against her chest. She personified feminine beauty.

The couple on the elevator stayed there. "Do you need us to call the police?" the man asked, giving Gareth a wary glance.

"No, it's okay. Really," she added when they didn't look reassured. "He's my—"

"Tooth fairy," Gareth supplied. He stepped inside the apartment, closed the door and threw the dead bolt for good measure. He and Stacy were going to have a long talk.

"That wasn't funny," she told him, turning her back and retreating to the kitchen. She checked a Crock-Pot on the counter by the stove.

Her shorts were the type used for jogging. They had slits cut up the sides so they wouldn't bind across the thighs. Her legs were good. He'd noticed that often enough. Her rear was rounded and fit his hands nicely when he'd caught her there and hauled her against him.

"That smells good." He was suddenly ravenously hungry. For food. For her. For anything she wanted to give him.

What did she want from him?

She stirred the ingredients, tasted the broth, then turned the pot off. "It's just pot roast."

He waited, knowing she was too polite to ignore him.

"Do you want some?" She was far from gracious.

"Yes."

She frowned, but didn't protest. She opened a cabinet and took two plates down with her free hand.

"Here, let me. Tell me what to do."

"Get the silver. In that drawer. Napkins there." She pointed them out.

He set the table, poured two glasses of milk and filled their plates with roast, potatoes, onions and carrots.

"Rolls in the oven." She placed the baby in a swing and wound up the spring. The merry tinkle of a nursery rhyme tune filled the room.

After finding an oven mitt, he removed two rolls and placed them on a saucer. He waited at the table for her to be seated before he took a chair opposite her. Their knees brushed when he stuck his legs under the table and pulled forward. She moved hers to the side.

"Weren't you going to answer the door?" he asked, cutting a slice of margarine from the stick and layering it on a roll. He did the same to the other one, placed it on the saucer and pushed it toward her plate, keeping one for himself.

"I didn't feel like arguing." She took a bite of roast, chewed and swallowed. "This is *my* time, you know."

"Yeah." He bit into a carrot, then closed his eyes in ecstasy. It was cooked to perfection, still firm, but done all the way through, sweet and tasty. The meat was falling-apart tender. He mashed the potato with his fork and added more gravy from the Crock-Pot. "You want more gravy?"

"No, thank you." She ate primly, one hand in her lap clutching the napkin, the other tucked close to her side as she ate in small, ladylike bites.

Her hair was pulled into a loose ponytail, making her neck bare. He had to fight a strong urge to kiss her there.

Returning to the table, he turned his appetite on the food. It was so damned good. He ate firsts, then seconds, then after due consideration, had a small third helping.

"Off your feed, huh?" she suggested snidely.

He grinned, scooped up the last bite and put it away. "I was hungry." Now that he was inside with her and the boy, he felt much more relaxed. Happy, even. He stared at her mouth.

He liked watching her. She chewed daintily, with her lips pressed together, a frown of disapproval nicking two faint lines between her eyebrows. The lines would deepen with time.

In her fifties, she would fret about them. His mother had. She said they made a person look like a grouch. Now in her sixties, she no longer worried about a few lines.

"Do the women in your family age fat or thin?" he asked.

She looked at him over the rim of her milk glass. After swallowing the last sip, she patted her mouth with the napkin. "I don't know. My mother was in her thirties when she died. I never knew either of my grandmothers."

"Too bad," he murmured.

She immediately looked suspicious of his sympathy.

He wasn't going to win her that way. Win her? He wanted her to return to work. That was all. He watched her wipe her mouth and recalled how soft her lips could be.

"Did you drop by to discuss family genetics?"

"No." He pushed his plate back with a sigh of satisfaction and crossed his arms on the table. "I came to apologize for my behavior at the office. Your resignation took me by surprise."

She gave him an uncompromising stare.

"However, I didn't have the right to tear it up."

"No, you didn't."

"I'll miss you." He glanced toward the swing. "I already miss the boy."

"His name is Billy."

"Yeah. William Bainbridge Gardenas."

He witnessed the slow buildup of heat in her face when she realized he knew she'd named Billy after him as well as the baby's father. "I thought, after all I put you through that day, it was…it seemed the least I could do."

Gareth smiled at her stiff little speech. She was on the defensive. Good. Maybe it would give him a small advantage with her. She could be stubborn at times.

"It was an excellent thought. I was honored when I saw the birth announcement in the paper. Thank you."

"Oh. Well, you're welcome."

"My mother was pleased, too. Did she tell you?"

"No."

Very stubborn. "Will you stay at the office until we find someone else and get her trained?"

"Pat could take over easily. She's very capable."

His patience snapped, suddenly and without warning. "Dammit, I don't want Pat! I want you!" The thunder of his voice died away into the silent room.

"I want you," he said again, amazement filling him. A glow ignited inside him, like the sun coming up, warming the earth after a cold, dark night.

Somehow, without quite knowing how it happened, he was standing and she was standing. He reached right over and lifted her off the floor and into his arms.

He saw the protest forming on her lips. Before she could say it, he covered her lips with his.

Oh, God, she tasted good. Ambrosia. Honey. He sampled her with a wild roaming of his tongue on her lips, her teeth, in her mouth. He wanted a response. So far she was fighting it. That gave him hope.

"Stay," he mumbled against her mouth.

Her breasts heaved against his. Passion or anger? He didn't know.

He kept her busy with forays of his hands and mouth. She tried evasive tactics, then she became aggressive, trying to catch his hands and remove them, shaking her head from side to side to dislodge him. He held on, staying with her every move, feeling the glow grow hotter, the heat pouring out of him, surrounding them both, melting them together.

She freed her mouth and gasped for air. He pressed his face into her hair and breathed deeply of her—shampoo and cologne, the twin sweetness of baby powder and mother's milk.

"God, you smell good," he whispered, overcome with needs and emotions too strong to name. He couldn't. He'd never felt anything like this in his life. "We need to talk."

Taking her hand, he pushed her into her chair. For a minute, he stood there, his hands on her shoulders. Her smallness was deceptive. She had more inner strength than most men he knew.

He released her and paced about the kitchen. "I've been thinking about us for days…weeks."

Stacy raised her head and looked at him suspiciously.

"We've shared things this past year that a lot of people don't share in a lifetime." He searched her eyes. "Death. Birth. Desire."

She nodded. Her husband's death. The birth of her child. Desire from both of them. Her love for him, although he didn't know that. She folded her arms on the table and looked away.

He rubbed a fingertip along her jaw, then slipped it under her chin and caressed the sensitive skin there. "For most people, those things would form the basis of a solid friendship. For us, they seem to have raised a lot of problems. I think we need to solve them."

She couldn't think how.

"If I asked, would you be my lover?"

Every cell in her body went into suspended animation at the softly worded question. *My son is an honorable man. Take whatever he offers.* His mother's advice. Should she take it?

"Would you?"

"I don't know."

"We've nearly made love three times. That has to mean something, doesn't it?"

She shrugged as if her heart wasn't about to pound right out of her body.

"If I asked you to live with me, would you?"

She recoiled instinctively from the temporary nature of such a relationship. Her expectations were so much more. "No."

"Then…perhaps we should consider marriage."

It was several seconds before she could think again.

"Yeah, I find the idea pretty daunting, too." He gave her a rather uncertain smile as if perplexed by the stormy relationship between them. "But I think it would work."

A chill flashed over her. "Do you?" He didn't catch the ice in her tone. "Why?"

He gave a ragged sigh and leaned both hands on the table. "I think about you all the time. I rush to the office just to see you. When you're near, all I want is to hold you and kiss you. It makes me angry when I can't. Before this grand passion, we used to work well together. I think marriage would solve several problems."

"I'm not like other women you've known. I'm not blasé about things like commitment or fidelity."

"Believe me, that won't be a problem." His smile was wry, conveying more than the words expressed.

She studied him, trying to arrive at a logical reason for this sudden offer of marriage.

"You're the only woman I've even wanted to touch in the past three years," he told her.

He had to be speaking rhetorically. "You've dated."

"Dated, yes. Nothing more. It's as if I'd died below the waist. Until you."

The impact of his words hit her. He hadn't made love to a woman since his fiancée died? No. She couldn't have understood him correctly. He was too sensuous, too virile and powerful...a handsome, healthy male who could have any woman he wanted.

"You can't mean...no women?"

"None."

He lifted her hand and kissed the tip of each finger, sending sparks up her arm and down into her abdomen. "At first, I wasn't sure what it was with you. That weekend at the cabin, I wanted to hold you. You were in my bed. I felt I should be there with you."

"You felt like that after the delivery?"

"Maybe it was insane, but yes, I did. I liked being with you. Sometimes it was peaceful. At others, it wasn't." His eyes blazed, reminding her of those times, not so peaceful, when their kisses had burned away any thoughts of self-preservation.

"Are you saying you love me?" She just couldn't believe this conversation.

"I find you sexy and exciting and very, very tempting. I want to make love to you. I've thought of those grandchildren we might give my mother. If that's love, then..." He left it for her to finish.

"You were in love once. You know what it's like."

His face closed. "I'll never feel like that again."

Cold and immediate, those words of denial. She flinched as if he'd slapped her.

"I didn't mean that," he said at once. "What I feel for you is hard to explain. I've never felt this way before. There's passion, but there's also admiration. I care for you. I'll be a good husband to you and a good father to your son. You know I'm a wealthy man. If something happens to me, you'll have enough money to live where and how you wish. Billy can go to Harvard—"

"No." She couldn't bear his logical, sensible explanation. "No more," she said, furious with him and with herself for letting herself hope.

"What is it?"

"You. This." She stood and moved away from him. "You intend to feel so much and no more. You'd parcel out your love like a miser." She shook her head. "It isn't enough."

Not when she knew the depth of tenderness that existed in him. Not when she could see the potential in him, the very force of life that he kept buried deep inside. She would eat her heart out for his complete love all the days of their marriage, and he might never share it with her.

His carefully drawn lines that she mustn't overstep would drive her insane. She could never be spontaneous in her love. She would forever be watching the boundaries. She loved him more than that. She wouldn't accept limitations.

"It isn't enough," she said again and faced the fury that bloomed in him.

"What is?" he demanded. "I've offered you my name, my money, a future of security for you and your son. What else do you want?"

She met his furious gaze. "I think you know."

He took a step toward her, then whirled and walked away. She listened to his steps in the hall, then the snick of the dead bolt as he opened the door. When the door closed, she sighed and looked at the swing.

A mother wasn't supposed to bawl like a kid. She had too many other things to do. "Poor baby," she murmured, bending over the sleeping child. "You've been such a good boy."

She froze in a half crouch, her arms reaching, but not touching. Something was wrong…very, very wrong.

"Billy," she screamed. "Oh, God, no…"

Chapter Ten

Gareth heard Stacy's cry before he stepped more than a foot away from the door. He froze for an instant, then spun around and grabbed the doorknob, praying it didn't have an automatic lock on it. It didn't. He raced to the kitchen.

"Billy?" Stacy whispered.

Her voice sent a chill down his spine. He crossed the room in four strides. "My God," he said.

Billy lay utterly still. His skin was white, like frostbite, except around his lips and eyes. They were mottled with blue. His hands, too.

She cradled him against her. "He's not breathing! Gareth, he's not breathing!"

"Bring him to the table." He slammed the dishes aside with one sweep of his arm. A glass hit the floor but didn't break.

She laid Billy down and opened his shirt. Gareth held two fingers in the groove of the tiny neck. He finally detected a beat, thready and weak. "Thank God, he has a pulse."

He licked his finger and held it under the boy's nose. No cooling effect of air passing over the wetness.

"Do you know CPR?" he asked.

"No. I don't."

"I do. You'll have to drive to the hospital. First we'll get some air into him."

Bending, he opened the rosebud mouth and put his lips over the baby's mouth and nose. The papery skin was smooth against his lips, as cool as tombstone marble. *Ah, God...*

He breathed into the boy's lungs in a short huff. Against his hand, he felt the thin rib cage lift. He raised his head and the air soughed out of the infant.

After ten breaths, the delicate eyelids faded from blue to white. Better. Billy wasn't breathing on his own, though.

"Get your keys," he told her. "Let's go."

They went down the elevator with him inhaling, huffing air into the tiny mouth, and exhaling the rest of the breath with the child. Stacy watched without a word, her face as white as her son's. Pity rose in him.

Inhale, huff, exhale.

In the ute, he ministered to the boy while she backed and drove out of the garage into the flow of Friday night revelers with the stoic courage of a warrior. *God...please...*

Inhale, huff, exhale.

The hot sting of tears shocked him. He knuckled them back with one hand. He could hardly bawl in front of her. She didn't need that from him. But inside, there was a tight, hurting sensation, as if some primal need gathered in upon itself. It coiled tighter, like a tiger crouching, ready to spring.

He forced the odd feelings at bay. There was no time for them. Billy grew cold to his touch. Gareth prayed one minute, cursed the next.

Inhale, huff, exhale.

Time condensed into this moment and this tiny human clasped in his hands. Next to the delicate limbs of the boy, his fingers felt like overgrown zucchini.

Inhale, huff, exhale.

They seemed no closer to the hospital than when they'd started. Billy lay limp on his lap, the matchstick arms and legs trailing along his thighs, shifting with each bounce of the ute as if they contained no bones at all.

The streetlights bled all color from the parchment-fine skin. Death caressed Gareth's neck with a sharp, ragged nail, flirting, teasing, mocking.

But he knew it was the boy that was wanted.

He locked his own fears inside and ached for Stacy. The control she displayed as she wove through the traffic, silent and courageous, tore at him.

Gareth lifted his head and swiped the sweat with his sleeve. Beneath his hand, the plum-size heart fluttered and skipped. The fragile connection between body and soul shredded until only a heartbeat held the torn threads intact.

He'd prayed before. For his dog to live after being hit by a car. For his grandfather to survive a heart attack. For Ginny to wake up and smile at him.

Now, as he placed his mouth over Billy's cool face, he prayed for Stacy and her son.

Please, God. Not Stacy. Don't do this to her.

He took a breath, huffed part of it into the boy's mouth, then lifted his head to release the rest of it. The air slipped from the blistery lips. None went in. He bent his head and willed life to remain.

I'll do anything. Anything. But don't take this child.

Inhale. Huff. Exhale.

I'll give her up.

Maybe it was too late for them anyway. He'd been a coward about her and the feelings they'd shared. Hurt once, he'd been afraid to trust life again. Stacy had lost her parents and her husband, yet she'd carried on without a whimper. She'd had her child and went on with living.

A man would be a fool to lose a woman like her.

The carefully guarded vaults of emptiness expanded and shattered. His heart filled with pity and anguish and the love he hadn't been able to admit. What a fool.

"We're here," Stacy said.

She wheeled into the semicircle of the emergency entrance, her hand on the horn blasting for help. She stopped at the curb. He was out of the ute before the engine quit running. Stacy was behind him by the time he ran through the sliding glass doors.

A male nurse shoved a gurney toward them. "What's the problem?" he asked, already reaching for the infant.

"He's not breathing," Gareth said. "I can't get him to breathe on his own."

"Right." The nurse called out a code.

In less than one minute, the medical team assembled. A doctor gave crisp orders.

Respirator. Heart monitor. IV.

Stacy stood by the white-tiled wall. The side of herself that was able to do what needed to be done in an emergency directed her movements. The other side screamed in silent fury at the unfairness of it all, at a fate that could allow this insult to her soul, this wound to her heart.

Gareth put his arm around her shoulders. She stood stiff and unyielding, the anger clutching at her throat, a mad thing clawing its way out. If she opened her mouth, she would scream.

"He'll be all right," he whispered to her.

She heard him, but she didn't believe him.

A big hand covered hers and rubbed gently at the fist she pressed to her stomach. She glanced at him.

Pity gleamed in his eyes. She sighed and let the anger go. "He has to be," she said simply. "He's all I've got."

The male nurse came over. "His heartbeat has picked up," he told them. His smile was cheery, as if this was news they'd been waiting for.

She nodded and tried to remember the miracles of modern medicine. Until the doctors told her differently, she had to believe her son would live.

"Is he breathing?" Gareth asked.

"Not on his own. Not yet." It would only be a matter of seconds, minutes at the most, his tone implied. "We're taking him to the ICU in Pediatrics. Fourth floor. There's a waiting room right outside the ICU main doors. You can go there."

A spurt of panic set in at the thought of them taking Billy away. She fought it back. "I want to go with my son."

The nurse was already walking off. "Soon," he called over his shoulder, taking a position beside the gurney. "As soon as we get him stabilized."

No, now, she wanted to say. She wanted to hold the tiny body that lay so pale against the faded green sheets of the gurney. She wanted to nurse him and make the life come back into him. When they wheeled him behind No Admittance doors, she trembled uncontrollably.

An arm closed around her waist. Gareth hauled her to him. "Let them do their job," he advised.

His strength flowed into her, firming her shaky legs. "I'm scared I'll never see him again," she told him.

"I know." He looked at her with such tenderness, she had to turn away.

A gray-headed woman bustled forward. "You'll need to sign the admitting forms."

"Where do we go?" Gareth asked.

"Through those doors. Admitting is on the right."

Gareth propelled her along. Her skin was icy to his touch. He hated the pain she was going through.

"It'll be okay," he said.

"Yes. Yes, of course it will." She managed a smile. It was so brave, it made him ache.

He guided her to the office, then answered the questions the girl behind the desk asked. The form was on the computer.

The admitting clerk was about twenty-two, bored with her job and indifferent to their suffering. Her long hair stuck out like a spiral mop around her head. The fluorescent lighting made her skin sallow, the blush on her cheeks magenta.

"Next of kin?" the girl asked, twiddling a corkscrew curl around and around one finger.

Gareth gave Stacy a little squeeze, telling her to answer.

"I am. I'm the next of kin," she said.

"Someone who doesn't live in the same household," the girl said. She clicked her artificial nails on the keyboard, impatient for the answer. "In case you skip out and don't pay the bill."

"There isn't anyone."

The girl shot her an irritated glance.

"I'll take care of it," Gareth broke in, his patience at the edge of control. He gave his name and address, his telephone number, the address of the office and the number there.

At last it was done. Stacy signed the forms.

"Let's go." Gareth swept her around and toward the bank of elevators next to the lobby.

Stacy felt his arm around her. His warmth enfolded her. She wanted to lean into it, but didn't dare. It would be that much worse when she had to stand on her own again. She knew just how wonderful he could be during a crisis, but she couldn't let herself depend on him.

In the waiting room, he ushered her to a seat, then brought coffee for each of them. It was hot. She set it aside.

After an hour, she stood and paced, moving from the door to the windows lining one wall. It was dark out. Night.

She leaned her forehead against the window. The heat of the day lingered in the glass, making it warm to her touch. She went back to the sofa and drank the lukewarm coffee.

"I'll see what I can find out," he said.

She nodded.

He left the room. After a while he came back. A doctor was with him, a woman with dark hair and soulful eyes, a kind smile in a tired face.

"He's stabilized," she told Stacy. The smile faded. "However, he hasn't started breathing on his own yet. I have a call in…"

Stacy saw the doctor's mouth moving, but she couldn't hear the words. At least it seemed that way. But she must because she knew what the woman was saying. Some research doctor had a new drug…a strong stimulus…could be dangerous…

More dangerous than not breathing?

"…permission to use it. Would she sign the form?"

She signed a form. She'd already signed a bunch. She'd sign as many of the damned things as they wanted.

The doctor left.

Gareth seated her on the sofa and sat beside her. He pulled her close, folding her against him.

She resisted. He was warm. She was finding it harder to be strong and brave and all that. She wanted to wail.

"Stacy," he said. He sounded strange. So hoarse and strained. So sad. "Don't close me out." His hand crept up and cupped the side of her head. His arm tightened. "I know I deserve it, but don't shut me out. Let me share this with you."

His eyes were so sad. She reached up without thinking to soothe him. "It'll be okay," she said. She dropped her hand, having given as much as she could at the moment. There was so much sadness in his eyes, but she couldn't do anything about it.

"Ah, God," he breathed against her temple. His fingers kneaded her scalp.

Time passed. An hour. Another. Fear revived, becoming stronger. "Is my baby dead?" she asked.

"No, he isn't. His heart is beating." Gareth searched for words. People had said words to him when Ginny had died. Surely he could remember some of them.

They hadn't comforted him.

There must be others, some truth he could tell her. He found it. "He's got the strongest little heart. It just went on and on, beating like sixty. I breathed for him, but that heart… It keeps on and on."

"He's so little."

"He'll make it. His heart is like his mother's—too strong

to give up, just like you've never given up on life no matter what it threw at you. Billy won't give up, either." He willed it to be so.

"He's such a good baby."

Her love broke his heart. He realized it was the same love she'd offered him, whole and complete.

She'd wanted the same from him. But he'd held back, thinking to give only a little of himself and so escape the greater pains of life. Love didn't work that way. A person had to take it all—the joy and the hurt.

Stacy understood. That's why she'd refused him.

"I know, love." He rubbed her, soothed her. He held her when she would have pushed him away. "He'll be okay. Have faith in him, in his heart. I do."

She leaned her head back on his arm so she could see his face. He held still and let her look into his eyes. She shook her head as if confused. She was too tired to understand the message he was trying to give her. That could come later.

"Hang on to this thought, darling," he murmured to her. "No matter what happens, I'll be here for you and the boy."

"You don't like children."

"I love your son." He couldn't hold in the words. "I didn't want to. I was afraid. To love someone meant I might be hurt again. I am hurting, Stacy. For you. For Billy. For myself. For all the years we might not get to spend together because I was too blind to see what life still offered."

Stacy laid her hand over his and stilled its movement against her face. "I can't think about that right now."

"I know." He kissed her palm, then held her hand in his lap. She felt his warmth flow around her.

Once she'd thought love would be like that—a steady

warmth to keep a marriage going through the coldest of winters, with an occasional flare-up to keep things lively. She wasn't sure about that anymore, though.

"Don't give up," he said as if reading her mind.

"All right," she whispered.

Gareth prayed that her faith would be rewarded. If he could have moved heaven and earth to save her child, he would have. But all he could do was wait with her and tell her silently of his love.

Stacy was allowed to see Billy for a few minutes each hour. At dawn, she drank the tenth cup of coffee Gareth brought her.

The pediatrician returned before she finished it. "The medicine is in. The chief of pediatrics and the hospital board have given their approval to use it. We're ready."

Stacy felt Gareth's arm slide around her waist. She leaned against him. "Good," she said, drawing on his strength.

"You two can come into the room, but stay out of the way."

"We will," Gareth promised for both of them. He smiled at Stacy. "It'll be okay. Come on."

Together they followed the doctor into the ICU area. Billy was in an open incubator, a respirator hissing rhythmically close by. The heart monitor indicated a regular heartbeat.

The medical team stood ready. The doctor removed the IV and inserted the hypodermic needle. She slowly administered the drug. When she finished, she removed the respirator. They waited in total silence.

A second went by. Ten. Fifteen.

A shudder went through Billy's tiny body. His arms jerked. His fingers tightened. His legs kinked up, and his mouth dropped open. He drew a breath and let it out in a wail. His face turned an indignant red. He was breathing!

The seven adults laughed. The more he cried, the more they laughed. He stopped and gazed around.

Gareth pushed Stacy forward. She bent over her son and smiled. He smiled, then yawned as wide as his mouth would go. For the next three hours, he fussed and fretted. Stacy played with him. When that wouldn't do, Gareth walked the floor until his cries quietened.

At last, after he settled down enough to drink his fill of his mother's milk, his eyelids drooped and closed. He slept, looking perfectly peaceful and perfectly all right.

"The sleep of the innocent," Gareth murmured.

Thank you, God....

It was past nine. The hospital bustled as shifts changed and routines, suspended during the night, were resumed. Billy was doing fine. No signs of any trouble at all after the trauma.

Stacy sat beside the incubator, her hand constantly touching her son. She looked up and smiled. Fatigue showed itself in the lines between her eyes, the shadows beneath them.

Gareth's heart did a nosedive, righted itself and spun around dizzily. He'd forgotten what strange things love did to the human body. But he was willing to learn again.

That's what he wanted to tell Stacy. He understood why his proposal of marriage had hurt her. He'd offered reasons when she had wanted love. He'd wanted her, but he hadn't wanted to call it more than passion.

Stupid, really stupid. He could have lost her as easily as they had nearly lost her son. It was unthinkable. They were his, those two. She'd come to him to birth her son. That made him the surrogate father. He'd tell her so as soon as possible.

The pediatrician with the beautiful eyes of a Mona Lisa came in. She examined Billy and checked his reflexes. "He's right as rain," she declared. "You can take him home."

Stacy's eyes went big.

"You'll have a monitor like the one on him now. It sounds an alarm if he pulls another of those breath-holding tricks on us." Her smile was reassuring.

"He'll do fine," Gareth told Stacy. He meant to see to it. Eventually, they sorted through the checkout ritual and got on their way. Stacy sat in the back seat to be closer to Billy.

At the apartment, she carried the baby while Gareth brought up the monitoring equipment. The couple who lived across from Stacy opened their door just as they stepped out of the elevator. They took one look at him, then closed and locked their door.

Gareth chuckled.

Stacy flashed him a sparkling glance. "They probably think I've gotten mixed up with a madman. You're lucky they didn't call the police." The long hours of the night strayed into her eyes. "So am I. I couldn't have made it without you. Billy wouldn't have—"

"Hush," he admonished softly. "We'll talk later." He pushed open the door when she unlocked it and allowed her to precede him inside. Sixteen hours had passed since they were last there, but it seemed to him that it had been a lifetime.

He set up the monitoring equipment, checked to make sure it worked. It did. The alarm woke Billy, who started, then cried loudly. Smiling, Stacy picked him up and settled into the rocker-recliner. Gareth went to put on a pot of coffee while she nursed her child.

Later, when she came into the kitchen, he told her to go to bed. She shook her head.

"I couldn't sleep," she explained.

"You didn't sleep last night. I doubt if you'll sleep tonight, so you'll need some rest. I'll stay to make sure you don't sleep through the alarm or any of the other things that you're afraid might happen."

She tried to protest, but he insisted. At last she gave in and went off to shower and change into pajamas. He settled into the comfortable chair in the baby's room and read a magazine.

He thought over the revelations of the night. He stood and looked at the sleeping boy. This time when his heart tightened, he smiled. After patting the sleeping child, he resumed his vigil.

Stacy woke with a start. She sat up and frantically gazed around the tranquil bedroom. The apartment was silent. Her nightmare came back to haunt her. Fear sluiced down her back—cold, sweaty, mind-numbing.

"Billy." She flew out of bed, down the hall and into the baby's room.

She stopped just inside the door, her heart thudding. Relief left her weak and trembling.

Billy was there. Safe. Asleep. On Gareth's chest.

The rocker-recliner was tilted back as far as it would go. The monitoring equipment, mounted on an IV rack, stood sentinel beside them. Gareth's hands were laced together across the baby's bottom, holding the child securely in his grasp.

It was the most beautiful sight she'd ever seen.

Gareth opened his eyes. For a long minute, they watched each other without moving. Then he smiled.

It filled her with a radiance so bright, she could hardly

stand it. She smiled, then she laughed. She skimmed across the floor to her two men.

Gazing into her eyes, Gareth saw the words weren't necessary. He'd say them later, but she knew. She knew....

Chapter Eleven

The month of June was the most perfect for weddings. The second Sunday dawned bright as a robin's egg. Stacy looked out the window of the Clelland home in Virginia and laughed softly.

Mrs. Clelland was directing the caterers, the florists, the minister, her husband, their guests and Gareth. Maudie sat in the front row, the bassinet in the aisle beside her, decked out in festive ribbons, which Billy persisted in trying to eat.

He would get a bite of wedding cake later.

"Ready?" She faced Pete and nodded. He held out his arm. She tucked her hand into it and walked outside.

The photographer snapped pictures while Shirl's pilot husband filmed the procedure. Stacy felt quite beautiful in her white silk suit with pink accessories.

And indescribably happy.

No one could be luckier than she was—a handsome husband, a perfect child and a cruise in the Mediterranean to all the places she'd read about. Italy, Greece, Turkey, Egypt, Spain, Portugal. She couldn't believe it.

Billy and Maudie would be with them in a separate room across the parlor from the master suite. It was too wonderful.

Shirl, dressed in champagne silk with an Egyptian necklace sparkling in the sun and long spiral earrings dangling from her ears, stood at the end of the white satin carpet. The music started. She gave Stacy a wink, then walked with stately dignity down the aisle.

Stacy and Pete moved into place behind the matron of honor. At last they came to the bower of flowers where Gareth, his father and the minister waited. Her eyes widened.

When Gareth turned fully toward her, she saw he held Billy in his arms. The love in his eyes made tears form in hers. She sternly forced them back. No tears today, she warned her shaky emotions.

She listened to her husband's voice and followed his vows with her own. Billy was cradled securely against Gareth's chest. And he squeezed her hand and held it clasped in his after they exchanged rings.

At last it was finished. He bent over and kissed her.

Everyone clapped. Pete claimed a kiss from her while Shirl did the same with Gareth. Shirl leaned against her own husband and fanned her face. "I can see why you fell for Gareth," she told Stacy in a stage whisper. "He's got a kiss like a twenty-mule team kick."

That brought more laughter. The afternoon passed in a happy daze. Then it was time for them to go to the honeymoon

suite where they would spend their wedding night before beginning their trip.

Gareth went with her to the nursery quarters to change clothes
and let her feed their son once more before they left. There was
extra milk in the freezer to get him through until morning.

"You're beautiful," he told her when she sat in the rocking
chair in her slip while Billy tugged hungrily.

"You, too."

They smiled at each other.

"I can't wait for our next child. Dr. Kate says she'll let me
do the delivery," he said, never taking his eyes from his bride
and new son. "I figure about nine months from tonight…"

A blush suffused Stacy's cheeks. Tonight. It was what
she'd been waiting for. Gareth, too. They'd already agreed
they wanted another child as soon as may be.

"Me, too."

"A girl," he told her. "A bossy little sister for Billy.
Someone to take my side of our arguments."

He looked so pleased, she had to smile. The big lummox,
grinning like a politician on the campaign trail.

Stacy let her breath out in a deep sigh of happiness.

"Smile," Gareth ordered, producing a camera and proceed-
ing to take several snapshots of her and Billy.

A picture of love, Stacy thought. She had many such
pictures. There would be more. Of Billy on his birthdays.
Fishing with his dad and grandfather. Sticking number tags
on items for the annual auction for his grandmother. Making
cookies with her and a sister or brother, or both, someday.

"Ready?" Gareth asked when she finished and put Billy in
the crib. His voice was deep, husky and very, very sexy.

"Yes."

He enfolded her in his arms after she had slipped into a simple summer dress. Her breath snagged for a second when she saw the look in his eyes.

Tenderness. Love. Desire.

"A steady love," she murmured. "I always wanted a steady kind of love."

"It'll always be there for you," he promised.

He leaned over so he could hold her closer, his warmth pouring over her.

She laughed.

"I love it when you do that," he said, becoming serious. "When you laugh and look at me with love in your eyes." He nuzzled his face into her hair. "I never thought I'd have another love in my life…and then there were you and the baby, invading my mountain retreat, refusing to let me hibernate in my own self-pity, driving me crazy with longing—"

"I couldn't help but love you," she whispered. She batted her lashes at him. "When you helped me with Billy, I realized what a catch you were. All that valuable experience. Now when we have another child—"

His lips cut off the rest of the statement, but he finished it in his heart. *Our love will expand to include it, too.*

She'd come to his house to deliver a briefcase of law reviews. Instead, he'd had to do an unexpected delivery, one that ended up bringing him joy and happiness and peace. And the greatest love he'd ever known. It was a fair exchange.

* * * * *

Romantic reads to
Need, Want

...International affairs, seduction and passion guaranteed
10 brand-new books available every month

Pure romance, pure emotion
6 brand-new books available every month

Pulse-raising romance – heart-racing medical drama
6 brand-new books available every month

From Regency England to Ancient Rome, rich, vivid and passionate romance...
6 brand-new books available every month

Scorching hot sexy reads...
4 brand-new books available every month

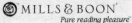

MILLS & BOON
Pure reading pleasure

M&B/GENERIC RS2 a

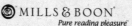

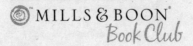

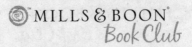

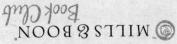